P9-DEV-303

THE UNIVERSAL LAWS OF MARCO

Also by Carmen Rodrigues

Not Anything

34 Pieces of You

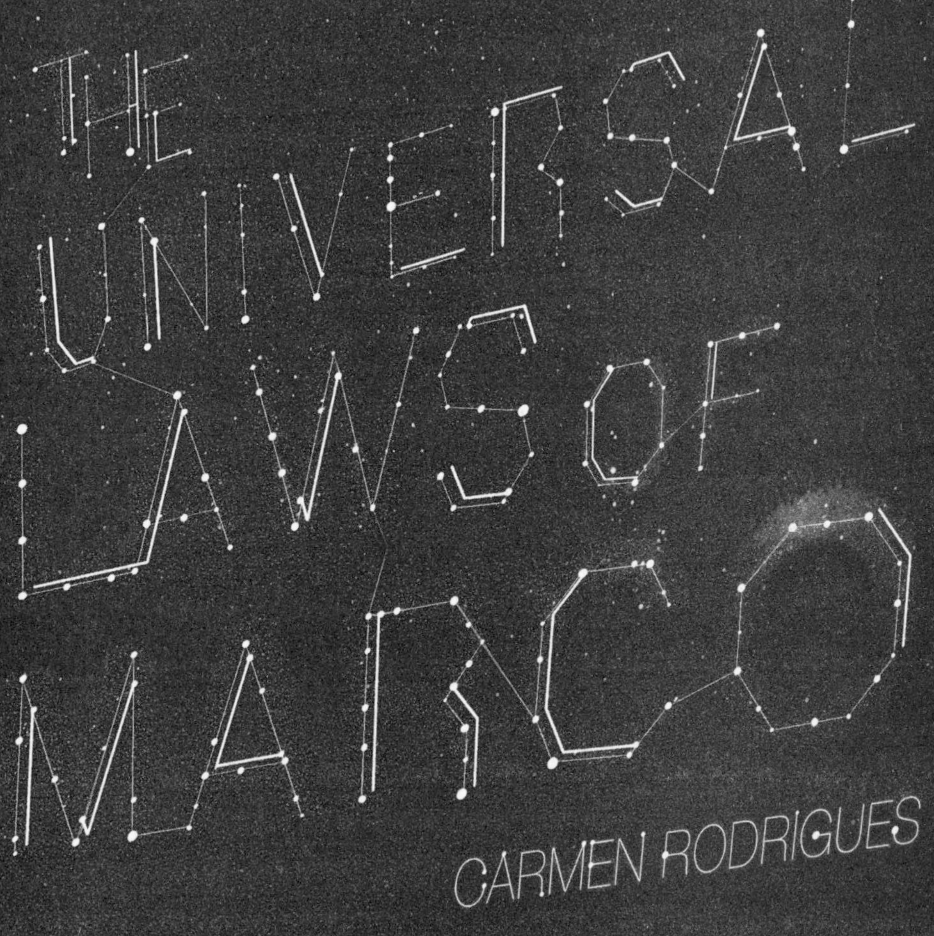

Simon Pulse
New York London Toronto Sydney New Delhi

This book is a work of fiction. Any references to historical events, real people, or real places are used fictitiously. Other names, characters, places, and events are products of the author's imagination, and any resemblance to actual events or places or persons, living or dead, is entirely coincidental.

SIMON PULSE
An imprint of Simon & Schuster Children's Publishing Division
1230 Avenue of the Americas, New York, New York 10020
First Simon Pulse hardcover edition March 2019

For information about special discounts for bulk purchases, please contact
Simon & Schuster Special Sales at 1-866-506-1949 or business@simonandschuster.com.
The Simon & Schuster Speakers Bureau can bring authors to your live event.
For more information or to book an event contact the Simon & Schuster Speakers
Bureau at 1-866-248-3049 or visit our website at www.simonspeakers.com.
Jacket designed by Jessica Handelman
Interior designed by Tom Daly
The text of this book was set in Venetian 301 BT Std.
Manufactured in the United States of America
2 4 6 8 10 9 7 5 3 1
Library of Congress Cataloging-in-Publication Data
Names: Rodrigues, Carmen, author.
Title: The universal laws of Marco / by Carmen Rodrigues.
Description: First Simon Pulse hardcover edition. | New York : Simon Pulse, 2019. |
Summary: With girlfriend Erika, a full scholarship to college, and a busy life with his
tribe of close friends, high school senior Marco Suarez holds tightly to his carefully
choreographed life, until Sally, his first kiss, moves back to Miami.
Identifiers: LCCN 2018019246 |
ISBN 9781442485099 (hc) | ISBN 9781442485112 (eBook)
Subjects: | CYAC: Friendship—Fiction. | Love—Fiction. |
Cuban Americans—Fiction. | Miami (Fla.)—Fiction.
Classification: LCC PZ7.R61875 Un 2019 | DDC [Fic]—dc23
LC record available at https://lccn.loc.gov/2018019246

For my mom—

one of my best friends and my first champion.

I love you.

Omnia mutantur, nihil interit.

Everything changes, but nothing is truly lost.

—Ovid, *Metamorphoses*

THE UNIVERSAL LAWS OF MARCO

FIRST SPARK

THE FIRST TIME I KISSED SALLY BLAKE WAS on a hot summer day.

In early August.

The summer before my last year in middle school.

And it mostly happened because of a bottle, glass and old-fashioned—a classic Coca-Cola bottle, not too hard to find in Little Havana. The older Cuban men, the ones who wear guayaberas and play dominoes in the dusty streets of Calle Ocho, are fond of such novelties. And living near Miami, I had a Cuban great-grandfather who brought me such things, and I, in turn, brought them to my next-door neighbor Jade's house on that hot summer day.

And, damn, it was hot. The air was heavy with buttons of dew that floated in the way cotton-like fibers of dandelion seeds float when you make a wish.

A wish flower. That's what my mom had called it the first time I'd picked a dandelion seed head on a trip to visit her people in Ohio.

Make a wish? I had asked.

Yes.

I puckered my five-year-old lips and released a stream of air, never realizing that eight years later one of my wishes—a wish I didn't even know to have—would come true.

A kiss with Sally.

"Spin the bottle," Jade had announced.

We were thirteen and huddled behind a shed in her backyard: Sally, Jade, Diego, and me. Sweat dripped down my back, and Jade laughed nervously, running her fingers across the side of her jaw like she did whenever the shouting inside her house spilled into her yard.

"I don't know." Sally looked at me and then at Diego, Jade, the bottle.

"Why not?" Jade replied. She set the bottle in the middle of an old piece of cardboard we had pulled from behind her shed and gave it a spin. The gaping mouth pointed to me, and Jade leaned across the grass, her curly brown hair curtaining her face. She gave me a quick peck on the cheek. "That's just a demonstration. When we do it for real, it has to be an actual kiss."

"Like . . . ?" Sally's pale skin turned pink. Her freckles rose to the surface, little warning lights. "Like . . . with, you know . . . ?"

"Tongue?" Diego finished dryly.

Jade studied the bottle, unsure. "No, not tongue. Not"—she glanced shyly at Diego—"not unless you want to. Just, you know, it has to be on the lips. Not on the cheek, like I just did with Marco."

Everyone nodded, and Jade licked her lips. "Okay, so you go first, Marco." She pointed at the bottle, long neck still aimed at me. I also licked my lips, excited and nervous.

We were all best friends back then: Me and Jade and Diego and Sally and even Sookie, who that day was at her Jewish day camp, because that's what she did every summer. ("No, not Jewish Day Camp, Marco. Stop calling it that," she'd say to this. "It's called the Jewish Community Center, or the JCC, or really, everyone just calls it the J.")

I flicked the glass and the bottle spun again. I kept my eyes on something inconspicuous, like the tip of the bottle. I heard my heartbeat, heavy and reckless in my chest, and my mom, one yard over, singing as she washed that afternoon's dishes.

And then the bottle landed.

On her.

On Sally.

I shifted my gaze to her mouth: Pink. Chapped. Scooting closer. "It's me," her mouth said.

"Go on," Jade said, her brown eyes stuck on Diego. "Go on."

I scooted too. Time sped up, or rather, my view of time distorted. My body's tempo became at odds with my thoughts—one measurably increasing while the other slowed down. The rest was hazy, condensed. The images spottier the closer Sally came.

Too much licking of the lips before—me.

Too much shaking of the knees—hers.

Jade said something I couldn't make out, and then Sally's lips blurred into bits of her face: the bridge of her nose, wide; the sweep of her ash-brown eyelashes, tinted blond at the edges; and, finally, the corner of a gray eye.

I heard a little sigh.

Hers.

Then our lips clashed, the moment too quick. Way too quick. Barely enough time to marvel at the softness.

Time unfolded, widened, stretched out like a cat trying to get a back rub. Then, somehow, I returned to the circle. Again the bottle spun with ferocity.

Sally kissed Diego while I looked away.

Diego kissed Jade.

Jade kissed me. Quick. More like a peck.

All possibilities exhausted, we stopped.

We stopped.

But the story didn't stop.

The story of how I came to kiss Sally a second and third time would continue on. I just didn't know it back then.

Senior Year

1. I HAVE A GIRLFRIEND

FOR THE LAST SIX MONTHS, IN FACT. AND right now she's sitting on my stoop, dressed in jeans and a T-shirt, hair up in a ponytail, makeup at a minimum. Basically, she's just the way I like her, but if I say that, she'll be like, *Are you serious? Liking me when I'm a disaster is not a compliment.* So I don't say that. I keep it simple with a kiss.

She tugs me down so that I'm sitting beside her. Her finger slips across my skin, the skin moistened by my sweat. She turns to give me a tight hug, her hands resting on my shoulders. "You're sexy today." She touches the hem of my tank top. Normally I'm covered up, T-shirts or hoodies. But today is hot, summer-right-up-against-us hot, and it hasn't rained in days. I tell her that. Then I put my finger to the bridge of her nose, a place where her makeup has run thin, and whisper, "*Besitos del sol.*"

She touches her face self-consciously and pulls away. "I just don't know *why* you love them. They're like little pieces of lint I can't get off my face. You should love yours more instead." She taps my nose and cheeks, touching the ten freckles that wave across my brown skin.

"Do you love mine?" I ask her.

"Yeah," she says, and smiles.

"Then I'll love yours." I connect the dots with my fingers, trailing light kisses across her face until arriving at her mouth. "Corona Borealis . . . ," I say into her lips.

"What?" She pulls back.

"The crown of Ariadne . . ."

"Marco." She groans, shoving me away. She returns to the stoop.

"It's a compliment."

"It's a *what*?"

"Comparing you to a constellation is a compliment."

"What's with you always finding constellations on my face?"

For the past four years of our friendship and even into this "new stage of our relationship" (as Erika calls it), she has insisted on sparring with me like this. I'm easy bait, she says. Like even now when I see that mischief in her eyes, I'm still quick to offer an explanation. "*Really.* She helped Theseus—"

"Very romantic and also not listening anymore." She glances at her phone and then holds up the device as evidence. "I'm too busy waiting for your text to arrive. But it doesn't."

"Oh, man, I'm sorry. I got distracted."

She raises an eyebrow, because for as long as Erika has

known me, I haven't gotten distracted, not when she texts, not when she talks. So today is kind of unusual.

But I can explain. I was thinking about wormholes, which I've been trying to get down on paper for my final physics assignment. Or maybe—and I realize this is it—I was traveling down a metaphorical wormhole, returning to that first kiss with Sally, and I forgot to reply at all.

Either way, I never make Erika wait on replies. She says that's what makes me "different" and "mature" and a bunch of other superlatives. Which is bizarre. That being punctual through the rapid tapping of two fingers can earn me bonus points. But it does.

"So what was it?" she asks.

"Huh?"

"That distracted you?"

"Huh?"

She sighs. "You said you were distracted when I texted."

"Wormholes?" I offer up.

Erika rolls her eyes, and in her predictable way of zoning out most things that have to do with cosmology, says, "Okay, then, fight over."

"Wait, that was a fight?"

Because Erika and I don't fight. That's why Erika says we're "perfect" and "meant to be." I say we like to "avoid conflict." But Erika says we don't have to "avoid conflict" because "we're not conflicted."

Anyway, fight avoided, I pull her back to that space on my chest. That space that feels better when she's there.

"You're sweaty," she says.

"I'm purified."

"So I'm absorbing your outcast toxins?"

"Possibly . . ." I squeeze her in tighter, and she struggles to break free. Finally, I let her go. We're both smiling. "So what's going on?"

"Oh *that*. My mom."

"Your mom what?"

"She's . . . I don't know. Her sister, you know the one who always has some boyfriend drama . . . ?" Erika lowers her voice so my mom won't hear, not that my mom could hear over the "twin nightmares" (that's what Erika calls them), who are yelling at each other inside the house.

"What is it this time?"

"It's always the same—*he said this, but then he does this, and then he didn't come home, but then he said he was working late. I think I should trust him, but is that naive? It's naive, right?* And blah, blah, blah, nonsense."

"Sounds fun." I squeeze her hand.

"Yeah. I was around the corner at Gabby's, trying to wait it out, but her mom kicked me out because family-only dinner and more blah-blah-blah nonsense. So, now I'm here . . . Are you glad to see me?"

"Yeah," I say, but she hears the hesitance in my voice and replies, "No, you're not."

"I'm surprised, that's all. I was in the middle of doing this . . ." I hold up my hands to mean, *my thing.* My I'm-not-working-or-running-ragged-from-homework-so-I'm-going-to-sweat-it-out routine. I get to do this thing maybe once or twice a week. "I still have to—"

"Hit your bag?" She laughs, her hand returning to the edge of my tank. "And you know I don't care if you're Mr. Six-Pack Abs. That's not my thing."

"It's not that. You know it's not that."

A long time ago, I had been small. And small in middle school meant easy target. I was okay if Diego was nearby. Even back then he *was* Mr. Six-Pack Abs. But when he wasn't around, which was most classes in the sixth and seventh grade, I felt my smallness like rocks in my pockets or a splinter beneath my skin. The burden followed me everywhere—up the school stairs, into honors classes, into restrooms, (*especially restrooms*, where someone could easily force your head under sink water), in the corners of the PE locker room (where I was pantsed on the reg).

I hated being small.

"Oh, so that's why you've been eating left and right," Pop had said back then, the one time he caught me staring plaintively at the scale. "Trying to bulk up like me?"

"Not left and right," I had mumbled, stepping off the scale and staring at him—six one, two hundred and twenty pounds, rippled with muscles, and a smile that most of the ladies around the block couldn't withstand. At least, that's what Mom always said.

"Nothing wrong with being skinny," Pop said, using his toe to slide the scale beneath the bathroom sink.

"Pop."

"You know, Bruce Lee was skinny." That was Pop's thing, referencing people and places that you'd never heard of before. But I knew about Bruce Lee. When I was five, Pop introduced me to his sick martial art moves through a bunch of old films. Bruce Lee could kick ass. I couldn't kick a stick.

"Pop, that's like comparing a steak to a potato."

"And you're what? The potato?" Pop turned me so that we faced the mirror. "You've got a good symmetrical face on your shoulders, just like him. The ladies dig a symmetrical face. And you know, you got my eyes." He offered me his signature wink. "You should practice that move. It works. Got me your mom's engagement ring at half off."

My mom's solitaire was so microscopic that half off must have meant free.

He winked his left eye, followed by the right. He was an ambidextrous winker. "Go on," he urged. "Try it."

I glared at him. "No."

"That's a mistake," he said, and gave me the wink version of the wave—left, right, left, right. I became dizzy. "That wink is perfection, but it's your call, my man. If you don't want to harness the power of the Suarez wink, you can travel down your lonely road alone." He stepped back and sized me up from a distance. Then he lifted my shirt and stared at my concave belly. I tried to squirm away, but he held on to my shoulder. "You know what? You could be a little more athletic, a little more like Bruce Lee, especially here." Again, a tap, tap to the belly. "Why not?"

"Because Bruce Lee had training. Bruce Lee had skills," I muttered.

"You could get those things."

"How?"

"What about that studio my buddy runs down in South Miami?" he said, letting me go.

"Pop, that costs money."

"Yeah. True." His foot tapped the tile floor as he gave that part of the plan some thought. Then he smiled.

"What?"

"You just gotta get the money on your own."

It was nearly the summer between seventh and eighth grade. And for weeks after that talk, I let the conversation slide. Pop was always coming up with these ideas on how to "be better" and "maximize your potential." That's because he was always reading books on self-improvement and jotting down possibilities for the future in one of the many journals he kept.

"Third act," he used to say when I watched him scribbling away, palm smudged with still-drying ink.

By "third act" he meant when we were grown—me and the "twin terrors"—he'd follow up high school and parenthood by taking himself back to school. College. Pop was big on always having a next act.

But sometimes Pop tried to push me into my next act before I was ready, and that was just what happened when, a few weeks after finding me on that scale, he walked into my bedroom with a stack of papers. Each was the size of a postcard, the wording laid out like a bad advertisement.

Helper for Hire ($8/hour)

Lawn mowing

Babysitting

Light housekeeping

Tutoring for elementary kids

Call Marco at 305-555-0112

"*Pop*, what's this?"

"Acceleration. You've got to pick up speed to push past the friction and into your future. Use the momentum you gather along the way to take a few breaths, but acceleration is the only way to start from point A and make it to point B. And trust me, you need to keep moving, because *life is now.*"

He was speaking in riddles, but that was another way Pop talked. He loved telling me about acceleration and momentum and friction, and I loved listening. But right then it didn't exactly tell me what I was supposed to do—not in practical terms.

"Okay," he said, sensing my confusion. "Take that around. And, hey, don't just leave it in the mailbox. Okay? You gotta knock on the doors. Talk to the people inside. Sell yourself."

A good plan, except I was pretty quiet back then. In many ways, I still am. Everyone knew that, especially Pop. "I can't."

"You can't? Or you won't?" He turned to glance at

Mom, who had slipped into the doorway, wrapping her arm around his waist. She looked small next to him—barely five three, all hips and curves, a mouth almost always open in a smile.

"What are my guys talking about?" she asked.

"Pop wants me to accelerate."

"That doesn't sound like a bad thing," she said, and Pop kissed the crown of her head, squeezing her in closer.

"Where there's a will, there's a way. Accelerate," he commanded.

But I didn't. Not that summer—the summer of Spin the Bottle. Eventually, I'd make good on Pop's command, just not then.

"Hey, you don't have to stop doing your thing. I'll be fine," Erika says, sensing the "dark thoughts" hovering. That's what she calls it, when my face "closes off" and my eyes "look somewhere far away, like you have a stormy cloud dropping dark thoughts into your head."

Erika knows this sweat-it-out routine helps keep the dark thoughts away.

"Yeah?" I say, relieved that I don't have to figure out a way to make us both happy. I try to be that way with Erika, give her what she wants. It seems only fair, since she's been such a good friend to me for all these years.

"Girlfriend," I could hear her whisper, but only in my mind. Ever since we switched things up before winter break, Erika likes to remind me of her new title. "It's just different," she'd explain.

"Like you're a friend I can now kiss?" I'd tease her.

"No." Her face would screw up. "That's the least of it. It's like a best friend you can kiss, and you never want to kiss anyone but me, and we become closer and closer until who knows?"

"We disappear, like you're a black hole that sucks me in like a ray of light?" I sorta joked, because, to be honest, sometimes what she said about our growing closer reminded me of one object disappearing into the other the way light disappears into a black hole.

"You're ridiculous with your universe stuff!" Erika said, laughing. "But you get it, right?"

"Sure," I said because that seemed to make her happy.

Now she's trying to make me happy. She slips her hand into mine and leans up, onto her tippy-toes, her mouth right there. Oh man, *right there*, at the curve of my earlobe.

I know what's coming. It's the maneuver that makes me sign over power of attorney.

This is a talent—whatever she is doing, it is definitely her talent.

Gently, oh so gently, she slips that earlobe between her teeth. The smallest of bites, the tiniest of licks, and then her secret weapon—a hint of breath. The breath is important. The breath is what sends goose bumps up and down my arms, over my chest, down, down, down until I can barely think.

A little more and then, suddenly, she steps away. It takes a second to get back to a place where I can think.

When I do, though, I have to pull my shirt until it's low. She glances down, laughing. "You like that, huh?" she whispers.

Like it? This is acceleration and displacement and in . . . um . . . certain . . . um . . . parts—a directional movement of—up, up, up, aka velocity.

"Let's compromise. Take off for *just* a few hours," she says. This is her new tactic: compromise me into compliance. She flattens her feet and stares up at me with her pale-blue eyes. *Please*, she mouths, her fingers rubbing the inside of my palm.

I give myself the speech: *Don't do this. You have responsibilities—your own things. This is a trap. Don't do this. Don't do this. Don't do this. Don't do this. Don't do this.* There's a lot of *don't do this* in speeches that concern Erika and her talents.

"How about we compromise by you staying here? Work on your homework while I finish up?"

"And then what? We'd do more homework together?"

I nod. Because as much as I try to make Erika happy, I also have to keep my parents happy. And nothing makes them happier than having a son with straight As.

And I've had straight As every quarter since ninth grade.

But that takes work and dedication.

She laughs. "I don't think I have that much homework to do. Anyway, I told Manny we could study for the chem final together. And he's right around the block—"

"Oh." I make a face. *"Manny."*

"Stop," she says, smiling.

"What? You said you want me to be more jealous." I push out my chest, like I'm Superman or something, about to take on Manny, her track buddy, who I'm pretty sure is a pacifist. At least, that's what most of the stickers on his backpack imply. "If he makes a move on you, I'll kick his—"

"Oh my God. No, no, no. You're terrible at this." She laughs again.

"It's not something I want to be good at," I say, half seriously.

She's silent for a few seconds, watching me carefully. Then the easiness returns. "Well, I said *sometimes* it hurts my feelings that you're not jealous. There's a difference." She bends over to pick up her purse, slinging the strap across her chest. "I have to go, scholarship boy. You just keep your focus on that GPA. Or else we'll never get the shiz out of here." She slips her hand under my shirt, pulling me closer by the waistband of my shorts. When she steps away, she tugs down my shirt for me. "There. No one will notice."

I smile, embarrassed.

"So, call me later?"

"Sure," I say. "*Later*'s a much better name than Erika."

WORMHOLES

BUT EARLIER THAT DAY, WHEN ERIKA TEXTED, I was traveling down that wormhole. I was on that journey because that's what happens when someone reappears after four years. And suddenly that someone, that her, is standing in the middle of your high school cafeteria as if she had never left . . .

You is what you think. *You are here.*

And for a second you wonder if you're hallucinating. Because, let's be real, you've imagined this day more than you'd like to admit. You've seen it play out in your head hundreds of times. But when it happens, in your cafeteria—man, of all places, the cafeteria—you stand there, watching her with her lunch tray in hand, eyes searching for a place to fit. For a friendly face. And you can't move because your feet are paralyzed. You're holding up the lunch line, and everyone thinks you're acting weird. But what they don't know is that you're traveling.

Through time.

You are a time traveler.

On a mission through a wormhole, the past suddenly connected to the present through a not-so-simple bending of the space-time continuum.

Just one-quarter shy of graduation.

Meanwhile, your responsible girlfriend, the one who never disappears, is texting you. Her unheard words circulate through the machine in your pocket. But those words can't reach you. Because you're not in *the now*. You're in *the then*.

You're with a bottle that spins and a girl who kisses you, a girl who hasn't yet disappeared, taking your heart with her.

And with all that going on, you forget one of the fundamental truths about wormholes.

A wormhole can kill you.

Middle School

2. MARTA, AN EPIC STORYTELLER

BACK IN THE DAY, I KNEW THIS GIRL NAMED Marta Ochoa. Marta was a big-eyed girl with an even bigger heart, who loved nothing more than to tell a story from the absolute beginning. The first time I heard Marta tell a story was in second grade, on a field trip to the Miami Seaquarium. That's when Marta pressed her face to a stretch of glass and recited every detail about her "very, very first trip" to the Seaquarium with her stepdad. And how she'd "never had a dad before," but this one was "pretty good" and felt like a "real *papá*" and much better than her mom's last "*novio*," who was a "freeloader." Or, at least, that's what her abuela called that *novio* all the time: *Juan, un conchudo.* And the story went on and on, circling backward in time until I knew the name of every boyfriend, the *conchudos*, the *idiotas*, and the one guy that her *abuela* declared, "*Más feo que un carro por debajo,*" which meant that he was pretty ugly, even uglier than the underside of a car.

You're probably wondering why I'm even bringing

Marta up. Well, it's because she had an unwavering belief that every story had a beginning and those beginnings deserved—no, *needed*—to be told, which is why I'm taking us back to four years earlier, in middle school.

Back then we did everything together. We took the bus together. We ate lunch together. We hung out after school together. We even went through the extras together: Jade's cheerleading competitions, Sookie's chess matches, Diego's football games, and Sally's runs.

Sally was fast, maybe the fastest girl in the county. She won first place at a lot of meets. They had a bookcase at her house, in the living room, that was weighed down with Sally's trophies: a collection of gold-colored, plastic medals hanging from various colored ribbons. First place was Sally's standard place. And it should have been no different on that day, except it was.

It was because something singular happened. Something that had never happened to Sally before: *She fell.*

She fell hard and twisted, tangled up in the legs of another runner as they rolled head over torso over legs until they came to a stop at the edge of the track. Still, she persisted, bleeding her way across the finish line, arriving second to last.

Another first for Sally.

The coach called out, "Blake, get over here! Let me see that." But Sally waved her away, pointing firmly to her dad. Coach Sami nodded after a second, used to Sally's dad taking the lead on everything. He was, after all, an almost Olympian, a star runner at the University of Miami before an injury ended his career, but now he had a legacy. That legacy was Sally.

On the way to her dad, Sally stopped to talk to us. She looked a mess—blond hair askew, hands scraped and dirty.

"Are you okay?" Sookie asked, staring at the bleeding knee.

"Eh," Sally said, smiling through her pain as she lowered herself onto the ground. "Did you see that, though?" There was a twinkle in her eye, her voice slightly excited. "The girl from Hammocks cut into my lane, and I couldn't stop myself from hitting her. And it was so strange because it was one of those moments where, like, your brain clearly sees what's going to happen and you get these warning messages, but it doesn't send the message fast enough to your legs. Like, I knew I was going to hit her, but I couldn't stop myself, so bam!" She laughed, only wincing again when Sookie bent over to assess the scrape, skillfully palpating the skin around Sally's cut.

"Hmm . . . ," Sookie said while she continued her examination.

Sally glanced at her father, who watched us from the bleachers, his lips twisted with . . . worry? Disappointment? Anger?

It was hard to tell with Mr. Blake. There were days like yesterday, when he had us over for pizza, handing out T-shirts that shouted: RUN, SALLY! RUN! And there were days like last week, when he didn't answer their front door—didn't let Sally or her brother, Boone, answer either—even though we knew they were home because the car was in the driveway, the lights were on inside, and we could hear the TV blasting as we walked up the sidewalk.

"That's just how he is," Sally would say, and then she'd crack a joke or tell a story, all the while shrugging off her father's peculiarities. We shrugged his peculiarities off too, because we did everything together, even ignore the obvious.

"Should we clean it?" Sookie asked, leaning back. The skin around the wound was red and puffy. The cut wasn't deep, but it was caked over with dirt.

"Why bother? My father's gonna kill me anyway. It'd be nicer to die from an infection." Doubt etched her lips, little frown lines appearing like parentheses.

"Yeah, but that looks harsh. You should clean it," Diego said.

"Yeah," Jade echoed, pressing her shoulder against his. "Harsh."

"That's it. I'm getting the first aid kit." Sookie headed off to the bleachers.

Diego placed his finger close to the scrape, tapping lightly on the skin. "Does it hurt?"

"What do you think?" Sally snapped, wincing again. She looked up at the sky and then over to me, knowing that I was always queasy around injuries. "This is making you sick, right?"

"Maybe." Fresh blood oozed from the wound, and for a second I bent down, putting my head between my legs.

"Wimp," Diego coughed, and Sally kicked him with her good leg. "Stop."

"Sally?" Mr. Blake called out from the stands. "Sally!" I glanced back. Sookie was talking to him, pointing at the first aid kit and nodding her head.

"Ignore him," Sally said to me then. "I've been thinking about that dream you had."

"Huh?" I asked, caught off guard.

She fingered the charm at the end of a brown leather necklace, a mustang in mid-gallop—a gift from us on her thirteenth birthday. "The one you told me about during lunch the other day?"

We had played this game since seventh grade when once, during lunch, Sookie had described a recurring nightmare that ended with her being chased by a monster and unable to scream.

Diego had been like, "That's messed up."

Jade was like, "I'd have been so scared."

But Sally glanced up from her PB&J and asked casually: "So if you can't scream, you can't get help. Maybe there's something you need help with but you're not getting?"

This response might sound weird, but Sally was one of those super-smart kids. Every year when we got back the scores from our standardized assessments, I fell short of her results. My ten *X*s—the ones that marked my position on the chart—always began at the center of the page, the tail end of average, and flowed right, into above average. That fit. I was the kind of student who had to work hard to get *A*s. Sally was the kind of kid who read something once and could recite it back to you word for word.

"Oh, that's called verbatim," she had told me in fifth grade, when I noticed that her answers on a difficult science test were exactly what was said in the textbook. I thought she was cheating, but she said, "Nope. I can repeat things with the original words that I read, aka verbatim." So it wasn't a surprise that Sally's chart showed only three to four *X*s on the far right of the above-average spectrum. The rest, like Sally, were somewhere beyond the chart.

It turned out Sally really liked dream interpretation. After Sookie's dream, she always asked us about ours. The dream I had told her about took place in school and seemed pretty standard, except that I had experienced the dream again and again for eight months, from September to now, in early May.

"Okay." I played along. "What does it mean?"

"Well, you keep showing up to class, but you don't have your homework, right? Even though you know you've done it. And it's like that for every class, right?"

"Yeah. That's what it seems like."

"And you feel frustrated?"

That was the trick behind Sally's dream-interpretation skills. She never focused on what the dream was about exactly. She always focused on how the dream made you feel.

"Yeah, I do."

"Anything else?" Sally's eyes darted momentarily to her

father, talking animatedly to Sookie, who was practicing her listening nod.

"I don't know." I thought about the dream, scanning for any other feeling. "I guess I feel angry."

She nodded, closing her eyes as she mulled over this detail, my feeling of anger. A minute later she said, "I think it's about you being prepared for something, like you've done your homework, but you can't complete the final step. You can't turn it in. So you're frustrated and angry with yourself."

She paused again, considering. "Is there something you're ready for but haven't done?"

"Oh." Jade leaned in, always a sucker for Sally's dream analysis. "Like complete the task to get credit?" Jade shot me a look. "Is that it, Marco?"

"Yeah," Sally said. "Exactly." She squeezed her fist as another wave of pain hit. "There's probably something you need to do to make the dream stop."

"Turn in the homework," Jade encouraged.

Diego laughed, always skeptical of Sally's gift. "Oh, please. Pretty sure dude just needs to check his backpack before he leaves the house."

"Shut up, Diego," Jade said. "Well, Marco?"

"Maybe? I'd have to think about it."

Mr. Blake's voice rose again from the bleachers. I glanced back at Sookie, who was practically body-blocking him.

"Yep. He's going to kill me." Sally groaned and fell back onto the grass, her lips moving as she counted—a calm-yourself-down technique her mom taught her when our kindergarten teacher, Mrs. Bryant, wouldn't stop calling home despite all of Sally's promises to "be gooder."

"Fifty." Sally sat up, looking at the fields of Seagrove Middle, the grass patchy from the thousand or so kids walking back and forth to the portable classrooms.

Sookie returned, waving her first aid kit. "Can you scoot?" she said to Jade, who nodded, happily grabbing Diego by the hand with a "Let's give them space. Right, Sookie?"

"Yes, please," Sookie said.

"Can you tell my dad I'll be there soon?" Sally asked.

"Sure," Jade said, and dragged Diego off to the bleachers.

"Should I go?" I asked, but Sally said, "No. You stay, Marco, okay?" And then she took my hand and squeezed it.

I tried not to notice the blood as Sookie worked to clean the wound or Sally holding my hand. I tried to breathe, really. But that's hard when there is a girl like Sally touching you.

My logical side said: *Maybe she just needs a hand to hold, something to help her get through this.*

My hopeful side said: *Maybe she needs to hold* my *hand the way Jade always wants to hold Diego's hand.*

It was possible, right?

A few minutes later Sookie said, "There. Done," and Sally let go of my hand. I took a gulp of air. "Better?" I asked, and Sally nodded.

Sookie applied Neosporin and placed a Band-Aid over the

raw skin. "You'll want to clean it again later today and let it air out for a bit before you put a new Band-Aid over it."

"Okay," Sally said as Sookie helped her to her feet. She gave Sookie a tight hug. "Thanks."

"Ha. Don't thank me. Thank YouTube." Sookie had a belief that every problem could be solved on YouTube. "If there's an apocalypse," Sookie had once said, "and you have Internet access, you only need YouTube to survive. But without Internet, you'll probably need a public library."

"Everything okay?" Erika—the before Erika—called out as she passed us on her way to her next race. Erika was Sally's teammate, the second-fastest runner in the group, and she and Sally were friendly enough.

"I'm okay," Sally called back. "Good luck!"

Sookie rolled her eyes. "I can't stand that girl."

"Still?" I asked.

We had gone to school with Erika since second grade, but Sookie hated her because of an incident that happened during a pretty intense kickball game in the fourth grade. That's when Erika had said to Sookie, "You can't be Jewish. You're, like, Asian." And Sookie, who was specifically Korean *and* Jewish, on account of Jewish parents who adopted her while teaching abroad in South Korea, said, "You can't be pretty. You're mean."

And then Erika spat on her.

The loogie landed in Sookie's thick hair, and she began to cry. Sally's response was to pat Sookie on the back. Jade's response was to shove Erika to the ground and kick her in the shin. On occasion Diego liked to reenact the scene by falling onto the ground in the middle of anywhere—the park, the grocery store, someone's backyard—and screaming, "You kicked me!" while holding his shin.

"I'll hate her forever," Sookie continued, eyes narrowing. "And I think she has a thing for Marco. She keeps making love eyes at him in science."

"*No,*" I protested. "The only eyes I see are the ones she's got on her face, which are, like, regular eyes."

I watched Sally, hoping for signs of jealousy, but other than a coughing fit, she seemed unfazed.

Sookie tapped her back. "You okay?"

"Yeah. Swallowed wrong. So . . . wait. What are love eyes?"

"Oh, it's like . . . like this . . ." Sookie's eyes widened until they were so big they nearly popped off her face. "You know, like a tarsier."

"A what?" Sally laughed.

"A tarsier. You don't know what that is? It's a primate, but it's small, looks like a squirrel, but a squirrel with bizzaro eyes. Did you ever check out the link I sent you to *Nature Unleashed* on YouTube? It's totally there." Sookie shot me a dirty look. "Marco, you better not ask her to the dance."

"What?" Sally's back stiffened, and I wondered if she was making a connection between the upcoming dance and me and Erika. Maybe she was jealous?

I took a deep breath, deciding to hope. "I won't ask her. I swear."

The eighth-grade dance was still weeks away, and I hadn't asked anyone yet, mostly because of courage—or my lack of it. But if I did ask anyone, I'd ask Sally.

Truth be told, I'd been practicing asking her for months, maybe even the whole school year. Not out loud. Not even really in the conscious part of my brain. But deep inside, I was always trying out those words. . . .

Would you . . .

Could you . . .

Be my date?

Later, I would connect the dots between Sally's interpretation of my dream and my hesitance to ask her to the dance, but I didn't see it then. I stood too close.

"Enough already, Sally Pearl!" Mr. Blake waved his arms, gesturing for her to come over to him. "Now!"

Sally limped off, and Sookie asked, "Think she'll be okay? He was pretty mad when I went over there, but what's new?"

"I mean, he's not the worst." I glanced at Jade, who sat in the stands with Diego, her knee pushed against his. Lately, Jade's dad was the worst.

Sookie started to pack up her kit. "I'm serious about the love eyes, BTdubs." She made her tarsier face and nodded toward Erika, who, coming off that race, looked sweaty and tired and the opposite of love struck.

"Nope. The girl barely knows I'm alive."

"Ha," Sookie said, and walked off to run interference between Sally and Mr. Blake, whose agitated hands vacillated between the track and the injured knee. Even Coach Sami eyed them warily.

So by now you're probably thinking, "Hey, Marco, why pull a Marta here? Do we really need to know all this?" And I'd say, "Yeah, you do." Because if you don't know about that particular day and that particular run and that very first fall, you won't understand what happened next, something equally singular.

That night, at midnight, Sally Blake showed up at my house.

Senior Year

3. I WORK HARD FOR MY MONEY

THAT FIRST BLAST OF AIR IS HEAVEN. I stand in that space between the double doors that lead into Grendel & Son's Market with my eyes closed, arms raised to the ceiling in triumph. The fact that I am here, on time for my shift, is a slight miracle. Just thirty minutes earlier, I was standing in my kitchen, slicing up tomatoes and refereeing another fight between my eleven-year-old twin brothers.

```
                    THEM
You told everyone I wet my pants!
Well, you do!
No, I don't!
You did that one time!
I was sick!
So?
That's different!
Yeah, right.
And you told Melanie that I liked Celia.
```

```
But you do!

No, I don't!

                    ME
Stop! Just stop! Seriously stop!
```

When it comes to conversations between me and my little bros, three phrases always take center stage: *No—don't do that! Just stop! I'm warning you!*

So, it's probably no surprise that many afternoons, including this afternoon, are spent in Principal Johnson's office at Seagrove Middle. There, I make promises I haven't been able to keep: that my brothers can do better, that they'll stop giving each other smacks and shoves, that they'll cease and desist on the not-so-occasional kicks in the nuts (at least on school property). So far their violence remains localized—the fights, only between the two of them. But Principal Johnson insists that it is only a matter of time before we witness the spillover. Apparently, sibling fighting is like a gateway drug to fighting among the general population.

Anyway, I make promises, and sometimes (less and less so) Principal Johnson buys my promises. He's got a soft spot for my family because he's known Pop from when they were "scraggly sixth graders" together at Seagrove Middle to when Pop worked here, as a custodian, back when I was that "scraggly kid" making tarsier eyes at Sally. And even though Pop no longer works at Seagrove and they're not really close like that, he knows that Pop is a "good guy" whose life was on track until the end of eleventh grade, when Pop knocked Mom up with me.

But all that goodwill doesn't stop his concerns over my brothers' "fumbling transition" into sixth grade. Principal Johnson is always surprised by the twins' nonsense because, to hear him say it, I was "always a sensible kid" and the twins act like they're "out of their minds." This is all the kind of stuff he says when he's "reached his limit." Today he delivers a hell-and-damnation lecture.

PRINCIPAL JOHNSON

Your brothers need to learn to control their tempers. Your brothers need more individual attention at home.

ME

But I—

PRINCIPAL JOHNSON

Yes, I know you give them your attention, Marco, and yes, I know your mom has to work and your father—well, I know that he is . . . sometimes . . . unable to focus. I'm sorry about how . . . about what happened. But . . .

ME

We're trying. We're doing our best.

PRINCIPAL JOHNSON

I know. But you . . . it . . . it has to be better.

Better is what we've all strived toward these last four years, since Pop had his head injury followed by his diagnosis with TBI.

For those of you not in the know, TBI stands for traumatic brain injury. And it's something that can change you for good. TBI is something that can make Pop sit at home while I deal with a middle school principal who always wants more than we have to give.

TBI can mean that on bad days, I have to be the one to stop my brothers from fighting at the kitchen table while Pop sits in the living room, staring out the window. The noise level epic, but Pop not hearing one bit of it. Or, at least, not saying anything about it.

Pop's random quietness is better than the first year after his diagnosis. That year—the year I started high school—was filled with sudden outbursts. TVs were broken, and dishes were flung across the room at Mom. Mom would fling them back at Pop because, at some point, you lose it. You forget what the doctors tell you. "It's not him. It's the injury. The injury can create the outbursts. But we believe that his brain will heal more. That this will stop."

"That he'll be the same?" is what Mom wanted to know.

"We don't know about *the same*. The injury is different for everyone. Only time can tell," they had said. "But we believe that he'll get better."

One thing I learned from Pop's injury is "better" is a relative term.

And so we waited, repeating, "It's not him. It's the injury."

Mom cried a lot that year. The twins stayed outside most days. And, yeah, I guess that was when the boys started fighting. I did my best to change the dynamic. To not be the "jerk of a big brother" I had been before Pop's injury. I stopped shoving them into walls and eating the last of their favorite cereals. I tried to put them first because that's what Pop would have done. But my changing hasn't stopped their fighting.

Still, even I need an escape, and Grendel's has become my salvation. I take pride in restocking shelves, in making order out of disorder, but I also goof around with Diego as we break down boxes in the stockroom, and there's a lot of relief in that.

Plus, you know how they say repetitive tasks calm the mind? It's true. When I'm at Grendel's I feel my blood pressure drop. Maybe that's because not a lot of drama can happen while you're putting up cereal boxes in aisle nine or watching your best friend wield a box cutter while demonstrating a how-to on the Kid 'n Play kick step. (Don't know about Kid 'n Play? Oh, son, look it up!)

Grendel's also saved us financially. I get paid to be here. And that paycheck has helped a lot these past few years, especially after Pop's extended leave from the Middle turned into a permanent one and the disability checks weren't enough to get us through.

But despite my brothers today, there are many days when things flow well enough, when Pop is pretty on point and the money doesn't feel so tight. On those days, I imagine a different future. A future with a dorm room that doesn't have the "terrible twins."

No more talks with Principal J about "strategies" to "develop the boys' sense of self-control." A street without yowling cats. Grass as far as the eye can see. No more of Pop's random quietness and Mom's stress face.

I'd be free.

I just need to get the twins in line. I tried to talk to Mom about that today.

ME

It's getting worse.

MOM

They'll grow out of it. They're young.

ME

They're hoodlums.

MOM

They're your brothers.

ME

I feel like we're the only thing keeping them in check. And when I leave? You'll be down a man. Wayne is far away.

MOM

Well, good thing I can handle it.

ME

How? It's two full-time jobs.

MOM

Marco, I said I'll handle this.

But can she? Without me? That question keeps me up at night.

I lower my arms. That feeling of triumph is gone.

When I step into the grocery store proper, I pull a collared shirt from my backpack and head to the men's restroom, where I wipe the stench from my creases with a wad of paper towels. Semi-presentable, I slide my Grendel & Son's shirt over my head, tucking the edges into my jeans. I'm ready to clock in exactly when my shift begins.

"Yo, that is some *funky cold medina*," Diego says when I enter the stockroom. He slashes through the seams of another cardboard box with his utility knife as he sniffs the air. "Why don't you go buy some baby wipes from aisle seven? Take a poor man's shower."

"Nope. Gonna funk it up. *That's my prerogative.*"

Alex, a guy who's a few years older than us, works his own magic in the far right of the room. He smirks at our bit and then tries to slyly glance at his phone. "Nah, Alex, you either can speak twentieth-century pop song or you can't," Diego says.

"Dude, I'm learning." Alex exhales heavily. "I'm new to this. You guys have been doing this forever."

"Alex, it's not hard," I say. "*You just listen to your heart.*"

"*You may not know where it's going or why, but . . .* ," Diego repeats, monotone.

Alex rolls his eyes. "Just listen to your heart?"

We crack up, even Alex, who never wins the pop song game. When we're done laughing, I admit, "*And . . . I missed the bus.*"

"Dude." Alex groans. "Did you literally miss the bus?"

"That is literally the first time you've used 'literally' correctly," I reply.

"You know what? Forget it," Alex snaps, genuinely flustered. He walks away.

"That gets easier and easier," Diego says.

I glance around at today's offerings, about a hundred or so boxes waiting to be emptied and broken down. Their contents will be used to restock the shelves. I pull out my box cutter and start on a stack of emptied boxes. I break the box apart in seconds, feeling the tension from my day leave, little streams of frustration puffing out of my fingertips as I work my hands back and forth, up and down.

After a while I notice that Diego's shirt is tucked in *and* ironed to a crisp. Even stranger, his five-o'clock shadow has gone the way of a clean shave and his hair is twisted into a . . . "*Dude,* what's up with them dreads?"

"*He works hard for his money,*" Diego sings, arms raised as he spins. "Looks good, right?"

"Looks like a man bun."

"Dude, this is the cleaned-up look I gotta have if I wanna get some respect 'round here."

"Respect? For what?"

"Oh, bro, you lookin' at Grendel & Son's next management trainee." He stands stock-still. Then, extending his arms like he's the goalpost at a Dolphins game, he begins some new dance moves. Looks like the robot. "I. Diego. Sanchez. Am. The. Latest. Version. Of. An. Excellent. Employee. I. Will. Get. This. Job. And. Become. A. Pioneer. The. Grandmaster. Flash. Of. Grocery. Stores."

"Stop playin'." But it's kind of infectious, so I start my

own robot dance routine. We pop and lock for a few seconds. Then Diego leaps into the air, lands on a cardboard square, and slides a good three feet, shoulder checking me along the way.

I crack up. "All right, though. Seriously, D?"

"What? Yeah, seriously." He returns the box to its band of brothers and glances at the security cameras. There's one above the door and another near the dock. "You think they saw me? I gotta get better at this *being managerial* stuff. Bro, you think you could help me with my application? It's due next week. I want it to be super tight. I could ask Jade, but you're our Ivy League boy."

"The Ivies are in the northeast—Harvard, Princeton. I'm just going to Wayne." Which, not to humble brag, is only one of the most selective science-driven private colleges out west. It took four years of straights As, stellar SAT scores, and a killer essay to get in there.

"This school is the school for you," Pop had said back in the Middle, when he handed me my first brochure to Wayne. "Great science program, scholarship opportunities."

I looked at the brochure. "Pop, I don't have the grades for that."

"But you have the smarts. You only have to apply yourself more."

"Apply yourself more" was a phrase that Pop had grown fond of that year, ever since my guidance counselor had sent home a note that said I wasn't "living up to my potential."

As if potential was something we had to live up to. It wasn't that my grades were bad back then; they just weren't great. I had some As, some Bs, and every now and then, for a quarter only, I'd pull out a C. Pop said the problem with my grades was my daydreaming. "You sometimes go off in your head, and your concentration goes . . ." He took a hand and let it plummet, like a car losing control going down a steep hill. When he said that, though, Mom laughed and pointed from him to me and said, "Tree, apple."

But besides the whole "potential" debate, I had never been west of the Mississippi River. "What if I want to stay here, in Florida?"

Pop slapped his hands together, suddenly animated. "I want you to see the world. I never got to do that. I want that for you."

I laughed. California was far, but not that far. "It's still the United States, Pop."

"California is about twenty-five hundred miles away. You know what else is that far away?"

I shook my head.

"Brazil, British Columbia, Greenland. Those seem exotic to you?"

I nodded.

"Well, same distance as California. See the world," he commanded, and stuck the brochure in the top desk of my drawer, where after all these years, the pages became bent and stained with fingerprints and food. Still, even when Wayne sent my welcome packet with a glossy new brochure inside, I kept that wrecked collection of paper, a symbol of Pop's dream for me.

"So you'll help, right? You owe me," Diego says with a wink.

"For what?"

"What?" Diego rolls his eyes. "How 'bout for every time I stopped someone from stomping on you in the Middle?" He flexes his muscles, making like he's the Incredible Hulk or something.

"Dude, you protecting me in the Middle when I weighed a buck nothing doesn't make you look like the hero."

"Don't it, though?" Diego cocked his head to the side. "Anyway, you serious about applying?"

"Like a corpse."

"What?"

"Man, 'dead serious' is played. 'Like a corpse' is the new thing."

"I'll help, 'cause with jokes like that, you *need* this to be your future."

Diego jabs quickly in my direction, pulling his fist back inches from my face. I don't flinch.

"Damn, hard-core lately."

I tap my belly. "Nickel, iron, and sulfur."

Diego slow claps. "Them dad jokes, though." He turns back to his boxes, breaking three down in record time. "So, you really take the bus?"

"Yep."

"Where's your truck?"

"No gas."

"What happened to your gas money?"

"Twins and cavities, timing belt on truck." I didn't add paying rent or making minimum payments on the high-interest credit cards Mom opened when Pop got injured because Diego got my point: Blah, blah, blah, money nonsense.

In these parts, the struggle was real.

"That blows. I'd have lent you money—"

"Nope. Bus is free with student ID, so no biggie. I'll be good again after tomorrow's paycheck."

"Okay." Diego moves on to another stack. We're quietly working until he asks, "So, what about that Sally being back?"

"What about it?"

He slowly raises an eyebrow for dramatic effect. "You gonna play me like that?"

"Like what?"

"Like you didn't have your thinking face on for all of lunch."

"Dude, that's what I do. I think."

"About ghosts." His voice has an edge to it.

I shrug. "I don't believe in ghosts. I *do* believe in thinking all the time. What do you do in that big old head of yours?"

"Store spare change. Old McDonald's wrappers. Wanna make a deposit?"

"I only make deposits when I can get a return for my investment."

"Deposit this," he says, grabbing his crotch. Then he pauses, glancing nervously at the security cameras. "Damn, I gotta remember those cameras. You think they got volume on those things?"

I shake my head and return to breaking down boxes. Soon I'm lost in my thoughts. Mostly I'm compiling a list of things I have to accomplish when I get home: review study guides for tomorrow's exam in calc, work on my part of an English project with Sookie . . . I've got a list of three items and a stack of flattened boxes when Diego smacks my arm.

"Hey, they're calling you." He points upward, to the speakers.

The Supermarket God says, "Marco Suarez, Mr. Grendel would like to see you."

"Ooh. Do you want that ass of yours sliced thin?" Diego snaps.

"A deli pun?" I slide my box cutter into my pocket and tidy my shirt.

Diego smiles crookedly, shrugs. "Yo, just remember when you get in there, you got to deny, deny, deny."

"Deny what?"

"Everything. Prisoner's dilemma. They'll always say someone's ratted you out to get you to confess, but if everyone just denies, denies, denies, it's all good, see? My old man taught me that before he went to the resort."

Diego's dad went to "the resort," aka prison, four years ago. Not really the best example to follow.

"Well, I didn't do anything wrong."

"Just trying to help," he says sincerely. Then he turns his back to the cameras and mouths, *You dick.*

Middle School

4. AT MIDNIGHT

ON THE NIGHT OF SALLY'S FALL, SHE CAME to my house at midnight. I had just finished a big project for physical science and couldn't sleep with all that accomplishment buzzing around me. So I snuck outside and sat on our front stoop. Just a quick look at the moon was all I wanted because I liked the moon. Have ever since I was four years old and Pop explained that the moon wasn't creeping on me.

"But . . ." I had pointed up at the silver globe during a long car ride. "It never goes away!"

"No, kiddo." Pop had laughed. "It's not following *you*. It's following *everyone*." And he explained that because the moon was so far away—about 230,000 miles—that it seemed like it was always in sight, no matter how far we traveled. "See, we're traveling around a curved earth and the moon is orbiting the earth. So the moon is really following the earth, not us specifically."

"Or-butting?"

"Or*biting*. It means that the moon is circling a celestial object."

"Cel-cel-es-tel?"

"Celest*ial*," Pop corrected. "That's something for later. Just keep checking to see if the moon is following us."

I'd learn what celestial meant a few years later: "an object in the sky or heavens"; "heavenly"; or "supremely good." I liked the last definition best. A planet was obviously supremely good. And in this case, the moon was orbiting the celestial object of our planet earth.

What a weird thing, to go in circles around something else. But I guess that tied in to ideas of gravity, the earth and the moon pulling toward each other the same way our family—Mom, Pop, me, and the twins—did, the world a series of large and small orbits: the earth orbiting the sun (large) and the moon orbiting the earth (small). The tribe orbiting school (large), Jade orbiting Diego (small).

Me suddenly orbiting Sally.

So my mind was pretty much all over the place that night as I thought about orbits and Sally and how ever since that first kiss, that first spark, I wanted to be around her more than any of our other friends.

Just us. Alone

That's what I was thinking about when out of nowhere a voice whispered, "Gotcha!"

A few seconds later I sank back into my skin and found Sally there at my gate, laughing. "I gotcha. Didn't I?"

"What? *No*. No, you didn't."

"Puh-lease. I crept up like a ninja." She pantomimed ninja moves, but she looked more like Scooby-Doo trying to sneak away with Shaggy.

This was one of our things: a never-ending game of "Gotcha" that began in the second grade and had escalated in the last year with some pretty elaborate pranks:

Springing up from behind a car during her walk home from track practice—Gotcha! (She fell backward.)

Jumping out of my closet one random Sunday afternoon—Gotcha! (I ducked and slid under the bed.)

"Falling" out of a tree one Saturday afternoon to suddenly block her path as she and Sookie walked home with ice cream—Gotcha! (She tossed her ice cream so far it landed in the street.)

We were "Gotcha" fanatics.

And if I were being honest here, she had gotten me. But that wasn't how the game was played, so I said, "That was lame."

"Score 444, me; 442, you."

"That doesn't count." I walked over to the gate, keeping my voice low so I wouldn't wake my parents. "I . . . I wasn't expecting anyone. Besides, you didn't know that I'd be outside. That was an accidental gotcha. They don't count."

"Nope. That was opportunistic. And that always counts. That's practically the essence of gotcha. *Carpe diem de gotcha!*"

I held in my laughter. That would give her too much

satisfaction. Instead, I asked, "So, what are you doing out this late, anyway?" I stepped onto the sidewalk and glanced at the quiet street: just a bunch of parked cars and darkened houses and the occasional stray cat sniffing around for scraps.

"What I just did. Prank you."

"Ugh, stop."

"You stop."

"Okay. Fine," I admitted. "You got me."

"Thank you." She bowed, and I realized that she was wearing her pj's—shorts with sheep on them and a matching tee. But on her feet were running shoes. And in her right hand was—

"Is that Mace?"

She glanced at the small black plastic cylinder strapped around her palm, the nozzle in the off position. "Oh, yeah. My mom got it for me. You gotta be safe, and it's late."

"It'd be safer not to be out."

"Gramps, I am not even here for that."

"Do your parents know you're out?"

"What do you think?"

I made a face. "What's going on?"

She crossed her arms over her chest, almost like she was hugging herself. "Nothing."

"You don't do this, though."

"What?"

"Sneak out."

"Oh, you're so after-school special with that sneaking-out bit. I didn't sneak. I climbed out the window *loudly*."

I laugh. "Because . . . ?"

She sighed. "Because my parents are having a pretty epic fight right now, and Boone never came home. Or maybe he came home, heard them fighting, and just didn't come inside. Which would be smart."

"What are they fighting about?"

"The usual. My dad dreaming up some wacky plan that's never gonna happen anyway, that's for sure." She smiled her wry smile. That was the smile she gave whenever she wanted to communicate that life was fine. That she could manage. That she wanted to get off the subject of her parents and on to something more fun. "Anyway, how'd you get out?"

"I walked out the door. My parents fell asleep at, like, ten."

"*Asleep*," Sally said suggestively.

"Stop." I knew where she was going with this. Last year, when Sally stayed over for dinner, she walked in on my parents in the kitchen, sharing a "passionate kiss" and had insisted ever since then that my parents still "did it."

Which was true.

Also true was that Sally's parents didn't do it much or at all. They were the kind to hold hands every now and then, *maybe* kiss on the cheek, but they didn't rub each other's backs. Or stand in that half sway, half hug as they asked about your day. They didn't have inside jokes that stretched across the dinner table, leaving them with goofy smiles on their faces. I couldn't imagine my parents apart, but Sally's parents? Who knew?

I glanced at Sally. Her gaze was focused on the far end of the street. "What?"

"See that?" She pointed to something in the distance.

A few seconds later I saw a car driving slowly toward us with the headlights off. Sally gripped her Mace a little tighter, straightening up into what seemed like a fighter's stance, but I wasn't a fighter. I had more experience running. So I took a more practical approach and dragged her into my yard, pulling her back into the shadow of a tree, the bark rough against my neck.

I was holding her.

One hand around her waist, no air between our bodies.

I noticed her breathing deepen. Mine too. A tingling that began in my chest spread across my body.

The car crept closer. At Jade's house, it swerved left, the engine revving as it mounted the curb, stopping two feet from her fence. The driver's door flung open, and her dad stumbled out.

We watched him stagger up their walkway, falling into the front door as he fumbled with the knob. The porch light flicked on. Then the door opened, a hand pulling him inside.

"Was that Mr. Acosta?" Sally asked.

"Yeah."

"Was he . . . ?"

We heard a voice yelling (Mrs. Acosta) and unintelligible slurs (Mr. Acosta).

I let Sally go. But for a second she didn't step forward,

the two of us as close as books on a crowded shelf. And then she took a deep breath and moved back into the yard.

We didn't speak for a few seconds, but finally Sally said, "Can't she hear them?" She pointed to Jade's room at the front corner of the house. The light was still off, but that didn't mean she wasn't listening. If we heard them out here, she had to hear them in there.

"Probably."

Sally cocked her head to the side, all her earlier playfulness gone. "I didn't know." Her eyes widened. "Did you?"

"It's kind of how they are," I said quietly. I had lived next to Jade the whole fourteen years of my life, and for all of those years Jade's parents had fought just like this.

"She never told me."

I waited a while, thinking about that. "Well, that's just Jade."

"I'm always telling you guys about my wacky parents."

"Well, that's you."

At the time I didn't know how to explain the difference, but later, when I thought back to that night, I realized that it came down to escape velocity.

In physics, escape velocity is the minimum speed an object needs to gain in order to break free of a planet's gravity. And the greater the mass of a planet, the greater the speed needed to escape. On earth, for example, an object needs to reach seven miles per second to break free, but on the sun, a star that is about 333,000 times the mass of our planet, that same object would have to accelerate to 384 miles per second.

That's a big difference in escape velocity.

But it makes sense. The sun is huge, and all that mass means it has more gravity to pull objects back to it. The shorter the distance between the two bodies, the more powerful the attraction.

I'd like to think that back then Jade lived in a house filled with mass.

The mass of shouting and fighting.

All that a short distance from Jade's body.

Sally's house had mass too, but where there was anger, there was also laughter. Even Sally's dad, on his better days, could surprise you with a joke, or Sally with a genuine hug. Those were the days that her parents clasped hands and Sally came to school with an easy smile. And so, yeah, while Sally's home life had a lot of mass, more mass than mine, those good days meant that not even she had had the escape velocity Jade needed to break free of the gravity of her parents' messed-up relationship.

Sally kicked at the pavement with her shoe and then looked up at me, her eyes uncharacteristically sad. "But if we can't tell each other, who can we tell?"

I nodded my agreement. It wasn't right—what Jade had to go through—but there also didn't seem a lot that could be done about it. How many times had neighbors, even my mom and pop, called the cops on Jade's drunken father? But Jade's mom never pressed charges and Jade's dad was pretty good at playing sober enough once the cops showed up.

So why talk about it at all?

Except I did try to talk about it a few times, but Jade would always shut me down with, "So? They fight. It's not all the time. It's only once in a while . . . when . . ."

When he had been drinking.

And for a while his drinking had been every now and then. But when he lost his job, the drinking became more and more, until we started talking about it in that language of neighbors.

"But what can we do?"

"It's not our problem."

"You can't fix the world. You just take care of your own."

My parents said to me, "It's not like we don't see it. We do."

Mom added, "I've talked to Jade's mom a few times, when I got her alone, but she says it's under control."

"I feel bad for Jade," is what I said.

"We feel bad for her too, but there's no law against fighting loudly."

Mom and Pop tried to be good to Jade in their own way. They invited her over for dinner and movie nights. On parent-teacher nights, they took both of us around the school. When report cards came, Jade showed my mom and pop first and then her parents. She always got good grades. She had to.

"People like that, they look for reasons to be angry," my mom had said. "But you hear me, Marco: There are just as many reasons not to choose your anger."

I watched Jade's house until I couldn't take it anymore. Until I needed to get out of there more than anything. So another singular thing happened that night: I took Sally's hand. I took her hand and tugged her toward the end of the block. And while, at some point, the tugging stopped, I never let her hand go.

I'd like to say that the walk felt romantic. That all I wanted was for the world to disappear, so that we could be alone. But looking back, that moment felt more like an act of survival, an act of staying in my own skin, an act of forgetting about Jade and all that I couldn't do. An act of being with another person and that other person being there, with me.

WORMHOLES II

IT WAS SOOKIE WHO RETRIEVED ME FROM my time travel.

Sookie who finally nudged me forward with a finger poke to my back until my feet began to move. Until I began to breathe again, returning to *the now* of the cafeteria from *the then* of that first kiss.

The tribe talked around me.

JADE

Is she taller?

DIEGO

No, but didn't she used to have blond hair?

JADE

It's only been four years. You remember that she had blond hair.

DIEGO

I remember nothing.

JADE

Yeah, not even how much you used to like her.

DIEGO

Nothing.

SOOKIE

You okay, Marco?

ME

Huh?

SOOKIE

Are you okay?

ME

Yeah, why?

SOOKIE

Because

(another poke in the back)

you stopped moving again.

The second nudge shoved me into full motion. Like Lot's wife, I tried not to look back. Because, you know, when she does, she turns into a pillar of salt. Look it up.

But when I was at the front of the line, I turned my head to the right. Just a simple flick of my chin, and our eyes locked.

And I didn't turn into salt.

But I stumbled back down that wormhole—back again to that first spark.

Somehow, despite the laws of physics, still alive.

Senior Year

5. PERFECT LIKE US

WHEN I TAKE THE SEAT OPPOSITE MR. Grendel's desk, all I can think about is Diego's advice: deny, deny, deny. Only problem is, I'm not sure what I'm denying. I haven't done anything wrong, but I also haven't done anything right enough—at least, nothing out of the ordinary—to be called into Mr. Grendel's office.

So, yeah, I'm nervous.

Truth is, I haven't had many one-on-one interactions with Mr. Grendel. Like most, I see him at group functions—monthly meetings and holiday parties—or around the store, his hobbit-size body bustling here and there while he smiles broadly at everyone. I get dosed with that smile as soon as I settle into my seat. That makes me think that this thing—this being-called-to-the-office thing—isn't bad.

"So, I noticed that you've been picking up a lot of shifts in the last few months. What's going on? Do you need more hours?" is how he begins.

Eh, so not a good start.

I'm scheduled for thirty hours a week, but I try to hustle closer to forty, always keeping an eye on the employee board for the telltale Post-it notes.

Can anyone cover cashier tomorrow? I have to go to the doctor.—Mike

Trying to sneak away this weekend. Can anyone take my bagger shift on Sunday night?—Jesenia

I'm the king of the pickup game, plucking Post-it notes off that board like they are sweet-and-sour candy.

"I help out with my family," I explain to Mr. Grendel. "So I like to pick up shifts. Is that okay?"

Mr. Grendel nods. "Well, I appreciate your work ethic, but I just want to make sure you don't go into overtime like you did last week. Okay? Overtime is expensive. So I need you to be a bit more careful."

"Oh, sorry. We had a last-minute emergency with a delivery, so I stayed late to take care of it, but I won't let it happen again."

"Good, Marco. I'm curious, though. If you always need the extra hours, why haven't you signed up for the interviews? It's a full-time job, so you wouldn't have to pick up hours. They'd be guaranteed. And it's a huge bump in salary, plus full-time would mean benefits. You've seen the new sign, right? At the employee station?"

"The management-trainee sign? Yeah, I saw it." Of course I saw it. The sign was big news from the moment Mr. Grendel tacked the flyer to the bulletin board. The interview sheet had filled up so quickly that Brenda, the operations manager, had to post a second sheet the next day. Besides Diego, there were a ton of hopefuls: Callie, in produce, who'd started wearing long shirts to cover up her tattoos and Pax, in the meat department, who'd taken to shaving off his daily scruff and Stefania, who was a new mom going through a divorce. It was a sweet deal. Even the year spent training came with a bump in salary, and afterward, a new title and even more pay. Everyone wanted a shot at that trainee spot.

Everyone but me.

Okay, that's not exactly true.

I had thought about it for a second or two. In that way that your mind wanders and you see this other path. This one that would let me stay closer to my family, working my way through college while I kept an eye on Pop and Mom and my foolish brothers.

But what about being free?

"How long have you been with us?" Mr. Grendel asks.

"Started in ninth grade, so almost four years."

"Well, I came on in 1975, when I was just sixteen. Brenda came on in 1980, when she was twenty. We've spent half our lives here, together. I always thought we'd leave here together. But life happens, right? Now that Brenda's in her last year before retirement, I've realized that I don't have a talent pipeline. That's why I'm starting this program. I want to identify the Brendas, nurture them, keep them invested in Grendel's." He launches into a speech about Brenda's best qualities: *She is nice, and so when customers have complaints, she always listens empathetically and provides a reasonable and timely solution. She is trustworthy. You can tell Brenda the biggest secret in the world and she won't say a word.*

I know all of this firsthand. The time Brenda caught me tearing up in the back room after one of Pop's bad days, she patted me on the back and just listened to the few words I had to say. Afterward, she never mentioned it again, not to me or anyone else. But she always seemed ready to listen. And when she found out I was accepted to Wayne in March, she made sure to write up an announcement for the company bulletin, even slipping a gift card into my locker with a note that said, *Best of luck!* I really appreciated her acts of kindness.

"So if Brenda thinks you should apply"—Mr. Grendel taps his hand on his leg—"I agree."

My mouth opens and shuts. If I could speak, I'd say, *Wait? What?*

"I've been watching you for the last few weeks," Mr. Grendel continues, a little smile playing over his lips. "You're good at what you do. You're on time, efficient, always willing to lend a hand. You smile a lot. I like a smiler." He pauses to flash me his effusive smile. "I asked Brenda last month, who's the best? And she gave me a few names, but at the top of her list was you."

"Me?" I finally push out, looking around like you do when you can't believe that the thing happening is happening to *you*.

"Yes," Mr. Grendel says, that smile still holding. *"You."*

• • •

"You?" Erika says, her eyes lighting up. "Brenda suggested you?"

"Yeah. Me." It's about an hour after my meeting with Mr. Grendel, and we're standing outside, next to her car, talking.

"But that's good, right? I mean, even if you're going to Wayne and your plans are settled, it's still good to know that Brenda really likes you and that Mr. Grendel agrees."

"No, it's good. But Diego . . . It'll kill his confidence," I say.

"If he knew, sure. But you don't have to tell Diego what Grendel said."

"But I told Grendel I'd think about it."

"Because he wouldn't take no for an answer. But you're not going to do it, right?"

"Right," I agree.

"So," Erika continues, "why tell Diego at all?"

She had a point. I smile, squeezing her hand. "You're so smart," I say, and she laughs.

"Does this mean you're not annoyed with me for showing up 'unannounced?'" She raises an eyebrow, her part of the hand squeeze turning into a playful death grip.

At least, I hope it's playful.

"I never said that."

"No, but you acted like that."

"Like how?"

"Did you give me a big ol' kiss?"

"I'm at work."

"Did you give me a hug, then?"

"Again, work."

She sighs, and I say, "I'm happy to see you, but . . ."

"But what?" she asks, like she knew there was a "but" all along.

"I'm at work. I have to really do a good job here."

"You do a good job at everything."

"That's because I have to."

"Not because you want to?" she asks, veering toward one of those logic twist-ups, where she takes every little thing I say and examines it for the "deeper meaning."

But there's no deeper meaning here. I'm at work, and work is sacred. The real problem is that she doesn't understand that. This is her third visit in the last week. The first time it was, "I needed butter to bake cookies for track's end-of-the-year party and Grendel's is the only one that carries the vegan brand, and you know Kelsey's vegan."

The second time, "I needed to find those all-natural eye drops, and Grendel's is the only one that carries it. You know I'm allergic to the kind with preservatives."

And today it was, "Coach suggested that we keep track of our heart rate and blood pressure. She says that's good for athletes. And the machine at Publix is broken."

"Oh, really," I had said, raising an eyebrow.

"Yes." She had laughed. "Stop shading me. I don't have any other motives."

Except to get me to walk her to her car so she could drop a loaded question on me:

On visit one, she asked: Where did I see things going? How did I feel about graduation?

On visit two: What would things be like when we lived away from everyone else?

Today I didn't offer to walk her to the car, but sure enough, when I turned to leave, she called out, "Actually, wait! Take your break. I want to show you something."

And that's why right now I'm wiggling my bloodless fingers from her grasp while standing next to her car.

"You know," she says, "you'd think you'd tell me how awesome it is to have your girlfriend drive out of her way to break up your monotonous workday."

"So you admit that you're coming here is a stretch from the usual path."

She scoffs. "I plead the Fifth."

"Humph."

"Anyway." She clicks a button on her key chain, and the locks of her hand-me-down Honda Civic pop up. "I have something amazing to show you."

When she opens her passenger door, the overhead lights flick on, illuminating the back seat and a pale-pink dress sheathed in a clear plastic cover. I recognize it from one of Erika's many Pinterest boards: mid-knee, silk, and form-fitting in a 1920s style. The neckline is the kind that resembles a heart—a sweetheart neck. Yeah, that's what she called it when she showed me the dress in January.

"Isn't it perfect?" Erika raises the dress delicately to her chest.

"Yeah," I say, exhaling my relief that there are no questions today. Just this.

"Perfect like us." She swirls around, the plastic fluttering in her wind. Then she returns the dress to the car and wraps her arms around my neck, sidestepping a slow back-and-forth dance like we're already at prom. "It's all happening. Everything we've planned."

"Everything *you* planned," I say with a smile, because there is a certain appeal in her unwavering belief that life can be plotted out moment by moment. That all you have to do to be happy is follow your plan. Step one foot forward after the next and everything you want will be yours in time. I lost that type of certainty after Pop's fall. But sometimes, for the briefest of moments, I find it again when I lean into the feeling of Erika there in my arms.

Middle School

6. GOTCHA

"DO YOU WANT TO CLIMB IT?" SALLY HAD asked when we arrived at the park.

She pointed to a tower constructed of stretchy blue rope and silver joints that stood at the center of the park. We walked closer, passing the swing set, the jungle gym, and a small shelter. At the basketball courts, we turned right and continued up a narrow path until we stood at the tower's base, our necks craned upward.

At times, when we were younger, we'd pretend the tower was a rocket about to launch into space. Back then we'd take turns being "Captain" and "Astronaut." The captain was in charge and stayed at the very tip of the tower, focusing on navigation. The astronaut got to zigzag around the rope tower's web, fixing all the things that could break.

Since Sally was a more confident climber than me, she was mostly Astronaut. That left me with the cushy job of Captain, shouting out commands like, "Prepare to launch, Astronaut Blake. Ready the fuel tanks!" And Sally would scramble over to the right quadrant of the ship to ready the tanks, her hands working quickly to pull herself along the rope until she reached the imaginary panel with the imaginary buttons, completing all the imaginary tasks I had assigned her.

We loved the game. We loved the imagination. But at some point we outgrew it. Probably around the time that we exchanged our toys for cooler clothes and Spin the Bottle.

That night, I stared up at our tower, wondering if we could go to Mars or, like in another version of the game, discover an enchanted tree house that overlooked Camelot. Or we could pretend that we were eating dinner atop the Eiffel Tower. I could be Captain or Knight or Parisian. Or, I thought, glancing shyly over at Sally, whose hand I'd held until the minute we entered the park, I could be Marco, and she . . . she could just be Sally. And we could be alone, up there. Two stories higher than the rest of the world for miles around.

I started to climb, and Sally followed, a little slower than normal because of her knee. Our hands worked quickly. Foot found joint after joint. Hands found new levels of rope. Before long we sat at the top of the tower, our feet dangling over a square platform just wide enough to hold two bodies. We contemplated the neighborhood below. Squat houses, simple block construction, yards that were mostly concrete, as if grass were a luxury only those with money could afford.

"I wonder what next year will be like," Sally said suddenly.

"More of this," I said without much thought.

"More of what? What is *this*?"

Looking back, I think she met philosophically, but I answered her literally. "This is us hanging out."

"Yeah, but what about the future?"

"Oh . . ." I dug deeper, imagining that future being pretty much a continuation of the now. "Well, you'll run track. We'll take AP Geometry. Sookie will play chess. Jade will continue cheerleading. Diego . . ."

I didn't know what Diego would do. He had announced about a month ago that he didn't want to play football anymore. "That was my dad's thing, but I just want a real job, not some blown-up dream." I guess Diego had come to some conclusion that his dad's stint as a high school all-star who didn't have the grades to make it in college wasn't the path for him.

"D," I finished, "will do his best to be a law-abiding citizen."

Sally laughed. "Do you think high school will be hard?"

"Nah. We're smart. We can handle it."

"No. I mean, like, transitionally. Do you think the older kids will be mean?"

I glanced at Sally, waiting for her to crack some joke, but her expression was pretty serious. "You'll be fine," I say. "Me? We'll see."

"Wait. Why am I fine and you're not?" She turned to

me, her hand accidentally brushing my thigh.

I took a deep breath. Because, you know, her hand, my thigh.

"Marco?"

"Um, sorry."

"Why am I going to be okay, and you're not?"

"'Cause." I didn't look at her, but I let my hand sweep up and down like I was saying, *All this*. But I guess Sally didn't get it, because she said, "What's that supposed to mean?"

"Well," I hedged, "you're taller than most girls, so they won't bother you. Easier to pick on someone smaller, right? And the guys will . . ."

I paused. I couldn't exactly say what I was thinking. . . . *The guys will find you pretty with your wide gray eyes and front teeth that lean in together like some kind of old married couple and the cute little bump on the bridge of your nose.*

"Guys will what?" She studied me.

"Guys will . . . like you," I settled on.

"Why?" she pushed.

"Because." I stressed the full word to make it clear that was explanation enough. But Sally kept going. "Because what?"

"Because you're . . ." And then I decided we were on top of a magical world. Maybe some of that magic would rub off on us. "You're pretty."

She smiled, the edges of her lips rising triumphantly toward the tips of her ears. "I knew it," she whispered. "You think I'm pretty."

"You're a jerk," I said, and I did something else that was brave. I pinched her side. She laughed, expanding so that our thighs pressed together, her left hand just inches from my right. And then the magic kicked in and her pinkie extended, our fingers suddenly linked.

I sighed.

Even looking back, I'm sure that sigh was audible.

It was a sigh of *Yes. This. Is. Happening.*

Sally didn't sigh. She looked out over Camelot. I watched her in the dim light from the streetlamps, finding us now that we were up here. A wrinkle rippled across her forehead as she worked out a new thought, then settled in that space between her eyes. She cleared her throat. "Actually, I'm thinking about not running next year."

I didn't say anything. I was too surprised.

"Does that count as another 'gotcha'?" she finally asked.

I laughed, unsure. "So, you're joking?"

"No." She glanced at me. "I'm not. I mean, 'gotcha' because you're surprised."

"Yeah, I am." I tried to imagine that bookshelf in Sally's house, the one lined with trophies, growing dusty. "But why?"

"I know I don't act like it, but it's a lot of pressure."

"Would your dad let you quit?" I thought about earlier, how her dad had yelled at her on the bleachers until Sookie "had enough," interrupting the tirade with instructions about the care and maintenance of Sally's wound.

"That's the problem," she said, her voice quieter. "I don't think so."

"Could you . . . ? Could you talk to your mom—"

"I don't think she'd do anything about it."

"But I could go with you. I could help—"

She sighed. "It's dumb. I can't quit."

"But you could. He can't force you."

"No. He can just bother me every day."

"But after a while he'd stop."

"It would just be easier to try harder, to be better." Her voice picked up speed. "If I'm better at it, it won't feel so hard. And I won't fall again. Maybe I could be just as good as my dad. Maybe even better if I trained harder."

I stared at her knee, the shape of the bruise somewhat like the outline of a cauliflower. Even though Mr. Blake couldn't compete professionally now, he still trained, pushing Boone and Sally just as hard as he had pushed himself. In fact, I couldn't remember a time past the age of eight that Sally wasn't training.

"Sally, you spent all of last summer training. You do work hard."

"Not hard enough," Sally said.

"Says who? Your dad?"

"Can we not talk about this anymore?"

"But—"

"Please, Marco."

She let go of my pinkie and scooted to her end of the platform. I could barely make out the glimmer of her eyes through the curtain of wavy blond hair. All my words, all my solutions left me.

I stared up at the moon, the moon that had thought to follow us all the way here, and then back at the world below. All those boxes on the ground filled with more boxes inside. Boxes that people slept in, their bodies resting on little squares and rectangles made of sharp corners, and all of this contained by a world that is round.

I wanted to tell Sally that we could lose all our sharp corners and become round too—supremely good, celestial beings with no clear beginnings or endings, always in orbit of each other. I wanted to tell her that she was Astronaut, unafraid of space or dark matter or being untethered from this rocket and floating toward the brilliance of the sun. And that as Captain, I would be there to make sure that wherever we were going, we got there okay.

I wanted to tell her that she *could* quit running.

But I didn't say any of that. Because for all the things I could say—like *you're pretty*—I still had an inability to vocalize greater truths.

That's what being young is all about.

Instead, I said, "Sally?"

And she ignored me.

"Sally?"

"What?"

"I like . . ." I stalled. "I like . . . peanut butter and jelly sandwiches."

It was another game we had played when we were younger.

Hours and hours lost to listing everything in the world that we liked.

"And chocolate," I said. "And"—I imitated her voice—"summer rain." I took a deep breath, adding in my own voice again. "The ocean . . ."

"I don't want to play," she said.

"Butterflies," I said in her voice. She was still silent. "Try, please."

It took a while, but finally she sighed and said, "No. Moths. You know I like moths more than butterflies."

"Okay." That rapid beat of my heart lessened. "Moths. And Pluto, for me."

"It *is* a planet," she said, slowly inching her way back toward me and the safety of good things. "Thunder."

"Warm benches."

She laughed a crinkly laugh anchored in sadness, but still a laugh.

"Mr. Snuffleupagus," I said.

"Bert."

"Ernie."

"Miss Piggy."

"Kermit."

She laughed again. "Always Kermit."

"Better?" I asked.

"Almost. Oranges and bananas."

"Blueberries."

"Smoothies."

"Peanut butter," we both said simultaneously.

She leaned closer, until our eyes met. I glanced at her pinkie, an inch or two from mine now.

"Playing gotcha," she whispered, that wry smile settling back onto her lips.

I took a deep breath, finding the last of my courage for the night. "You."

"My turn? Again?"

"*No.* I like . . . *you.*"

"Me?"

We were so close, I felt her exhalation on my lips. And then I felt all the other supremely good things that I liked swirl inside of me—ocean breezes, hot sand between my toes, the coolness of a sun shower. All of that waiting to be found, right there in Sally Blake's second kiss.

Senior Year

7. DRIVING AN IMPALA TO THE MOON

"OH, JIGGETY-JACK LOOKS GOOD." A FEW hours after the unveiling of Erika's prom dress, Diego and I clock out of Grendel's and head over to his souped-up Impala. I climb in, pausing to run my hands over the fresh topcoat—a sparkling emerald gloss that makes his old ride look as good as new. "How'd you score the new paint job?"

Diego beams proudly. "Moms knows this guy from church. I helped paint his house; he gave me a pretty new sweater for baby boy." Diego uses the edge of his shirt to wipe away a smudge from the hood. "Almost getting too pretty to drive, right? Gonna have to be on the bus like your ass when I get Old Jiggetty a spot in the classic car museum."

"Nah, don't do that. Something this pretty has to be shown off, right?"

"Yeah, that's true, and with Jade riding shotgun, it'll be like I have all the beauty in the 'hood right here, in my ride."

We slide into the leather bucket seats Diego had repaired last year—another bartered restoration from another dude at his mom's church—and I settle into a few minutes of heavenly rest, sipping on my coffee while Diego gives me the side-eye.

"It's only half full," I reassure him, because spills aren't allowed in Old Jiggety, but I'm willing to risk his wrath because this tiny dose of caffeine will help me power through the last of my homework. I yawn, and when I glance at Diego, he's yawning too.

"This," he says, pointing at his mouth, "is because of you. When you start with that nonsense, I can't even stop till tomorrow. I'll yawn my way through all my beauty rest."

"Sorry."

"Sorry is as sorry does." He yawns again. "So, what did Grendel want with you?"

"Huh?"

"You know, in the office?"

"Oh . . . that?" That's a conversation I'd like to avoid, so I yawn again, face thrust at him. Sure enough, he takes the bait, yawning too.

"Stop."

"You know, it's good that you yawn back. Means that you're not a psychopath."

"How'd we go from yawning to psychopaths?"

I shrug. "It's about empathy. If you yawn back, you're basically feeling my exhaus—"

"Let me guess, you read that somewhere?"

"I read everything somewhere."

Usually we can banter like this for hours, but tonight Diego has tunnel vision. "Nah, but seriously, what he'd say?"

"Huh?" I yawn again. "Who?"

"Grendel."

"Um . . ."

"Come on, now." Diego takes a turn at a red light, slowing down suddenly to let a cat pass.

"Okay, well . . ." And I tell him about the problem with my overtime, leaving out the part about Mr. Grendel encouraging me to interview for the management-trainee program. Like Erika said earlier, that part isn't relevant.

"Couldn't Brenda tell you that?"

I shrug. "I guess, but . . . Grendel did."

"That's some watchful eye Mr. Grendel has."

"Yep. Eyes everywhere."

Diego pulls into my driveway and looks at me, all thoughtful. "Think those cameras have sound? 'Cause maybe the volume was turned down the last time I was in the office."

I know they don't because when I was in the office with Mr. Grendel, I managed to casually ask that question, but I decide to have a little fun with him anyway. "Bro, best to think they do. If you wanna be a Grendel man for life, you're gonna have to look, act, and *sound* the part."

"Piece of cake." Diego smiles confidently. "I'll just imitate corny-ass you."

• • •

Inside, I knock off fifty push-ups just to relax, followed by a shower to get the grit and grime from my skin. After, I sit at my desk, spending one last hour working on my physics final. This project is just the kind of assignment that only our teacher, Mrs. A, could come up with. First we have to complete a "deep dive" into one of our favorite physics principles or concepts. Then we have to explain how that principle or concept applies to our everyday lives.

MRS. A

You have to be slightly philosophical.

KID AT BACK OF CLASS

Say what?

MRS. A

(smiles patiently)

Physics is practical, but there's also a beauty to all of these rules about the way the universe operates. These are principles of organization, of interaction between objects that are visible and invisible to the naked eye. Think about the principles that dictate the way you live your life—both visible and invisible.

KID AT FRONT OF CLASS

How do you live an invisible life?

MRS. A

(laughing)

You don't live an invisible life, but much like physics, a lot of why we act the way we do is a result of the invisible forces at play. Forces like love, sadness, fear, and pain. I want you to consider how those forces complicate and influence the trajectory of your lives. What are the universal laws that you use to manage those forces?

KID AT BACK OF CLASS

Say what?

You've probably figured out that Mrs. A is that teacher who smells of essential oils, wears clothes made out of organic materials (hemp, for Mrs. A), and washes her hair with mixtures of baking soda and apple cider vinegar.

My friend Mrs. Banks says Mrs. A is the most hippie teacher I'll ever meet. And you know a thing or two about the kind of teachers you'll meet in a lifetime when you get to be Mrs. Banks's age. Although, technically, no one knows how old Mrs. Banks is. The only clue is a crinkled black-and-white photo of her as a toddler, standing outside a row house in Washington, DC. Sookie is Mrs. Banks's neighbor, and she says her parents believe that picture was taken some time between World War I and World War II. That would make Mrs. Banks as old as a hundred or as young as eighty—so, pretty old *or* super old. As a nod to all that oldness, the tribe calls her Old Mrs. B when she's not around. When she is around, we just listen, because like I said, Old Mrs. B knows a thing or two about everything, including teachers.

Anyway, up until now it is true that I haven't had a more hippie teacher. But hippie or not, I like Mrs. A. I like that her Jamaican accent is still strong, since she's only been in the United States for a few years. I like the faint smell of lavender when she passes by my desk. I like the depth of her brown eyes. I like that when she looks at me, I feel like more than just the sum of my GPA and attendance record.

Yeah, I like Mrs. A, but I don't really like this assignment, because I'm good at science, but life? That I'm not so sure about.

But the paper is due soon, so tonight I force myself to work on the first part of the assignment: wormholes. Truth be told, I've been fascinated with wormholes ever since Pop introduced me to that old nineties movie *Contact* when I was about seven.

That part at the end, when that blond scientist Ellie travels through a series of wormholes to arrive in this new place—maybe a new galaxy!—to meet an alien who looks just like her dad? Wow.

And even more impressive is how all of that goes down. On earth, Ellie is gone for just a few seconds. But her video camera—a nineties version of a GoPro—captures eighteen hours of static. What does that mean? How can you reconcile the time difference?

Back then Pop tried to explain it to me, but all I remember are the series of words he used: wormholes, speed of light, something about Einstein.

I've watched *Contact* a dozen times since then. Now that my brain has developed more, I get how it's done now, at least in theory.

In theory, even though Ellie's gone for only a few

seconds of earth time, she could still be gone for eighteen hours Ellie time because the wormhole could pick her up, at say 3:05:02 p.m. and return her back to earth at 3:05:04 p.m. That's one of the reasons why wormholes are so amazing. If real, they could cut through the fabric of space and time. (At least in theory.)

After an hour reading up on wormholes and jotting down notes, I make a list for what I'll try to find tomorrow at the library. At two a.m., I crawl into bed. You'd think I'd fall dead asleep, but instead, I'm awake in the dark, watching my ceiling fan whirl above me. And then I do something that I often do late at night. I whisper the words I heard almost four years earlier from Pop's doctors: *He's suffered a traumatic brain injury.*

Those words are like a cancer that sits inside me, metastasizing to my bones, my skin, my heart.

Many versions of the story have been told over the years—by me, by others—but the shortest version is the one I return to tonight: After the eighth-grade dance, Pop got hurt and our lives changed forever.

I roll onto my back to stare at the moon outside my window. I try to calm down, step away from my thoughts—the night Pop got hurt, Sally in the cafeteria yesterday, Mr. Grendel and our talk, Erika and her questions about the future. I play a game Pop taught me when I was six. The game is "How Long Would It Take You to Get to the Moon?" And the answer is, "Depends." Here are the options:

1. If a dude tried to drive to the moon in his Impala, it would take him about five months.
2. But if a dude tried to get there on a rocket, it'd take him thirteen hours.
3. But if he hitched a ride on a wave of light, it'd take him 1.52 seconds.

You might be like, "Marco, the moon is 238,900 miles away. That's an outrageous destination for a dude with an Impala. But if I have to choose, book me a first-class ticket on that wave o' light."

But I'll tell you what Pop used to say to me. "Think of all that you'd miss along the way. That first break from the atmosphere, the earth full-out behind you. The lights as they brighten our globe at night. Think about that, little man."

And even though I'm not a little man anymore, I think a little about that tonight.

About all that I'd miss along the way.

About all that the twins have missed along the way.

I think about Pop.

About who he is and who he used to be.

About wormholes and Ellie bending space and time to see her father again—at least some version of him.

And then I remind myself that wormholes exist only in theory. And me and Pop, we exist in real life. And for us there is no going back.

• • •

The following Tuesday night Old Mrs. B hands me a yellow sticky note covered in her slanted handwriting. The ink is bright purple; the quote stretches from edge to edge. "Have you gotten to that part of the book yet?" she asks.

We are sitting on a courtyard bench outside of Seagrove Branch Library, taking a "breather," which Old Mrs. B defines as five minutes of fresh air and companionable silence. I'm at the library because we, the tribe, meet here every week. Sookie came up with the idea at the start of our senior year because . . .

SOOKIE

Well, Jade's always busy with cheerleading, and I'm always busy with my committees. Marco, you've got school and work and your family and, Diego—the same—so, like, when do we really hang anymore?

ME

We hang all the time.

SOOKIE

Not *outside* of school.

ME

I swear I just saw you on Friday.

JADE

I saw her last night and this morning and at lunch. . . . I think sometimes she watches me while I sleep.

DIEGO

That's creepy.

SOOKIE

Untrue, but if true . . .

(points to Diego)

pot to my kettle.

DIEGO

What is that? Old-people metaphor?

JADE

You two are fighting over who stalks me more.

(winks at me)

I'm beloved, Marco. I am.

SOOKIE

Anyway. We need a guaranteed midweek meeting. Our high school experience is almost over. We're about to be *Petals on the Wind* and you all are *Beloved* by me, so let's really think about *The Way We Live Now*.

DIEGO

Huh?

SOOKIE

(winks at Diego)

Welcome to twentieth-century pop novel.

And that's how Tuesdays—part study group, part smack talk, part potluck madness—became our thang. Now, I know you're not exactly supposed to talk or eat in the library, but since Sookie is a library aide and Old Mrs. B runs the reference desk, we got hooked up with a janitor's closet to do just that. The space is tight. One overhead light illuminates five-by-five feet of crammed furniture—a rectangular wooden table, five chairs, and a storage shelf that holds cleaning supplies, extra toilet paper, paper towels, and the like—but since it's connected to the library's main space by a long hallway, we have our privacy. Although Old Mrs. B makes us keep the door wide open because "rules" and "being the adult here" and also "common decency is dependent on transparency."

I use the closet to study more than the others, so above the table I've hung posters of my heroes: Einstein and Newton and Hawking and the little-known Emmy Noether, who, to paraphrase Einstein, was a helluva mathematician.

If you don't know about Emmy, look her up.

The rest of the space is filled with random, mostly inspirational quotes that Old Mrs. B taped to the wall. Though we've added our own over the years.

And then there's one corner, the far-right corner, that's sort of an altar for Trayvon Martin, the South Florida kid who was murdered in 2012 for just being a teen who wore a hoodie and walked through a neighborhood that wasn't his—*a black kid like me* is what Diego had said when it happened. *I know how it can go. I see how some people look at me when I got my hood up.*

He's right. When you're a young person of color, who knows how it can go? But to be knee-deep in that reality every day is hard. When I said that to Diego, though, he was like, "Man, we got to think about it every day. We've got to remember."

So, we remember.

It was Diego who taped Trayvon's picture to the wall. And Sookie who handwrote the index card affixed below, the words of an old Jewish proverb: "*As long as we live, they too will live; for they are now a part of us; as we remember them.*"

And it was also Sookie who, on our eighteenth birthdays, presented each of us with several voter registration applications wrapped in red, white, and blue ribbon—one to register and a few to pass out to whomever because "we've all got to fight to make things right, to make them better."

Anyway, this is our thing. Each Tuesday we're here dutifully to have one another's backs. That is, unless it's this week and we're talking about something like this weekend, when Erika sorta asked me to move in with her freshman year of college.

DIEGO

Wait, What? Whoa.

ME

That's hard-core alliteration.

JADE

Freshman year?

(sucks on lips)

That's major, huh?

ME

Says the girl who started a savings account to move in with this dude

(nods at Diego)

this summer.

JADE

Yeah, *but* we've been together for almost four years. You and Erika got together when? November?

DIEGO

And mostly because she straight-up kissed you.

ME

No. *No.*

SOOKIE

Yes. *Yes.*

ME

No, I kissed *her*.

DIEGO

Back. Bro, you kissed her back.

ME

No. I got that party started.

JADE

Eh . . .

(tilts hand side to side)

Did you?

SOOKIE

You were very good at receiving the kiss, Marco.

ME

There was a mutual lean-in!

DIEGO

Eh, you took a step back, like *way* back. But damn . . .

(whistles)

You closed the deal. Eventually.

JADE

Yeah, but if it weren't for that wall behind you, who knows? You'd be stuck in lonely heart city.

DIEGO

But, damn, Erika's been after you for, like, what?

JADE

If you count eighth grade . . . about four years plus before the eagle landed.

DIEGO

(eyes Jade)

Eagle landed?

JADE

It's a common idiomatic expression.

DIEGO

Idiomatic expression?

JADE

Stop. I got mad vocab.

(smirks)

That better?

DIEGO

(smiling, proud-like)

Humph.

SOOKIE

Anyway, Marco. It was four years. But that's okay. You had to heal from your broken-heart syndrome.

ME

From my what?

SOOKIE

You know, because . . .

(exchanges looks with Jade and Diego)

ME

. . .

SOOKIE

But you opened your heart again.

ME

She . . . I . . . *I* . . . We were just friends back then. I wasn't *healing*, and she wasn't *waiting*.

SOOKIE

Except she had the love eyes for you. Like, in eighth grade.

ME

Regular eyes. Normal eyes. Everyday eyes.

SOOKIE

Tarsier eyes. Nature unleashed.

JADE

Love at ten thousandth sight.

ME

And I'm out.

DIEGO

Bro, c'mon . . . Hey! *Wait!* You said no, right?

"I did say no," I tell Old Mrs. B while I pick at the bark of a shady palm tree.

She nods sagely. "Best to not breed false hopes."

"False hopes that I'm ready for that step?" Because who knows about the future? Maybe Erika is *the one*, whatever that means.

Old Mrs. B raises an eyebrow. "Best to live in the reality of your situation, as one who runs away from a Pinterest board."

"That? *Again*?"

"That is everything."

Old Mrs. B is talking about Erika's San Francisco Pinterest board, the one she began weeks ago, when her application to San Francisco State jumped from wait-listed to accepted.

"It's gonna be great," Erika said when she started the board. Two days later she said, "Just check it out. You'll love it!" On the seventh day, she moaned, "Have you looked yet?"

I hadn't. I was still busy processing. Had been for months now, ever since I had been accepted early decision to Wayne and Erika had immediately started applying to schools nearby.

"That's normal, right?" I asked Sookie back in January. "Erika says it's important, if we, you know, want to, like, have a future."

"Erika says?" Sookie sighed. "I mean, if you guys break up, that's going to be uncomfortable."

"But it's a big city."

"Yeah, but . . ." She rolled her eyes. "It's the *same* city."

"Well," I said optimistically, "we won't break up."

"Never ever ever?" Sookie deadpanned.

"Maybe?"

"So, you're saying she's *the one*?"

"*No. No. No*," came out fast. Then I backtracked, "I mean, who knows, right?"

"Um . . ." Sookie shrugged. "I'm thinking Erika knows if she's willing to move to the same city for you. Wasn't Florida State her dream school? What happened to that?"

Sookie was onto something—I knew that—but I also argued that it couldn't be *that* bad. Erika was just thinking ahead. Planners do that. Nothing was locked in.

When I shared that with Sookie, she snapped, "Just look at the board! If it's terrible, at least you'll know and you can stop talking my ear off about it!"

So last Monday I looked. I was at Erika's house, checking my grades on her laptop, when I took a deep breath and navigated to her Pinterest page. Maybe I should have asked. Or used the specific link she sent me. But then I wouldn't know this: Erika also has a wedding board.

With wedding cakes.

And lacy white dresses.

And flower arrangements.

And a new section of "Happily Ever After" banners that she had started earlier *that* day.

That day!

I reasoned that Erika had fallen prey to *Happily Ever After* Disney Princesses Wedding Culture and this was her version of playing dress-up for the very, very faraway future. But then I remembered something else. Something that happened a few months earlier.

We were at her house, rewatching *For Keeps*, a late-eighties film that was part of her mom's ancient VHS collection, when Erika cuddled into my chest and whispered: "Don't you think it's sweet that your parents got married at eighteen?"

ME

Please don't be seduced by preggers Molly Ringwald and this fluffy-haired baby daddy.

ERIKA

(laughing)

Oh, c'mon! They fall in love, have a baby, get married. It's cute. And your parents did it too. That's sweet, right?

ME

No. Teen pregnancy is not sweet.

ERIKA

It can be. Don't be so judgy.

ME

What's sweet about my mom dropping out of school?

ERIKA

Yeah, but that's because you were a difficult pregnancy. Teens don't always have to drop out. You just made her throw up all the time. *And* she did get her GED.

ME

She didn't want a GED. She wanted her actual diploma and to go to prom and to not have an episiotomy at the age of seventeen.

ERIKA

What's an episiotomy?

ME

That's when the baby is too big to come out so they . . .

(makes snipping motions with fingers).

ERIKA

That's disgusting.

ME

That's having a baby.

ERIKA

Well, no matter what, I think your parents got married because they loved each other. . . . And you can get married and not have a baby right away.

ME

But *they* wouldn't have.

ERIKA

You don't know that.

ME

Yeah, I do. They'd have gone to college, traveled, and had more—

ERIKA

More what?

ME

Options.

ERIKA

Well, all I know is, they are *still* married.

ME

What does that prove?

ERIKA

(kissing me)

That young love wins.

"I just needed space," I tell Old Mrs. B now. "I couldn't breathe."

"You ran."

Technically, when I found the wedding Pinterest

board, I walked. To the kitchen, where Erika was making us grilled cheese sandwiches. And then I made a reasonable excuse—"Oh crap, I forgot I picked up a shift at Grendel's"—and took my grilled cheese to go.

I headed straight to Old Mrs. B's house. I needed a safe space to rant about how seventeen's too young to get married or to think about getting married or even to be creating boards about getting married. Seventeen is for sneaking out of the house. Bombing tests. Making mistakes.

OLD MRS. B on that day
But you haven't done any of those things, Marco.

ME
I want the . . . the . . . possibility.

OLD MRS. B
Do you?

ME
Yeah.

OLD MRS. B
Maybe . . . Or maybe you just want *possibilities* . . .

ME
What's the difference?

OLD MRS. B
I'll let you figure that out.

And then she smiled that sage smile of hers. A smile just like the one she wears now. She runs a wrinkled, brown hand over her 1950s dress, probably one of her own from that time period, before patting her silver hair appreciatively.

"Aged like a fine wine," Pop's *abuelito* has said about Old Mrs. B. So smitten that he gets his younger neighbor, Marcelo, to drive him to the library on Sundays, so he can give her the "the chit-*y*-chat."

"You mean chitchat, Lito?" I always ask him.

"Sí, eso fue lo que dije, the *chit-y-chat."*

An octogenarian love story waiting to happen, I tell you.

Old Mrs. B stands. "I should get back. As always, Marco, a lovely bit of respite. Wouldn't you say?"

"Sure," I mumble, rising. And then I see her—that her—in the parking lot. She is there because she is everywhere these days.

Old Mrs. B smiles at me slyly. "Apparently, she was practically a full-time library aide in North Carolina. Obsessed with books is how the librarian who called put it. So I've hired her to be an aide here. Today is her first day."

"Sally?"

"Don't sound so surprised," Old Mrs. B says softly, but I am. Between running and school, when did Sally ever have time to be obsessed with books? "People change, and it's important to see someone as they are and not as they used to be."

Sally stops a few feet from us and smiles tentatively.

"Excited for your first day?" Old Mrs. B asks, and Sally nods. Her bag slips to the crease of her elbow, and a dog-eared book tumbles out, landing on the pavement with a *thud*. She quickly drops to her knees and slides the book back into her bag. When she stands, her eyes are on the floor.

"Ready?" Old Mrs. B asks without missing a beat.

"Yeah," Sally says. Her eyes dart to mine for just a second.

Just a second before she is gone.

Middle School

8. YOU LOOK BEAUTIFUL TODAY

A FEW DAYS AFTER OUR SECOND KISS, I noticed Sally's hand shaking.

The first sighting was on the morning bus, as her fingers hovered above the strap of her backpack. The second sighting was in English class as she turned the pages of *The Curious Incident of the Dog in the Night-Time* during sustained silent reading. Even at the end of the day, her hand shook. This time, in math class.

Maybe Mr. Weaver, our algebra teacher, couldn't see the shaking from the front of the classroom, because he called on her, fingers in mid-pulsation.

"Yes?" Sally replied after a second.

"The answer?"

"Oh . . . um . . . I don't know."

The class's laughter bounced around the room.

"Hey now," Mr. Weaver said to the class. "Just give it a shot, Sally. Begin by simplifying like terms."

She stared at the board—the sharp blue lines of Mr.

Weaver's sloppy but best handwriting—like she couldn't make sense of it. I stared at her hand; the shake had increased to a tremor.

The class laughed again, and I waited for Sally to go cross-eyed or something, giving others a reason to laugh at her antics, not her, but she didn't do that this time. Instead, she stared at the board going, "Um . . . um . . . um . . ." under her breath.

"Twenty-one," I coughed.

"Twenty-one?" Sally repeated meekly.

"Yes . . . that's correct," Mr. Weaver said, looking at me. Then he began narrating a new problem on the board. "And so, as you can see . . ."

"Hand," I whispered. When Sally's palm slid back, I pressed a piece of paper into the pad of her hand, holding for a second like I could absorb whatever was making her tremble. She brought the note around to her desk, head dipping as she unfolded the creases and glanced at my drawing of the rope tower before flipping the note over to read:

1. Sneaking out is kinda fun.
2. I drew this b4 I realized u might not be OK.
3. R u OK?

She glanced at Mr. Weaver before jotting down her reply, balling the paper, and tossing it lightly over her shoulder. The ball landed at the center of my desk. Her note said:

4. I did 2. A LOT.

5. I'm ok.

6. Am I being weird?

I scribbled back:

7. ☺

8. Not weird.

9. + u look beautiful today.

Number eight was a lie. She was definitely acting weird, but I wanted to make her feel better. Number nine was true. That day she wore a white dress, dotted with blueberries; her hair was up in a sloppy bun, her eyes "wide and dipped in tragedy." Those aren't my words. I had read that somewhere in some book that Mrs. Bartell had assigned us. But those were the words that struck me when I looked at her eyes. And I knew then that this was what that same book had called "a tragic sort of beauty," the beauty "of a heart laid bare." I know. I know. Who talks like that? But, damn, if it weren't true about Sally on that day.

She never saw number nine. Right before I slipped the paper into her hand, I tore the words away.

I tore the words away because, back then, I suffered from the middle school worry that you could say too much, do too much, show too much. And writing down that I saw her as an exquisite creature definitely qualified as *too much* of something. I thought I was being slick, but after she read the list, she twisted in her seat, her fingers running across the frayed edges.

The bell rang, and the class shifted. Some hurried toward the door. Others stopped at Mr. Weaver's desk to ask questions. We were used to traffic jams, so we took our time packing up. Sally was slower than me, and while she pulled and prodded at her backpack, I worried at the slip of paper in my pocket and stared down at my clothes: the best pair of jeans I owned, a collared shirt that didn't have a hole. On my feet, last year's pleather kicks, shiny from lack of use but tight as hell. I'd even used Pop's date-night hair gel, so that my hair had what the bottle called "body" and not "frizz." To me, though, it gave me what my mom called "helmet head."

And the biggest reveal: I plucked the field between my eyebrows.

"About time," is what Jade had said that morning at the bus stop. "I've been bugging you about that forever."

"Dude." Diego chuckled. "What's up with all the man-scaping?"

"YouTube has a really good tutorial on that," Sookie said.

Thankfully, Sally wasn't there yet, because she might have asked me *why* I had done all this. And the answer would have been: to ask you a big question—would you . . . ? Could you . . . be my date to the last dance of our middle school lives?

More and more I knew I wanted a chance with Sally. A

chance to sway with her on some stupid dance floor, even if everybody was watching. A chance to kiss her a whole lot more. A chance for her to be my girlfriend.

My first girlfriend.

Yeah, this was pretty serious stuff.

So I followed her out of the classroom, the question clogging my throat. I hardly paid attention to where I was going until—

"Ow!"

I stumbled backward, a direct hit to my head. Tears stung my eyes, but I sucked them back, focusing on squeezing my fist in and out.

I glanced up at Erika, standing a foot away, rubbing her brow.

"Sorry," she said quickly.

"Are you okay?"

"I've had worse hits," she said, smiling slowly. "I played soccer in elementary school, remember?"

"Oh, yeah," I said, even though I didn't. Later, after we started hanging, I would see pictures of her in her soccer uniform—the green and gold jersey—and form those memories secondhand, but back then Erika was nearly a blank to me.

"That was really cool of you today," she said.

"What?"

"Giving Sally the answer." She smiled. "You always do things like that."

"What? Give answers?"

"No, like, nice things . . . for your friends . . . I've noticed that . . ." She blushed, looking embarrassed, and I thought about what Sookie had said, about the love eyes. Maybe, maybe there was something to that. I glanced back at Sally, who had pressed herself against the far wall, trying not to be swept away by the exodus.

"I should go," I said to Erika.

She laughed nervously. "Okay, but hey, I . . . I want to ask you something." She tugged at her lip. "It's . . . it's about the dance. I'm going with a group. And we got a Hummer, and it's with my cousin and her boyfriend and some of the other girls from track. They all have dates, but I don't. . . . Do you . . . have someone to . . . ?" She gulped. "Like a date?"

"Me?"

"Yeah." She didn't wait for my answer. "I mean," she backtracked. "Like, it could be . . . We could, you know, go just as friends, but you'd be my date is what I mean. . . ."

"You and me?"

She paused, her cheeks flushing red. "Yeah . . ."

"*Oh.* Yeah."

"Yeah? Really?" She grinned ear to ear, suddenly rambling on about texting and pickup times and the colors of her dress.

"Wait," I said. "I mean no, I can't. I'm . . . I have . . . I meant, yeah, there's somebody . . ." My eyes shifted to Sally, who was waiting in an almost patient daze.

Erika's gaze widened. "With Sally?"

"No," I said. "I mean, I haven't asked, but yeah. I'm going to."

"Oh. Okay." She was obviously disappointed. She started to turn, and this time it was me who called out, "Wait!" Because I realized that Erika might tell a friend who might tell another friend and so on. And everyone would know before I even had a chance to ask Sally. "Would you not say anything? 'Cause . . ." I searched for the best way to explain it. "'Cause it could be weird."

"Would you not say anything either?" she asked. I nodded, and to this day we've both kept our word.

Sally and I hustled to the bus, boarding just as the driver reached for the door lever. Once settled, Sally asked, "What did Erika want?"

"Um . . ." I stalled, trying to think of a not-lie but also a not-truth. "She was just sorry about hitting me on the head is all."

"That was a long apology." Sally's gaze slid to the window. When she looked back, she asked, "So what did the rest of that paper say?"

"What paper?"

She took out the note, ironing the creases with her palms. Her hand was steadier now, a slight tremble but nothing compared to the little earthquakes that had been happening all day.

"Are you okay?"

"Why?" She glanced at me.

"Because, you know, before, you were . . ." I didn't want to say shaky, but I didn't have to exactly.

She offered up, "Spacey?"

"Yeah," I said, even though it was obviously more than that.

She glanced out the window again, her lips moving in a silent count—one, two, three, four, five—until she turned to me with her usual smile. "My grandma in North Carolina fell. She broke a hip. Because . . ." Sally laughed. "That's what old people do. But seriously, I was really worried. My dad was talking about going up there, and he and Mom are still fighting, so things have been kind of a mess. But I decided in math that I just can't think about it anymore. I decided she's going to be okay, right? And my parents will just do what they always do, get over themselves."

I nodded, even though I didn't know much about either. Lito was steadier than a cat with nine lives, and my parents never had to get over themselves. "She'll get better. For sure," I said. "And your parents will stop fighting. They always do."

"Right?" Sally said, and then she made one of her faces: lips suddenly inhaled into a twist, eyes bulged until she looked like a goldfish. She crossed her hands in front of her chest, fingers waving like fins swimming through the ocean.

I laughed. And then I made my attempt, but my lips wouldn't form the fishy *X*. I ended up with a pout instead.

"That really sucked," Sally said with a smile. "So, what

did that last bit say? The part of the paper you tore off?"

"Nothing," I said. My tone was light, even though I was still trying to push her away from that vulnerability that had stuck a turtle-like head out in math class.

We were so late that we had to sit at the front of the bus, away from the tribe. I craned my neck to look to where Sookie, Jade, and Diego had squeezed in, three to a seat. I could hear them fighting from here.

JADE

Why don't you shut your legs and there'll be space?

DIEGO

Girl, how 'bout you sit somewhere else?

JADE

I want to sit with Sookie. You sit somewhere else.

DIEGO

How about *you* go—

SOOKIE

(squeezing past both of them)

I'll go. Just shut up already.

Sookie rolled her eyes as she headed up the aisle. When she settled into her empty seat, she smiled like she could finally enjoy some peace.

"Well?" said Sally, still beside me, still waiting.

I shrugged, acting tougher than I felt. "Don't know what you're talking about."

Her fingers went into my pockets, lightning fast. First

the pocket on the left and then the one on the right, rooting around for the torn piece of paper.

Let me pause and say that again: Her fingers went into my pockets.

Even if she didn't touch anything, that was about as close to a *touch* as I had ever gotten, and afterward, I had to slide my backpack onto my lap. Breathe deeply. Take a second.

She waited a few beats before she unfolded the sliver of paper in her palm.

She read the words silently to herself. And then she tucked her chin to her chest and smiled, her rosy cheeks glowing like a candle suddenly lit. And when her pinkie slid across the seat to link with mine, I said in a voice so low only Sally could hear, "Gotcha."

WORMHOLES III

THE TRUTH IS WE TRAVEL DOWN WORM-holes all the time.

Not the kind you'll find in outer space. That hasn't been proven yet, but I have faith that one day we will be able to move between time periods, jumping forward and backward into other points of our lives.

But until then we can only travel through the worm-holes in our mind.

Check it. You're walking down the street one day, with your boy, and you smell something familiar. It's coming from the house of the woman at the end of the block, the little old lady you call *abuelita,* not because she's your actual grandma but because she asked you to call her that. The title makes her feel good.

Anyway, that little old lady is cooking *arroz con bistec*, and you get a whiff of those sizzling onions and the juicy steak, and maybe you can't smell the rice, but you know it's fluffy and that the recipe is just right, the way your real *abuelita* used to make that dish before she died. And suddenly you're not on NW 27th Avenue no more; you're three blocks over, where your real a*buelita* used to live, and you're sitting in her kitchen, on those seats that are vinyl, and it's a hot day, and you're sweating through your basketball shorts, but you're happy because you're eating her *arroz con bistec*. And she's telling you those stories she used to have on the repeat, the one about the doll she only got to play with every Christmas. The one about the doctor she almost married, before she settled down with your working-class *abuelito*. And you're staring at her, because it's the part where she talks about that doll with such longing, her brown eyes sad and far away. She's in her dark place. And you reach out and touch her wrinkly skin, skin that's so soft and thin, it would tear wide open from just a paper cut.

And you're just there with her. In that kitchen. You're there.

But then your friend says something, bringing you back through that portal. And if you had timed the whole journey, maybe thirty seconds would've passed. The person next to you, the one you were talking to before you got a whiff of that magic, wouldn't even know that you had disappeared for that fraction of a minute. He'd look at you and say, "Bro, so what'd ya think 'bout that?"

And you'd remember enough of the conversation to reply, "Nah, he didn't hafta do you like that."

And your time-traveling self would be there in the real world.

But at the same time, you just spent a whole afternoon with your *abuelita* in her kitchen.

Try and tell me otherwise.

Try.

Senior Year

9. PHYSICS IS WISDOM

"IF THE BUDDHA GOT STUCK," I REPORT back to Sookie ten minutes later. I've returned from my "respite" with Old Mrs. B to find Sookie and only Sookie sitting there, in the janitor's closet, writing in her AP notebook. Beside her is *Their Eyes Were Watching God* by Zora Neale Hurston, the primary source for our AP English small group paper. But she doesn't try to push us into work mode. Instead she says, "Diego and Jade went suit shopping. They made me promise to tell you to not move in with Erika. Not, not, not."

In return I tell her about Sally's suspicious book.

"Why are you whispering?" Sookie asks at one point.

"Because," I say, swinging my eyes to the door. Beyond that is the hall. And beyond that, somewhere in those stacks, is Sally. And Sookie gets that I'm saying, *She could be anywhere!*

But Sookie points out, "The chances of her stumbling into this janitor's closet on day one is nearly zero. I didn't know this room was here until my second year on the job."

But I insist on whispering, so Sookie follows my lead.

"*When the Buddha Got Stuck*, huh?" Sookie asks again.

"If. *If*, not *when*."

"Hmm . . ."

"And there were Post-it notes and folded pages. The book looked well worn."

"Hmm . . . ," Sookie repeats. "That *is* interesting."

"Right? Do you know what the book is about?"

"Let's see." Sookie clicks her MacBook awake. A few minutes later she reads from the library's online catalog: "'Notice Where You're Stuck; Show Up; Pay Attention; Live in Reality; Connect with Others, Connect with Life; Move from Thought to Action; and Let Go.' That sounds . . . intense."

"Yeah," I agree. "It does. And she could barely make eye contact. Again."

"You noticed that too."

"It's hard to miss."

"Maybe she feels guilty." Sookie slides the laptop toward me. "Maybe she should. Maybe it's only right."

"Yeah . . . maybe."

"It was a total ghosting," Sookie says. "Diego's right about that. And, you know, we don't have to engage. Jade's right about that, too."

Sookie's repeating fragments of the conversation we had after we saw Sally in the cafeteria. After we took our lunches outside to the picnic tables. After the first five minutes when we ate in dumbfounded silence. Well, they ate. I stared at my burger and fries like they weren't edible, until Diego snapped, "Bro, this is the one meal the cafeteria knows how to make."

"I'm not hungry," I mumbled.

"Why? Because you saw a ghost? Well, ghosts don't exist. So eat."

And I did, slowly, bite by bite. The food tasted like paper.

"I don't know if I can ignore her like that," Sookie was saying now. "I know that's what Diego thinks we should do, but it feels weird. What did you say when she came up to you and Mrs. B?"

"Nothing. I was . . . I don't know . . . surprised, mostly."

And confused. I've been low-key confused since Sally reappeared. There were questions. Of course there were questions: Why did she stop talking to us? To me? How did she keep it up for so long? And what brought her back after all this time?

"Yeah, that's how I felt when she came in for her interview. I was nice enough, professional, but I didn't really engage, and it wasn't because of Diego's speech, but more like, I just didn't know how to engage. It was hard . . . different from all the times I imagined I would confront her if I ever saw her again. . . . Does that make sense?"

I nod. "Is it like, you want to be angry—and you are—but the anger just isn't as big as you thought it would be?"

"Yeah," Sookie says, chin bobbing. "Maybe I'm too exhausted from final papers to care, and life is just too short to be mad at anyone like that. But I think there's more to the story. . . ."

I stare at the screen. "Live in reality, connect with others, connect with life," I say. "That sounds so heavy." But then again, the Sally who had returned to us was that type of heavy—quiet and sad in a way that couldn't be covered up with a wry smile.

"And you know"—Sookie sighs—"I've been thinking about what she said to me that day at the beach, about time not being infinite. That changed my life."

"How?"

"It got me to go see South Korea, and that got me asking questions, and my parents really wanted me to have answers. I found my birth dad. . . . I learned about my birth mom, you know, about her dying a little bit after I was born. I learned the story of how I came to be separated. And I got to meet my half sisters when they were still so young that meeting me wouldn't freak them out. None of that would have happened if Sally hadn't pushed me." Sookie's eyes go misty. "I mean, if it weren't for Sally, who knows if I would even listen to K-pop?"

I laugh, because Sookie has whole Spotify playlists dedicated to K-pop. She's a hard-core fan.

Sookie smiles. "Seriously, how can I hate someone who pushed me into figuring out more of who I am?"

We stare at the wall of quotes, and then my eyes fall back to Old Mrs. B's Post-it note, the one she gave me during our respite. " 'There are years that ask questions and years that answer,' Zora Neale Hurston," I read aloud.

Sookie's gaze is on the empty hallway. "I wish this were one of those years that answered. Like what if we had a magical wish list that the universe sent us answers to?"

"What would you ask it?"

"What wouldn't I? How about you?"

"Nothing." I laugh. "Everything."

"So . . . what would you ask?" This time her smile is a challenge.

"Okay," I say slowly. "Okay . . . Um . . ."

She hands me a sheet of paper. "Just write down the first three questions that come to mind."

"Seriously?"

"Yep," Sookie says, "seriously." And her pen starts to scribble across the page.

I wait a minute or two, not even sure if I'm going to write anything, but then the pen starts moving, almost independent of me:

> Why does Erika have a wedding Pinterest board?
>
> Will time travel through a wormhole ever be possible?
>
> Why did Sally leave?

"Done," I exclaim. Sookie grabs for my paper. "Whoa! You first!" I slide the page out of reach. Sookie sighs and then begins to read:

> Will I get a date to prom? (Will the guy from science ask me? Should I ask him?)
>
> Will I be happy at Northwestern?
>
> Why did Sally come back?

Sookie looks at me. "'Cause, like, she didn't have to. The school year is practically out. That's another reason I think there's more to the story. Why come back here? Why not finish the last quarter in North Carolina? Why face us at all? Seems like a choice."

"Hmm . . ." I hadn't thought of it that way.

I hold up my list and point to my number three.

"Wait." Her eyes grow wide. "Erika has a wedding Pinterest board?"

"You like a boy in your science class?" I counter.

Sookie plays along. "I don't know. He's cute. You think wormholes will ever really be a thing?"

I shake my head.

"So." Sookie sighs again. Then she reaches for a blank index card and draws a Venn diagram. In the intersection, she writes one word: *Sally*. "That's the question we both want answers to."

"Think Old Mrs. B was being clever when she gave us this quote?"

"Of course." Sookie laughs. "Of course."

On Thursday Erika skips English to eat with me. "It's not exactly skipping, Marco," she explained. "It's more like choosing how to spend my time. We're done with all the assignments. All we're doing is watching movies. So I checked in, and when the teacher dimmed the lights and started grading papers, I said I'm sick, got a pass, and came to lunch. Easy, right?"

"Easy" is a word Erika loves. She likes taking easy classes, likes making easy friends, and for college she wants to major in something easy as well. "I'm thinking physical therapy."

"That's got a lot of science."

"But I'm good in science, so that will make it easy."

What's not easy is the way Erika's been reacting to Sally today. As soon as we sit down at the lunch table, she swivels her eyes around the room until she locates Sally sitting about three tables away.

"So, Sally has lunch with you?" she asks. "You didn't tell me that."

The edge to Erika's voice puts me on the defensive.

ME

Not with me. She's over there, and we're over here.

(I point to my table and tribe, who are ambling over from the lunch line.)

DIEGO

(plops down at table. To Erika)

You lost?

ME

She's trying out skipping.

ERIKA

It's not skipping when you have a pass.

ME

The pass is to the nurse's office.

DIEGO

So you're lost?

JADE

Tsk-tsk. And right before graduation.

ERIKA

They're not gonna fail me because I skipped before graduation.

DIEGO

(eyes her up and down)

Maybe not *you*.

ERIKA

What does that mean?

SOOKIE

(sighs)

Just that statistically your whiteness makes you less likely to be suspended, while Diego's blackness makes him almost three to four times more likely to be suspended for that same offense.

ERIKA

Seriously?

SOOKIE

Yeah, seriously.

(returns to nibbling on a pretzel)

DIEGO

Which is why I'm not playin' with that paper. Damn *near* perfect attendance this year.

JADE

D, I think you did get perfect attendance this year.

DIEGO

Man, really?

JADE

Really.

ERIKA

(nods at Sally)

It's just sad, right? Sally sitting by herself over there.

ME

. . .

SOOKIE

She's gotta eat.

ERIKA

(softly)

Yeah, but she has no friends. Right?

SOOKIE

Maybe we should invite her over here.

ERIKA

(coughs up soda)

No. No. I mean, that would be awkward, right?

SOOKIE

I don't know. What do you guys think?

DIEGO

I don't see ghosts and I don't talk about ghosts because ghosts don't exist.

SOOKIE

(innocently)

But Erika thinks we should, right?

ME

Sookie.

ERIKA

Um, no . . .

SOOKIE

I thought you felt sorry for her.

ERIKA

Um, it would be weird. At least for Marco? Right?

ME

(invested in my sub)

I don't have an opinion on it, honestly.

ERIKA

Really?

(scoffs)

You had lots of feelings about it in ninth grade.

ME

I don't remember talking about it to *you* in ninth grade.

DIEGO

Damn. Savage, bro.

ME

What? I don't remember.

ARI

(passing by with goofy grin)

Hey, Sookie. Thanks for the chem notes.

ME

Wait. That's science-slash-possible prom guy?

SOOKIE

Um, maybe?

ERIKA

(recovering)

Didn't you go with Ari to the dance? In middle school?

SOOKIE

Yeah.

ERIKA

So, what happened?

SOOKIE

I went away that summer and so nothing. When I came back he had a girlfriend.

JADE

I remember that. She went to another school, right?

SOOKIE

Yep. And then after that he had another girlfriend.

JADE

Lisa, right?

SOOKIE

Yep, and so on and so on and so on.

DIEGO

(snapping his fingers)

Big-eared Ari is getting the ladies? *That* Ari is taking hearts and breaking hearts?

JADE

Uh-uh, D. *Stop.*

DIEGO

Total eclipse-ing of the heart.

SOOKIE

Diego!

(pauses)

Anyway, he's all broken up with the latest what—

DIEGO

Making love out of nothing at all.

JADE

Seriously, shut up!

ME

(laughing)

Bro.

DIEGO

(smiles wickedly, returns to burger)

ERIKA

So, you want to go to prom with him or something?

SOOKIE

I didn't say that.

JADE

Uh-huh.

ME

(glances at Sally, who's reading a book, strains to see title, accidentally bumps Erika in shoulder)

Oh, sorry.

ERIKA

(follows my stare)

Well, I don't think the back-and-forth thing is good. Right, Marco?

ME

(shrugs)

ERIKA

I mean, we should just all keep our eyes forward.

(nudges me)

Right?

ME

(whispers to Erika)

You okay? You're acting weird.

ERIKA
(whispers back)
You're acting weirder.

SOOKIE
It's not like it didn't work out. It's like it didn't have a chance to work out. I think that's different.

DIEGO
Sooks, if you want to get your Ari on, get your Ari on.

SOOKIE
Thank you, Diego. I salute your advice and your perfect attendance.

ERIKA
But—

ME
(taps her thigh, whispers)
She gets it. So, don't.

ERIKA
(closes mouth)

ME
(looks back at Sally's table)

ERIKA
(taps my thigh, nods toward Sally's table, and then whispers)
You don't.

ME
What?

But I know what.

• • •

On Friday after school I stop by Mrs. A's classroom for some clarification on our physics project. The first part, explaining a physics concept and how it applies to my life, I've got. I like digging into wormholes, and yesterday I found a slew of books at the library that will help me, like *Unveiling the Edge of Time* by John Gribbin. And I think I can figure out how wormholes apply to my life. Who wouldn't want to travel through time?

But the second part, the whole managing invisible forces with my own universal set of laws? Yeah, that part has me completely baffled.

"You're taking it too literally," Mrs. A says now. She's standing at the front of the classroom, cleaning off her whiteboard. She's so short she had to drag a chair over from her desk. Then she climbs up, wiping away the date and the last bit of yesterday's notes with her eraser.

When she steps down, she says, "Think about gravity. Without it, we'd just fly away, but gravity keeps us locked here, on the floor of this classroom. We may not realize it, but we depend on gravity every second of every day. Gravity is literally one of the most important parts of our lives, but we give it zero thought."

I glance at my feet, planted right where I left them, and realize how right she is. And when I think about those gratitude lists that people are always making, the ones that are supposed to help you appreciate life more, I recall how so many have listed "the air I breathe," but not one has ever listed "gravity." And we couldn't even breathe earth's air without gravity! We'd be too busy suffocating in outer space.

"Okay, but how do I turn that into my own law that I use to . . ."—I consult my notes—"use to manage those forces?"

"Well . . ." She tucks the chair back into place and slips around to the front of her desk, perching at the edge. "What sayings do you live by? The ones you use to calm yourself down when you're angry or sad or overwhelmed?"

She sees the doubt on my face. "Let me guess—you're thinking that you don't feel any of those things."

I shrug. I'm sure I do, but I try not to dwell on those feelings. "This project seems awfully personal," I say.

"It might be. But I think it's important to send you off into the world with an understanding of the tools you have in place to survive it."

And there goes Mrs. A, being all hippie again. She smiles, patiently waiting for me to catch up.

"So, I have to think about my feelings first and then figure out what?"

"Figure out what bit of wisdom you're carrying around." She rubs her head. "Okay, so whenever I'm having a hard day and I can't do anything right, I think about what my grandma once told me. She'd say, 'Little Lily'—that's what she called me—'all of life is a practice. You don't have to get anything right the first or second or third time. You just try to get better every day. You do that and you'll be fine.'" She smiled again, a little lost in her own memory. "And that has helped me more than you know."

What were the little bits of wisdom I had been carrying around inside of me? And had those sayings been guiding my life? I thought about our wall of quotes. So many of those words were what I pulled out whenever I needed to find the courage to walk into the unknown. And I had walked into the unknown a few times—as a gawky fifteen-year-old applying for a first job at Grendel's. As a seventeen-year-old applying to an elite college.

"So part two of this project really isn't about physics; it's about wisdom."

Mrs. A wags her finger at me playfully. "Marco, physics *is* wisdom."

I leave Mrs. A's classroom in overdrive. It's like I'm watching some kind of Tetris game in my head—quotes and phrases floating by as I try to find the right spot in the construction of the narrative that will likely form my paper.

Maybe that's why I don't really see Sally in the parking lot until I'm slipping my key into the ignition of my truck. That's when I focus on the real world, the one where me driving on autopilot could end someone's life, and I see her, in profile. She is two aisles over and she doesn't see me because she's looking underneath the hood of her car. A second later, her palm slams against the car's side. A universal sign for, *My car's acting like a piece of crap and I don't know how to fix it.*

For whatever reason, I hear Erika's voice in my head: *It's sad, right?*

And it was sad, Sally being out here with no friends. But maybe it was deserved? Or maybe there was, like Sookie said, more to the story. Because there's always more to the story. People do crappy things in reaction to the crappy things that have happened to them. But does that make what they did less crappy?

Nope.

What I'm saying is, I should leave her stranded here, even if the night school crowd can be a little rough. And the security guards aren't exactly good at providing security. And she is like a sitting duck with her mopey eyes and poor eye contact.

I should just go about my day, because what do I owe her? Wasn't she the one who told me to leave her alone?

And so that's what I do—I turn the key in my ignition, and I'm about to back out when the other me, the better version of me, says: *Enjoy that guilt if something bad happens to her.*

And then Mom's voice chimes in: *Or, you could help.*

Pop's too: *We raised you to help.*

And then the opinions take over my headspace:

OTHER ME

You know this girl. Like really, really know her, and you're gonna treat her worse than a stranger.

ME

What do I know about her anymore?

OTHER ME

For starters, how about she saved up her money for three months to buy you a pass to Disney World so you could go with her? You gonna pretend that never happened? That she didn't do a bunch of nice things for you throughout most of your life?

MOM'S VOICE

So you can help.

POP'S VOICE

You *will* help.

Two minutes later I'm standing a few feet away. "Sally?"

She jumps and hits her head on the inside of her hood. *"Damn."*

My thoughts exactly.

She looks at me. Full-on eye contact. I swallow hard.

"You okay?" I indicate her head.

She nods, letting her rubbing hand fall to her side.

"How about the car?"

No words, just big eyes and a shrug. Her fingers ripple at her side. I remember that ripple down to that day it first showed up in Mr. Weaver's class.

Not everything has changed.

"Maybe I can help?" I ask.

"Okay," she says, and her eyes get a little wet, magnifying her irises. She looks like an anime character in distress.

I step forward until I'm looking down at an engine

and some other . . . stuff. What that other stuff is, I'm not sure, because I don't know jack about cars. When Old Ancient hits the fritz, I call on Diego. But I've marched over here like some dude to the rescue, so I pull out the stick marked "oil" and inspect that. Looks oily. Then I unscrew the cap marked "radiator" and see some green stuff there. And then, just as I'm out of ideas, my phone chimes.

"Hold up," I say, grateful for the rescue.

"Marco? It's Principal Johnson."

Or maybe not.

When I hang up, Sally clears her throat. A quick glance reveals that her eyes have reduced in size. Somehow that makes it easier to breathe.

"I have to go," I say. "It's my brothers. They're in trouble."

"Oh." She looks worried.

I shake my head. "No, it's not like that. They're always in trouble."

"Oh." And worry turns into surprise. Last she saw Lil' Jay and Domingo, they were sweet kids. She doesn't know this newer hell-on-wheels version of them.

"Is anyone on the way? To get you?"

"No, but it's okay. You go. I'll . . ." She glances at the mystery beneath her hood, those fingers rippling double time. "I can figure it out."

I shift back and forth on my heels, with this kind of buzzing inside that shouts: *Not a good idea. Don't do it.*

But then there are those eyes—pale gray, rimmed in ebony, growing in diameter by the second.

A souped-up Mustang rolls up next to us, even though there are empty spaces all around. Two guys pile out, the driver pulling on a T-shirt as he rises from his seat. Outside, he pauses to look Sally up and down. Then he smirks and says, "Hey, girl, you need help?" He saunters around to the front of the car, followed by his boy. We'll call him Scary Eyes.

Sally glances nervously from me to the guys. T-shirt Guy steps closer, like he's trying to inspect the engine. Sally steps back—one, two, three, until she's inches from my side.

"This is looking bad," says T-shirt Guy. He looks at me, like, *Son, I'm about to school you in front of your girl.*

And let's be honest, he can school me. Because I know nothing about cars.

But the way his eyes keep roaming over Sally, like she's the quick meal he's about to catch before getting his education on, has me saying, "We got this."

"Got this?" T-shirt Guy repeats, straightening. He gives me the once-over, like, *Yeah, right.*

Now, I'm pretty sure that if this ends in a fight, I'll take a good old-fashioned beatdown. But Diego's taught me enough to know that you gotta stand your ground with certain types. You gotta throw out that vibe that you're willing to take the beatdown to protect the things you care about. And I'm not saying that I care about Sally. I'm just saying that I don't *not* care about her. You get the distinction, right?

So, I roll my shoulders back—present all six foot two, two hundred pounds of me—and repeat slowly, "Yeah, *I* got this."

Scary Eyes asks dryly, "So, what's wrong with it?"

I'm one foot forward when Sally grabs me by the arm, playing off that power move by slipping her hand into mine. She smiles kindly and, in that soft voice of hers, says, "He's got it. Really. But thanks. Thanks a lot. It's nice of you to try to help." She doesn't break eye contact with them. Not once. Instead, her smile grows, calm, confident, reassuring.

After what feels like a minute, T-shirt Guy says, "We got class anyway." Then they walk off, Scary Eyes looking over his shoulder every now and then.

When they enter the school, Sally looks at me. "That was weird, right?"

For a second I'm silent. I'm coming off an adrenaline high. Then I go with, "Okay. How about this? I'll give you a ride home, and then you can figure it out from there."

She looks at me, surprised. All that projected confidence is gone—the best fake out in the history of the world. "I actually have to go to the library. I have to be at work by five. Is that okay?"

I nod. "Yeah. No biggie. We just have to make that one small stop first."

"Okay," she says, and when her gaze drifts down my arm, I realize that we're still holding hands.

Or, maybe, what I realize is, I haven't let go.

A few things: The stop will not be small. Principal Johnson does not know how to deliver short lectures.

And it is not a "no biggie" that Sally is riding shotgun in my truck.

It's a big biggie. A huge biggie. A huge-ie.

But I've worked it out, see? Because that feeling that I needed to protect her from something terrible—even though, honestly, I was just hella afraid—that's me tapping into some kind of learned response that goes all the way back to our childhood.

And you know how these kinds of learned responses go. You just can't help yourself. It's like when I'm stocking the cereal aisle at Grendel's and I get to the Honeycombs. The kid in me remembers the sugar high, and my brain, sensing a reward, sends a message that's like, *Oh, man, want that. Have that. Buy that.* But because I've conditioned the adult in me to make better choices, I also hear, *No, sugar. That has absolutely no nutrition, and who invited you to come here and tell me what to eat?*

And I don't buy Honeycombs. Haven't in years. But you can see how both responses are automatic.

Well, that's how it was in that moment with Sally.

And, you know, studies also show that being in stressful situations with someone can make you feel closer, which explains why, right now, it's perfectly normal for me to sneak sidelong glances at her at just about every red light. So far there have been six red lights and six sidelong glances. She doesn't seem to notice. The windows are rolled down, since Old Ancient doesn't have working air-conditioning, and Sally's head is about an inch or two out the window. Her hair takes flight in the wind, trailing across bodegas and bus stops and guys on the corner offering up window washes for a few quarters.

This darker hair, I reason, is what magnifies her eyes. Makes them more serious. More tragic. That adds to my susceptibility to her. (Because who doesn't want to protect an anime character?)

And then there's the way she fills out her white T-shirt a little more than she did in the Middle.

How the angle between her waist and hip is greater, too, accentuating the slope of her curves.

How her hand felt in mine, different from the first time Erika and I held hands, that jostling for position: Whose thumb goes first? Just the link of a few fingers? Or should we go for an index and pinkie grab?

With Sally, the alignment has always been perfect. The thumbs fall into place. There's no air between the palms.

And she squeezed my hand.

That's what I remember now that my adrenaline has settled.

And I squeezed her hand back.

On light seven, I glance up from my inspection of her book bag—a button that says MAKE LITERATURE NOT WAR—and find that her head is back inside the truck and she's studying me too.

We speak at the same time:

"Your button is cool."

"You're bigger. Like, a lot bigger. Which is good. Because back there . . ."

A car honks. The light turns green. I move again, seeing the Middle rise up in the distance. Outside, after-school buses load up the extracurricular kids with their practice tees and soccer cleats and socks pulled up to their kneecaps.

"You were just . . ." She glances at the kids outside the school. "You were like that, small . . . *before.* But you look the same, face-wise, just not . . ." Exhausted by her explanations, she falls back against her seat.

"So, what you're saying is we finally see eye to eye?"

It's not a good joke, but she smiles. Our eyes meet, and she asks, "So, did turning into a giant make high school better?"

"Huh?" We're in the parking lot now.

"You thought it would be easier for me because I was tall. So, was it easier for you because you weren't so . . . ?" She's trying to find the least-offensive word.

"Small?"

"Yeah." The next smile is embarrassed, toothy. She

swipes a hand over her hair, brushing back windblown strands. I smile too, because I remember that conversation was the night of our first real kiss.

She looks away, at the parking lot. "You've stopped."

"Stopped what?" Her words don't make sense. But neither does this. Us, in this truck. Her, different, but the vibe still like old times.

"You stopped driving. The truck."

"Oh." I lift my foot off the brake. We glide forward.

Man. What is going on?

I park near the front of the lot, hopping out of the truck like I'm all business. So much so that I'm three feet from the school door when I realize she's still sitting in the truck, chin resting on the lip of the window, watching me. "Are you coming?" I shout. She can't wait in the truck. It's too hot.

(*Too far away,* other me whispers.)

Like I said, too hot.

"Really?"

"Unless you want to die from a heat stroke, yeah."

"Okay." She smiles.

But I don't smile back.

I've got this under control now.

Except for that tingling in my stomach.

Whatever that means.

Middle School

10. I'M PROUD OF YOU

JADE FLOPPED DOWN ON THE SAND IN HER polka-dotted bikini. "We should do this every day of the summer."

"Right?" Sookie said, shielding her eyes from the sun.

I looked at the stretch of sand filled with kids from the Middle—tossing Frisbees, chasing waves, or lounging, like we were, on the hot earth. This was our final class trip, and we didn't go to Disney World or Universal Studios like most eighth graders around here. We went a few miles down the street from our very own 'hood—Key Biscayne. Principal Johnson got one of the hotels to donate a private beach and a few wealthy businesspeople to fork over the dough for buses—and not just school buses, coach buses, the kind that had TV screens and reclining seats. That trip highlight had Diego saying, "Man, it is super legit to do your business while moving. I felt like I was ballin' hard." Which made all of us crack up, because . . . well, because.

And being on the sand is never bad, which was why Jade was plotting out how to get back here over the summer. She rolled onto her belly, inches from Diego, and continued. "But how can we get here every day is what I want to know. Maybe we could take a car?"

"Like a cab?" Diego asked.

"Yeah," Jade said.

"Girl, you ain't ever heard of a bus schedule?"

Jade giggled. "I take the bus every day, including *today*."

"Sheesh." Diego sucked his lips. "No, the one for grown folk, not this luxury ride we had today."

SOOKIE

Well, I can't do much this summer, turns out.

DIEGO

Yeah, yeah, you'll be at the J. We know, Sooks.

SOOKIE

More like South Korea.

JADE

What?

SOOKIE

Yep.

JADE

Why?

DIEGO

I get it. Visit the motherland. Show you them roots. Be down with your *OK* people.

JADE

Her what?

DIEGO

Original Koreans.

JADE

My mom's never taken me to Antigua, even though I was technically born there. But I guess I've been to Jamaica to meet my dad's mom. Some of my OJ.

(beat)

Original Jamaicans.

DIEGO

(shaking his head at Jade)

But you also got some of your OP's here. You live with them. Sooks doesn't have any of that. She's got her AP.

(beat)

Adopted People.

SOOKIE

(rolling her eyes again)

I like my APs.

DIEGO

For sure, but, you know, there's more peeps. That's all. I'm just saying. You adopt a Korean girl—

SOOKIE

South Korean—

DIEGO

Bring her here, make her Jewish, give her that bar mitzvah—

SOOKIE

Bat mitzvah—

JADE

That was such a fun part—

DIEGO

That's just a whole lot of identity fusion if you ask me.

SOOKIE

You mean identity *confusion*?

DIEGO

(locking his hands together)

Nah, fusion. 'Cause you got all your identities fused.

SOOKIE

(laughing hard)

DIEGO

Me, droppin' some hard-core truth bombs, but you laugh it up, Sooks.

SOOKIE

Sorry, D. It's just the other day, my parents made this Korean Jewish fusion food.

JADE

There's Korean Jewish food?

SOOKIE

Yeah. It's a whole thing. But a lot of what my mom is doing is just, like, what can you put kimchi on? So far, there's kimchi matzoh brie, kimchi hummus, kimchi latkes.

JADE

What's kimchi?

SALLY

(sounding like she's reading off a *Webster's* dictionary)

A traditional Korean food made from Chinese cabbage fermented with lactic acid bacteria.

DIEGO

That's disgusting.

SALLY

Says the boy who'll always eat my leftover yogurt.

DIEGO

What's that gotta do with it?

SALLY

(shaking her head)

Anyway, kimchi is really good. My dad buys it from this pricey gourmet store, which pisses my mom off, and we put it on our tacos for Taco Tuesday.

DIEGO

You guys have tacos every Tuesday?

SALLY

Yeah, because it's Taco Tuesday.

SOOKIE

It really is good. But my mom is, like, on kimchi overdrive, so I'm a little burnt out. I feel like she might put it on my Bran Flakes next.

DIEGO

Sooks, you eat Bran Flakes? That's so BO.

SOOKIE

What?

DIEGO

(winks)

Boring *and* old.

SALLY

There's a lot of other types of Korean food. Maybe you can ask for something different.

SOOKIE

```
I know. That's kinda the point of our trip, to
"expose me" to all the types of everything that
I'm missing.
                    (sighs)
Let's just not talk about it anymore. Okay?
```

Sookie looked at the water. Silent. Jade sat up, grabbed a floppy hat from the beach blanket, one of several that my mom had bought just in case, and wound her curly hair into a bun. She shoved the hat onto her head, but her hair was so thick, the seams bulged. When she brushed the sand from her shoulders, Sally reached out to touch Jade's shoulder blade, where there was a faint bruise the size of an apple.

"Does that hurt?" Sally asked.

"Nope," Jade said. "It's old. Cheerleading."

"Cheerleading?" Sally said, looking confused.

"Yeah."

"But isn't that over—" Sally began, but Jade cut her off with, "So, do you want to go, Sookie? Sounds like it could be fun. I'd like to be anywhere but here this summer, especially on an adventure!"

Sookie nodded. "Yeah, but it's a lot. Like, a lot, a lot. I'm just trying to figure out high school, and now I have to figure out this, too?"

"Could you not go?" Jade asked. "And then your parents could take me."

"Ha ha," Sookie said. "But seriously, I'm thinking that

I'm not gonna go. It's too much. And also, I still don't want to keep talking about it."

We were quiet, watching the others play in the surf. Calvin Thompson called to Diego to play football, but Diego waved him off and began to bury himself with the help of Jade and a plastic shovel, another offering from my mom. Sookie silently chipped away at her toenail polish. Sally watched the waves, sneaking glances at Jade.

I walked over to where my parents sat, closer to the water so they could keep an eye on my brothers as they played in the tide. Mom handed me a picnic basket, the brown wicker frayed from wear. "We got everyone subs from your favorite place, DeMatteo's."

DeMatteo's was an Italian place off US 1. The owner was this guy from Buffalo, New York, who made subs based on recipes his grandmother brought over from Italy. My favorite was the classic meatball sub, which had the best red sauce I'd ever tasted.

"Mom." I shook my head. "DeMatteo's is . . ." I rubbed my fingers together.

Mom laughed. "It's your last year in middle school. Today is special."

Pop squinted in my direction. "We know how much that cost. Want us to eat it?"

"No."

"Then?" Pop said as Mom tossed him a baseball cap. "And cover this great head of hair?" He ran his fingers through curls that tumbled over his shoulders. Mom's eyes narrowed, and Pop begrudgingly put on the cap. "What are you waiting for?" Pop asked.

"Okay." I hefted up the basket. Then I thought better of it and squatted down to give Mom a peck on the cheek.

"What about me?" Pop asked, throwing up his hands.

"Pop." I looked around.

Mom raised an eyebrow.

"Fine." I leaned in for a quick hug, but Pop wasn't having that. He held on for a while.

"Damn, Pop."

"Whoa." Pop smacked the top of my head lightly.

"Yeah." Mom laughed. "Watch that mouth."

"I saw that." Diego said when I got back to my blanket. He was flat on his back, buried up to his belly in sand.

"You saw nothing," I said, and then as a bribe I took out the first sub and held it over him.

"*Bueno, yo vi todo, pero no voy a repetir nada*!" Diego popped up, sending sand everywhere.

"I was almost done," Jade said, pouting as she brushed the scattered sand off her torso.

"And you got it all over my book," Sookie, said, shaking out the pages.

"Girl, this is DeMatteo's!" Diego exclaimed. *"DeMatteo's.* You don't eat this buried in sand. You enjoy it, sitting up like people do." He unwrapped the wax paper. "I can't believe your mom did this."

"Yeah," I said. "Me either."

Jade eased herself free, took the sub, and smiled.

"I think you should go," Sally said when she took her sub.

"Go where?" Diego asked, mouth full.

"Sookie. To South Korea," Sally said, and Sookie's fingers froze.

"Dude." Diego groaned. "We're trying to enjoy this meal."

"Yeah, but—"

"No, Sals. This meal is so good I'll lick the wax paper when I'm done." He eyed everyone. "Seriously, you pass me that paper when you're done."

"What if I want to lick my own paper?" Jade asked.

"That's good too. But don't throw it out like that ain't half the treat is all I'm saying."

Sally placed her sub in her lap. "Okay, hear me out. You could wait, Sookie, but you'd lose time knowing more about who you are. And time isn't infinite."

"You sound like Marco's dad with that infinite shiz," Diego said.

And she did. But she also sounded like someone whose grandmother was in the hospital, doing better—yeah—but still recovering. "I wish," Sally had said earlier that day, on the bus over, "that I had gone there for Christmas when she asked me." But she hadn't, not Christmas or Easter. Sally had waited for the summer. But this summer she wouldn't have the same grandmother at all. She'd have one who sounded older on the phone. "Weaker" is what Sally had said.

"I just think," she continued, "that we imagine that we can wait on things, but that's you believing that those things will wait for you, too. But some of that could disappear while you're waiting to be ready. Sometimes we have to do things when we're not ready. Just think about it," Sally said to Sookie, who was quiet, her fingers still frozen.

"She's thinking. Now can we eat?" Diego said, and started on the second half of his sub.

"It's good," added Jade, and Sookie slowly unwrapped the wax paper while Sally took her first bite and chewed silently.

Later, Sally and Sookie joined Principal Johnson and Coach Sami in a volleyball game: chess versus track. Surprisingly, the chess team seemed confident. Something about "out-strategizing the jocks." I was pretty sure it didn't work that way, but Jade, who was the scorekeeper, said, "You never know. Strategy is everything. Strategy is how you win the long game." And then her eyes drifted toward Diego, who was tossing a football around with some of his teammates in the waves.

On the sand, the twins built a mega castle. Mom used the distraction to covertly slather on more sunblock, keeping the pink away while their skin deepened into a darker brown.

Somehow, Pop convinced me to go on a run with him.

No socks. No shoes. Just bare feet hitting the shoreline.

"Very hard-core," he'd said, and took off in a sprint, leaving me to double-time. When I finally caught up, he smiled, and his stride suddenly hit quadruple time.

I wished Sally had been there to take him on, because I never caught up until he stopped.

"Better," he said when I collapsed beside him.

"Than what?"

"Your *bisabuelo.*"

"Than Lito? That's super harsh, Pop."

"Well, at this age. When he was in his fifties, he'd have smoked you."

"Man, I'm charcoal here. You wanna keep going like that?"

He laughed, and I glanced back a few miles. Everyone seemed small in the distance. I couldn't make out Mom, the twins, or the tribe, but I heard the faint shouting, the trills of laughter.

Pop smiled. "Seriously, you're getting faster."

"Thanks." I smiled too. Pop wasn't the type to lather on praise, and I decided to bask in his words, tilting my head up to him and the sun.

"A little more focus on your school, a little bit nicer to your brothers, a job after school," he added a second later, and I rolled my eyes. "Okay, Pop. What is this, a to-do list?"

"Just a thought," he said. "A path forward."

"More like a push forward."

"What? When I was your age, I would have liked someone to push me forward. Instead I had to figure it out on my own, but you," he said wistfully. "You're in this pretty great time in your life . . ."

I gave him a sidelong look, wondering what kind of talk was coming my way. I wanted today to be about sand and heat.

"What?" he said.

"Just don't, Pop."

"What? It's not like that. Come on, now. I was reminiscing about, you know, where I was when I was your age, about to start high school."

"And?"

"Took me back, that's all." He looked out at the water, like Sookie had earlier that day, all silent now.

It's true this was a weird time, and even I felt myself getting nostalgic. Just yesterday I walked through the science wing of Seagrove Middle to stop by my sixth-grade locker to look for a little bumblebee that had been carved into the lower-left-hand corner of the metal. The tattoo would have been barely visible to the average sixth grader, but I was so small back then that the carving fell at my eye level. So every time I returned to my locker, there it was, waiting. I got into the habit of touching the indent, rubbing the pad of my thumb over the tiny circles that served as the bumblebee's wings. I rubbed those miracle wings through a lot of bad.

That one time that Max Castillo tripped me on purpose, sending me sprawling in the middle of science class.

That one time an eighth grader snatched my backpack and I had to chase him up three flights of stairs to beg for it back.

The one time a pair of seventh graders pantsed me in PE and Diego gave the taller one a black eye.

And all the other times after that. There were more than I could count. More than I cared to remember. But what I did remember was how I'd come back to my locker and find that bumblebee there, those tiny wings raised in midflight, and feel better.

Pop had taught me about the aerodynamics that go into keeping bumblebees in the air—the wings' stroking the air like a swimmer, backward and forward instead of up and down, the angle of the sweep creating the effect of "small hurricanes" above the wings that creates a low-pressure system that will send the bees up, up, up.

And, yeah, bees flying despite it seeming impossible, well, that made me feel hopeful.

And I held on.

Yesterday, though, when I looked, the bumblebee was gone, painted over, probably by my very own pop. And so I committed my first and last act of vandalism: I carved that bumblebee back into the metal.

"You're welcome," I said silently to all the sixth graders who would follow, because they deserved a little bit of hope too.

"Seagrove Middle was different when I was there," Pop was saying. "It was different back then. Smaller. About four hundred, maybe five hundred students."

"That would be like cutting my classes in half." I couldn't imagine what we'd do with all that space.

"We didn't have portable classrooms. We didn't need them. Believe it or not, Principal Johnson was in a few of my classes."

"Which ones?"

"Let's see." He looked off for a few seconds, trying to scale back the twenty years since he had been a middle schooler at Seagrove. "We had advanced geometry and English together. Maybe science."

"Were you in all advanced classes?"

"Yep, just like you."

"And Mom?"

"Yep, although she was at Orange Grove until eighth grade. We met at Seagrove High."

I had seen a picture from the year Mom met Pop. They were both gawky—skinny legs and arms and heads that were bigger than their bodies. Pop might have been a lady killer now, but he grew into that well after ninth grade.

"So, were you and Principal Johnson friends?"

"Hmm . . . not really. He was a little too popular for me."

"You were a nerd?"

"I was a science nerd," he said proudly. "Physics and chemistry clubs."

"How many members?"

He laughed. "Before or after I recruited your mom?"

"After?"

"Three," he admitted, "including me."

I tried to imagine this other version of Pop. The one who always had his head in a book, and then I tried to imagine the day all that changed, when he found out Mom was pregnant with me. I wanted to ask him about that day, but it seemed like something I should ask later, when I was older.

Looking back, I wish I hadn't waited. I wish I had known that memory—like time—isn't infinite.

"What would you have studied, if you had gone to college?" I asked Pop.

He sighed. "Who knows? One thing is this: People always think college is going to be one way and then it's another. I don't know that firsthand, but that's what it was like for my friends who went on without me. Start off studying physical science and end up being an English or theater major. Who can predict who you'll become, especially into your twenties?"

But Pop's life was pretty much set by the time he hit seventeen. After having me, he was a dad and then, a year later, the youngest custodian at Seagrove Middle. Nothing much had changed for him in the last seventeen years.

That was the first time it hit me, what he had given up for me.

I've come back to that thought over and over again, but

it was there, sitting with him on a beach in Key Biscayne, that I saw what his life might have been: Principal Johnson vs. Custodian Suarez.

And the thing is, what can you say to someone who gave up who they could have been so you could exist at all? How much gratitude is enough?

At the time I didn't know the answer, but now I know that there isn't enough gratitude in the world.

We returned to camp in two waves.

Pop arrived first, doing his best Rocky Balboa impression. You know, that scene where Rocky runs up seventy-two flights of stairs to stand before the Philadelphia Museum of Art, with his fist pumping in the air. (If you don't know that scene, look it up.)

But the thing you need to know is this: In that scene, Rocky is triumphant.

And in that moment in my life, Pop was triumphant. Powerful. Strong.

I arrived minutes later, holding on to my side as I dropped to my knees in the surf, the sand creeping into places unmentionable.

(Seriously, don't mention it.)

That's where Erika found me. She crouched down, hands on knees, and asked, "Are you okay?"

"Oh, yeah," I huffed. "Just playing it cool so Pop feels good about himself."

Somehow I managed to get up. When I looked around, I saw Pop sitting on his towel, laughing and pointing at me. Mom was smiling like a goober.

Parents of the year.

"Well." Erika shifted her feet. "We need one more."

"One more what?"

"For tug-of-war. Can you play? You look really . . . red." She drew a circle around her face with one finger.

"Yeah," I said, trying to slow down my breathing. "I'm good. I can play."

To be honest, I hadn't really played much tug-of-war. But with me, we were an even ten on each side. Erika led me to the middle of our team, the blue team, and indicated that I should get behind her. I was still on the small side, exhausted, and overall not a good tugger, I assumed, but I followed along with whatever she said to do. I adjusted my grip on the rope a few times until my grasp felt "snug." I dug my bare heels into the sand until I felt "no give." And then I leaned back as far as I could so that the weight of my body seemed to "pull the group back" an inch. We were close enough to touch, her long brown hair hanging over my abdomen. When she grunted, I grunted too.

A crowd watched as we set up. Sookie and Jade waved. Diego smirked. And Sally smiled, even though her eyes held on to that worry.

"On the count of three," shouted Principal Johnson. Everyone took a deep breath, then released a synchronized groan. "One-two-three!"

Erika shouted, "Go! Harder! Harder! Harder!" and I crouched to get more resistance from my legs. My abdomen tightened until every rib was visible. I grunted again and again, and that bought a few steps backward. Erika stepped backward too, and so did the person in front of her. Blue moved so quickly that our line became a compressed accordion.

And then red was over the line.

Over!

"Blue team," Principal Johnson shouted, "is the WINNER!"

We all fell like dominoes, a tangle of bodies. I landed on the sand. Erika landed on top of me, flipping over seconds later, so that her stomach was against mine, her hair falling into my eyes. "You were so good! You grunted like wild," she said, laughing. I started laughing too, because it was a high. This winning thing. And maybe that high led to what happened next.

Erika kissed me.

Senior Year

11. SURPRISE!

PRINCIPAL JOHNSON IS SURPRISED TO SEE Sally Blake outside his office. At least, that's what he says when he calls out to us. "Sally Blake, is that you? What a surprise!"

I am surprised he recognizes her, with the whole taller, not a blonde any longer thing, and missing the wry smile, but I guess beyond that, she's pretty much the same.

"Hi," she says, waving shyly.

"Come in. Come in." Principal Johnson meets us at the door. He gives me the normal shoulder clasp and Sally an enthusiastic hand pump.

"I haven't seen you in years. How . . . ?" He shakes his head, like he's shifting gears. "No, *where* have you been?"

"North Carolina," she states matter-of-factly.

"North Carolina?" He whistles, his brown lips puckering into a small O. "How's high school up in North Carolina?"

"Same?" Sally says.

"And the running?"

"Um . . ."

"Bet Coach Nia, over at Seagrove High, was crying when you didn't end up on her team!"

Sally's shoulders slump; she mumbles something.

Principal Johnson and I exchange looks. He asks, "Can you say that again?"

She squares her shoulders and in a loud, practiced voice repeats, "I quit running."

"Quit running?" Principal Johnson steps back, a look of wonder on his face. "Were you too busy your junior year? That can happen, but you can get back in again. Didn't your coach talk to you? Help you come up with a plan?"

"Actually"—Sally's voice rises—"I haven't run on a team in years."

"Years?" says Principal Johnson.

"Years," Sally confirms, her eyes drifting to the floor.

It's uncomfortable—this exchange—about as uncomfortable as my brothers, who sit opposite the admin's desk, heads also slung low.

I glance at my watch and say pointedly, "Principal Johnson?"

He nods, giving Sally a shoulder pat. "Remember, it's never too late to start again. Sometimes a stop can also be seen as an extended pause. You just have to hit the unpause button."

"I'll remember." She glances at me like, *What do you*

think? Can a stop be an extended pause? But that silent question is even more uncomfortable than the exchange, so I head into the office with an, "It shouldn't be long." But, of course, like most things today, I'm wrong.

My brothers' fight continues all the way to the library.

LIL' JAY

He started the fight.

DOMINGO

I started it? I was helping you not get your as—

ME

Whoa. When did you start cursing?

LIL' JAY

See? He's the one getting me in trouble.

DOMINGO

I'm the one saving you from getting your butt kicked.

SALLY

(bumping into me when I take a fast turn)

Sorry.

ME

It's okay.

(to the boys)

Just shut up, okay? Seriously. Shut it.

DOMINGO

But—

ME

Shut up. Or I am going to pull over and show you some of Diego's justice.

Silence.

Finally.

So, two things here: Diego's justice is pretty much whatever I threaten the boys with when they get out of hand. It's based on a story that Diego told the boys about how in the Dominican Republic, if you get too mouthy your Pop might get you with a switch. "You know," he said, "it could be a branch of a tree. Thin, though. Hurts like hell."

```
                    DOMINGO
You're lying.
                     DIEGO
Nah, kid. I've got the marks to prove it.
  (pulls up his pant leg to reveal a scar about
                an inch long)
                    LIL' JAY
That's abuse!
                     DIEGO
Not in DR. That's justice.
                      ME
                  (laughing)
Diego's justice?
                     DIEGO
When my kids get out of line like these punks?
Yeah.
```

Okay, side note so you don't freak out because that would seriously be abuse: The scar is actually from a motorbike accident. Diego got burned by the muffler. But

I keep this story alive because the fear keeps them in line.

Second thing: The seating in the truck is either ideal or not ideal, depending on how you look at it.

First, the seats are really one long bench. So we're squished four to the bench: me in the driver's spot; Sally on the hump, and the twins on the passenger seat. Every time I hit a bump or take a turn too fast, Sally practically falls into my lap.

This arrangement wasn't my idea. The twins refused to sit on the hump, and after a few minutes of fighting, Sally said quietly, "I'll sit there."

And now we're four bumps in, and you'd think I'd slow down. But for some reason I'm taking the turns faster today.

And there are a lot of turns.

By the time we arrive at the library, we're battered from smashing into one another and sweaty because Old Ancient has no AC and we're four bodies deep. Sweat drips down my back; my palms are wet, and yet for a second after I put the car in park, I wait in that heat, feeling the pressure of her shoulder against mine for one more moment. Then, feeling guilty, I get out.

On the pavement, Domingo raises his hand to speak, still afraid of Diego's justice.

"Go ahead," I say benevolently, fanning my shirt away from my skin.

"What are we doing here?"

"Dropping off Sally and picking up some books for a project."

Lil' Jay raises his hand next.

"Yes?"

"Can we go to the graphic novel section?"

I nod, and they take off running.

Sally waits, her eyes low, around my hips, watching me pull my shirt up and down. When our eyes finally meet, she turns pink a little. "Your . . . ," she mutters.

"What?" I say, shaking my head.

She clears her throat, runs a hand through her hair, her face inching toward red. "Sweaty," she finally says, and I do my best not to laugh. Because I know what that's about.

And damn.

I try to change the subject. "I can ask somebody about the car. He can probably take a look tomorrow if you can leave it there overnight."

"Yeah?" She looks surprised. "You'd do that for me? Help me more?" Again she clears her throat. "I mean, you've already helped me a lot today. . . . I don't know why."

I tell myself what I tell her. "My mom raised me to help, so . . ." I hold out a sweaty palm, and Sally takes it like she's trying to shake it. But my hand doesn't move, and all I can think is, once again, we're holding hands in a parking lot.

"Keys?" I say slowly, letting our hands slide apart.

"Oh. Yeah." Her face is neon. She fumbles with her key ring before handing over the key. "Thank your mom for me," she says, making a big show of glancing at her watch. "I'm late. I should . . ." And then she sprints off across the parking lot.

Inside, I make my way over to Old Mrs. B, at the reference desk.

"I've got your books," she says, eyebrows raised. She nods toward Sally, who clocks in nearby. "You two came here together?"

"Her car broke down. She needed a ride."

Old Mrs. B chuckles, like, *Is that all?*

"I couldn't leave her stranded."

"No, you couldn't," she says, chuckling again.

"What?"

"You know, for an old bird, I have near-perfect vision."

"And?"

"And?" Old Mrs. B chuckles again. "*And* I have a perfect view of the parking lot."

"I didn't hold on," I mumble.

Old Mrs. B smiles innocently. "To what?"

On Saturday night the tribe hangs out at Sookie's house. Unlike the yards in my part of the 'hood, her backyard is full on green. Her patio is even more legit, laid out with large slabs of tile and comfy white couches. Twinkle lights are strung from tree to tree.

Tonight, even though it's hot, we sit beneath those lights, roasting marshmallows over a cast-iron fire pit.

"How many more nights do we have left like this?" Sookie asks, and Jade sighs. "Not enough."

"Man, speak for yourself," Diego says. "I already worked it out with your moms. Even after you're gone, me and Jade are still gonna be here on Friday nights. I got the adoption papers in my backpack."

Sookie laughs. "Ha! They've always wanted to adopt more. But I assure you that *nothing compares to moi!*"

Jade kneels beside the fire, holding four sticks to the flames. The marshmallows start to glow orange, the slow creep of a crackle, the eventual blackening of crust along the edges.

"Your hair," Jade says for the third time that night, and Diego swipes a hand over his almost-bare scalp and says, "Gotta look the part, right?"

I glance down at the paper in my hand—it's a drawing of the Venn diagram from Tuesday. Earlier in the night, Sookie tried to get the tribe on board for "a mature exploration about what happened when Sally disappeared."

At least, that's how she'd put it.

The "mature" part was lifted from a conversation with her parents because Sookie is the type to be like, "Hmm . . . let me talk to my mom about that problem." And her mom was all like, "You can't know what Sally was thinking unless you ask her." And even Old Mrs. B agreed, because to be honest, after that whole "to what?" nonsense, I had a little chat with Mrs. B about how I had a girlfriend and I couldn't be tingling for other girls because I'm pretty sure girlfriends don't like it when you tingle for someone else.

That's when Old Mrs. B launched into "Life can be confusing, especially when something you think is settled turns out not to be settled at all."

"Like Sally?"

"Yes."

"But I'm not confused."

"Well, if you were, that would be perfectly normal."

"But I'm not, because, again, girlfriend."

"All I'm saying is that it's more grown-up to walk toward the things that scare us than to run away from them."

"I don't run away from the things that scare me."

"Well, you do."

"No, I don't."

"Like the Pinterest board . . ."

To that I said, ". . ." Because, *I know*.

Anyway, now Jade is asking how Sookie knows that Sally is back at her old house.

"Because I looked at her file."

"Because it was just hanging around?"

"No, not exactly."

"So you stole her contact info?"

"Not exactly."

Jade gasps, and Diego lets out this high-pitched whistle. "Sooks, that's straight-up mafioso."

"No, it's not," Sookie says with a slick little smile, because Diego is saying she's a badass, and Sookie's never been a badass at anything but tests and quizzes.

Jade shakes her head in disbelief. "What do you think, Marco?"

"Um . . ." I think that I haven't told them about that car ride to the library. "I think . . ." That I haven't told them about how I bartered a fix for Sally's car earlier today. "That . . ."

"*Dude.* What?" Diego snaps.

"That it makes the most sense for us to just ask her."

"Ask a ghost?"

"She's not a ghost," Sookie says. "She's real. She was our friend."

"And so what? We forgive her?" Jade asks.

"Or realize that all she did was lose touch. That happens all the time when someone moves," Sookie argues. "We at least remember how it used to be. Doesn't anyone miss her?"

No one answers.

Jade pulls the marshmallows out of the fire, edges burnt, the centers soft and vulnerable. She nods at Diego, who presses them between graham crackers and squares of chocolate. We eat quietly, lost in our own thoughts.

"I'd never shut you guys out," Sookie says after a while.

"You think we're shutting her out?" Jade asks.

"I don't know. Maybe. But I'm also saying that just because I'm leaving and Marco's leaving doesn't mean things have to change. There's video and group chats and e-mail. Right?"

"Absolutely," Jade says.

We're quiet again because we see an unintended parallel between Sally's leaving in the past and our leaving in the future. Would we move on? Maybe not at first, but eventually? I think about my parents, who have zero friendships left over from childhood. Then I look at my tribe, the faces I know so well. Will I know them a year from now? Two?

"Would we even be having this conversation if we didn't miss her?" Jade asks, and for once Diego doesn't argue.

Mrs. Blake answers the front door wearing a birthday hat and holding a wineglass. "Wow. You guys! Everyone grew up!" She peers past us at the street. "Where did you park?"

Sookie looks confused, but still points to her beat-up Dodge across the street.

"The van?"

Sookie nods.

"Okay, good thinking," Mrs. Blake says, ushering us inside. "I'm so glad you're here. I know it's a late invite, but I'm glad that Boone got it to you. When Marco came over earlier today to drop off Sally's keys, I was so excited to find out that you all were friends again and I said to Boone, we really should invite them all over. And he promised me he would, but sometimes he forgets or doesn't listen. . . ." She interrupted her rambling to laugh. "But oh, never mind! You're all here, and that's all that matters." She paused to look at each of us, thirty seconds on every face. "You all have really grown up—especially you, Marco! You're a giant now."

I smile down at her, recalling how tired she'd looked earlier today when she'd answered the door. But maybe she wasn't tired. Maybe she was hungover.

"Okay, let's find some places to hide in the kitchen.

They'll be back soon. Enough time to—" She grabs birthday hats from the living room and quickly snaps a cone onto each of our heads, except for Diego, who bobs and weaves himself away. Then she scoots us into the kitchen.

"Keys?" Diego hisses in my ear.

"Her car didn't work," I whisper. "And . . . I wanted to help."

"And so that's why you needed that dude's number from my church?" Diego mutters.

"I said I needed car repairs. I just didn't say for who. Besides, it's my barter." And it wasn't cheap. I'd agreed to spend ten hours tutoring the mechanic's son this summer.

"Later," Sookie hisses, nodding at Mrs. Blake, who is going on and on about the birthday surprise.

"But it's not her birthday, right?" Jade whispers, eyes drifting off as she calculates dates. "I thought it was April . . ."

"April 29," I say, no hesitation. Today is May 12.

"So her mom's completely confused?" Jade mimes drinking a big glass of wine. *Lush?* she mouths.

Maybe? I mouth back.

Probably.

"Well, we can't stay here," Jade whispers. "Does Sookie think we're gonna stay here?"

Nearby, Sookie compliments Mrs. Blake's birthday decorations, pointing out the yellow and white streamers, the gold balloons.

"I just have to get one more thing," Mrs. Blake says, heading toward the bedrooms. *"Don't move."*

We look around. The house is crammed roof to tile with partially unpacked boxes and yet-to-be placed knick-knacks.

"This is a sad party, even for a ghost," Diego says.

Jade steps closer to the dining room table and peers down at a sheet cake. "Is that a baby pic of Sally?"

We move in and see baby Sally—wispy hair, hazel eyes, pink lips.

"Oh," Sookie says. "She had those chubby legs, you know the kind that . . ." She makes this chipmunk face, and her voice elevates. "Like you want to bite them and squeeze them all at once."

Diego whips his head around. "Sooks, that's some Hannibal shiz right there."

"No!" Sookie laughs self-consciously, looks to me. "It's not, right?"

I shrug.

"It's not," Sookie insists.

Diego inspects the party items crowding the kitchen counters—chips, sweet and salty *pastelitos*, a half-empty bottle of wine. He takes a swig of the wine and hands the bottle to Jade. She waves him away.

"Maybe we should . . . *beat it, beat it,*" Diego says.

"*Beat it, beat it* . . . ," Jade harmonizes, but nobody moves.

Because we've come to another realization tonight: that

this is not the life we imagined for our missing Sally. The life we imagined included a better house, a better family, everything better. We had constructed an elaborate lie, in which Sally sailed off into the sunset unharmed by her losses, when what really happened was Sally left everything she knew, every anchor to her happiness, to trudge through the abyss alone.

We're somber when Mrs. Blake reappears, juggling a gift box, a rose-filled vase, and an empty wineglass. I rush forward to take the vase. Diego rescues the box. Mrs. Blake clings to the wineglass. When her hands are mostly free, she sighs and tops off the glass. Then she takes a large gulp and sighs again.

"Let's see," she says, centering the vase and gift box on the table. "Perfect." She takes another big gulp.

"Pretty, Mrs. Blake," Jade says, her voice unnaturally high.

"*Ms. Martin*," she corrects. "My maiden name . . . I took it back after the divorce."

We exchange looks that say: *This is getting worse by the minute. I'd like to sneak out the front door now.*

But it's Sookie, always Sookie, who regains our equilibrium. She says, "*Ms. Martin*, the flowers are beautiful."

Ms. Martin smiles gratefully. "You only turn eighteen once and . . . and . . . we missed it. I missed it. I . . . I completely forgot. The real day, that is. With everything that's been going on . . ." She glances around at the house. "Anyway, there's a rose for each year of her life."

We admire the roses, the buds still tight, a few petals straining to bloom.

A car door slams outside, and Boone's boisterous voice urges Sally up the walkway.

"I guess we're staying," Diego whispers.

"Life is what happens to us while we are making other plans," I say, quoting Allen Saunders. Old Mrs. B taped that life lesson to our janitor's closet wall a few weeks back.

"I don't like that quote," Sookie says as we crouch in the dark behind the dining room table. Collectively, we inhale our breaths, and when the door swings open, we yell, "Surprise!"

Middle School

12. ALWAYS

ERIKA'S KISS LANDED ON THE SIDE OF MY mouth. One-quarter lip, three-quarter chin. No big deal. And not my fault. "She kissed *me*" is what I said to Sally afterward.

But did I take it in for a second? Two? Three?

Was I curious, caught up in the whole shift from barely noticeable to kissable?

Maybe.

Probably.

The Monday after the kiss, Sally brought me a bag of Hershey's Kisses. "In case you need some today. There's a lot to choose from. I got the variety pack. You can try them all out."

That Tuesday, in the cafeteria, she tripped me. When I hit the floor, she snapped, "The floor can kiss it and make it better."

On Wednesday she tried ignoring me.

But on Thursday, as we printed out our English papers in the school library, she finally started talking. "Look,

Erika likes you. Sookie was right. She is all 'love eyes.' So, admit it. And admit that you wanted her to kiss you."

But I didn't want her to kiss me. I couldn't have predicted that end to tug-of-war if I'd tried.

"Then why didn't you push her off you?"

"I was surprised, and anyway, it was like here." I pointed to my cheek. "Not here." I pointed to my lips.

"It was here," Sally said, and placed her index finger on her lip and the middle, on the skin beneath her lip. "If you moved your head, it would have been here." She moved the two fingers square onto her lips.

"Nope. It would have been here." I put two fingers square on my cheek.

She glared at me. "You're avoiding the question. Do you like her?"

"Too much noise. If you want to make noise, go back to the cafeteria," called Old Mr. B from the circulation desk.

Old Mr. B was our school librarian and the man who gave Old Mrs. B the last name Banks. If she hadn't married him, her name would have been Old Ms. D for Dumas. But as of middle school, they had been married for almost forty years. The fact that our school librarian was married to our city librarian always cracked Diego up. Every time he stepped foot into our school library, he'd be like, "You know how Old Mr. B met Old Mrs. B? He checked her out."

"Sorry, Mr. Banks," I called out, and looked at Sally with a big smile.

"Why are you smiling?" she hissed.

I shrugged, even though I knew why. I was smiling because she was jealous, and if she was jealous, then she didn't just like me; she really, really liked me. And if she really, really liked me, then I could ask the thing that I had been wanting to ask.

"You're being really creepy," she said.

Smile got bigger.

"Stop!" Her voice rose again.

"Sally Blake and Marco Suarez," Old Mr. B called out. "You need to take that outside."

"But we're sorry," I called back.

"Outside."

"See?" Sally said, obviously frustrated. "See?"

She stood, and I popped up behind her, grabbing my books.

"What are you doing?"

"He kicked us both out."

"No."

"No?"

"Yes."

"Which is it?"

She walked ahead, pausing every now and then to give me a dirty look. Outside, I began to laugh.

"Why are you laughing?" She turned to me—arms wide, palms up.

"Why are you so pissed?" I asked.

"Because . . ."

"Because what?"

"Because you're kissing two girls, and one of them is me."

In that moment I had more courage than ever before. I grabbed her hand and tugged her close enough to feel the inhalation of her breath.

"What?" she whispered.

"I like you. I keep telling you that, you know."

Her eyes darted to the side, and her mouth formed a stubborn little line. "That doesn't mean anything if you're kissing Erika too."

I moved closer, until my lips were next to hers. One-quarter lip, three-quarters cheeks. I waited to see if she would move away, but instead she moved closer. Her hand squeezed mine. She looked at me with big gray eyes.

"Only you," I said. And even though I knew that dismissal bell would ring at any moment and the tribe would come pouring out of lunch, I held us there a little longer. I let my hand curl around her waist. I let my lips inch along hers until we were four-quarters lip to lip.

One hundred percent. Together.

Sally leaned in to me, our bodies aligning, not perfectly, but close enough. And I said the thing that I had been wanting to say all along.

Will you be mine?

Not just to the dance.

But for always?

I used that word, "always."

"Always?" she said.

"Always."

Senior Year

13. WE WIN

AFTER WE YELLED SURPRISE (AND WHAT A surprise it was!)

After Ms. Martin went on and on about the good old times.

After Boone gave us the death stare because he knew he had not invited us.

After Sally, wide-eyed and nervous, blew out the birthday candles.

After the cake had been cut and the birthday presents opened: a gift card from Ms. Martin, a BuLiMaL (BUDDHIST LIVE MANY LIVES) poster from Boone, and a voter's registration application from the supply that Sookie keeps in her Dodge van—*because you never know when I'll run into someone who isn't registered!*

After all that, we declared the ceremonial festivities over, and Ms. Martin took a fresh bottle of wine and headed to bed. We sat in Sally's backyard and tried not to think about the crying attack that had hit her in the middle of cutting her cake and had gone on until Boone had led her away with, "Hey, Sally, let's go to your room and get you right again," Ms. Martin trailing behind, a hand nervously fluttering in the air.

DIEGO
That was . . . Wow.

JADE
Yeah, and . . . and, like, really sad.

SOOKIE
Yeah, this is . . . not what I thought it was going to be.

DIEGO
This is, we win life.

JADE
And not in a good way.

Diego pointed to the church pamphlet stuck to the refrigerator door. Circled in a bright marker were times and dates for a divorce support group. Scribbled beside the circle in Sally's familiar bubbly handwriting was one declarative sentence: *Mom, please go to this.*

"And that"—Sookie pointed to the recycling bin in the corner of the kitchen, overflowing with empty tin cans, milk cartons, and wine bottles; she sighed heavily—"at least three or four?"

"Wow," Diego said again. "Her recycling game is strong though."

I glanced at Jade, who looked a little teary-eyed. "I get

it. Like who wants to tell anyone about this? I might have disappeared too."

And yet the night went on. Diego snuck a few more sips off Ms. Martin's stash. Sookie took stock of the rest of the house, and I checked the text messages on my phone while we waited. Erika had texted me an hour ago.

Erika: 0 tips. 2night sux.

Me: ☹

Erika: so bored, on Pinterest. Just wanna b out 2 meet up. Where R U?

Me: surprise-ish bday

Erika: 4?

Me: Sally

Erika: ex Sally?

Me: ex bff

Erika: + ex

Me: ?

Erika: . . .

So Erika wasn't happy about tonight.

When they returned, Boone suggested we sit on the back patio. One by one we dragged the dining room chairs outside. A small neighborhood kitten appeared, and Sally pulled him onto her lap, stroking him until the purring became as loud as an engine.

We pretended that everything was okay—maybe we did it for Sally; maybe we did it for us. But the more we let go of the past, the more Sally came out of her shell. Eventually, we were talking about safe subjects, like last-minute school projects, prom, and the colleges we'd selected.

"I'm staying here," Jade says. "Florida International."

"And I'm going to be a management trainee," Diego says, all confident, tugging on his fitted khakis.

"You look good in those," Jade reassures him.

"Hmph," Diego says. "Good-boy pants are tight. I feel like I'm murdering all my future sons."

"Why didn't you take them off after work?" Sookie asks.

"Method actors stay in character."

Sookie rolls her eyes, but the rest of us laugh.

"So where did you get in?" Jade asks Sally.

"Um, UM. I got a scholarship." We nod because we remember that this was the plan, since Mr. Blake had once run for UM.

"So, you're running for them?" Jade asks.

Sally clears her throat, looks surprised that I didn't tell them.

"I stopped running," Sally says.

There's that collective gasp again—Diego's at the tail end of it with his high-pitched trill, so high that Boone chuckles.

"It's not a big deal," Sally says. "I stopped a while ago. I got a merit scholarship. Turns out when you're in need with a photographic memory, you're a pretty likely candidate for a merit scholarship."

Diego shakes his head, always fascinated by Sally's

photographic memory, always testing her with ridiculous requests: *Recite "The Star-Spangled Banner." Name all the countries in North and South America. What did JFK say to Coretta Scott King when he called her?*

I could see him working up to a question now. His forehead wrinkles, and then he spits out, "Last sentence of the Declaration of Independence."

We had been asked to memorize the Declaration of Independence for extra credit in seventh grade.

Everyone laughs, except for Boone, who says, "What?"

"Just watch," Diego instructs as Sally closes her eyes. For a minute she looks peaceful. Her mouth begins to move as she remembers. Then, with eyes still closed, she slowly recites, "And for the support of this Declaration . . . with a firm reliance on the protection of divine Providence, we mutually . . . pledge to each other our lives . . . our fortunes, and our sacred honor."

Diego claps like a kindergartener. "Wow!"

Sookie and Jade also applaud. When Sally meets my eyes, I do something unexpected. I give her the Suarez wink. Flawlessly executed.

Sally laughs, an honest-to-goodness laugh.

"But seriously, look at this." Diego holds up the last slice of cake for us to admire. "You know, Sals, Sookie is really into your little baby rolls. But that's not creepy, not even a little bit, right, Sooks?"

"Wait. What?" Sally's forehead ripples, little lines of confusion form like a mountain range across her skin. But her smile deepens. Maybe it's because Diego called her Sals. He's the only one who ever did.

"It's not creepy. Haven't you guys ever thought a baby was so cute you could literally gobble up his chunky thighs? Like . . ." She scrunches up her face like that overexcited squirrel and goes, "*Nom, nom, nom, nom.*"

Cannibal, Diego mouths, and we bust out laughing, especially Sally, who laughs until tears roll down her face. She says, "This night is so weird and spectacular. Isn't it weird? Us together again."

Silence follows, because the conversation suddenly got deep. I offer up a lifeline, because the lightness feels too good to wash away. "Life's weird. But that's okay."

"True," Diego says, and chuckles, shrugging his shoulders like, *What are you going to do?*

Sally takes a deep breath, her eyes a little glassy. "I know that when I left . . . The way I left was . . ." She takes a few more deep breaths as her lips form silent words: one, two, three, four . . . She stops at ten instead of one hundred, and then aloud she says, "It was . . ." Sally lowers a vibrating hand to her belly "I—"

"Not you." Boone interrupts, his knee bouncing up and down. *"Dad."*

Sally nods, eyes wide. "Dad . . . ," she begins again, and my phone chirps—the sound of my mother's ringtone.

"Sorry." I send the call to voicemail.

"Our dad—" The phone chirps again, and everyone

looks at me like, *What the hell?* But the phone won't quiet. It goes: *chirp, chirp, chirp.*

"I'm sorry." I pull the phone from my pocket. "Mom?"

"Marco?" Her voice is small, nearly breathless. I hear noises in the background: an ambulance siren. My heart speeds up.

"Mom? Where are you?"

"I'm at the hospital," she says. "It's Pop."

"Marco!" At the hospital, Mom rushes up to hug me, squeezing extra tight. I hold on too. A few minutes ago I was with the tribe, in Sookie's van, rushing past every yellow light while Sookie sang under her breath the *Mi Sheberakh*.

"What is that?" Jade asked, rubbing her jaw.

"It's a prayer, kind of, for your dad's healing," Sookie said, giving me that *I'm sorry* look. But all I could think about was how the day had gone: s'mores at Sookie's house, a surprise birthday party at Sally's house, and now Sookie was saying some kind of Hebrew prayer for my pop.

How did we get here again? Pop hurt. Pop almost dy—

I shake the thought away and pull Mom in closer. "Where's Pop?" I ask when I let her go for good. We stand in a room of sorts—one wall, three curtains. Next door, I hear a patient cough. A man asks, "Do you want more water?" Across the hall is a little kid about the twins' age with an arm freshly wrapped in a neon cast. And in front of me is my mom, who left home dressed for sleep: yoga pants and a grubby T-shirt.

Her voice shakes when she speaks. "They took him for tests, but he's awake. We think . . . He, um . . . The doctors think he had some sort of a seizure when he was in the shower, and when I found him, he was lying on the floor with a . . ." She takes several deep breaths. "A gash here." She touches the right corner of her head. "He needed stitches for that."

I also take a deep breath, trying to find space from the feelings that push up inside me. That will have to wait for later. Right now I need to help Mom gather facts and make decisions. "But he's here now, and that's good. The doctors will set him right. What did they say?"

"They're running tests—right now it's a CT scan to make sure there's no bleeding in the brain and . . ." She pauses, trying to think of the right terms. "An EEG because of the seizure."

"Where are the twins?"

"Mrs. Banks has them."

I stare at the empty bed; my need to do something is strong. "So, now we just, what?"

Mom holds up her arms helplessly. "We wait."

They wheel my father into the room around midnight. I'm texting with Erika, who checked in after work, and the tribe, who went back to Sookie's house to hang out. Mom sleeps in the chair beside me, but the minute the attendant says, "Here you go, Mr. Suarez," she jumps upright and blinks into the light. "Sammy?"

"Mom, he's here." I squeeze her shoulder.

"I'm here," Pop echoes, reaching for her hand. Once they're linked, the lines ease from their faces, their breaths deepen.

Pop, though, looks a mess. His hairline's been shaved. An inch of his forehead is covered with gauze. Slumped in his wheelchair, he seems as fragile as Mom's voice on the phone.

After the attendant helps him into bed, Mom tucks him in, making sure that he's warm. That he doesn't need water or ice or—

She runs out of *ors* and finally asks, "How are you feeling?"

"A headache," Pop mumbles. "Too bright." He points to the fluorescent lights spilling in from the hallway. I close the curtains and the light dims. Pop nods his appreciation.

Mom climbs into bed beside him and rests her head on his chest. She looks like she's trying not to speak. Not to say what we are all feeling: that we're scared. That we don't know what this means. That to be back here, in this place where we almost lost him the first time, is too much for anyone.

And yet, somehow, we continue to survive. To push our way through to the other side.

I try to remind myself of this as Mom bites her lips and makes the murmuring noises she sometimes makes when she is overstressed. I sit at the edge of the bed and reach for his hand. It takes a Herculean effort not to cry, especially when I meet Mom's eyes and she whispers, "You're a good son, Marco."

"You're a good mom, and you"—I squeeze Pop's hand—"are a good pop."

Pop smiles limply, and Mom looks away, wiping at her face with the back of her hand.

I run my hands through my hair, and with eyes wide open, I pray.

At some point I slip away for a few minutes and take the elevator up to the hospital's rooftop observatory—an open deck that is closed late at night, but with my Grendel's-issued pocketknife, I manage to jimmy my way past the door (a trick Diego's dad taught us before he went to the resort).

On the rooftop, it's just me, the moon, and a smattering of stars. And it is here that I complete a ritual I started four years ago. I close my eyes, stretch up to my tippy-toes, and walk the perimeter of the deck, with the handrail as my guide.

I name the star patterns, beginning with the asterisms: Summer Triangle, Keystone, the stars that make up the body of the Hercules constellation—Eta, Pi, Epsilon, and Zeta Herculis. On and on until the ritual—this prayer to let Pop stay with me and Mom and Lil' Jay and Domingo—is finally complete. Then I return to solid ground and head downstairs.

• • •

An hour later Mom's exhaustion has gotten the best of her. She is asleep on the chair beside Pop's bed. We're waiting on word from the doctor about tests and a transfer to another floor for further observation. It'll be a while. The ER is hopping tonight. The examination bays are as full as the waiting room, and the nurse looks harried when he sticks his head through the curtain to ask, "Everything okay?"

"Yeah," I say, and Pop, who is trying his best to stay awake, offers up another meek smile.

The nurse leaves, and I take Pop's hand, settling onto the edge of the bed. "How you holding up, Pop?"

"Eh," he says. His voice is scratchy. "Seen better."

"You'll see better again."

He nods but doesn't look convinced. "Hey, you know, you know I'm real"—he pauses the way he always does when he's forgotten the word he wants to use—"proud of you. I am."

"Yeah, Pop, I know that." I lean over to give him a kiss on the forehead.

"And you know, I'll try to be there more. I'll try to . . ." Again he pauses, looking for the words. "I'll try to talk more, be less in here." He raises a finger toward his head. "Be more with . . ."

I wait a while and then say, "Us?"

"Yeah. It's hard sometimes to . . ."

"Find the words."

"Yeah."

"That would be good. I don't mind waiting for you to find them."

"Yeah, and I don't want you to worry about this because you've got, you know, stuff . . . You got . . ." He stares off at the TV, his mouth trembling slightly, like the words are stuck on the tip of his tongue. His eyes are so focused—almost like a dead stare—on those words, on where they live in the distance.

"With college?" I prompt, but he doesn't respond, except his hand starts to shake. Then, suddenly, he jerks forward, and his whole body begins to convulse, like ocean tides are rolling inside of him.

"Mom!" I hold him steady so he doesn't fall off the bed. "Mom!"

"What?" She sits up, looking from me to Pop. "Sammy? *Sammy!*" She reaches for the call button, shouting, "Nurse! Nurse!"

And then the scrubs arrive, pushing us from the room. We stand in the corridor, watching as one holds Pop and the other turns him on his side, stretching out his neck. A doctor appears, spewing out a bunch of medical jargon. Bed rails are raised and pillows are shoved in the gap. Someone calls out, "We're at three minutes. It looks like it's winding down."

Pop's eyes open. The shaking suddenly stops. His body sinks into stillness. Mom is next to me, crying. I wrap my arms around her and whisper, "He's okay now. He's okay." But the words sound hollow, even to me.

• • •

"So, how is he?" Old Mrs. B asks when I stop by her house to check on the twins.

It's eight a.m. and I'm away from the hospital. Pop has been moved from the ER to another floor for further testing and observation. The seizures, his doctors say, are something that can happen years after a head injury, and because Pop had more than one seizure, they're inclined to think that it's not just a two-time deal but signs of epilepsy. Something else that can happen with TBI. There will be a neurological consultation later in the day, but for right now they've got him medicated and resting comfortably.

I give Old Mrs. B the short version. I tell her about the other seizure. I don't tell her about how it happened, how I was holding his hand when he convulsed, how I thought he'd bite off his own tongue because that's what they always shout out in movies: *Put something in his mouth for him to bite down on or else he'll bite off his tongue!* That the minute Pop was okay, I left to hit up a single-stall restroom and lost my shit, holding my T-shirt to my mouth to muffle the sounds.

I only say, "He's okay." And then I give her the facts as briefly as possible, because this is the way I'm operating now: straight-up survival mode. And I need to talk about anything else, just for an hour, just until my insides stop shaking.

Old Mrs. B takes the hint and moves on to taking care of basic needs: She feeds me. I scarf down three over-easy eggs, a pound of chorizo, and gulp my *café con leche* like it's a cold glass of water after a hot-as-hell walk through the desert.

"More bread," she says, and holds up half a loaf of Cuban bread, toasted and smeared with butter.

"Yes, please," I say, and she hands me a huge chunk.

"An appetite is important. Even when life is hard, it's always wise to keep up your strength."

That's never been my problem. My appetite increases with stress.

"Oh, but slow down, okay?" she says as I swallow that chunk nearly whole.

"Sorry. I'm starving."

"I know." She clicks her tongue. "I know." And then she touches my back and says, "You're okay. You're safe."

And man, my heart pauses as those words wrap around me. Warm words, like a blanket right out of the dryer. When I'm fully sated, Old Mrs. B clears the dishes and tells me to follow her outside, to her front porch, where we rock on her old-fashioned rocking chairs. We don't talk, just sip our coffee and enjoy the world as it is, in that moment: The moss-draped palm trees that shade the roadway. The family of ducks waddling through the front yard. The little girl that comes outside to draw on the sidewalk with chalk. Even Old Mrs. B's broke-down mailbox, which I keep fixing, the one that random kids keep taking out with a baseball bat in the deep cover of night.

Inside the house, my brothers sleep that sleep of

children who are too young to feed a worry. And four houses over is Sookie's home, where yesterday we sat around her fire pit. In the driveway is her rickety Dodge; Jade's baby-blue scooter sits off to the side. Inside the house, Jade and Sookie are probably out cold. And somewhere farther out, Diego is most likely dreaming of how to be more managerial. I glance at my watch. Erika's dreams are about to end; her alarm clock is always set for nine a.m. on the weekends. In a few minutes, she'll jump out of bed and hustle to get ready for her next shift at the diner.

I close my eyes and let my mind continue to drift. And that's when I allow myself to think of her—of Sally. Of what she almost said last night. The truth so close I could have reached out and grabbed it. But what did it matter anymore? The truth couldn't change us. Couldn't change Pop. No matter how far we stepped into the future, we couldn't escape our past.

Middle School

14. UNTIL A PATTERN FORMS

"WHAT IF . . . ? WHAT IF HE HITS HER?" SALLY angled her body toward me so that our knees overlapped. This was Friday, day one and a half of Sally being my girlfriend, and new things were already happening. We went to the library during lunch, not only to finish studying for our English test but to have "private time." That's what Sally called it—"private time." Just us, sitting in the far corner of the library, where autobiography turns into auto mechanic, alone except for Old Mr. B. He sat at his desk, hunched over a book, one finger robotically lifting a baby carrot to his mouth.

We were also studying, our backs pushed against the stacks, knees tented so that the spines of our books hung in the gaps between our thighs. But it was hard to concentrate with her being so close. Hard not to reach over and kiss her. Hard not to say, "Hey, you" and have her say, "Hey, you" back.

Because when you got together, words like "hey" and

"you" meant so much more. They meant, *I like you. I want you. I'm here with you.* Sally must have felt the same way because she kept touching me—a hand reaching for mine, a squeeze of my knee, a finger sweeping my hair from my face.

I didn't want her to stop.

But she did.

She stopped at that part in *The Curious Incident of the Dog in the Night-Time* when Christopher uncovers the letters from his mom, proving that she is still alive. That his dad had lied. That's when Sally twisted her body toward me and said slowly, "What if . . . ? What if he hits her?"

"You think the mom ran away because she was afraid of Christopher's dad?"

"*No*. I'm talking about Jade, about *her* dad, about that night he was out-of-his-mind drunk, about the bruise at the beach. About the sweater. It's too hot for sweaters. Why is she wearing a sweater?"

Jade had worn a sweater the whole week. A hot week. A week where most kids were trying to sneak by in as little clothes as possible. And there was Jade in long sleeves.

I shut the book. "Maybe she gets cold?"

"Suddenly she gets cold?" Sally sounded agitated. "Okay, then explain this to me: Why, in the locker room today, when she took off her shirt, did she have a huge bruise on her arm—like a *huge* bruise—"

"A new bruise?"

"Yeah."

"Because, cheerleading?"

"Except cheerleading is over. Their practices ended before track's did. And what about that bruise at the beach? She changed the subject when I tried to ask her."

"You're sure? There's no way it could be cheerleading? They couldn't be practicing inside? Because it's hot?"

"No. That's not it," Sally said. "Today, in science, I asked Genevieve about the last time they had practice. It was weeks ago."

"I don't know." As far as I could tell, everything had been quiet on Jade's home front. But maybe there was something I missed? I scanned my memories of the last few weeks, looking for anything that stood out. Now that I'm older, I see that our brains work like that, picking up pieces of information, storing them until a pattern emerges and a picture forms, solving a puzzle you didn't even know existed. Which explains why people say, *I knew, but I also didn't know.* That's because the subconscious mind slowly gathers information while the conscious mind remains unaware of the investigation.

That's where I was right then, in the library, somewhere between my subconscious and conscious minds—a bridge being built between the two as I sat there. The puzzle pieces moving around until the pattern formed a picture. A picture that I couldn't quite see. Just fragments:

The sweater.

Mr. Acosta and his drinking.

The bruises.

What if he hits her?

My stomach turned, my conscious mind reaching for something that was still too far away to grasp.

But there was something I knew for sure—there were repercussions for suspicions like ours. In our neighborhood hitting wasn't all that uncommon—kids got smacks to the head, swats to the butt. But that was survivable. That wasn't hitting until there were bruises. Bruises meant kids got taken away from their parents, put into "the system." And if we weren't right, an accusation like that would make a bad situation worse for Jade. And I didn't want that.

The bell rang and with it came the sound of Old Mr. B from the other side of the library. "Time to go," he called out. "The books will be here just the same tomorrow."

I helped Sally to her feet. When we stood eye to eye, she paused, her legs slightly bent.

"I'd feel better if you talk to your dad. See what he thinks."

"Pop?"

"Yeah. He'd know what to do."

I thought this over. If I moved quickly, I might be able to find him in the custodian's office. Even if he wasn't there, I had the electronic key code and could wait for him. Give myself a moment to be alone and think.

"You'll ask him?" Sally pushed.

"Yeah."

She smiled. "Okay. That's good. I feel like we're doing something."

We. My mind stuck on that word. We—like someone had taken an invisible rope and bound us together—Sally and me, a team. And for a few minutes I didn't think about Jade, about who was on her team. I just thought about Sally and the newness of our private world.

Senior Year

15. FRAGMENTED AFTERMATH

THAT TUESDAY–THE DAY BEFORE POP CAME home from the hospital—Diego showed up at my house with an armful of groceries: premade foods from the deli, a rotisserie chicken, and some veggies. "For your mom to be satisfied with your healthiness and all that, kid!" he said. Then he held up Klondike bars, the twins' favorite treat, and added, "But never keep the devils hungry."

When I whipped out my wallet, he said, "Don't even try." And to be honest, I was relieved. There were only a few dollars in there. "I used my Grendel's gift card—the one I got for my three-year anniversary—and besides, I know your moms isn't working right now. Times be tough, but don't you worry, 'cause you got Big D to the rescue."

"Who's gonna rescue you?" I joked.

"When I need rescuing, you'll be there, right?" He punched me in the shoulder. "Besides, you know my motto: Responsible to my j-o-b, to my lady, to *mi familia. Es parentesco sin sangre una amistad verdadera.*"

Which means something like: If someone feels like your blood even when they ain't your blood, that's a true friendship.

"Thanks, D," I said, and I might have taken a little pinkie to the corner of my eye. Whatever. It was a moment, that's all.

"So what's this?" Diego stared at the spreadsheet I had up on my school-issued Mac.

"Trying to figure out this money situation." I started tracking our finances after our electricity got cut off the summer of Pop's first hospitalization. That's when I noticed the bills piling up on the kitchen table. That's when I walked into Grendel's to ask for a job. That's when I decided kid time was over and I had to do my best to pretend I was a man. To take my pop's advice and keep on accelerating.

And my motto then was kinda like my motto now: Fake it until you make it.

Right now I'm trying to fake my way into figuring out the hospital bill. We hadn't paid off our medical deductible for the year, so I knew that bill was going to be high, about twelve G's—if my math was right—before our "maximum out of pocket" would kick in on our medical insurance. Mom had missed nearly a week of work, and the gist of what I had worked out so far was that we were screwed. Even with a payment plan, the hospital bill threatened to topple our house-of-cards debt.

But maybe with a plan we'd be okay. Maybe we'd be fine.

Okay, not fine, but we'd survive.

"Well, let me know if you need a loan. I got some money saved up for a rainy day," Diego said seriously, and once again, I had to look away.

Truth be told, I had already made a list of people we could ask for money if it came to that. Diego's name was on the bottom of that list. Taking from him would mean taking away one of his dreams: to get an apartment with Jade after graduation.

"I've got money saved up too," I said.

"For college," Diego said. "That money's for college."

My college fund had about fifteen G's in it. Enough to cover all the first-year expenses my college scholarship wouldn't.

"I got money for what needs money." I was trying to be funny, but the moment grew heavier. Diego knew how to fix it. He pulled out the Klondike bars and shook the box like he was baiting a pair of wild animals. "Hey, little shits!" he shouted out to my brothers. "Uncle Diego brought some treats!"

"I looked it up, and the water is like sixty degrees," Erika told me later that day. We were in my bedroom, around ten p.m. Mom was staying at the hospital overnight, and the boys were finally asleep. Erika snuggled up to me on my twin bed, the covers half across our legs. "We're going to miss the Atlantic."

"You mean 'cause it's as warm as if someone peed next to you."

"I like the heat."

"Yeah, me too."

"If you want, I can pee next to you in the Pacific, so that you feel more at home."

"Hmm . . . maybe."

Earlier that afternoon, I stood in the doorway of the boys' room and nibbled on a Klondike bar. The room was a mess. "When are you gonna clean up?" I pointed to their beds, littered with clothes, old plates, and games.

LIL' JAY

When ya gonna stop being creepy?

ME

What's creepy?

LIL' JAY

Licking that bar and staring at us. And I heard Diego. That's our treat.

ME

Ha! Not when you get two days indoor for hitting someone.

DOMINGO

He called Pop "Forrest Dump."

ME

It's Forrest Gump.

DOMINGO

Who's Forrest Dump anyway?

LIL' JAY

So we had to hit him.

DOMINGO

Yeah. Because respect.

ME

(bites into Klondike)

This is so good.

DOMINGO

We had to! You're not being fair!

ME

Did you have to kick him in the nuts and shove him inside his locker, too? Was that fair?

Erika pulls the covers over us. The boys have fallen into such a deep sleep in the room next door that we can hear their snores. "I could spend the night." She scoots up, until her body is fully over mine. Her legs straddle my hips. "We could . . ." She shakes her hips. "Have fun."

I let my hand slide up her thigh. "Like this?"

"Yeah," she says, a little breathless. "Or"—she leans over and kisses me—"like this." And then she tilts her head to the left and lets her tongue slide across my ear. That thing she does. That power of attorney. It's hard to think after that.

Hands sliding over each other's skin.

Hands sliding under each other's clothes.

Hands sliding up.

Hands sliding down.

Our lips everywhere.

"We could do more," she says, when our shirts are crumpled on the floor. "We could . . ."

ME

Like messed him up bad, bad?

PRINCIPAL JOHNSON

Not the worst I'd ever seen. No. But they seem angrier than usual. And if this kid hadn't initiated the fight—and he's initiated quite a few—I'd have given your brothers more than an indoor suspension. I'm trying to give them a break, with your dad in the hospital again. But we all need to think about what's going to happen to them.

ME

What's gonna happen to them? They're fine.

PRINCIPAL JOHNSON

They're not fine. Not even now with you at home. They're struggling.

ME

I'll get them back on track. I always do.

PRINCIPAL JOHNSON

But this is your senior year. You're not always going to be there. Who's going to keep them on track when you're gone?

Erika leans down to kiss me, her tongue like a wave over mine.

I want more.

She wants more.

It would be so easy to take it to this next level. I have condoms in my dresser. "Just in case," my mom had said, when she'd slipped the box in the drawer. "I was young once too," she joked. "And not responsible. That's how I got you. The best—"

"Mistake you ever made," I finished for her.

"Yes." She smiled. "The best mistake I ever made. I wouldn't change a thing." She laughed. "But you haven't made any mistakes yet." She pointed to the box of condoms. "And you've got a full scholarship."

"I won't make a mistake," I promised her.

But here is Erika, twisting her hips in that way that makes me want to sign over that power of attorney. "I want to," she urges. "I do."

It would be so easy.

Except . . .

Sally.

In that moment—I don't know why; it makes no sense—I think about her.

Of the past Saturday: Sally in front of her birthday cake, slicing the square into smaller squares, her mom beside her, holding the paper plates. That one moment she stopped slicing and looked around the room, her eyes lit by hope.

And our eyes meeting and, without thinking about whether I was still mad or angry or whatever, I mouthed *Gotcha*, and she smiled—her first smile since we had surprised the crap out of her.

That smile felt like coming out of a freezing-cold school to stand beneath a June sun.

That smile felt like that day when her car broke down and I took those curves extra fast, her shoulder pushing into mine.

We had promised each other always.

We had broken that promise.

And here is Erika—who has told me she loves me but I have never told her I love her back. But that's okay, she says, because I've been "hurt" because "of what happened to your dad."

Erika is in my bed, her mouth curved up into an excited smile.

We've been together for six months.

In so many ways, I want this to go further. But . . .

```
                    JADE
          (leaning against locker)
I feel terrible.
                     ME
Don't.
                    JADE
I do. I feel like this is my fault.
                     ME
It's not.
                    JADE
It is.
                     ME
You were a kid. It's not.
                    JADE
But your dad, he saved my life.
```

Erika pulls the covers around her shoulders, hides her nakedness.

"I'm really sorry. I should have thought about being . . . prepared . . . and having something . . . on hand. . . . I didn't think tonight would be . . . the night. . . ."

"No. It's okay. You're right. We have to be safe." She slips off my lap, sits with her legs crisscrossed, and watches me, a little warily.

"I really am sorry," I say.

She nods, tilting her head like she's thinking.

"You okay?"

"Yeah," she says. "I'm just confused."

"It's not you," I try to reassure her.

"I know," she says. She leans across me, slides open the top drawer of my nightstand. The shiny box of condoms gleams in the light. A ten-pack.

"Well?" she whispers. "Couldn't we 'be safe' with these?"

My heart thumps in my chest. I'm speechless.

She sighs. "Is this about Sally?"

"What is she, psychic?"

"Maybe? Maybe she saw the condoms earlier in the night? Or at some point in the last few weeks? I don't know."

"No, I mean about Sally."

"What about Sally?"

Diego raises an eyebrow.

"I don't know why she said that. I don't have feelings." I pause. "I have nostalgia, but not, like, feelings."

Diego's eyebrow inches higher.

"I have memories. . . . It can be confusing. . . . That's all."

"Mm-hm."

It's the next night, after work, and we sit outside Grendel's, at a picnic table, enjoying a rare Grendel's perk: end-of-the-night deli freebies.

Rare because usually by the time Diego and I get off, the freebies are more than gone. But tonight, thanks to some new relationships Diego has made among our colleagues in the deli—*Doing recon, bro, for the interview*—we have a feast before us: risotto, chicken wings, kale, tuna salad.

Diego shoves some tuna salad into his mouth on the tip of a freshly baked pita chip.

"So, she just popped into your head, mid–you know?"

"Yeah, mid-exactly."

"And you don't know why."

"I don't know why."

"Humph." Diego washes the chip down with some water. "When I'm mid–you know with Jade, I've only got one girl on my mind."

"So what? So that means I'm into Sally?"

"Just curious timing, man."

"I really . . . you know . . . wanted to . . . with Erika. Before that. Maybe I should have tried to . . ."

"No." Diego shoves a forkful of risotto in his mouth. "You did the right thing."

"I did, right?"

"Yeah. Something like that . . . You have to be sure."

"And I wasn't?"

"Nope. You weren't."

• • •

"You don't want to get an apartment together. You don't want to do *this* together." She was listing facts, and her legs had moved from crisscrossed to a tent perched protectively in front of her chest.

I slid up the wall behind my bed. "I'm sorry." I stopped myself from saying reflexively, *I'll try to do better.* I was starting to think that maybe I couldn't.

"Well, I think this all started with Sally being back." She watched me closely, like she was trying to find an answer in my body language, but I stayed calm, relatively still. I moved my hands into my lap, quietly waiting for whatever came next.

"Is it?" she repeated, her tone more urgent.

"I don't think so," I said finally.

"Think?" Her voice went up.

"Erika." I leaned over to touch her, but she moved away, standing as she put her clothes back on. "Erika?"

"Did you know," Diego says as we walk toward our cars, "that Grendel's has been here, in this spot, since 1902? Place started with a crew of six, including the OG." Diego winks, a sure sign he's about to deliver a punchline. "Original Grendel."

"Jokes and facts." I laughed at his corny ass. "You got them both, huh?"

"And heart. I got serious heart for *this* place." He touches the center of his chest, and I can see, in his eyes, that he does have heart for Grendel's. He clears his throat. When he speaks, his voice deepens, the words carefully enunciated. "And, thanks to you punks, my interview skills are straight." Earlier that day, we all sat around the lunch table, asking Diego a variety of questions.

JADE

Where do you see yourself in ten years?

SOOKIE

What's your best contribution to Grendel's?

ME

Have you done anything that made the operations of the store better?

JADE

What's your strength as an employee?

ME

What's your weakness?

Diego had laughed at that last question. "Um, twentieth-century pop songs?"

"Your answers were pretty tight," I say.

Like, I learned that last year when we switched to ergonomic box cutters, that was because of a suggestion made by Diego. "My wrist thanks you," I had told Diego, and he smiled proudly.

"Bro, my interview skills are tighter than two strands of a licorice stick. I feel ready for tomorrow."

Diego was the first to interview for the position, with preliminary interviews continuing on until Tuesday.

The final interview would be held sometime after, most likely the week of prom. "Not nervous?" I ask.

"No, excited. Tomorrow's interview is do-or-die, and when it's do-or-die, you grab on to your future and hold on tight."

"I want to move forward," she said, slipping her shirt over her head.

"We are moving forward," I said gently.

She sighed, sitting on the bed as she laced up her shoes. "We're crawling forward."

"Crawling is moving," I argued. "Babies start off by crawling."

"So, we're babies?" She turned to me, her lips twisted.

"We're only six months old," I continued. "That's pretty much baby-relationship status, right?"

Her eyes searched mine. "Six months is a turning point—"

"Into what?"

"Serious or not serious."

"Says who?"

"Marco."

"Says who?" I repeated, but I knew who—everyone at our school. We saw the pattern happen over and over again. Six months and couples either fell like dominoes or turned into iconic high school sweethearts. We stood at that precipice of forever and never. Erika wanted to move forward, and I . . . I wanted some more time to think about it.

"Are we serious or not serious?" she repeated.

I looked away. I didn't have an answer.

There are moments when everything can change. You cross a threshold and step into a new world. All possibilities that were open before are suddenly closed. But that's okay.

That is, if you choose correctly.

Thoughtfully.

The night of my eighth-grade dance, I crossed a threshold. Only, I didn't really see that I was making an irreversible choice. I didn't see the consequences that would follow. And, really, you can't see the consequences. Crossing over a threshold doesn't work like that.

But as you grow older, wiser, you start to see that there are thresholds, these irreversible moments that will change you and all the possibilities that follow.

On that night with Erika, I saw the threshold. And I wasn't ready to make that choice, to close those doors.

Because some part of me still clung to the possibility of more.

Middle School

16. WHEN THE TRUTH IS SHARP

THAT DAY WHEN I LEFT SALLY IN THE library, I didn't talk to Pop. Or go to my next class. I walked the halls, past rows of orange lockers, trampling bubble gum wrappers and lost homework with my knock-off Adidas. At the end of several long hallways, I found an exit sign and, beyond that, the sun and grass and, beyond that, a fence, and then I was free.

It shouldn't have been that easy to be free. Schools in Seagrove have security guards who have attitudes and golf carts to zoom around campus. They have school-issued cell phones to set up their sting operations and good track records for catching kids who skip. But I was lucky that day. I somehow managed to walk right out, like I was one stealth mother, like Pop's favorite hero Bruce Lee.

I walked for about a mile or two, head down, barely noticing the boxy houses or the gray gravel that made up most driveways. At some point I stopped at a bodega and bought a bottled water with five quarters I found at the bottom of my backpack. It was only then, when I paused to lift that cold bottle to my hot lips, that I let myself think about the puzzle piece that came to me, suddenly, on my walk to Pop's office an hour earlier.

It was a memory of Monday, day one of the sweater. Jade and I were walking to the bus stop together. I was in a T-shirt, sweat trickling down my armpits and over my ribs, but Jade wore that sweater—light green and patterned with small white fish, the sleeves rolled all the way down to her wrists.

"Aren't you hot?" I asked, and she yawned in my direction, her hand covering her mouth, and walked on slowly.

We could afford to be slow. Our departure time was designed to get us to the bus stop twenty minutes before pickup—a throwback to the first day of middle school, when I had a freak-out about missing the bus and told Jade, "We have to be on time," because my dad always said, *Be on time. Be ready. Be great.* And Jade shrugged and said, "Okay."

Jade never cared much about getting up early, because she didn't sleep that much to begin with. I knew that because from my room I could look across our yards and see Jade's bedroom window, the light glowing long after my ten p.m. cutoff time and shining brightly when Pop shook me awake at six a.m.

Today, though, she looked extra tired. "Your dad's back again?" If he was back, it was one of his quieter phases, like that time last summer when he returned home with carnations and a freshly shaved head, a look of shame that marked every step up their crooked walkway.

Jade glanced at me wearily, yawning again but this time forgetting to cover her gaping mouth. "He came home last night."

We rounded the corner, making an automatic left onto NW 30th Street. I could see the kids down the way, some mingling beneath the trees, some standing a few feet apart, wet hair pressed down by hats and old-school headphones. One kid smoked a vapor cigarette, his hand moving up and down mechanically as he took in short puffs; a girl beside him waved her hand in front of her face.

"Was it okay?" I asked. "Him coming back?"

"It was . . . ," Jade said, and stopped for a second, tucking her hair behind her ears. I noticed her earrings, silver peace signs, and above those, a pair of birds, rising, like they wanted to fly away from here.

"What?" I stopped too, waiting for what came next. Because it seemed to me that Jade was opening a door that had never been opened, one that led into her family's home, and I wanted to step through that door. I swear I did, but Jade was so quiet for so long that my eyes slid back to the bus stop—maybe out of habit or out of searching, searching for something—no, someone—I had been waiting to see all night. *Sally*.

After my kiss with Erika on the beach, I hadn't heard much from Sally. The whole weekend was spent in radio silence. But I wanted to know if we were still a thing about to happen. Or if that kiss had ruined it all. And there Sally was, arriving at the bus stop from the opposite direction—short skirt, strong, athletic legs, laughing at something Diego had just said. And in my gut, there was this feeling of jealousy that held on to me until Jade touched my shoulder and said, "Are you even listening?"

"Yeah," I said reflexively, and she ran a nervous hand across her chin and asked, "So, do you think you can love someone even if they're hurting you?"

I glanced at Sally and Diego, talking animatedly beneath a tree now, and with that jealousy still wrapped around me, I realized that this thing for Sally—whatever it was—mostly felt good but sometimes, like this weekend, it also felt spectacularly bad. "Yeah, I think that's how it goes. That's normal, right?" I said, assuming she was thinking about Diego, who still hadn't asked her to the dance, no matter how many hints she dropped.

But what I realized walking to Pop's office was this: What if that question hadn't been about Diego? What if it had been about her father?

Years later, on those nights after Grendel's, when I lay in bed watching the fan swirl above me, I'd think back to that moment and the moments that followed and wonder why I didn't ask, *Who's hurting you, Jade?* Later, much later, in college, I realized that there are moments in life that you back away from, moments where the truth is too sharp, the path forward too uncertain. So you take a break—a mental vacation of sorts—and think about everything else. And that's what I did in the week that followed Jade's question at the bus stop. I backed away, keeping my attention on Sally and what was happening between us.

But on that day that I left school—one of only two times that I would ever skip in my life—I couldn't exactly find the why of my discomfort. I could only feel my failure. So I went to the rope tower and sat at the very top, in the exact spot where I had kissed Sally, and even without the why, I knew that I had gotten it wrong. I had gotten so much of everything wrong.

Senior Year

17. SHOULD I GO?

"I THINK YOU'RE ON THE RIGHT TRACK," says Mrs. A. She peers over her laptop, reviewing my explanation of wormholes on our shared Google Doc. "Albert Einstein, Nathan Rosen, check. Description of mouth and neck, good, check. Problems with stability, possible use for time travel, exotic matter, size. Good. Good." She pauses, glances up at the ceiling of the room, thinking. Then looks back at the screen, her fingers hovering over the keyboard. "Just going to add a few comments for you to review later—a few grammatical errors, and then take another look at Einstein's theory of relativity. Make sure you're explaining it so that a sixth grader could understand it."

"A sixth grader?" I tried to imagine explaining Einstein's theory of relativity to Domingo and Lil' Jay, but all I could see was one of them yelling at me, "Deez nuts!" Because that's something they'd been doing lately.

"Yep. That's the goal. That anyone who reads your paper,

even a sixth grader, could keep up with the content."

"Okay." I watch the screen as comments pop up in the document's margins.

"What about your list of laws?" She clicks her mouse pad a few times to another page. "Do you have a separate doc for that?"

"Um, yeah," I hedge.

"Oh." She glances up from her screen, brown eyes waiting. "Did you share it with me? I don't see an e-mail with the link."

"Um, no."

"Okay." Her eyes widen slightly as she processes this. "Why not?"

"Well . . . it's blank."

"Oh." She says this in the teacher language of *Oh no. Get it together. Come up with a plan.*

The project is due in less than a week, and I'm nowhere near a list of my universal laws. It's not that I don't have contenders. Yesterday I went by the library and stared at the wall of wisdom, all the sayings shouting out to me, like, *pick me, pick me!*

But I couldn't pick just one. In many ways I needed all of them.

The thought of asking for an extension crosses my mind. I could tell Mrs. A about Pop being sick, about Erika and me . . . being . . . what? Something unknown? Presently unhappy? *Presently taking a break* is how she put it.

I could tell her about Sally, the girl who was once my

best friend (okay, more than a best friend), suddenly coming back to Seagrove in the last quarter before graduation and how that's kind of messed with my head.

I could tell Mrs. A about how life is what happens while you're making other plans. A saying that should definitely go into my list of laws.

But I don't talk about any of those things. I wait, staring off at the whiteboard, like I've got a bad case of senioritis. Mrs. A flips through my notebook, stopping when she reaches a page titled WORMHOLE IV.

"What's this?" She's points at the sloped handwriting, so fast of an outpouring that my cursive looks like scribbles.

I grab the notebook and tuck it into my bag. "Nothing," I mumble.

"Looks like a pretty interesting nothing," Mrs. A says, her tone even. "Maybe you'll want to share that with your project."

"It's just for me."

"Okay." She looks like she wants to push the subject, but maybe my expression tells her that's not a solid plan. "So, mostly, I think you're overthinking the list of laws. Honestly, Marco, your grade is so solid in this class that I'll let anything go. Give me a top ten list or something like that. Do it David Letterman style."

"David who?"

She laughs and snaps the laptop shut. "Oh, do I feel old now. Just come up with ten of your favorites."

"But how do I narrow it down?"

"Well, how about you think of the top ten people in your life and offer up one wise principle from each of them. The list doesn't have to be definitive; it merely has to exist. Something for you to reflect on when you need it. But really give it some thought. If you had to hand this list over to someone else, say your brothers, what advice would you want to give them? Does that sound easier than what you've made it out to be?"

"Yeah, much." Although the assignment still seems a bit personal, more for English class than physics.

"Good. Why don't we give it a shot now?"

"Now?"

"No time like the present."

"Can I write that one down?" I ask with a smirk.

"Ha!" She smiles briefly and then her face turns serious. "Nope."

"Okay." I navigate to the blank document. "Let's begin."

Later that night, after my shift at Grendel's, I drive past green lights and nearly empty streets. I drive past my house, where the rooms are dark. My whole family is asleep.

I should go home, I tell myself. That's the responsible place to be. I could get in some studying for my calc final on Friday of next week, or I could continue to work on my physics paper. Mrs. A had helped me come up with an almost-complete list of names—Pop, Mom, Diego,

Sookie, Jade, Erika, Mr. Grendel, Old Mrs. B—and now I just needed to remember some piece of wise advice from each of them.

No big deal.

Or I could send Erika another e-mail, explaining that I didn't mean to hurt her feelings. That I'm trying my best over here to figure out what's true and what's not. That I don't know what she means by "taking a break."

"Just a break, Marco," she had said last night. "We need to figure out what we want."

"But we're fine," I had argued. I mean, sure, I was asking her to slow things down and there was something happening—a spark, maybe—every time Sally was around, but couldn't that be explained as nostalgia? Shock? I needed time to work past that. And I needed Erika to give me less space, so I could remember all the ways we made sense as a couple.

But she wasn't playing that. She said, "We're stuck, and I've already wasted four years waiting on you. And you know what? I don't want to wait anymore."

And so I drive, circling the question as I circle the blocks in my neighborhood.

At the stroke of midnight, I find myself in front of a house that's not my own.

I turn off my headlights and let the car idle across the street, like some kind of creeper. Then I take a few deep breaths and tell myself that I'll leave in a minute or two. That I won't replay another time I stood in front of this house when the rooms were empty, the For Rent sign posted defiantly in the yard. In my chest, the melancholy warmth of nostalgia is replaced with a much deeper ache.

I can hear Diego say, *That girl, that Sally—man, you've always been thirsty for her.*

Maybe in the before, but now? Still?

The feelings that follow are so unwelcome that I shift my truck into gear and head home. I'm parked in my driveway when I'm startled by a knock on my driver window. I slowly turn my head to find Sally there.

Two bodies in orbit of each other.

She wears shorts and a tank top. An ancient iPhone is strapped to her arm. She smiles, almost apologetically, stepping back so that I can exit. When we stand opposite each other, she says, "Hey."

"Hey."

"Did I scare you?"

I shake my head and then slip my hand, left to right—a seesaw teetering. "Okay, a little. More like surprise. What are you doing here?"

She pulls her earbuds out and coils the wires into a tight bundle she slips into her pocket. "I couldn't sleep," she explains. "And when I can't sleep, I run."

"I thought you gave that up," I say, surprised.

"I did, competitively, but I could never give it up entirely." She laughs, a little hollow, "But don't tell my dad. He thinks I gave it up completely. . . ."

I mull this over, this not telling her father, who isn't

even inside state lines. Like even though he's far away, his influence over her never feels far at all. "Were you waiting for me?"

She shrugs, half smiles. "Maybe? I didn't see your truck, so I thought you were still out. I wasn't going to wait all night."

"Why were you waiting at all?"

She rubs her palms on her shorts, drawing my attention to her thighs. Strong thighs. Smooth skin. I quickly shift my gaze forward.

"I wanted to see how your dad's doing," she says.

"You came to ask me about my dad now?"

"I would have asked you in school, but . . ." Her voice trails off. She squints a little, like she's studying something far in the distance, and then she turns those gray eyes on me and sighs. "You don't really talk to me at school."

Which is true. After her birthday party, though, I'd begun to give head nods in the hallway and *heys* if we passed close enough to touch. It was an improvement, but not exactly friendly.

"I mean." She sighs. "I get it. I didn't exactly end things between us in the best way. . . ."

"No," I say quietly. "I guess you didn't."

She nods, swallows hard. "But I'd hoped that after you helped me with my car and also the . . . my birthday . . . thing . . ."

Our eyes meet. I wait, and she finally says, "I wanted

to talk to you about what happened after I left, but then everything happened with your dad. It just . . ." Her voice cracks for a second, and she takes a deep breath. "It kind of sucks." She looks down at her hands and then up at me, steeling herself for the thing she's going to say next, the thing she probably wanted to say all along. "It kind of sucks not knowing you anymore."

And then there is silence.

Because I don't really know what to say. I find my own something remote to stare at—a cat meandering around a bush.

"Should I go?" she asks, her voice smaller.

"No." Because that's the one thing I do know: that I want her here.

I want her here because I have questions. But I don't know how to ask them yet. I know that for sure too. I need to work my way toward them. So I decide to change the subject to something safer. I tell her about Pop, about coming home from the hospital today. I leave out other details, like how his return is part of my restlessness. That earlier that day, I carried his suitcase into his house and then watched his excruciatingly slow journey from the car to his bedroom, his unsteady gait causing him to take baby steps.

"The new medication to control the seizures gave him some issues with his balance. We've switched to something else, but the side effects still haven't worn off," Mom had explained.

Side effects.

After Pop's first injury, all we heard about were the side effects.

The sudden agitation.

The depression.

The getting stuck on words, so that Pop repeated the same thought over and over again.

I am tired of side effects. I am tired of trying to move beyond them. Of almost getting to the other side of it all. Because here we are again, square one: 2; Suarezes: 0.

When Sally asks if he'll get better, I say, "I don't know. Better is a relative term. We'll see."

"Give it time?" she suggests, and my heart gets stuck on her phrasing. *Give it time*, I can hear Pop say. *Time will always tell.*

"You okay?" Sally steps forward. I step back.

"Yep. Just tired."

"I should go," she says again, but she doesn't move. "This is weird." Her fingers ripple along her thigh.

"Life is weird," I say, and her nose crinkles, a little smile like a bridge across her cheeks.

"So you keep saying."

"Must be true, then."

"Must be."

That nervous hand slips into her pocket. She rocks on her heels as she glances around my street. I imagine she's looking for differences, but there are barely any. The houses are still small, utilitarian abodes. Some have been repainted over the years—a teal house, now mango. A mango house, now gray. The sidewalk, still dimpled with cracks. A cat still meows urgently in the distance.

Her eyes settle on the house next door. The yard is different, alive with flowers. Mr. Martell has lived there for the last three years, and all he does is garden and plant trees in his retirement. The canopy of his avocado tree hangs over our fence.

"Did Jade start living with Sookie because of what happened?" Sally asks.

"Yep, about the start of ninth grade."

Our eyes meet. "And her parents?"

"Not there anymore." I don't offer a further explanation. Something in her body language tells me she already knows. "Who told you?"

"I had tea with Old Mrs. B today." Sally takes a deep breath. "She thinks that we should talk about that night . . . the night of the dance."

I lean against the truck, crossing my arms in front of my chest. Her eyes flash to mine, and she steps forward, a hand reaching out to me. But I flinch—because I don't want to talk about that night. I don't want to be comforted by her either. The hand falls away quickly, but Sally pushes on, determined. "That night . . . You couldn't have known how it would turn out."

"You did," I say quietly.

"I had more experience." Sally's shoulders rise, hovering around her ears. "You did the best you could, okay?"

"Did I?"

"*Yes* . . ." She pauses, takes a deep breath. "I also regret what happened that night. . . . I didn't have to put everything with Jade on you. I could have used my own voice, but I was so wrapped up in my drama with my dad and leaving to North Carolina. And I made some really bad choices, and I believe those choices hurt you."

I stare at the ground, taking my own deep breaths, wanting these parts of our history—the parts that she is trying to drag out into the light—to disappear.

"Marco," she says. "I am so sorry about your dad." Her voice breaks. When I look at her, there are tears in her eyes. Her hand rises up again, bit by bit, until it rests on my chest. "Marco—"

I step back. "You should go home," I say, and the hand falls limply to her side. She nods. "Okay," she says. "Okay."

I watch her leave, her head cast down, hands working to pull the earbuds out of her pocket, her silhouette growing smaller and smaller with every step she takes.

Middle School

18. LOOK HARDER

THE NIGHT THAT I WALKED OUT OF THE Middle, I came home to Pop in the kitchen, cooking his signature combo of black beans, white rice, *bistec*, and *tostones*. Lito was there, too, sitting at the kitchen table, snacking on a little bit of *pan* with butter.

"Hey, there you are," Pop said when I walked through the door. "Where have you been?"

It was after five, and I was sweaty, my hair plastered to my head, droplets clinging to my brow. Lito took me in, his lips fluttering, and then he went back to his newspaper, the kind you hold in your hands because "*Tu sabes, con la computadora ellos pueden reescribir el pasado.*" Which meant something like, On computers, you can rewrite the past.

"So?" Pop said.

"I left school early," I admitted, not wanting to lie to Pop.

"I know."

"How?"

"I work at the school. You don't show up to class, I get

a messenger from your teacher asking if you're sick. So, why'd you skip?"

"I don't know. I got . . . I got claustrophobic."

Lito looked at me then. *"Mira, tu no puedes hacer niños a hombres en la escuela. ¿Pero en el campo con un machete? Bueno, sí."*

"Abuelito, por favor," Pop said, because Lito had grown up in the fields and was fond of saying you made men out of boys by sending them into the fields with a machete.

"*Bueno.*" Lito held up his hands. *"Es verdad."*

Pop cleared the steak from the skillet and set it on a plate. He picked up another piece of meat—slender and raw—and dipped it in a concoction of whisked eggs and spices, then bread crumbs. Front and back until the steak was coated brown. He dropped the steak onto the skillet, watching the steady sizzle. When he turned back to me, he repeated, "Claustrophobic?"

I felt that pressure on my skin, that tightness in my lungs again. "Yeah, like I couldn't breathe if I stayed there."

"Come here." Pop opened his arms, a safety net to fall into. The truth is I cried for a while, all to the sound of Lito's fluttering lips, a fluttering of approval, because Lito believed two things made a man:

1. The ability to handle a machete.
2. The ability to have a good cry.

"A man can protect and be brave, but a man can also be sad. For what is any of this for if you can't feel it?" he told me later.

I didn't know what any of it was for, but I knew, without a doubt, that I could feel it.

I wasn't the hero, if that's where you thought this was going. I didn't march over to Jade's house that night to confront her parents or to demand that Jade roll up her sweater and settle the mystery of the hidden bruises. Maybe, for a minute, though, my best self—that self you never quite are but imagine one day you could be—had intended to do that, but my real self sat on my bed, my patchwork quilt wrapped around my shoulders. The night was too hot for a quilt, but I needed that feeling of weight on my bones.

My bones hurt.

Really, my whole body hurt, a current of pain radiating outward from my chest. And for a long time I just stared at a poster of the solar system and tried to make sense of how we got on this planet. And why was this planet, of all planets, the only one that had life—at least life as we know it? We weren't the biggest or the heaviest of planets. And yet all the elements aligned, and—bam—there we were! Life.

And life was hard.

Around seven p.m., there was a knock on my bedroom door, followed by the audible sound of wood scraping against tile. The lights flicked on and Sally entered, her T-shirt and running shorts sprinkled with sweat, a goofy smile on her face.

"I escaped," she said. "Your mom let me in."

"Who'd you escape from?" I sat up, subtly rubbing the sleep from my eyes.

"My dad. I'm on a"—she did the air quotes gesture "run. He's up in arms with my mom, so he couldn't come."

"They're still fighting?"

She nodded, rolling her eyes. "It's this whole thing with grandma."

"I thought she was getting better."

Sally sighed. "She is, but you know my dad. He always has to make everything dramatic."

"Like how?"

She shrugged, her eyes drifting to the right. Then she smiled that wry smile and said, "Can we not talk about it? I'm happy that he's in my mom's business and not mine."

I smiled, because that sounded good. "Okay."

"Anyway, I predict my fastest time."

"For what?"

"For this run."

"How long?"

"Well, I'm claiming five miles." She glanced at her wristwatch, bright yellow and plastic. "I'll give it thirty minutes, I think."

"A six-minute mile." I whistled.

"Like I said, I am the wind."

"Think he'll buy it?"

"He's not really paying attention, so yeah."

She was in my room by then, leaning back against the

dresser, one foot perched on my bedframe. She studied me for a second, her expression turning somber. "You weren't in math. Where'd you go?"

I turned my eyes back to that poster and its unanswered questions. "I kind of left," I admitted.

"Left? Like skipped?"

I nodded. "I guess. It didn't feel like that though. It felt like . . . like leaving."

"Where'd you go?"

"Nowhere really, kind of around."

"But why?"

"I don't know." I debated telling her about the pain in my chest, but I hadn't brought those feelings to any kind of conclusion. So I settled on saying, "I just couldn't be there anymore."

Her foot fell to the floor. A few seconds later she sat beside me, her hand next to mine. That pinkie of hers slowly made its way over until our fingers were linked.

For a second I marveled at this touch. How casual it was. How easy. How her pinkie might always be available to me for such clandestine meetings.

"I get that. I feel that way sometimes too. So, did you tell your dad?"

"About leaving?"

"No, about Jade." I shook my head. "Why not?" she asked, clearly disappointed.

"I was going to. . . . But come here."

I pulled her to my window. We stared at Jade's house

across the lawn. The windows were open and, for once, music—not fighting—floated out onto the lawn. I had heard the music earlier as I sat on my bed. I had also heard their laughter. I turned off my light and pointed to the dining room window. Jade and her mother sat across from each other, eating and talking quietly. "They look okay, right?"

"For now," she said, her voice a little harder. "But what about when her dad comes home tonight drunk?"

"But I think we're wrong. See? She's fine." I pointed back to the house, to Jade, who looked like any other girl having dinner with her mom.

"You don't get it." Her voice went from hard to firm. "It can be both."

"Both what?"

"Both okay and not okay. It can be both all the time. And from the outside you don't know what that means, but on the inside"—she looked back at Jade, who was up now, clearing the dishes—"from the inside it's terrible."

"How do you know that?" I asked. "How can you be sure?"

"I just am," she said quietly, and I think I knew, even then, that she was speaking from her own experience. She clicked on the light. "You *have* to tell your dad."

"But—"

"No." She held my stare. "You have to tell. Promise me."

"Yeah," I said, agitated that she was pushing me into something I wasn't sure about, especially when I could see with my own eyes that Jade was fine and Sally was overreacting. That telling anyone about her suspicions—*not facts*—would only make a bad situation worse.

She checked her watch. "I have to get home for dinner. When Dad can't run, he cooks. We're having meat loaf." She was trying to get us back on steady ground.

I knew that, so I teased, "Who still makes meat loaf?"

Later, when Pop came to say good night, I looked out the window and heard only silence from Jade's house.

"You better?" Pop asked as he leaned in to give me a hug good night.

"Yeah."

"You sure?" His brow wrinkled. I could tell he didn't believe me. "What was today all about, anyway? It's not like you to skip. Or . . ." He didn't say cry, but I knew that's what he meant.

"I know," I said. "But . . ." I looked for a way to tell him about Sally, about Jade, but all I could get out was a question. "What do you do when you're not sure about something?"

"Ah . . . I see." Pop mulled that over, his thumb rubbing the space above his lip. "So all this is about a girl?" he asked, a twinkle in his eyes.

"Sort of." I could tell he thought I was talking about Sally, not Jade. But I didn't see how his confusion would alter his response.

He patted me on the shoulder. "I say give it time. Time has a way of telling. You'll know what to do in time."

"In time," I repeated.

"Yep," he said, confident. "Time."

That night in the dark, I went back and forth between Sally's urgency and Pop's advice. And I reasoned that time was the better plan. Then I could see how things played out. Jade, I told myself, had been fine up until now. She'd be fine for a little while longer. And maybe, with time, I could find the right moment to talk to her about everything. To get her to tell me the truth. I went to sleep feeling like that was an okay plan. A solid plan, really.

But looking back, I see that I chose the easiest plan. The path of least resistance. A way to move forward by not moving at all. Because when you give something time, you also give it space to grow. That's fine if what's growing is good—a girl liking a boy, a boy liking a girl. But what was happening in Jade's house was dangerous. Sally saw that, but I chose to take my father's misplaced advice and look the other way.

I looked away when what I should have done was look harder.

WORMHOLES IV

THERE IS A THEORY, THOUGH, THAT IF YOU travel back in time—wormhole or not—you might actually end your life.

Scientists call this the Grandfather Paradox—*La Paradoja de Abuelito.*

The idea is that if you travel into the past and run into your *abuelito,* you could change the course of his life. And if you changed the course of his life, you could change everything that follows. In chaos theory, the idea of one small change leading to bigger—maybe even destructive—changes is called the "butterfly effect." The term goes all the way back to a meteorologist and mathematician named Edward Lorenz, who discovered this phenomenon while trying to predict the weather.

The weather.

Look it up.

So let's say your return to the past prevents your *abuelito* from meeting your *abuelita,* and as a result, your pop's not born and then you're not born. And if you're never born, then how can you go back in time to create the ripple effect that stops your own birth?

Scientists say the Grandfather Paradox proves that time travel to the past can't happen. Because how can you go back in time if you never existed in the first place?

But other scientists disagreed. They came up with a new hypothesis that asked: "What if it's more like parallel tracks running through a parallel universe?"

In one version of the parallel universe theory, you go back in time, you create that butterfly effect where your *abuelitos* never meet, and you're never born in the future. *But* in the past—that place where you created that ripple—you continue to exist. You jump the track from your current world into another kind of world, where every outcome of your *abuelitos'* meeting disappears *except for you.*

Strange, right?

Here's where it gets crazier: Scientist believe that the second world—the one where you still exist but your parents don't—is just one of "many worlds." That, in fact, there are unlimited versions of your life playing out simultaneously—one where you do go back in time, one where you don't. One where you go back in time, but you don't meet your grandparents, one where you do. The possibilities of what could happen would blow your mind.

And I guess the question is, if you could find yourself in another version of your life, what would you change?

For me, the answer is, What wouldn't I change?

Maybe my father never gets injured.

Maybe Diego's dad takes that football scholarship he was offered, but doesn't screw around while at school, thinking football is going to be his life. He gets a degree or a trade, takes the straight lane, and doesn't strip cars and go to jail.

Maybe I go back even further to a track at the University of Miami, and I stop Sally's father from being injured, so that he ends up at the Olympic trials like he planned.

Maybe I go back even further than that, and I stop Jade's dad from taking his first drink.

Maybe I go back further than that and stop Sookie's mom from dying so that her bio dad didn't have to give her up.

Or maybe I go back to the moment before ovum met sperm, when my parents were two kids my age with dreams that could still happen. I stop the moment of my own conception, giving back to them all that was lost the minute I was born.

Pop would go on to become a teacher and Mom, a fashion designer. And in this parallel world, I'd still exist, just not to them. I'd be on my own, and they'd be free from being teen parents. They'd be free to be whoever they were meant to be.

Instead of working so hard to make me the person I'm supposed to be.

Would I give my whole life up to make things right for

my mom? For Pop? They've done that for me. But could I, for them? Sometimes, late at night, watching that fan swirl around my room, I'd like to imagine that I could.

Because that would guarantee that all the wrongs I've done in my short eighteen years of life would suddenly be made right.

Senior Year

19. SOMEHOW, A PARTY

THE NEXT NIGHT I FIND SALLY PARKED along the curb of my house at midnight.

"See? I drove," she says, hopping out of her car, keys jingling. Staring at her, I am reminded of that talk with Mrs. A about Georg Friedrich Bernhard Riemann, a German math guy (with a really long name) who theorized in 1854 that space is curved. If so, that would make our universe a closed system—much like a circle. And what makes that cool is that the farther a traveler journeys from the starting point, the shorter the return. The traveler is living that expression of "coming full circle." And Sally was too, looping her way around our circular planet until she had—somehow—returned to me.

I watch as she gathers her hair into her hands. Long strands spill over her fingers like vines, which she threads into a teetering crown. When she steps farther into the streetlight, I notice she's wearing makeup—her eyes are wrapped in silky black, her lips luminescent in red. Her dress is loose yet fitted—a snug curvature here, a flow of fabric there. Hers is a body in three dimensions.

She stares at me staring at her. I clear my throat, point to her clothes, and say, "Not running tonight?" Then I move my gaze to the cracks in the sidewalk, the hopeful green that spears the concrete.

Her bracelets jangle as she speaks. "No. I'm going somewhere in a little bit."

"Where?"

"A party, maybe. I'm supposed to meet Boone there."

"When?"

"Now."

"But you're here," I say, eyes finally back on her.

"I really want to talk to you."

I look at my dark house, exhausted. Today was a hard day—Mom lecturing Domingo and Lil' Jay about their behavior at school, Pop sitting in his chair just beyond the kitchen, suddenly laughing. A chuckle that grew and grew until he sounded like a hyena, the vocals twisting at its peak until Pop's voice became the mournful cry of that same hyena dying. The twins twisted in their seats at the kitchen table.

LIL' JAY

What's wrong with Pop?

MOM

Sammy? You okay?

DOMINGO and LIL' JAY

Mom? Mom? Mom? Mom?

MOM

Sammy? Hey, Sammy, it's okay. Sammy?

(kneeling beside him)

It's okay.

DOMINGO

We're sorry.

LIL' JAY

We won't do it again.

DOMINGO and LIL' JAY

Sorry, sorry, sorry.

And afterward, the silence.

An "episode." Maybe these will become common again.

Pop in their bedroom, door shut, and Mom at the kitchen table, pretending to be fine while going through the mail, stacking up the bills into a little pile on her right-hand side. Later, she sat with her laptop, reading.

"What is that about?"

"It's a site the Dr. Khan mentioned for more info on epilepsy."

"What's it say?" I peered over her shoulder.

Silence.

"Well?"

"Nothing good, except your father seems to be out of the ordinary; most people with TBI who get post-traumatic epilepsy get it in the two years after the initial injury. But in the comments section, I read that one guy started having seizures twenty years after a car accident."

"Twenty years?"

"Yeah."

"Man."

"Some people have up to six hundred seizures a month. Some people get really depressed—"

"I don't blame them. That sucks."

"Yeah, it does suck. Others are, miraculously, able to try to function normally. Some benefit from medication; some don't. It's a crapshoot. Who knows?" Mom shut the laptop with a definitive *snap*. She shook her head. "Who knows?"

"Are you worried?"

Her eyes rolled up to me. They said, *Yes, very*. But her mouth said, "A little."

She tapped the bills on her right, as if they were an extension of the worry or maybe a primary source. I knew the money was dwindling. I had access to the accounts. We had a couple hundred in savings, if that. There was my college savings, but she would never ask for that. Just like I would never point to the bills and ask if we were going to be okay. I knew if I did she'd say, "We'll be fine. Don't worry." The truth could only be found in her eyes. So I stared at them every chance I got as she fussed about the house.

Her eyes said, *I am drowning. And you, you are watching me drown.*

Even the boys sensed her impending submersion. Lil' Jay kept coming up behind her and squeezing her in bear hugs, and when she sat down to watch the news after dinner, they sat beside her. Domingo pushed his left shoulder against hers, Lil' Jay, his right. I remembered when they were three and used to fight over who sat in her lap. But today they were like tugboats, ferrying her to shore.

And now Sally wants to "talk," but I just want to escape, to do anything but talk.

"How about that party?" I ask.

She is puzzled. "To talk?"

"Nope."

To remember why any of this is worth it.

I don't say this, but somehow she understands. Or I think she does. Her eyes seem to say, *To forget.*

"Okay, the party."

"I'll drive."

She was coming back in pieces. I could trace the arc of her return, the slow unfolding of herself that began with the admission that she didn't run competitively anymore. That continued with her attempt to joke around at her birthday party. And now here she is, talking on and on as we drive eastbound through late-night traffic.

SALLY

But my mom's up, watching sad TV at least two nights a week. And then she's crying, and when she cries like that and has a few glasses of wine, she wants to drag out the family photo albums—actual albums—and reminisce about how things used to be, how we were almost—so very close—to being a happy family. It sucks . . . . . . And Dad left Mom for an artist. Can you believe that? She creates wire sculptures, which are supposed to be protests that come out of her, quote, social consciousness. They look like large balls of yarn made out of wire to me. One looks like a fire hydrant, and I still don't know why. Are the balls the world? Is the fire hydrant something we should piss on? I seriously have no idea, and Boone is like, "Give it a rest." But I think it's a mystery that should be solved.

. . . And then Boone dropped out of school. Well, really, he didn't go back. Just his freshman year, and then he never went back.

. . . Is this okay? Me telling you all of this? I feel like I'm rambling. Suddenly. I don't know.

ME

It's okay.

SALLY

You sure?

ME

Yeah, it's fine.

Sally isn't coming back in pieces; *we* are, who we used to be *together*.

• • •

"So, this is a college party?"

The room is chaotic—beer bongs, neon bracelets, and a DJ who miraculously fits into the corner. Yet, somehow, through a window to my left, I see on the ground floor a small garden lit with twinkle lights.

An escape.

But we are up here, having the college experience. Sally scrutinizes my face, telepathically agreeing with me that this isn't the best. "Impressed yet?" she shouts.

"No," I shout back, just as Boone finds us.

"Sally Pearl!" He wraps her in a bear hug, lifting her off the floor. But he's wobbly, and they fall backward from his weight. I catch them before they hit the ground, and Boone looks at me, squinting. He shouts, "Marco, you are a big mother fu—"

"Boone," Sally screams. "You're crushing me!"

I set them upright, and Sally smiles at me gratefully. "Why is it so loud in here?" she asks.

"Because it's a party! And . . ." Boone's eyes focus for a second. He looks me up and down. "You are a big mother—"

"He's really drunk," Sally shout-whispers into my ear.

"I can see."

"We should get him somewhere else. I don't want to be here, but I don't want to leave him alone either."

"I've got him." A hand clamps down on Boone's shoulder, commanding yet gentle.

"Tuck?" Sally shouts.

"Yep. Hey, Sally Pearl."

"My cousin Tuck!" Sally shouts at me. "He goes to UM."

"Hey," I shout back.

"I'm taking him upstairs to my place. I told him not to try the beer bong. That shit is only for amateurs."

"Amateurs? I thought it was for the hard-core professional?"

"Professionals don't impress others by killing off brain cells and stumbling around incoherently," Tuck shouts back with a good amount of snark. He holds up a glass of brown liquid. "Whiskey neat, drink for enjoyment, taste, and quality. Thank you. This"—he points at Boone, who is now kind of weaving back and forth while Sally grips his shoulders—"is incredibly juvenile."

I decide I like Tuck.

"Can you?" He points to Boone. Then playfully he adds, "Because you really are an incredibly big mother—"

"Let's go," Sally shouts as a girl stumbles forward, spilling beer onto her sandals.

I heave Boone over my shoulder like a sack of potatoes.

"I think I'm going to be sick," Boone says, but instead of puking, he passes out.

Two floors up, I set Boone down next to purses and car keys tossed haphazardly on Tuck's bed. Boone moans, curling up with a leather handbag. I take a blanket off the foot of the bed and drape it over him.

"You're still thoughtful," Sally says from behind me.

"Yeah?"

"Yeah. Do you do that for your brothers?"

"Sometimes," I admit.

Sometimes I do it for Pop, too.

We head to the living room, a space slightly larger than our secret room at the library. Tuck lists off the names of his friends: "Gigi, Ravi, and Becks." When he says Becks, though, he smiles, like that name means more to him than all the others, and when he plops down on the sofa, it's Becks he wraps his arm around.

"Hey," says Gigi.

"You guys come from downstairs?" asks Ravi.

"Tuck rescued them," says Becks, smiling proudly at Tuck like he's a member of an elite search and rescue team.

Gigi and Ravi sit on twin beanbag chairs. Sally makes a cozy space for herself on the shag carpet. I settle down beside her, about a foot away.

"We were going to play a game," Becks says.

"What game?" Tuck asks, leaning in for a kiss.

"Again?" Ravi teases.

"Ravi hates 'cause he's single," Gigi explains.

Becks smiles; Tuck does too.

Sally leans over and whispers in my ear, "Becks and

Tuck have been together for years. They always need a room. They're basically cuddle bears."

"Cuddle bears?" I whisper back, laughing.

"We can hear you," Tuck says. "Yes, we're a fan of the cuddle."

"And the hand-holding," adds Gigi.

"And the constant kissing," gripes Ravi. "Which would be sweet if I were happily in love with my own person, which, as of now, I'm not."

"I can be your person," Gigi says with a wicked smile, and Ravi flushes all the way to the tips of his ears.

"Hmm . . ." Becks raises an eyebrow.

"So, what game?" Sally asks.

"Oh," Gigi says. "It's like a free association game. We played it in my theater class today. I say a word, and then the person to my right says whatever comes to mind, and so on, until we go all the way around the room—full circle."

"For example," Becks says, "if I say banana, Tuck says . . ." He nudges Tuck.

"Split?"

"Got it?" Becks asks.

We nod, and the game begins.

Yellow.

Sun.

Circle.

Universe.

Einstein.

Relativity.

Special.

Ice Cream.

Treat.

"Great," Gigi says, after our second go-around. "That's the warm-up. Part two is just like this, only it's with questions. I'll ask a question, and if I point to you, you have to say the first thing that comes to your mind. And if I want, I can say 'explain,' and you have to. Okay?"

Everyone nods but me, because this version feels personal. But when I look around at their faces—Gigi with her dark-brown eyes, Ravi with the tips of his ears back to an almond brown, Becks with the whitest teeth I've ever seen, and Tuck, with his habit of smiling, then puckering his lips—my hesitance starts to fade. I don't know this tribe, but around them I feel okay.

"You want to keep playing?" Sally asks, her tone gentle.

"Yeah," I say.

"Okay." Gigi points to Sally. "Favorite color."

SALLY

Blue.

GIGI

Biggest verbal tick.

BECKS

Actually.

TUCK

He actually says "actually" all the time.

BECKS

Actually, I do. But, actually, so do you.

GIGI

Last kiss.

RAVI

What?

GIGI

Rapid-fire, Ravi. Last kiss.

RAVI

Monica? Monique? Monica or Monique. Don't look at me like that. I'm not . . . *She* kissed *me*, and it was a really loud party.

TUCK

Please, Gigi. You know I kissed a guy hours before Becks told me he liked me. It's not a big deal.

BECKS

Wait? What?

GIGI

(sighs)

Okay! Moving on! First real kiss. Like with real . . . contact . . .

ME

. . .

GIGI

Come on. Rapid-fire.

ME

(glances at Sally)

SALLY

(looks down, smiles slightly)

TUCK

Oh.

ME

Um . . . Sally.

GIGI

Follow-up question. Favorite kisser?

ME

Um . . . safe space.

BECKS

Very interesting.

TUCK

My turn. Do you have someone special, Marco? Or are you like Sally? Free as the wind . . .

SALLY

Oh my God, Tuck. Seriously?

TUCK

What? It's a legit Q.

SALLY

His girlfriend's name is Erika. And I'm not "as free as the wind." I am happily tethered to myself.

ME

(glances at Sally again)

Um . . . actually . . . We're on a break. Whatever that means.

SALLY

Oh. Um, okay . . . I mean . . .

(coughs)

are you okay with that?

ME

It's only been a few days, so yeah. I guess.

BECKS

Well, *ex malo bonum.*

(claps his hands)

From bad comes good.

ME

Um, it's just a break.

BECKS

Exactly. Break is bad; figuring things out, good. Right? So figure things out, Marco. Figure. Them. Out.

Middle School

20. FOR RENT

IT WAS FOUR DAYS BEFORE I SAW SALLY again—another whole weekend of radio silence followed by a Monday when she didn't show up at school. This time I didn't take it personally. Nobody had heard from her. "But," Sookie said at lunch, "she's alive."

JADE
How do you know? She's not texting back.

DIEGO
Nope, she's not.

JADE
(narrows eyes)

ME
Yeah, I tried calling her and the house phone. And I might have done a little stalking.

DIEGO
Bro, there is no such thing as a little stalking.

JADE

Yeah, there is.

DIEGO

Example?

JADE

Like when you go a certain way to pass by someone's house. That's a *little* stalking.

DIEGO

Do that much?

JADE

(narrows eyes again)

ME

That's kinda what I did. Yesterday.

SOOKIE

And?

ME

You know how sometimes you can go right up to their door, hear the TV on inside, and nobody answers when you knock?

THEM

(nod heads)

ME

That.

JADE

Okay, so I checked all her social media. No activity. And I checked Boone's, too. Also no activity.

DIEGO

You don't think they're all dead inside their house from some weird carbon monoxide thing? That can happen. I heard that on the news.

JADE

Diego!

DIEGO

What? I'm serious. It can.

ME

Yeah, but they don't have gas appliances or a garage attached to the house. It would be really unlikely.

JADE

And her cell keeps ringing, which means she must keep charging it. So she must be alive.

DIEGO

Wow. Impressed.

JADE

Thanks!

SOOKIE

I feel like a bad friend for not stalking.

DIEGO

Says no one ever, Sooks.

SOOKIE

Well, I have a JCC thing today, but I could try to after.

DIEGO

Since I don't think it makes me a bad friend not to stalk, I'm gonna pass. My old man is getting me a fresh suit for the dance.

JADE

Isn't that, like, not a good idea? With his . . . parole?

DIEGO

Girl, hush.

```
                         ME
                      (to Jade)
We could go. Right?

                        JADE
Nope. My mom wants me to clean the house with
her. Says Dad's coming back tonight.

                       SOOKIE
Was he gone?

                        JADE
                    (rolls eyes)
Never gone, just away.
```

When I got to Sally's house after school, I found a few surprises.

Sally was sitting outside on her stoop.

At the edge of her lawn was a purple For Rent sign, the ground freshly turned at its base.

Past the sign was Sally, sitting on her stoop, staring blankly at the street. She wore running shoes, shorts, and one of her dad-issued MUSTANG SALLY shirts. Her skin was coated in its usual gleam of post-run sweat. I called out her name twice before she looked up.

"What's that about?" I rested my elbows on the fence and nodded to the sign, waiting. I was pretty sure this was typical neighborhood nonsense. When you rented the way most of us did, families moved around like the silver pieces of a monopoly board. Heck, Diego had moved twice in two years, the houses right next door to each other. "Sally?" I said when she didn't reply. "Do you have, like, family to stay with?"

She looked at me finally, confused. "What do you mean?"

"Where ya gonna stay when they put you out?"

"Who's they?"

"The people who own the house."

"Grandma Jane owns the house."

"Did you ever tell me that?"

"Why would I?"

Grandma Jane was Mrs. Blake's mom, and she was cool, not the type to kick family to the curb. But Grandma Jane didn't like Mr. Blake. Every time I saw her, she was always complaining to Mrs. Blake about how hard her daughter had to work while her "artist" husband "ran around all day" with the kids. Maybe Grandma Jane was tired of Mr. Blake's freeloading? But man, to throw your own family out was harsh. Still, I had to ask. "So Grandma's throwing you out?"

Sally cleared her throat, her eyes coming into focus. "*No.* We're moving. That's what my dad says, and—" She pointed at the sign, making her way over to the fence now. "That's what the sign says too."

A ball settled into the pit of my belly. Another one of Mr. Blake's grand plans, only I couldn't figure out who would give them better rent than Grandma Jane. "Where?"

"I don't want to talk about it," Sally said.

"Where?"

"I said I don't—"

"Where?"

"Fine." She kicked at the fence, the metal clanging.

"North Carolina, by my Grandma Pearl. She has a gallery there, an art gallery in Asheville. Her broken hip isn't healing well, and my dad has this bright idea that he can take over the studio because he studied art in college. He acts like taking over Grandma Pearl's business is his big break."

I laughed reflexively, the sound sharp. Sarcastic.

Sally's eyes narrowed. "This isn't funny."

"It's not," I agreed. "But you said *his* big *break*. It's a pun. . . . Because it's actually Grandma Pearl's big break . . . you know, because she broke—"

"Yeah, I get it. Still not funny."

"It's not," I said earnestly. "Just the pun part," I whispered.

I couldn't believe Sally was moving to North Carolina. Away from here. From us. From me. Inside the house, I said, "Maybe you could stay with Grandma Jane? Or if Grandma Jane says no, maybe Sookie . . . Or maybe, don't you have a cousin? What's his name?"

"Tuck?"

"Yeah, what about his parents? Couldn't you stay with them?"

I was spinning. And with every spin, I tried to figure out a new living arrangement for Sally. For a second I wondered if I could house her in my closet, with blankets and a mini-fridge I'd procure from Diego's father, and she'd only have to be in there for maybe eight hours a night and . . . I grew dizzy from my thoughts.

"I don't know. I've thought about that. About asking Grandma Jane—not Sookie—maybe Aunt Ana but . . . My dad's not gonna let me stay. He's obsessed with my training."

"Maybe he'll forget about that with the store. Maybe that's your silver lining." I smiled hopefully. Wasn't that what she wanted anyway? To be free of him?

She sighed. "I really can't talk about this anymore. I feel sick. Like . . ." She put her open palm over her stomach and then contracted her fingers into a fist, moving the entire ball counterclockwise. Like that same weighted ball I had felt earlier had left me to twist deep into her abdomen.

I nodded. I understood. "Sorry."

"Let's just talk about something else. Anything else."

"Okay." I looked around and then I listened for a second. Nothing. No noise. "It's quiet in here."

"Mom went with Boone to the library. He has a final paper in history and zero out of ten parts done."

"And your dad?"

"Gone. Left yesterday for North Carolina."

I was relieved to hear that. It would have been hard to pretend to like Sally's dad today. I glanced around Sally's living room, wondering if I should sit. The space was much like mine, a decent enough couch made better with the help of a bright throw blanket. On the walls were pictures of her family—her mom and dad on their wedding day; Boone as a baby; Sally as a toddler, dressed up as a ladybug; her dad in college, holding up medals;

Sally in middle school, also holding up medals. There was a small TV on a stand, the second shelf holding a DVD player.

And, ironically, zero art on the walls.

I moved toward the couch and then stopped suddenly.

"What?" Sally asked.

"That." I pointed to an arachnoid, brown and fuzzy, the size of a quarter.

"You mean Issa?" she said.

"I mean the spider."

"Yeah, Issa the spider."

"You named a spider? Shouldn't you, like, kill it?"

"Not if you're my dad. If you're my dad, you become more attached to that spider than your own kids' happiness. He's the one who named it."

"But he's gone now."

"Yeah," Sally said, peering up at Issa. "But she really is harmless." She glanced around the living room too and sighed. "Let's go to my room."

She headed toward the hallway, but I held back. Sally wasn't allowed to have guys in her room. This had been a hard rule since the day I had met her, but Sally waved me forward and said, "They're not going to be back for a while. Ten sections!" And for a second there was a gleam of familiar Sally, who didn't sit on stoops and stare blankly at the street, so I followed.

In Sally's room, I leaned against the wall, a foot or two from her doorway, telling myself that I could make a fast escape if her mom and Boone came home early. Sally's room also mirrored mine—small, maybe six by six, with one tiny window on the wall that faced the front yard. My room was painted sea green from before time began or, at least, before my memory of time; Sally's was a pale yellow, the color still rich, like it had been refreshed only a year back. Where I only had blinds, Sally had blinds and curtains—the sheer fabric hanging off the wall dramatically, as if air were trapped inside the panels, a perpetual billowing. On the bed was a plush white comforter that looked like something you'd want to sleep in forever. I wondered how Sally ever got out of bed. My comforter was a patchwork quilt that my dad's mom had brought over from Cuba and passed down to him when he was born. He again passed it down to me when I was born, a ceremony of quiet giving from one to another.

I liked to imagine that *mi abuelita* had mended the quilt along the way. I could see the crooked stitches on different patches—a hand that wasn't as steady as the first. And Pop said that when his mom was alive, she liked to sew but she wasn't very good, not like his *bisabuela* or like my mom.

Sally sat on the twin bed, tucking one foot beneath her leg and letting the other dangle onto the floor. "You can sit on the bed," she said, and scooted to make space, her back now flush with flowers etched into her wooden headboard. The headboard made her room look like it belonged to someone who was seven.

I moved a few feet over until I was leaning on her dresser. Then I slid down, into a seated position on the floor, near the foot of her bed. "I'm good here."

"Okay." She kicked off her shoes and flipped onto her belly. She stretched her legs out behind her. One toe absently traced the etchings. We were close again, her head a few feet from my tented knees. She rested her chin on her hands and stared at me.

I shifted my eyes to the lavender area rug, picking at the shag fabric nervously.

Because it had occurred to me that something had changed since the last time I was in Sally's house.

Sally was my girlfriend now.

And I was her boyfriend.

I was her boyfriend, and I was in her room.

Her *bed*room.

All thoughts of her moving disappeared, and my nervousness grew. My mouth became dry. I picked at the carpet some more, and when I finally lifted my eyes, Sally was still staring at me.

"What?" I asked.

"Nothing."

"What?" I repeated.

"It's just not turning out the way I thought it would."

"How did you think it would?"

She sat up and hugged her legs to her body; she looked pretzel-like and small. "I thought we'd go to high school together next year. I thought we'd graduate together. I thought we'd always be together."

For a second I thought she meant only the two of us, and I could see our lives continuing on as they had always been: adjacent lockers and pushing our way, shoulder to shoulder, through the crowded halls of high school; our blue and silver gowns at high school graduation; the first jobs that we hated over that summer; and then the same college, probably University of Miami, because that's where Sally's father wanted her to go; and then we could travel. Maybe we'd see all fifty states or maybe we'd backpack across Europe or maybe we'd spend a year teaching English in a place like China or South Korea. Who knew, but we'd be together, just like we promised. For always. I looked at Sally, and she seemed to be daydreaming too. She sighed and said, "Yeah, all of us," and the dream expanded to include Sookie, Diego, and Jade. The bubble deflated a little.

"I thought," Sally continued, and then she paused.

"What?"

"I thought we'd have more dances."

The bubble inflated again. I leaned forward.

"Why wouldn't we?" I asked. "You can come back for all my dances. I can save up money to come to yours. North Carolina isn't that far away. I could take the train, or maybe it's not so much to fly. I could do all my summer jobs again and save up enough so that I could come to your homecoming."

Her eyes lit up. She held my stare. It was familiar Sally, there with me. A smile curved her lips.

"You would do that? For me?" she asked.

I pulled myself closer, into a squat so that my shins pressed against the edge of her bed. She did the same, folding herself onto her knees and scooting forward until our noses nearly touched. Our eyes seemed impossibly close. All I could see were her eyelashes and irises, but I felt her lips just a kiss away.

"Yeah," I whispered. "Of course."

"Because always?" she whispered.

"Yeah," I said. "Because. Always."

We closed the gap, a kiss that seemed to end only when we both ran out of breath.

Afterward, my confidence told me things—that we were meant to be. That no matter the distance, no matter the obstacle, our bond was unbreakable.

If Marta were here, she'd tell you some long story that ended with, *Love makes you think the impossible is possible. But sometimes the impossible is a mountain that love can't climb or burrow through.* She'd say that *life is complicated.* She'd point out how rare it is to know someone completely. To know yourself completely. She'd ask, *Anyway, what does a fourteen-year-old know about love?*

And to that, the older version of me would say, *Not much. Not much at all.*

Senior Year

21. A BREAK IS FOR THE BROKEN

ON THE RIDE HOME FROM SOUTH BEACH, Sally is silent. Her head is pressed against the passenger window, her hair falling across her face. I can't see her eyes, but I imagine she sees what I see: the cruise ships docked outside of South Beach; the lit runways of Miami International Airport; and, as we curve south along the highway, rows and rows of concrete-built suburban housing. When we get closer to our 'hood, she turns to me and says, "That's not what I expected, but it was good. Right?"

"Yeah," I agree. "Tuck and his friends are nice."

"He's always been my favorite cousin. Now you know why."

I nod, remembering that when we were young, she talked about Tuck more than any other cousin, about how he was "so himself." That's a quality that's easy to admire. For a moment I wonder what that would be like to just be myself, messiness and all.

"So, maybe we can hang and talk?" she asks when we

reach her block. "About . . ." She hesitates. "About . . . what I wanted to talk about earlier?"

"Now?" I ask, and she nods.

To be honest, some part of me doesn't want this night to end. Because sitting next to Sally, I remember the way our pinkies linked in the Middle, how I'd felt so high after our first and second and third kisses, how if I turned our history into a highway, the concrete would stretch from Seagrove to the ocean.

And I think about what Becks said, *ex malo bonum—from bad comes good*—and see that he's right: Why wait for Erika to figure out what she wants? Why not figure out what I want? Figure out why I can't stop thinking about yesterday, about Sally's hand on my chest. Figure out why it's so hard to hate her. And so easy to be around her.

In all of this, though, I've come to realize that I don't blame Sally for leaving. Where parents go, we must follow. It's what she did *after* she left, the way she completely disappeared from our lives. I took that to mean that she was done. That *we* were done. And I moved on. But clearly Sally isn't done. Because you can't be done and stand on someone's curb. You can't be done and return.

"So, can we? Talk?" she asks again.

"It's late," I say, because I still need space from this conversation. I'm just not ready yet.

At her house, I idle in the driveway, watching as she fumbles with her keys in the dark. I flash on my brights and see her tug on the door, knock, tug, knock. No answer. She disappears around the house, comes back a minute later. She pounds on the door. Still no answer. She starts back toward the truck, shielding her eyes from the lights. I cut the engine and hop out.

"I have no way inside," she says, her voice clipped by frustration.

"The key doesn't work?"

"No, it works, but there's a third lock at the very top. It's a dead bolt and you can only unlock it from inside. We don't really use it until everyone's home."

"So who locked it?

"My mom, I guess. She's not always the most reliable when she's been . . ." Sally mimes drinking. "And she was pretty much a bottle in when I left. I tried knocking on her window, but she isn't answering." She looks at her phone. "Let me try calling." She touches a few buttons and presses the phone to her ear. A few seconds later she hangs up. "She's not picking up her phone either. *Great.*" She sighs. "You know what? I'll text Tuck and tell him that I'm heading back." Her fingers fly across the screen.

I wait, noticing her droopy eyes, her tilted shoulders. When she yawns, I say, "You're tired," and then I yawn myself.

She smirks. "We're both tired. It's late."

"It'll take you another twenty or thirty minutes to drive back. I'll drop you off, or . . . get you an Uber."

"*I* can't afford that," she says. *"You?"*

I shake my head no.

"And if you drive me, then you'll be even more tired on the way back, and I'll be fine." Her voice softens. "Promise." She tucks her arms around her waist and hugs herself tight, looking down at her phone, waiting for Tuck's reply.

"You know, they say it's as bad to drive tired as it is to drive drunk."

"Marco . . ."

"But it's true. Studies show that—"

"I'll stop at a gas station to buy coffee or something. I'll drive in the slow lane."

"No. Don't do that. If someone enters on the exit ramp, because they're drunk—and that *does* happen—you'll be the first thing they hit."

"So the speed lane?"

"If someone's racing this late at night, you'll be the first thing they hit too."

"You worry about everything, huh?"

"I don't, just what could happen."

"But *hasn't* happened."

"But *could*."

She stares at me like she's finally figured something out. Her phone buzzes, the light illuminating her face. "Tuck says I can crash on his floor." She jiggles her keys. "I should go."

"It's too late. I'll drive you," I say again.

She sighs. "No."

"But?"

"No, no, no," she sings.

"Sa—"

"And Erika?" she asks suddenly.

"What about Erika?" I'm almost surprised that it's taken so long for her to get to this question.

Her chest rises and falls. "Are you guys gonna stay on a break? Do you want to?"

I'm silent for a while because . . . because the truth is, I don't know. "Why is that important?" I finally ask.

She steps closer until our toes touch, until we are almost eye to eye. Then she rests her head on my shoulder. And she smells so good. Even after that drunken party and the salty air, she still smells like coconut.

She slips her hands into mine. "Because I've missed this," she whispers. "I've missed *you*."

"I've missed you too? Bro, are you outta your mind?" Diego says the next day.

We sit outside of Grendel's at a picnic table on the green. We linger like the old men who wear pastel guayaberas and play dominoes on 8th Street. Our shifts are done, our polos untucked, and there's even a little daylight left. Maybe that's why it's easy to savor the *café con leche* and Cuban sandwiches. Diego straight-up prays before we eat this meal, thanking God for the "crispy bread, the perfect ratio of butter, melted cheese, and salty pork." Then he does the sign of the cross because that's "what good Catholics do."

But even this Cuban sandwich can't keep us from talking

about last night. About the party. About what happened after the party. About the holding.

"Erika will kill you *and* Sally if she finds out." He snaps his fingers together.

"But nothing happened," I protest. "You know, besides that—besides what I told you."

"*Y'all gonna make me act a fool, up in here, up in here* . . . ," he sings with a shake of his head. "And prom is this weekend, so you had to go and mess that up. And, man, Jade has been planning this out for months."

"Jade?" I lift an eyebrow. Diego's the one who sent out group texts like, "Which Escalade should we rent?" and "What colors is everyone wearing?" and "Who has the best camera phone?" On and on and on.

"Bro, keep to your side of the fence. I'm just thinkin' ahead."

We pause, considering how this can all play out.

"What if I tell her? Tell Erika and then, you know, we could move on."

"*Right.*" Diego smiles big. "So be like, 'Hey, Erika, check it. I hung out with Sally on Saturday for *four* hours and we held hands, super cas', and . . . Oh, yeah . . . I told her I miss her. NBD. So, like, what's up with prom? What time you want me to get you?'" He cracks up. "Something like that?"

"Or, how about, you put us on a break, and shit happens."

"Oh, yeah, go that way. I think that's a great opening

sentence to the story about how you got kicked in the nuts."

I stare at my empty plate, the afterburn of that Cuban sandwich, and my guilt, coming at me. "This thing with Sally—it's . . . it's not gonna happen again."

Except, even as I say it, I don't know if it's true. What would have happened if Sally's mother hadn't flung open the door and called out, "Sally Pearl? Sally, are you still out here?"

Maybe things would have gone further.

Maybe we would have gone further.

Because, honestly, I wanted to go further.

"What you need to understand is why you went on a break in the first place."

"Um, to figure things out."

"Nah, dude. You can't figure things out if you're not talking. That's like relationship 101: communicate. If you're gonna survive a relationship, you need to earn your PhD in talking. Jade and I talk *all the time.*" He sighs. "Like constantly. But you . . . You didn't go that way. Huh? You took 'a break.'" He shakes his head and gives me his classic I'm-about-to-drop-some-knowledge bug-eyed look. "Bro, you go on a break because you're broken."

Middle School

22. YOU'RE NOT OKAY. ARE YOU?

THE MORNING AFTER I WENT TO SALLY'S house and saw that For Rent sign, I showed up to school late.

Diego bounced over to my locker with a big old grin and said, "Dude, you finally made it. We were taking bets on whether or not you and Sally were kidnapped by aliens or something."

"Nah. I just overslept." The truth was I overslept because I had hardly slept. I got home from Sally's house and hopped into bed, eager to get to tomorrow because tomorrow would bring school, and school would bring Sally, and somewhere in all my fantasizing, the terror set in.

Sally was leaving.

In a week or a month, she could be gone.

It didn't seem fair. I was finally getting to be with her, and she was leaving. My mind went into a different kind of overdrive, plotting out how to earn money over the summer so that I could visit her in the fall. How I'd get my parents to let me take a plane to North Carolina on my own when I had flown only once before! The list went on and on until it was four a.m. That's when I heard the ruckus outside.

It wasn't too loud, but at four a.m., any noise counts as a ruckus. I told myself to be a good citizen, to investigate. See something, say something and all that nonsense that you stop caring about when your eyelids are heavy, but I forced myself onto my knees and pressed my ear to the window. I could hardly make it out: Maybe there were voices? Maybe there was the sound of a girl crying? Maybe I slid down the wall and fell asleep.

No, not maybe. Definitely. A few hours later Pop shook me awake before going about his usual business—grabbing coffee, packing his lunch, and dropping a book in his backpack, something to read on his lunch break. About fifteen minutes later, he knocked on my door and said, "Up?"

"Yep," I replied before rolling over and going right back to sleep. I didn't even hear Mom as she hustled the boys out the door. By the time I got myself together and asked my neighbor Mrs. Hernandez to drop me off at school, I had missed first period.

Diego slapped my back. "You look dead. What'd you get into last—"

"He looks fine." Sookie slid into the space between us. She took hold of my chin and studied the bags beneath my eyes. "Eh, okay, not your best. You feeling all right?" Her hand twitched, like she wanted to pull out the thermometer from her medical kit.

"I'm fine," I said with a blink, blink and a yawn, yawn. I looked at Diego. "Your face," I said.

"Your face."

"Your mama's face," I said, some alertness kicking in.

"Your mama and all her mamas before her," Diego clapped back.

"All your mamas. No," Sookie said. "Why not all the papas? Why not the mamas *and* the papas?"

Diego shook his head. "Because not everybody has a papa. Everybody's got a mama."

A tinge of hurt crossed her face, and Diego tried to correct with, "You got a mama *and* a papa, though."

"I know," she said pointedly.

"I just mean—"

"Anyway," she changed the subject. "Why were you late?"

"I was tired."

"Tired with love," Sookie teased as we began to walk to our classrooms. "Sally told me you were at her house last night."

"*And* I'm gonna bounce now," Diego said, rolling his eyes and heading in the opposite direction, even though his classroom was two doors over from ours.

"He's just jealous," Sookie said. "He thought he'd be taking Sally to that dance."

"I know," I said, my voice filled with pride. "But that'd

be weird, him taking my *girlfriend* to the dance."

Sookie laughed. "How long you been waiting to say that word?"

I sighed. I felt like I had waited forever to say that word, and with Sally leaving, I wanted to say it as much as possible. I wanted to say it so much that there was no question about it, not even with eight hundred miles between us. "That girl Sally *is* my girlfriend," I said.

Sookie smiled. "It's cute, but don't play it up too much." She paused, studying my face. I wondered if she knew about the For Rent sign, if Sally had told her this morning. "You and Sally make sense, you know."

"We do?" A current of hope ran through me.

Sookie shrugged, but her eyes were playful. "As much as anything else."

"But I've decided that the glass is half full," Sally announced midway through lunch, after letting the tribe know the big news: She was moving.

There had been questions and protests along the way.

"*Coño,*" was what Diego kept saying—basically, *damn*.

"I can't believe it," is what Sookie said.

Jade just looked at the table and muttered, "Today sucks."

I stayed quiet. I knew this was coming. Sally had told me before lunch that she was going to break the news like that. "Pull the Band-Aid off quickly! That's what I've got to do."

And she had, relaying the details of the move unemotionally, the way she might give you the lowdown on the answers to a quiz you missed.

"And I'll be fine," she had said somewhere in the middle. "I like North Carolina, and I like Grandma Pearl, and it's nice in the mountains, and . . ."

She went on and on about all the new and good stuff she'd find up there. And how it'd be better for her dad to be doing something and how her mom could work less. She smiled the whole time, but I had noticed that beneath the table her foot was moving at warp speed. And I was pretty sure this glass-half-full nonsense was an act.

"The glass is what?" Diego grumbled, moving his lasagna from one side of his tray to the other. "This is crap," he muttered, and shoved the tray to the center of the table. He fixed his eyes on Sally. "Is this some of that choose-to-be-happy bullshit?"

"Yep," Sally said. "And it works. I've been doing it all day, and I feel amazing."

"Lying to yourself feels amazing?" Diego scoffed.

"It's not lying."

"Yeah, it is."

"Nope. It's seeing a different angle. A better angle."

"No. It's like me taking a crap and you highlighting it in silver."

"You mean silver-lining it?" Sookie said.

"Yeah, that."

"You're just grumpy 'cause you're hungry," Sally said, sliding the tray back his way.

"That tastes like crap," Diego said, and slid the tray back.

Jade, who was eating the "thing that tasted like crap," looked up for a second and then went back to her food. She had been quiet all day.

"You okay?" Sookie asked for, like, the third time.

She didn't answer.

"Jade?" Sookie said.

"Huh?" She looked up, chewing slowly.

"You okay?" Sookie repeated.

"Yeah." She returned to her meal, lifting the fork to her mouth. She kept her eyes down while the rest of us exchanged looks.

"Did something happen?" Sally asked when we walked to our next class. The hallways were crowded, and we kept getting jostled apart. I was debating taking her hand to keep us together. And also, I just wanted to hold her hand. But there were practical concerns with this maneuver.

We had never really held hands in public before. The closest we had come to PDA was our touching in the stacks of the library.

Were we the kind of couple who did PDA?

Did hand-holding count as PDA?

I might as well have been on the moon when she started on her talk about Jade, because I didn't hear her until a second later, when she took *my hand* and said, "Marco?"

I looked down.

Yep. Hands interlocked. Mine and hers.

It felt weird-great and awkward at the same time.

Great because her hand was soft and warm and weird because her hand felt like a live electrical wire, sending a tingling current through the center of my body. I almost heard the buzz in my ears.

"Marco? Hello?"

"Yep. What?"

She glanced at our hands, still locked together.

"This okay?" she asked.

"Oh, yeah."

We were near our classrooms now. Same hallways, different doors. Sally stepped back so we were pressed against the lockers. "Did you hear what I said about Jade?"

I shook my head. "Sorry."

Sally sighed. "She's being weird today. Did anything happen?"

"How would I know?" I asked.

"You live next to her. Did anything happen with her *dad*?"

The quick answer was no. But then I thought about it for a second while staring at our interconnected hands. Even now, outside of the crowd, leaning against the lockers, we kept our hands together.

That was another kind of strange. Would we always be like this—linked together through palm, wrist, knuckles just for the sake of touching?

And while I was looking at our hands, another part of

my mind moved in a different direction, traveling through yesterday. Jade was fine yesterday. Fine at lunch. Fine on the bus ride home. But then I remembered what she'd said about her dad coming home, both at lunch and on the bus ride, about having to help her mom clean, so that the house would be ready for him, and that was why she couldn't come with me to Sally's house. I hadn't seen Mr. Acosta's car there when I came back from Sally's house. But then my mind jumped to those noises at four a.m. The muffled sound of fighting that was coming from somewhere. And that dream, the raspiness of a girl crying.

That *dream*.

"Did you at least talk to your dad?" Sally asked.

I hesitated, not wanting to lie to her but not wanting her to be mad either. But she knew the answer from looking at my face. She dropped my hand. "You said you would."

"*You* said I would," I argued.

"We agreed." Her voice rose as the warning bell rang.

"I still think you're wrong."

"Yeah? Is that right?"

"Well . . . ," I hedged, caught up in being right but also remembering that dream. Or that not-dream. Either way, we were having our first fight. In the hallway. I looked around at the faces passing by. One in particular stood out—Erika, whose half smile slipped the minute our eyes met.

"I can't believe you," Sally said, hoisting her backpack

higher until the weight rested on her hips. She narrowed her eyes. "I can't believe you lied." And with that she stormed off.

I didn't lie. I just didn't want to make a mistake. I'm sorry.

That's the note I slipped to her in Mr. Weaver's algebra class. She wrote back, *Prove it. Talk to Jade on the walk home. Ask her what's going on.*

So that's what I did. As Jade and I made our way toward our block, I looked for a moment to "talk." But it wasn't easy. She was, like before, pretty silent, opening her mouth only to yawn. About a block from my house, I offered up, "You're super tired, huh?"

"Yeah," she said, and yawned again.

"I had trouble sleeping too. I was up until about four in the morning. What time did you fall asleep?"

She shot me a look. "I don't know," she said quietly.

"Well, when I was falling asleep, I heard some noises. Did you hear that? If you were up . . ."

Her eyes darted away and then back to mine. "I don't think so," she said finally.

We arrived at her house, stopping in front of the gate. Her dad's car was parked outside. In my rush to get to school today, I must not have noticed it there, in its usual spot, hanging off the curb. And I could feel those puzzle pieces coming together as my lungs felt squeezed of breath. I decided to push. "So," I said, my voice low. "You didn't hear muffled fighting."

"No." Her voice was a whisper now.

"Some kind of crying?"

She shook her head. The words couldn't even leave her mouth, and her gaze traveled down to the ground.

"*Jade*," I said. "Come on." I reached out to touch her arm, still covered in that sweater, but she flinched, her eyes filling with tears. "You're not okay. Are you?"

She shook her head. A silent no.

My lungs tightened, and for a second it was hard to breathe. "Want to come inside my house?"

This time a nod. A silent yes.

But she didn't move, not until I took her by the hand—a hand that held no electric current for me but clung to me anyway—and led her home.

Senior Year

23. NO MONEY, MO' PROBLEMS

LATER THAT NIGHT, AFTER I'D GIVEN MY physics project three solid hours of work, I sit in the kitchen with my household-finances spreadsheet open on my Mac. I'm staring numbly at two columns—the left one shows our monthly income, and the right one shows our bills—when Mom walks into the kitchen.

"You okay?" she asks.

"Mom"—I look up at her—"when did you get this bill?" I hand her the "second notification" from the hospital, the number in red an astronomical amount.

She offers up a heavy sigh. "They gave me the bill at checkout, but I thought we'd worry about it when the time comes."

"And you thought that would be . . . ?"

"When they sent the bill again, in the mail."

"So now?"

"Don't lecture me, Marco. There's so much else to worry about."

She glances down the darkened hallway. Down that corridor is the rest of our family, asleep, but there is a new noise coming from the twins' bedroom. After a second, a sleepy Domingo appears in the hall and stumbles his way toward the bathroom. The light flicks on. The door swings shut.

"Too much water before bed. I tell him all the time," Mom murmurs, and then she sets her tired eyes on me.

"We'll be under," I say, pointing to a third column, TOTAL DEBT. "Way more under than we already are." As much as we tried, we were always about ten grand in the hole. Cars broke down. The twins needed more dental work. Mom got sick and missed work. And so on. But ten grand was manageable, even with the high-interest rates that credit card companies liked to force on people who lacked options. Now, though, with this increased amount, we'd be in real trouble—that can't-make-your-minimum-payment trouble.

"I know. I thought I could apply for help, but they're basing our neediness on last year's tax returns and we're above the qualification."

"So we're not needy enough?" I clarify.

"Yep, not enough."

"And a payment plan?"

"The hospital won't give us one."

My stomach turned. "Why not?" Mom looks down, ashamed. *"Why not?"*

"Because . . ." She sighs. "Because of all the payments

I missed on the last payment plan, the first time Pop was hospitalized. They say we're too much of a risk."

"But it's twelve thousand dollars."

Mom goes to the sink, picks up the sponge, and starts scrubbing the kitchen counters. "It's not the end of the world. I've applied for another credit card. See?" She pauses her scrubbing, walks over to the mail pile, and pulls out a thick envelope. Inside is a single square of plastic adhered to a letter several pages long. "And I qualified." She hands me the page.

"Mom," I say, pointing to the fine print. "The APR is high, higher than on any of our other cards."

"Yes . . . ," she hedges. "And?"

"And?" I pause to do the math in my head. "That's more than two grand extra a year in interest. And how long will it take to pay off? We could end up paying double what we owe by then. And wait . . . *look*," I point to the number at the top. "You only qualified for two grand. We'll still owe ten more."

"Then I'll keep applying." She scrubs the countertops like the Formica offended her. "I don't see what other choice we have."

"We have choices," I mumble.

Mom tosses the sponge into the sink. "Like what?" she snaps.

"Mom, come on. I'm just trying to figure out how—"

"Figure out *what*?"

"You know what," I say quietly, because she knows what.

She narrows her eyes. "No."

"Mom."

"No."

"Mom."

She takes a deep breath. "That is your money. You've been saving little by little since ninth grade."

"I'll have some left over," I point out.

"Still no."

"I'll get a job over there and make it up."

"Marco, you deserve a time when you don't have to work so hard. I don't want your first year at Wayne to be filled with you working yourself to death. That school will have academics unlike anything you've seen before—"

"Don't knock my public school education," I joke, but Mom rolls her eyes.

"You'll be up against kids who are coming from some of the top prep schools in the country. It's going to be an adjustment for you. That money means you can give your academics one hundred percent of your attention."

"Mom, I give my school right now one hundred percent. And I wouldn't even know what to do with myself if I didn't work so hard."

"You can't do both, okay?" She stares at the sponge like it's no longer her weapon.

"I think I can."

"This conversation is over, Marco," she says softly. She sighs, looks around. "You deserve better than this. That money is your way out."

"But—"

"It's over," she repeats without raising her voice.

I look back at the laptop, at that number in red—twelve grand. Without my college savings in play, that number seems impossible.

Scratch that. Without my college savings in play, that number *is* impossible.

"Bro, we'll take up a collection. I can give you two grand."

"Just like that?" I laugh. "Just a . . ." I snap my fingers. "You ballin' like that?"

"Nah." Diego chuckles. "But . . . I *could* is what I'm saying."

"Well, I couldn't borrow your money."

It's the next night, and Diego and I sit on my stoop, eating another round of deli castoffs. This is a true Southern spread, the kind you typically get north of Miami—fried chicken, collard greens, and corn bread. Food so good, it's nearly impossible to be upset about anything. Well, except for humongous numbers in red. I tell him about the spreadsheet, the high-interest credit card. "I want to go to Wayne," I explain. "I *need* to go to Wayne because of *future* and all that. But this? This feels like that time Kate didn't let Leo on that big ole' piece of wood when the *Titanic* sank."

"Dude." Diego sucks on a chicken bone. "That was mad harsh, right? Like, shiz, girl, flip on your side, and let a brotha on."

"Right? And that's *me*. I'm the Kate if I go to Wayne."

"But we can help you out, man." Diego reaches past the Southern food for some good old *arroz con gandules*. He digs into the plastic container with a spoon. No offer to me. *At all.* But that's okay, because the more I talk, the less I feel like eating.

"I can't borrow that kind of money from anyone, especially when I have it already. What's the sense in that?"

"I didn't say borrow. I said *give*. I don't want it back. It's for your pop. Your pop has been good to all of us, and your mom has, too. And Jade's got some guilt money from saving up that flow her mom sends every month."

"The money she's supposed to give Sookie's parents for living expenses?"

"The money Sookie's parents won't take for living expenses."

"They're good people," I say.

"Yeah. And we could ask Sookie. She probably has some cash just growing interest from her bat mitzvah stash. Remember that? I think she took in a couple of G's. And if we each give you two G's, that's halfway there. At least you won't have to work so hard when you get to Wayne. You'll need a job, yeah, but won't have to take on so many hours."

"I don't know. It's a lot to ask of you and Sookie and Jade."

"You're not asking."

"Yeah," I say, "but, man. I wanna be able to take care of this myself. I don't wanna make my bad situation into a bad situation for everyone else."

I'm quiet for a while because Diego saying that the tribe would do this for me fills me with a bunch of emotions.

"You okay?" he asks, trying to get a look at me, but I make a show of checking my watch and saying how I got that physics project to finish.

"Okay." He starts to pack up the supplies. When he's about done, he says, "You know, we're here—not locked up like my pop. 'Bout to get that diploma. We got options. And it'll be okay, I think."

"Yeah?"

"It's already better than it was for our 'rents."

"So, what? You come here to give me grub, money, and a pep talk?"

Diego shrugs, then chuckles. "Guess so."

"You know what that is?"

"What?"

"Leadership." I smile. "You'll make a good manager someday, D."

"Ya think?" He smiles so broadly, I see all of his teeth.

I clap him on the back. "Nah, man. *I know*."

I knew I had to come up with a plan—one that had me going to Wayne but didn't have my family dying in the Atlantic. So I thought on the problem all night, and the next morning I put on my good khakis, a nice button-down shirt, and headed to Grendel's.

I get there before the store is open, so I knock on the door, and Mike, one of the morning cashiers, lets me in.

He blows on his steaming cup of coffee and smiles at me. "You're here early, huh?" Mike glances at his watch. It's barely six thirty.

"Yeah, I'm tryin' to catch Brenda before school. Is she here?"

Mike shrugs. "If she is, she'll be up in the office."

I take the stairs two at a time, running through what I should say. That I need money? Nope. Too forward. That I need more hours over the summer for unexpected bills? Better, but probably should be more specific. How about *I need full-time hours over the entire summer, so that I can earn back a quarter of what I am about to spend on the hospital bill.*

Okay, getting there.

Finally, I would like the raise I'm due in September now, because I'm a good employee, because I'm loyal, and I've earned it.

I run through counterarguments until I stand at the threshold of the door, but it's not Brenda inside. It's Mr. Grendel, laptop open, notepad and pen to the ready on his right. On his left, a steaming cup of coffee and two jelly doughnuts.

"You're here early, Marco," Mr. Grendel says, wiping a smear of jelly from the corner of his mouth.

I scan the room, hoping Brenda will jump out of the shadows, delivering a "Gotcha!" worthy of Sally. But she doesn't. So I say, "Yes, Mr. Grendel. I was hoping to catch Brenda before school. Is she around?"

"She's on an errand. Can I help?"

"No . . . That's okay. I can catch her later."

"You sure? Must be pretty important for you to be here so early."

"Um, it was time sensitive."

"Well, lucky for you, I'm perfectly sensitive to time. Have a seat."

I sit, swallowing nervously. My agenda gone. My mind suddenly blank.

"Go on," he encourages.

Go on. Hmm . . . Okay. "Um, I wanted to talk to Brenda about this summer, and beyond . . ."

His smile falls a little. "I suppose it's that time of the year, almost graduation . . ."

"Yeah, a few weeks away, but—"

"When do you leave for Wayne?"

"August . . ."

"So this is about your exit strategy?"

"Not exactly." I take a deep breath. "It's more about my summer strategy. I'm hoping to be full-time, officially, over the summer." I clear my throat, letting the next words formulate. "I'd like to be guaranteed the hours instead of having to pick them up. If . . ." My voice falters. "If you think that would be . . . helpful."

Mr. Grendel tilts his head, like he's considering. "Well, I'd have to look at everyone else's hours. We'll want to give preference to those staying on. You understand, right?"

"Um, yeah."

"But if it's possible, I'm happy to accommodate."

"Thanks. I really appreciate that."

"Sure." He waits a few seconds. "Is there more?"

"Um . . ." I clear my throat again. "Um, yes, I am . . . um . . . hoping . . . that . . ."

"Yes?"

"That, um, I could have my review early this year. I'm due for one in September, but I'll be gone by then. So, I'm hoping that . . ."

"Hmm . . ." Mr. Grendel leans forward, his elbows pressed against the desk. "What's this really about?"

I look at the floor. The next words are hard. "My father, he, um, he's sick . . . again, and . . ."

"Oh," Mr. Grendel says, his voice softening. "I didn't know that. Does Brenda know?"

"Um, no."

"You didn't take any days off, did you?"

I slide my chin left, then right.

"Why not?"

"Money," I mumble, feeling embarrassed. When you're barely scraping by your whole life, money is a hard topic to discuss.

Mr. Grendel's quiet, his eyes sympathetic. Somehow that makes me feel worse. Because I don't want his pity. I want my review. "That's why I want the review . . ."

"For the raise? Yes, I see." His finger taps along the desk as he mulls this new request. "When I was your age, I needed money, too. I didn't have a father—at least not one that I knew—and my mother worked hard, but three of us depended on her. A maid's salary can stretch only so far." He pauses, that finger tapping again. "When I got old enough, just like you, I started working to take the pressure off her. To buy things that I needed—razors, school supplies." He pauses again. "What I'm saying is, I understand. It's one of the reasons why, when Brenda mentioned you for the position, the MIT position, I felt strongly about bringing you in here. I understand how hard it is to provide for your family at your age but to still find your own way."

I nod, realizing that wasn't pity on his face before; it was empathy.

"So how is your dad now?"

"Better." I don't explain that better is a relative term. "But . . ." I decide to be totally transparent, because what's left to lose? "There's the hospital bill, and things were already tight."

Mr. Grendel's eyes wander up to the ceiling. "So, you need more time this summer and an increase in your hourly rate? And that will be enough?"

"It'll help. If you think it's possible . . ."

"But will it be enough?" Mr. Grendel pushes. "Will it cover the debt?"

"Um . . ." I shake my head. "Not exactly, but . . . um . . ."

"Okay . . ." He places a jelly doughnut on a napkin and slides it toward me. "Settle back in that seat. Let's take a few minutes to figure something out."

At lunch, the tribe grills me about being late.

"And FYI," Sookie says. "Erika was looking for you.

She did not seem happy. Are you guys still on a break?"

I glance around the lunchroom, looking for Erika and Sally, but neither are here. Thank God.

Diego raises an eyebrow. "Bro, your girl Erika might seriously have ESP."

"What does that mean?" Sookie asks, looking from Diego to me.

"Nothing," I say, because I haven't exactly told the whole tribe about that night with Sally—the hanging out, the holding, the "I miss you." That stuff I'd like to keep between Diego and me.

"So, where were you?" Jade asks.

"I was taking care of some things," I say, digging into my sub to avoid talking and also because I'm starving. I haven't eaten anything but that jelly doughnut since my Southern feast with Diego, and my hands are shaking. I'm either experiencing a sugar low or a freak-out over the deconstruction of my carefully constructed life.

After Grendel's, I headed to the hospital to empty out my savings—my family's medical debt, paid in full. But I felt confident that I could earn back the money. Maybe not all of it but enough to get me started at Wayne. I just had to follow through on Mr. Grendel's conditions:

> Condition 1: Stick around until the very start of school.
>
> Condition 2: Interview for the management-trainee job.

According to Mr. Grendel, I wasn't "obligated" to take

the MIT job, but he wanted me to have "options" in case things changed or something else "developed."

That word "developed" hung between us like a cleanup on aisle nine, neither of us wanting to touch it.

Because what he was saying, really, was this: If your father gets worse, if there are more money problems, if your brothers don't stop punching other kids in the nuts, if your house of cards falls apart, Grendel's is always here for you.

And now I have to relay my choices to the tribe—more specifically, I have to relay my choices to Diego.

I look up, and Diego is watching me suspiciously.

"What?" I ask, a sautéed onion flopping out of my mouth.

"You don't want to know what Erika was here for?"

I shrug. "I'll text her."

"When?"

"D, mind your business."

"Okay," Jade says, frustrated. "*What* happened?"

Diego leans back. "That's for your boy to say."

"Say it already," Sookie demands, setting down her fork.

"It's nothing."

Diego snorts until he's laughing.

I cram a handful of fries into my mouth, chew noisily.

"You're doing that thing," Diego says.

Sookie studies my face. "Oh yeah. It's been a long time since I've seen that."

"Seen what?" Jade asks.

"*That.*" Sookie swirls a finger into the air, indicating

my greasy lips and fingers. "He's stress eating."

Diego gives me the once-over. "That's a nice shirt for taking care of things."

"I had stuff," I mumble, reaching for my napkin.

"What *stuff*? If this isn't about Erika, it's about Sally."

Jade sucks in her breath. "Wait. Is something going on with you and Sally?"

"No," I say, glancing around the lunchroom. Still no sign of her.

"Then what?" Diego pushes.

"I went to the hospital." I take a deep breath. "I paid off the bill—the *entire* bill."

"Why?" Diego asks. "We were coming up with a plan."

"I had to do something. I had to . . ." I sigh. "I had to make sure we were free."

"Of what?" Diego asks.

"Of . . ." I try to find the words to explain how that bill wasn't just a piece of paper. It was a thousand-pound weight leaning against the walls of our house until we'd be forced to stand sideways and eventually—because gravity pulls things down—crawl. "I had to, but I talked to Mr. Grendel this morning. I got a raise and more hours. If I work full-time over the summer, I can make up some of the money, and it'll be okay."

Sookie scrutinizes my face. "So why don't you look happy?"

Jade rests her head on Diego's shoulder, giving me her own once-over. "You don't."

"I . . . There are conditions—" I begin. But there's a tap on my shoulder. I twist around to see Erika, eyes rimmed in red. "Can we talk?"

"You okay?" I ask.

"Not here." She looks at the tribe. "Outside," she says, and walks away.

We sit at the picnic tables beyond the school—Erika on the table, me on the bench. This "break" has been a handful of days, but with everything that's happened in the gap, it feels more like months.

Around us is a thinning crowd of students, the end-of-the-year gap in faculty expectation has led to a lot of kids leaving early.

"Are you okay?" I ask again.

"Are we okay?" She looks at me.

"No." That much is obvious, given the break and all.

"But can we be? I need to know." Her voice is shaking. "I need to know, because I can't stop thinking about it, and I feel like I'm becoming my aunt, you know, making excuses for you at every turn. I feel that pathetic."

"Hey." I wipe at her wet cheeks with the tips of my fingers. "You're not pathetic. It's just . . ."

"What?" She stares at me with those brown eyes. "What is it?"

I stand, pull her to the spot on my chest, the one she's been occupying for the last six months as my girl. The same one she began occupying four years ago as my friend.

"Because being away from you is hard. Too hard," she whispers.

I pull her in tighter, trying to erase away the distance between us. Trying to forget the last few nights with Sally. To forget what might have been. To embrace what is.

"I want it to be over, okay?" She rises up to kiss me softly. And I let her.

But in that moment before I will myself into being the good boyfriend again, I come to a painful realization: The hardest part of the break wasn't being away from Erika. The hardest part was the feeling that no matter how hard I tried, I couldn't make our relationship right.

Middle School

24. JADE

WHEN WE GOT INSIDE, I WENT TO THE kitchen and made us both a snack. It might seem like I was waiting to "talk" out of sensitivity for her feelings or something. But truthfully, I waited because I didn't know how to begin. So I made us two bologna and cheese sandwiches, covering each slice of bread with a thick layer of mayonnaise, adding in a spoonful of mustard for Jade, because she liked it that way.

We ate quietly, sandwiches on paper towels, hands colliding as we pulled chips from a bag of Doritos. At one point Jade asked, "Have you ever had a mayo and Doritos sandwich?"

I coughed a bit, the idea catching me off guard. "That sounds disgusting."

"No," Jade said, eyes wide. "It's delicious, especially on white, especially with extra mayo."

"Why would you do that?" I asked.

She shrugged. "Sometimes you run out of meat."

"Then why not just put cheese?"

She shrugged again. "Sometimes you want more than cheese."

After we ate, we went to my bedroom. The house was still quiet. Pop and Mom were at work. The boys, at school. Jade stared out the window at her house, her foot tapping nervously against the floor.

I took a few deep breaths while I ran through my opening lines. Finally, I asked, "Did something happen last night?" The question felt big. And we left it there, between us, for a while. Jade sighed and sat on the bed. I sat too.

Finally, she nodded.

And I felt my heart catch against my ribs. I wanted to change the subject, to reach for the TV remote and flip the channels until I found something distracting to watch. But then I heard Sally's voice in my ear, *You have to look harder*. So I asked, "What happened?"

Jade started to shake, her eyes mournful. She took little gasps of breath and closed her eyes.

"Jade?"

Eyes still closed, she said, "I don't want to talk about it."

"But you can tell me."

"But I don't want to talk about it," she repeated, and only when I said, "Okay," did she open her eyes. The shaking stopped.

"Jade?"

"What?" she snapped, moving to the window.

"If you don't want to be here, why don't you go home?"

Because if everything were fine, she could go home. She could sit at her desk and do her homework, instead of standing at my window, watching her house from a safe distance.

She took several deep breaths. "I didn't hear the noise last night. I have these headphones that are pretty good, and so I put them on and blast some music and I . . . um . . . I put my covers over my head, and I just . . . I disappear."

"Why do you need to disappear?"

"No reason," she said quietly.

"Are you okay?"

She shook her head. A second later she said, "Your dad's home."

I glanced outside. He was coming up the walkway, his stride brisk. He opened the front door, calling my name before heading straight to the fridge to grab a snack.

"Hey, kid," Pop said when I entered the kitchen. He was in his work uniform, a navy shirt with matching pants. His name was sewn on the shirt, above the left pocket, the stitching redone every year by my mother.

He moved to the sink to wash his hands, scrubbing the skin beneath his nails with a stiff brush. "I was thinking *ropa vieja* for dinner. I've been marinating the beef since last night, and . . ." He turned off the water, drying his hands on a towel before holding up a fancy bottle of olives. "Don't tell your mom, but I splurged at Grendel's. It's worth the extra dollar, I think. Lito's coming by tonight, bringing Josefina." Pop laughed. "Wasn't last week Yesenia? Your Lito is a baller, I guess."

"I guess."

"You okay?" Pop turned to look at me. "Have another rough day at school?"

"Just didn't sleep well."

"You heard that too?"

I nodded. "Jade's here."

"Ah . . ."

"Is it okay if she stays for dinner?"

"She could stay forever as far as I'm concerned." Pop studied my face. "You sure everything's okay?"

I managed to push out a "Yep."

"Okay, well . . ." He handed me two apples. "Brain food for planning."

When I returned, I found Jade standing at the window again. I put the apples on my dresser and moved beside her. "He's gone," she said, nodding to her empty front yard.

"Jade, we could tell my pop. He'd fix it."

She stared at the wall, her eyes barely moving. "It can't be fixed."

"Maybe it could."

She shook her head.

"We should try. Okay?" I pushed.

Her eyes slid to the ground. "After . . ."

"After what? Dinner?"

"After the dance. We'll tell then." She looked at me pleadingly. "He'll be gone for a week. He explodes, and then he's gone. That's his pattern. And I just want this last thing. I want this last moment. I don't know what will happen after that. Because . . ."

Because sometimes kids got taken away.

Because there was still time to hold on to the now before things irreversibly changed.

I got that. I felt that way about the time I had left with Sally.

And Jade was right—there had been a pattern, and patterns were everything.

"Okay?" she said.

"Okay," I agreed. "But the very next day."

She nodded.

On the night of the dance, Jade wore a strapless purple dress. My mom had made the dress seven months earlier, when Jade had served as one of the *damas* in the *corte de honor* for her cousin's quinceañera—kinda like a dressed-up sidekick at another person's killer party. I wore a suit that my mom borrowed from a neighbor who had a son a year older than me. This was the same suit he'd worn to last year's dance, only Mom hooked it up with a mustard bow tie and a royal-blue vest made from fabric that she had lying around.

"You look different," Jade said when she came over to take pictures at Mom's insistence. "Taller. Have you grown?"

I shrugged, like it wasn't the miracle that it was, but in the last month I had been growing slowly. This week alone I had sprouted an extra quarter of inch, meaning that now I had to tilt my chin downward to see eye to eye with Jade.

"Wow, Sammy," said Jade when Pop walked through the door, dressed to the nines in a black suit and cap. He had gone all out and borrowed a black Cadillac for our trip. "Legit or what?" he asked, doing a Diego-like twirl.

"Super legit, Pop!"

"Very handsome," said Mom, coming up from behind to wrap her arms around his waist.

"Can we come?" begged Lil' Jay. He marched around the kitchen table like a robot. Domingo followed, arms outstretched like Frankenstein. I wondered what TV show they had been watching.

"Yeah, we can wear our suits and ties," said Domingo.

"No, Pop. *No*," I said.

"Tell you what?" Pop said to the twins. "I'll drop off big bro, and then I'll take you guys out for ice cream. You can ride in the back and pretend I'm your driver!"

"That sounds like a perfect compromise," said Mom.

"With waffle cones?" Domingo said, holding out.

"Yep." Pop leaned down to give him a noogie.

"Then okay," agreed Lil' Jay, and off they went, to march in the backyard.

"Okay, let's take some pictures," Pop said.

"Wait. Let me fix Jade's dress," Mom said, and fussed with her waistline. "What's that?" Mom asked, touching a spot on her shoulder that was darker than Jade's brown skin.

"Cheerleading bruise," Jade said, quickly.

"Oh." Mom's eyes met Pop's. She spun Jade around, studying her back closely. "Looks like you've got quite a few," Mom said, a note of worry in her voice.

"I tried to put makeup on them," Jade said. "Maybe I should put on a sweater or something."

"No. It's fine. They're faint, but I don't like the idea of you getting so bruised at practice."

"Well, season's over," I told Mom. "So, good news is Jade won't get any more bruises. Right, Jade?"

"Right," Jade said, her voice low.

After pictures, Pop waved me into his bedroom. "Want to give you something before we head out."

"Okay,"

He shut the door behind us and sat down on the bed, patting the empty spot next to him. "Pop, I don't want to be late."

"You won't be."

"Pop." He had a habit of long sentimental talks.

"I promise."

"Okay." I sat. "What do you want to give me?"

"A talk about the birds and the bees."

I groaned. "Are you serious? We've had this talk." When I was seven, Pop explained how babies were made, an awkward conversation that involved diagrams from a library book.

"We've had version 1.0, but there are least three more updates in your future, starting with today."

"Pop."

"Hear me out. With Sally moving and the dance, emotions might be heightened. So, first, girls have to be respected, okay? Let's say you try to kiss Sally tonight—"

"Pop."

"Marco, listen up—"

"But—"

"No. Listen." He waits for me to nod.

"Let's say you try to make a move, like kissing, on any girl, maybe Sally, and she says no or any version of no. She says something like 'I'm not sure' or 'I don't know,' or she even hesitates, you back off and say, 'Okay, no problem.' And that's it. You don't try to convince someone to do something they're uncomfortable with, okay?" He nods at me, eyes dead serious.

"Okay," I say.

"And the next time you see that girl, you act as nice as always. You don't hold a grudge because she wasn't sure or doesn't like you. Okay?" Again he waits, eyes dead serious.

"Okay."

"And you always be kind no matter what. Don't take anything personally. You respect whatever you're being told."

"Pop, what do you think is going to happen? This is just a dance." I stood, anxious for the conversation to be over.

"I'm planting seeds, young man. And those seeds need time to grow."

"Okay, Pop, well . . ." I looked at the floor. "They're growing. . . . So, we good? Can I go now?"

"What did I say?" Pop asked. "Say it back to me."

I gave him a look.

"Say it."

"That no means no. Any kind of 'I don't know' also means no. Back off. Don't pressure anyone. Don't hold grudges. Don't take anything personally. Be nice afterward."

"Exactly." Pop smiled.

"I already knew that, Pop."

"Then I'm doing my job, because I have to make sure you know it. So, if you don't mind, I'll keep doing my job while I'm able to. Okay?"

"Fine."

"Good." Pop stood and patted me on the back. "Now, let's get you to that dance."

Senior Year

25. I LEARNED FROM YOU

THEY SAY WE ARE BORN FREE. THAT FREEDOM is an inherent right. And I believe that. But sometimes I wonder if this country believes it too, because when you have to buy your freedom back, you learn that freedom comes at a steep price. For example, hospitals put a price tag on saving your life. If you survive, you're expected to pay that price. If you can't, you'll go into debt, maybe be sent to collections, incur more penalties and fees, and all of that will cost you your freedom.

The freedom to make choices, like taking time off from working like a dog to better yourself through school.

That's just how this life is.

Anyway.

I've basically decided to bury a bunch of things—either forever or until later. Most likely later, so I drag myself home, bloated with guilt and the need to interject a little bit of good into the world. That last part is to balance out my . . . lies of omission.

You know, not telling Diego about Grendel's conditions.

Not telling Erika about what happened with Sally.

Not telling Mom about using most of my savings to pay off the hospital bill.

I start simple. I make Pop a cup of decaffeinated tea because the caffeine in coffee might set off his seizures. Then I round up the boys for a quick game of Clue. I dust off the box and set up the board at the kitchen table, near Pop.

"You're playing with us?" Lil' Jay asks suspiciously.

"Yeah, why?" asks Domingo.

"I play with you all the time," I say, but they shake their heads hard, like they're suffering from a jammed neurotransmitter.

I split the stack into threes—weapons, locations, party guests—shuffle the deck, and slide a clue from each stack into the CONFIDENTIAL envelope. When I'm done, I glance at Pop, who's quietly sipping his tea while leafing through an old magazine. He has that look of comprehension in his eyes; so today is a "good day." At least for him.

Halfway through the game, Pop is watching us, like he wants to play. When I was younger and the twins were still babies, we used to play Clue all the time. Pop was always Colonel Mustard; Mom, Ms. White; me, Mr. Green; and Jade, when she was around, was Ms. Scarlet.

"Want me to deal you in?" I ask Pop.

"No . . . I'm good . . . watching," he says, resting an elbow on the table. He leans forward. A second later he ruffles my hair, and for a moment I am seven and he is twenty-four. And we're still okay.

"Are we gonna play or what?" Domingo whines.

"Yeah," I say, taking my eyes off Pop. "Hand me the die."

By the time Mom gets home, we've solved two mysteries—Mr. Green with the Rope in the Billiard Room and Ms. Scarlett with the Revolver in the Dining Room—and Pop has just done his "impression" of a "rich British dude." But, honestly, it sounds more like Madonna reading the announcement that precedes tests for the Emergency Broadcasting System.

Either way, it makes us laugh.

"Good day?" Mom sits beside Pop, giving his knee a squeeze.

"Good afternoon," I say, because the rest of this day—the bad parts—I could have done without. But that's the thing about good and bad: The distance between them isn't that far apart.

My plan to "bury my problems" doesn't work. Because, man, the truth really does have a way of finding you. That's the hard lesson Diego's dad had to learn after his arrest, that the theory behind "prisoner's dilemma" can only take you so far.

Truth came for me at two a.m. I was tossing and turning under my patchwork quilt when I heard its first tap. It took a second for my brain to register that someone was out there. Another second to hypothesize who that someone might be.

Sally was the first name that popped up. After all, a pattern had formed, with her showing up two nights in a row.

I've missed you.

I've missed you too.

But I knew that it couldn't be her. Because I saw her earlier today as I headed toward the school parking lot. And she saw me. With Erika. Holding hands. And the answer to her question—"Are you guys gonna stay on a break? Do you want to?"—was clear.

Because done is done is done. And even those words—*I've missed you. I've missed you too*—can't fix over.

No, this Truth had a shaved head and freshly laundered Grendel's shirt with the collar popped. This Truth was a gangster from a 1970s movie.

And he had come ready to fight.

The first thing I work out the next morning is that I can't bring myself to get ready for school. It's five a.m. and after tossing and turning for the last three hours in my bed, I've relieved two cases of the anxiety you-know-whats. Now I'm leaning on the countertop in the kitchen, staring at water dripping into the coffeepot. Not a good move, given my current condition, but this coffee will be the crane that pulls my eyelids open. So what else am I gonna do, besides drink coffee and replay last night?

```
                         DIEGO
    So you're not taking the job?

                          ME
    No. I just want my raise. I need it, man, to
    get some of my savings back, to save up again.
```

DIEGO

And you were gonna tell me? Even if your name hadn't appeared on that list for second-round interviews, you were gonna own up?

ME

Dude, I tried to own up already. At lunch. Remember? I said there was a condition, but then—

DIEGO

But then Erika came.

ME

Then Erika came. . . .

DIEGO

And now you're back together?

ME

Yep.

DIEGO

And I know that because I saw you later in the day and you told me about *that*.

(pauses)

Like that was your *only* big news.

The conversation nosedived after that.

To stop my ruminating, I skim old physics books and watch the sky lighten.

"I thought I smelled coffee," Mom says when she finds me around six a.m. She wipes the sleep from her eyes. "How long have you been up?"

"Too long," I grumble.

"Big project?"

I hold up a book. "One. Physics. But mostly movies in my other classes."

"Ah, the calm before the storm. But you'll see college will be different. At least, that's what I've been told. No wasting time, no feeling like you're being babysat. It'll be exciting."

"Would you be excited?" I ask, curious.

"Huh?" Mom selects her favorite mug from the cabinet—white veneer, blue waves, squiggly lines for birds, a cartoonish sun, my six-year-old "artist" signature on the bottom. "For what?"

"For college. Would you be happy to go?"

"Well . . ." She pauses to pour coffee. "I might still. Don't act like I'm ancient here. Who knows? Maybe after your brothers are grown."

"What would you study?"

"Hmm . . . Lots of questions this morning, huh?"

"Sorry." I twirl my physics book around, feeling that anxiety rise up.

"It's okay, but . . ." Mom studies my face, her eyes like an elevator. "You okay?"

I shrug. "Sure."

"Are you having second thoughts about cosmology?"

"No . . ." I spin the physics book again. "Not exactly."

Mom sits in the squeaky chair opposite me. "So what, then?"

"Just thinking . . ."

"About?"

"About this offer Mr. Grendel made me."

"For what?"

"Well, he's hiring a new manager trainee, and he thinks I'd be good for it."

"You would be, of course. You're good at anything you set your mind to. But that's not the plan, right? You told him about college, *right*?"

"I did, and he knows that's still my plan, *but* . . ." I clear my throat, deciding to drop some truth bombs. "But maybe . . . maybe I should." I wait for her to say, "No, you shouldn't. You should go to Wayne. You should live out your dreams." But she just holds that cup and sighs.

"I'd have a college degree no matter what. . . ." I continue. "There are, like, four universities here to choose from—"

"I know," she says with another sigh.

"And Mr. Grendel says this would give me options to help out with you, and dad, and the boys—"

"I know."

"So what do I do?"

She takes a deep breath. "Honestly? I don't know. When I was your age, I gave up everything to have my family—to have you. And I don't regret my decisions. But you have more options. I want you to have more. You know? But . . ."

"But?"

"*But*," she repeats, like she understands my doubts.

We're quiet for a while. Mom calls this "thinking on things." Eventually she walks over to me, crouching down until we're eye to eye. "Listen," she says, resting a firm hand on my shoulder. "You're the smartest kid I know. When you try to explain your homework to me, I have no idea what you're saying—"

"That's impossible, Mom," I say quietly. "Studies show that all my cognitive abilities are located in the X chromosome, and that came from you, not Pop."

"Well, there must be possibilities inside me that I've never explored. . . . And see? I didn't know that. *You* knew that, Marco." She rests her head on my knee, trying to keep our connection the way she did when I was child, those slender fingers always reaching for me. "I see how hard this is on you. I do. But you can't give up your future for us, okay? I know you keep trying to, but you just can't." She looks up at me, her eyes a little wet. "Okay?"

To be honest, mine are a little wet too. "Okay."

"Okay." She stands, reaching for my cup. "Where'd you learn to make such good coffee?"

Maybe it takes a while, but I answer, "I learned from you, Mom."

Middle School

26. THE DANCE

THE DANCE WAS HELD AT THE SCHOOL. THE student decorating committee, led by our very own Sookie, had turned our stinky cafeteria into "a magical undersea paradise," a transformation that involved gold, blue, and silver streamers blowing in the wind of strategically placed box fans. Taped to the walls were ocean scenes—giant fish and mermaids swimming through coral reef and above sandy ocean floors.

After the fourth dance, we collapsed on benches lining the walls, and Jade said, "It looks good in here, Sookie. I like it!"

Diego pointed to a far wall. "That mermaid is legit, Sooks. I ain't ever seen a Korean mermaid before."

"Actually," Sally said, closing her eyes like she was trying to remember a detail. "I read an article once on Korean mermaids, only they aren't real mermaids. They're women, some of them almost seventy, and they can dive up to sixty-five feet without taking a breath for two minutes."

"Seriously?" Sookie said, looking impressed.

"Yep, they're called the . . ." Sally paused, retrieving that picture from her photographic memory. "Haenyo and they're from . . . Gijang County. You should check them out if you go this summer, Sookie."

"So, you're going?" Jade asked.

"Yeah, I think so," Sookie said.

"So, is the mermaid supposed to look exactly like you?" Sally asked, laughing.

The mermaid was dark haired and pale skinned, with Sookie's big, almond-colored eyes. The smudgy dot of a beauty mark hovered above the mouth.

"Why not?" Sookie smiled, her own beauty mark rising. "I drew the mermaid three times before I got it right."

Sookie's date, Ari, said, "It's really cool, but why aren't there any mermen?"

"Mermen?" It was clear Sookie hadn't thought of that.

"Yeah, you could've made one with glasses and ears that stick out a little but is handsome, you know."

We laughed. Ari had just described himself.

"What?" Ari asked, playing up the joke.

Diego chuckled. "You got them ears right, though. . . ." He tugged on the lapel of his new suit. "*Or* you could have made a merman fly like me—a little macked-out 'fro, a little ebony skin, handsome as sure as that sun rises."

Everyone laughed but Jade, who stared at Diego with adoring eyes.

A slow song came on.

"Now, that's it right there." Diego looked around the room for a partner.

"I like it, too," Jade said, standing. "Let's go!"

"Um . . . ," Diego glanced from her to the dance floor, but Jade didn't wait. She nudged him forward, the whole time Diego going, "Damn, girl, be gentle."

Sally whispered, "Jade is not playing tonight."

Ari turned to Sookie. "Risk the Care Bear test?"

Sookie laughed and took his hand. "You know I came up with that," she said as they walked off.

"You want to?" I asked Sally, but she shook her head. "I'm still worn out from all your dad moves."

"What? This?" I shifted my hips left and right before shuffling back and forth on my feet.

Sally covered her eyes. "I can't look. It's so bad, even your dad would be embarrassed for you."

"Nah, as long as I got this covered. . . ." I waited for Sally to peek. Then I gave her the Suarez wink, stadium style: left, right, left, right.

Sally laughed, lowering her hands. "If you're my future, I'm in trouble."

I smiled all the way down to my heart.

"You're gawking," Sally said.

"Maybe . . . maybe not."

But the real answer was absolutely. She looked different tonight—a new version of Sally, one who wore charcoal eyeliner that made her gray eyes pop and a silver dress that fit her like nothing before. When I looked at her in that dress, all I could think about was the curve of those hips, and . . .

So many ands.

"You keep staring," Sally said.

I shrugged. "Not staring . . ." I searched for the right words and decided on something Pop always said to Mom. "I'm appreciating you."

"Appreciating?" She smiled, her cheeks glowing. "Well . . ." She took a deep breath. "I'm appreciating you, too."

The song changed, another slow jam. On the dance floor, Diego and Jade kept dancing. One of the chaperones tapped Diego on the back, motioning for him to step away from Jade until he could fit a Care Bear between them. Then he left them with their chaperone-approved space.

Sally nodded to Diego and Jade. "Something's happening there."

"What?" I watched Jade and Diego try to maintain their distance.

Sally smiled. "Love."

"See?" I said. "Nothing bad happened."

Sally looked at me, her smile fading.

"Nothing did is all I'm saying."

"Jade's dad could've come back at any time—"

"But he didn't—"

"But he could have—"

"No. There was a pattern—"

"Marco, stop."

We had fought like this for most of the week. Sally

pushing to tell. Me pushing to wait until after the dance. I knew there was a risk, but I set my worry aside and trusted that the pattern would hold. Watching Diego and Jade on the dance floor, I was glad I had kept my promise, but I was also glad that tomorrow was almost here. I wanted to stop fighting with Sally. I wanted Jade to finally be safe.

I scooted closer to Sally, taking her hand between mine. "I promise I'll talk to Pop tomorrow. Let's just dance. Okay?"

On the dance floor, we kept a Care Bear's distance between us.

"This sucks," Sally said. "I want to lay my head on your shoulder."

"That would be way better than this."

"We can pretend," she suggested.

"How?"

"Close your eyes."

"What?"

"Trust me."

I looked around self-consciously. Nobody was watching, so I let my eyes drift shut. "Now what?"

"Now," she said, "imagine me stepping closer, until I'm right against you. And I lean down to rest my head on your shoulder."

I imagined holding her tightly in my arms, my hand curving around her hips. I felt my face flush. I opened my eyes. "This is stupid."

She opened her eyes too, slightly hurt. "Sorry. I thought it would be fun to pretend."

"It's not." I glanced at the rest of the kids dancing. No one had their eyes shut. Not one.

"Okay." She took a deep breath. "What if we didn't have to pretend?"

I shook my head. "How?"

"What if we go somewhere else?"

"We can't leave the dance. Pop will pick us up in a few hours."

"Okay. So, what if we leave the dance but not the school?"

"Not the school?"

She raised an eyebrow. "There's got to be somewhere in here that we can go."

I thought about it and then smiled. "I have an idea."

Senior Year

27. FOR WHAT IT'S WORTH

ON THE DRIVE TO SCHOOL, I RETURN TO MY ruminations on last night, and another image pops up. This time, instead of Truth, it's a dude called Reconciliation.

Reconciliation is the kind of guy who swaggers, sweeping his fingers across his shoulders, like, "I got this; I can make this friendship take flight again," before jumping off Friendship Cliff. But the thing about Reconciliation is he forgot about gravity.

Gravity pulls him down with an acceleration of 32.2 feet/second ^ 2, *and* at a descent of 100 feet, acceleration causes an "exponential decrease of height." Mrs. A would tell you to imagine a line that curves sharply down. At one second in, Reconciliation falls sixteen feet. At two seconds, sixty-four feet. Around two and half seconds? Splat on the ground.

And that is the current state of my relationship with Diego.

Because, like I said, other truths came out last night. Here's the replay:

DIEGO:

I just don't get it, bro. I *killed* that interview. But if Grendel's out there recruiting, I guess he wasn't that impressed.

ME

No, it's not like that. . . . When the notice went up about the job, Brenda recommended me to Grendel, but I said no until yesterday. So, don't be down on your interview—

DIEGO

Brenda recommended you *weeks* ago?

ME

Yeah, but that's not the point—

DIEGO

And you didn't tell me that back then—

ME

Because—

DIEGO

Because *what?*

ME

Because I thought . . . I thought it would . . . mess with your head.

DIEGO

You don't think I'm good enough for the job.

ME

I never said that.

DIEGO

Actions, bro.

ME

D, I'm just trying to get my raise. Grendel's just trying to make sure I know my options—

DIEGO

Right. Your options are to go to that Ivy school—

ME

It's not Ivy—

DIEGO

Or become an MIT at Grendel's—

ME

Again, not taking it—

DIEGO

Right. Because if you want it, you'll get it. Because you're better than me.

And I couldn't think of a thing to say. Because I realized he was right. Some part of me thought he wasn't good enough to get what he wants.

Diego doesn't show at his locker. Same for Sookie and Jade. When the first bell rings, I walk slowly to calc, sliding into my seat before Mr. Mackenzie hands out our final exams. I try my best, but I'm pretty distracted. Afterward, I go through the motions: Locker, class, locker, class.

At lunch I sit opposite Diego. I arrive empty-handed because you can't take a beating and eat at the same time. But the response is quieter. Eyes down, he says, "You don't get to sit here today."

Sookie and Jade stare at the wall. Nobody will look at me. I expected a fight. An argument. Not this.

"You serious?"

"Yep."

"Dude, will you just listen to me?"

Silence.

"What about your pop's advice to deny, deny, deny?"

This gets his attention. He stands, fists on the table, stares at me until the moment gets so tense that Sookie says, "Just go, Marco."

"Yeah," Jade echoes. *"Go."*

"You guys, too?"

She nods. "For today, yeah."

I glance at Sookie. "Me too," she says.

And so I go.

I head to my truck and drive. I don't know where until Old Ancient pulls into the park, idling beneath the shadow of the rope tower. Nearby is the toddler playground where Diego and I played as little spits. I have an old-school picture of us on that playground in my room. There's Diego, big head and stocky legs. There's me, gummy smile and poofy hair. We're going down "the big boy" slide together. His legs are wrapped around me, and I'm falling back into his chest. You can be like that with your best friend when you're small. But it seems like part of growing up is growing farther apart.

Diego always makes fun of the photo. "Dude, you got me here, solo, like I'm your girl or something. Why don't you put up a photo of you and Erika or even your moms? This is like a bromance portrait."

But I keep it there because it reminds me that once upon a time our only jobs were to play and not fuss. Life is way more complicated now. But through it all, Diego's watched my back over and over again.

I wish he had hit me. It would have been simpler.

I get out of the truck and make my way to a picnic table near the playground. The park is empty except for a few moms with their chubby, knee-high kids running around, falling, and getting up again. Some stop to cry, but if the moms don't blow up the fall, they forget why they started crying in the first place.

I sit on the picnic table, leaning back until I feel the wood against my shoulders. I stare up at the sky, thankful for the way that sunny blue shows up, day after day. And then—I don't know why—I feel thankful for a lot of other things: for my job at Grendel's; for a mom and pop who stuck it out; for friends who, up until today, have always had my back.

And I'm hit with that nostalgia again, followed by a wave of sadness about what I did to Diego, about the aftermath in the cafeteria, about that coldness in his voice.

I think about Pop, about good days and bad.

About Sally, about how she looked that night when she said she missed me. And how she looked when she saw me back together with Erika.

I think about Erika, about if things are really right with her.

I feel a sadness in my chest, like that blue sky is crushing me.

There, in the middle of the park, wrapped in a blanket of trees and air and children laughing, I am hit with the messiness of this life.

The messiness of survival.

And how tired I am of just surviving.

How I want more than that.

This time I don't bring the tips of my fingers to my eyes.

I let it happen.

All that twistiness of hurt that crushes my chest. I let it out.

So I can breathe. So I can continue. So I can keep on surviving.

I'd like to say that there are no witnesses. But there is one. I see her when I finally sit up, on a park bench in the near distance. She wears a yellow dress, her black hair pulled up into a bun, and when our eyes meet, she lifts a solemn hand.

This is happening underneath this blue sky.

I am here.

I am *still* here.

And she is here too.

She stands, swiping at her dress, nervous hands easing out the wrinkles. Then she crosses the park, eyes slipping to the blades of grass beneath her bright red sandals.

A few feet away, I see her embarrassed half smile. She doesn't call out my blotchy face. She only gathers her skirt and climbs onto the table beside me, scooting over until our thighs touch—our pinkies just inches apart.

We look at each other.

And then her pinkie takes mine.

I've missed you.

I've missed you too.

And I know that it doesn't matter that I have a girlfriend.

Not to her.

Maybe not to me either.

That with Sally the past and the present are all mixed up. And the idea of a future with or without her seems impossible.

A heat spreads through me as I travel down a wormhole to the start of ninth grade. Early November. Her homecoming weekend. And I remember the weeks leading up to that day, all the excited conversations over the phone—Sally there, in North Carolina, her grandma or dad or Boone always screaming about something or other in the background of our nightly phone calls. And me, here in Seagrove, stopping our talks to tell Lil' Jay to put away his dishes or Domingo to finish up his math homework or to ask Pop if he wanted to go outside for some fresh air. The newness of being the man of the house, the separateness of having Sally so far away. But we were sticking to the plan, that no matter what, that no matter how far she was, we'd keep each other close. And then that day, that day in November.

"I showed up at the airport and you weren't there," I tell her.

She looks at the ground. When her eyes lift, they're wet. "I think about that every day."

She had bought me a return ticket home. Worse? She'd sent Boone to deliver it. He met me in baggage claim, wearing one long frown. He said Sally was "sorry." That she "wasn't feeling well." That I couldn't stay. I had to "go home." Two hours later, I was on a plane heading south.

After that she disappeared. No return calls, texts, e-mails. Not to me or any of the tribe.

Just gone.

And it just blows my mind that my biggest worry was that your corsage would wilt on the flight to North Carolina. I didn't worry about my mom being left alone with Pop. Or flying solo. I kept thinking about that freakin' corsage." I look at her, my eyes equally wet. "You sent Boone to tell me to go home."

"He didn't say it like that," she says quietly.

"It doesn't matter how he said it. What matters is that *he* said it, not *you*."

She picks at the dress, tugs the hem over her knees. She looks at me for a second before her eyes dart to the playground. "I tried—I did—but I couldn't get myself out of bed."

I imagine what that looked like—Sally of the infinite

"gotchas," suddenly stuck to a bed, like someone had glued her there. Sally, trying to push herself up with every ounce of willpower, first her shoulders and then her spine, but there is a snapback. That glue gives a little but doesn't break.

Sally stuck.

"Why?" I ask slowly. "What was wrong with you?"

She brings an index finger to the corner of her eye, her voice a slender breath. "I was really sad."

"About . . . ?"

Her calls were filled with talk of new friends, a demanding track and field coach, a part-time job in the art gallery. Her life seemed full. Happy even. My calls were about trying not to yell at the twins, trying to get a job to deal with a stack of bills.

But looking at her face now, I realize there were no friends, no team, no job.

"I was sad about everything. It was easy to pretend when you were far away, but I knew that when you came, you'd see. You'd *know*. And I couldn't face that. . . . I couldn't face you. Any of you. I didn't mean to lie. . . . I honestly believed it would get better. I thought it was the move, but now I know that moving made it worse. But, Marco . . ." This time when she looks at me, her gaze is unflinching. "I'd been sad for a while. . . .

"I think I tried to tell you before I left, but maybe I didn't say it in a way that you could understand. Maybe when I was with you, I said just enough to be okay for that minute, for that hour. Maybe another person can be like a Band-Aid, but if you remove the Band-Aid, the bleeding continues."

She stares at the ground, taking deep breaths. That nervous hand shaking.

I am quiet. I am waiting.

Her shoulders rise up to brush her ears. "After homecoming, I went further and further inside until I all but disappeared. Boone saved me." She wipes at her eyes. "He pulled me out, bit by bit. But by then so much time had gone by. I felt like it was too late. I . . . I went online. I saw pictures of you hanging out with everyone, with Erika—"

"We weren't together back then—"

"I didn't know that."

"You didn't ask."

"You're right. I should have. But I didn't even know how or where to . . . to start."

"And then you suddenly did?" My anger is sharp, but Sally doesn't toss that anger back at me. Here voice stays calm, resolute.

"Nothing about this was sudden." She takes another deep breath. "This year, with Mom, and the divorce, and reading—I've read so many books to just try to understand what happened." She looks at me, eyes pleading. "And sometimes I can't understand what happened, not entirely. A lot of what I did, the choices I made, are blurred. . . . But when Mom said she was moving back . . ." She offers me a shaky smile. "I knew that I wanted to come back here, to talk to you."

She tries to touch me, but I slide away, standing.

"Marco."

"You talked to me, okay? You can check that off your box."

"I know it's a lot. To take in."

She waits and waits, but I'm silent.

"I'll go," she says. "Give you some time . . . But if you want to talk about it more—"

"I won't," I say. But honestly, I don't know why. I just need this conversation to stop.

"Okay . . ." She's a few steps off when she turns back to me and says, "Wait, Marco, I want . . . I need—"

"*What?* What do *you* need?"

She nods, like she deserves that. Like it's okay if I snap at her a thousand ways. "For what it's worth, I really did love you." She waits a beat, glancing at her hands. When she looks back at me, she's determined. "For what it's worth, I'm pretty sure I still do."

Middle School

28. THE CUSTODIAN'S OFFICE

"THIS ISN'T BAD," SALLY SAID AS WE STEPPED into the custodian's office. "I've never been to the end of this hall before."

The custodial office was in the west wing of the school, up two flights of stairs. The room was small, tucked away beside a storage room, and had just the basics—a table, a few shelves, a sofa that could only fit two pushed up against the far wall of the room. We left the lights off, the illumination pushing in from the street and hall lights making the space bright enough to see.

When I shut the door behind us, Sally took my hand and pulled me closer. She nestled her head on my chest. There wasn't enough space for a teddy bear. There was only the feeling of her chest against mine, the smell of her coconut shampoo.

"We could probably get in trouble for this," Sally said as we glided left and right. Our first real slow dance.

"Probably," I replied, kissing her neck—another first

for us. Sally stepped back and smiled nervously, as if realizing the possibilities of us alone. I had already realized those possibilities, a puddle of sweat accumulating under each of my armpits. If Pop knew that I had brought Sally here, he would say that I was "crossing a line," and Mom would add that they had "raised me better." But in that moment, no amount of "better raising" would have stopped me from trying to get closer to Sally.

I led her to the couch. At first we were stiff. Shoulder to shoulder.

"Maybe . . . Maybe you should put your arm around me?" Sally suggested.

The obvious choice was my left arm, since it was the one between us. I commanded it to rise up. *Up,* my brain screamed. *Over her shoulder!* But for some reason my arm stayed stiffly between us until Sally looped it around her. She snuggled in closer. "Better?"

"Yeah," I whispered.

"Okay . . ." She laughed, shaking her head.

"What?"

"We're just so awkward. Like, so, so, *so* awkward."

"So awkward."

"This is super terrible." She scooted a little, so we were face to face. "We can do better than this."

"How?"

"We can just be us."

"But how?"

"What would we normally do? Before?"

I glanced around the room. "I don't know."

"We didn't used to do this."

"Yeah, we'd . . . watch a movie?"

"A movie," she said. "Yeah. So let's do that."

"Okay?"

She pulled her phone from her purse and loaded up her movie app. "What do you want to see? Only the old ones are free."

"Something classic?"

"Yep."

"Funny?"

"Yep . . . How about this?" She pointed to a *Goonies* poster the size of a thumbnail.

"Yeah," I said. "That one. That one exactly."

At some point we held each other.

We held each other until every part of me melded to her and I wasn't sure that my arms were awake.

We had learned that word in English class last week. And I told her that was what holding her felt like.

"You think we're melded?" she said, her head resting in the crook of my neck. I felt her mouth move upward into a smile.

"Yeah. Kind of. Right?"

She laughed, eyelashes brushing my skin as she closed her eyes to recall the vocabulary sheet Mrs. Bartell had handed out. "Melded. Noun. A thing formed by blending. *Oxford English Dictionary*."

"We are a thing formed," I said.

She looked up at me, her eyes shiny. "Together we form something new."

I smiled and then shook my head, suddenly sad.

"What?"

"You're leaving."

"I know," she said.

"I know too."

"I don't want to go."

"I don't want you to go."

She smiled and lifted her head defiantly. "Then I won't."

I squeezed her tighter. "Then you won't."

She fell back into me and sighed. Her sigh said, *We can stay here forever, right?*

I tried to respond with my heartbeat: Beat. *Yes.* Beat. *Forever.*

But she must not have understood the language of heartbeats, because she didn't sigh again. Instead she asked, "Did you hear that?"

"What?" I kissed her ear this time, another first.

"That," she murmured, but then we got lost in my kissing her ear and then her neck and—

"Marco?"

The light flicked on, and we pulled apart, trying to make order of ourselves.

"What are you doing here?" It was Gabe, Pop's supervisor.

"I . . . um . . . I don't know." It was all I could come up with.

"You don't know?" he repeated.

"I don't." But what I really meant was that I couldn't explain, not in a language any adult might understand.

Gabe called Pop, who came right away.

Pop tried to call Sally's parents, but there was no answer.

"They're not in town. They're too busy moving things to North Carolina." The bitterness in her voice was clear.

I squeezed her hand. My parents had made such a big deal about my first dance, starting with a special breakfast and ending with a photo session that made me pretty uncomfortable. "Like, how many times is your mom gonna say 'smile'?" Jade had said at one point. But here was Sally, alone on one of the last big nights of her eighth-grade life.

It didn't seem right.

"When are you leaving?" Pop asked gently.

Sally lowered her eyes. "A week from tomorrow."

I dropped her hand. "Next Sunday? Why didn't you tell me?"

"I . . ." Sally fidgeted with the seam on her dress. Then she finally said, "I didn't want to ruin tonight." When she looked at me, her eyes were apologetic. "I just wanted to have one more good night."

Pop sighed, putting his hands on our backs as he guided us out of the custodian's office.

When we got to the cafeteria, he checked his watch. "The

dance will be over soon. Why don't you finish it out? I'll wait in the Cadillac for all of you to come back out."

I looked up at Pop. "Thanks."

"Don't thank me. I'm pretty disappointed in you. And we'll talk about this more at home."

I shifted my eyes to the floor. "I know, Pop. I'm sorry."

"Are you? Look at me."

I lifted my eyes and nodded, but Pop shook his head like he didn't believe me. Like he knew that I wasn't sorry about what I'd done with Sally. I was sorry that he'd found out.

"Be careful, Marco," he warned.

"I will be," I promised.

But, of course, I wasn't.

The last song of the night was "End of the Road" by Boyz II Men. If you don't know the song, look it up. It's old-school, definitely twentieth-century-pop-song material. Diego slipped the DJ "a whole ten!" to get him to play it.

"Man, but it'll be worth it," Diego had said right before the song played, "because that's the song I'm gonna tell my kids about when they ask me how I fell in love with their moms."

In love.

After ten slow songs and five Care Bear violations, Diego had fallen fast and hard for Jade, only five years after Jade had fallen fast and hard for Diego.

Meanwhile, Sally and I snuck around to the make-shift stage at the back of the cafeteria, left up from the end-of-the-year play. We slipped behind the curtain and pulled each other as close as we could, swaying slowly to lyrics about the "end of the road" and not "letting go." About it being "so natural" and one person "belonging" to the other.

And I have to say, with every second that passed, I felt my heart being ripped out of my body because all I could think about was in seven days, me and Sally would have to let go.

At one point Sally said, "I'm really sad."

"Me too," I said, and pulled her so close that our faces were buried in each other's necks. All I could smell was her. All she could smell was me. All I could feel was her. All she could feel was me. There was nothing else but this wanting.

Wanting more summer breaks, lockers next to each other in high school, and crappy first jobs. Wanting all the things that Pop got to have with Mom—all those firsts. I wanted them all with Sally.

We were both lost in that wanting when the music ended.

When Principal Johnson ushered everyone out.

When our phones buzzed in our pockets.

When the teachers sweeping the cafeteria moved outside, called by the sound of sirens.

When the noise of the students reached an apex from the excitement of a drunk man coming at a friendly custodian.

When someone in my class must have whispered, "Isn't that Marco's dad? The custodian?"

And someone else must have said, "Isn't that Jade's dad? Is he drunk?"

When Jade's dad lunged for Pop because he wouldn't let him drive Jade home. When he swung and hit, one lucky shot to the temple, and Pop fell, slamming his head against the bumper of that shiny Cadillac he had borrowed to take me to the dance.

When there was blood.

When Jade started crying.

When Sookie used her purse to control the bleeding to Pop's head.

We didn't hear any of it.

We were lost in wanting what we couldn't have—Sally's leaving, a shroud that shut out the rest of the world.

Senior Year

29. HOW. YOU. LIKE. ME. NOW.

LATER THAT NIGHT I STAND IN FRONT OF Grendel's employee information board, staring at the list of names for the final MIT interviews. The list is short, just three names: me, Diego, and Amanda from produce.

For what it's worth, I really did love you. . . . I'm pretty sure I still do.

Once again I push Sally's voice out of my head and turn toward the heavy breathing behind me. Syed from the bakery stands a foot away, staring at the list of names.

"I didn't even know you interviewed for it," Syed says, rubbing his gray beard. Syed's a Grendel's lifer, been here for about twenty years, ever since he had his first kid. I know he wanted this job badly because on the day of his interview, he showed up in a three-piece suit.

"Diego never mentioned your trying for it, and aren't you going off to that big-time school in California?"

I drop my eyes to the floor. When the Grendel's bulletin came out with the announcement of my scholarship, Syed shook my hand. "Not surprised," he said, leaving me with a swollen head. And now I was on the list and he wasn't.

When I raise my eyes, Syed's gone and Brenda's fast approaching, money bag in hand. She pauses to stare at the board. "Saw Diego looking at this late last night, too. You got a minute?"

Upstairs, Brenda closes the office door behind us. "I know I recommended you, but I was honestly surprised that you accepted the interview. And I know—*I know*—it's just an interview, *but* . . ." She smiles encouragingly. "If you do your best today, show Mr. G that you're truly invested in Grendel's, only good things can come your way."

"Wait," I say, stuck on one word. "Did you say *today*?"

"Yep, today." She glances at my outfit—plain Grendel's shirt and usual khakis, a little stained around the cuffs. "You didn't know?"

"No." Truth is, a lot of that talk with Mr. Grendel was hazy.

"You'll be fine." She studies my face. "But you're worried about Diego, I'm guessing?"

It's a good minute before I say, "Diego is kinda done with me right now."

Now. Forever?

Brenda steps closer, gives my shoulder a motherly squeeze. "You have a right to take care of yourself, Marco. You have a right to take care of your family."

I look around the room. At the clock above the window overlooking the main floor. At an empty cash register balanced on a stack of ledgers. Over there, a calculator. There, a pencil and a pad. An empty money bag. Security cameras. People walking around on the security cameras. Six different boxes intersecting. One body pushing into the next square and so on. All those lives happening simultaneously, connecting in ways we barely see.

For what it's worth, I really did love you. . . . I'm pretty sure I still do.

I look back at Brenda; her statement rings false. Taking this interview isn't about taking care of my family.

Because Diego *is* family too.

About an hour into my shift of restocking shelves and breaking down boxes, Diego arrives in the back room wearing a sharp suit. He appears in good spirits now that his interview is done, whistling nineties pop songs like a themed satellite radio station. He ignores me and heads straight to the men's locker room. He emerges in his new but now usual uniform: fitted khaki pants and a starched Grendel's shirt that is every shade of clean. He runs a hand over that freshly shorn hair, the way you might stick your tongue into the groove of a missing tooth.

"How'd it go?" Alex asks when he settles into his stack of boxes.

"Better than good," Diego replies.

"Yeah?" I offer, trying.

Diego glances at me, mouths, *Judas.*

"That's great," Alex says, tugging on his mustache—wiry

and new. He turns to me. "You're up next. Better be prepared!"

"Mind your business."

"Just trying to be encouraging."

I give Alex and his stupid mustache a dead stare.

"What?" He checks to see if his fly is open. Then he looks at his shoulder like he's got a spider on it. Twists his head to the far right to see if somebody's standing behind him, but nobody's there. This isn't a "Gotcha!" *"What?"*

"That thing on your face."

"Sweet, right?" Alex rubs the intermittent fur.

"It's like caterpillars are congregating on your face."

Normally, Diego would hop in with a *ha*, but I'm a Judas now. So he continues to ignore us until Alex steps to me. So close I smell his Fritos breath. "Your ma-ma," he says slowly.

Diego laughs.

Encouraged, Alex exclaims, "Yeah, your mama!"

"My what?"

"Yo-u-r ma-ma?" he stutters.

"Say what?" I step forward; Alex steps back.

"Wor-d-d to yo-ur moth-ther?"

Diego's cracking up now, but when I look at him, his face grows serious. *Judas*, he mouths. This is Diego's Catholic upbringing coming for me.

"Dude," I say to Alex, "just be a farm boy from Oklahoma. 'Kay?"

Alex sighs, shoving his hands into his pocket. "I moved

here from Pennsylvania. I've never lived on a farm."

"Then just be cool about yourself. It's better that way. Trust me."

"'Cause that's the way, uh-huh, you like it?" Alex sings off-key, bustin' a move that can only be described as a spin-hop, a *spop*. There's no grace in the execution, but he tries to stick the landing by ending in a classic Beastie Boys lean back. "How you like me now?" he quips, but it doesn't really sound right. It sounds like, "How. *You*. Like. *Me*. Now."

"Did you go through some kind of messed-up urban boot camp?" Diego finally asks.

"I'm just trying to go with the flow," Alex whines.

"Well, flow your way right to your break, man," Diego says. "You're past due."

Alex checks his watch. "Fine, but when I come back, we're going to talk about letting me in on twentieth-century pop songs. Okay?"

Diego chuckles. "Maybe, *if* you promise to exterminate those caterpillars from your face."

"It's a mustache."

"It's a colony," I say.

"Whatevs," Alex says, and, simultaneously, Diego and I slow clap.

"*What now*?" Alex asks.

"That's the first time you've used *whatevs* right," I say.

Alex smiles, encouraged. "See?"

"Uh-huh," Diego says. "We see."

After Alex leaves, I glance at Diego. This feels like a

bridge, an Alex bridge, into a conversation, *the next apology conversation*, but Diego catches my eye and says, "Don't even. This is work, so I'm keeping it *profesh*."

I deflate. "So that's how it is?"

"Yep." He gets back to breaking down boxes and stacking new product on a cart.

"Come on, just hear me out," I plead, but he presses play on his phone. Music blasts—the clear intro of some old-school Nas. With his back to me, he loads up a cart with cereal boxes. And I return to what is possible for tonight—a room full of emptied boxes.

The Speaker God calls my name at ten p.m. I ignore Alex's attempt at a high-five. I ignore Diego's final mumblings of Judas this and Judas that. I take my sweaty self and head to Grendel's office.

The interview starts with a painfully long accounting of my general history at Grendel's as told by Brenda. A list of accolades from my file as told by Mr. Grendel.

And while I'm listening, I have a realization: Mr. Grendel said I had to take this interview because he wanted me to see that I had options. And the truth is, if I took this job, the increase in pay would be enough to help my family not only get out of debt but stay out of debt. I could go to school part-time while I worked here too. In a lot of ways, this job could save us.

But where would that leave Diego? Not just today, but tomorrow? Diego needed this job. More than that, Diego wanted this job. Even more than that, Diego would be better at this job. And me, I would figure it out.

Which brings me back to that realization: I have to be here, but I don't have to talk about myself.

"So, the first question we have for you, Marco, is where do you see yourself in five years? What's your plan?"

I clear my throat. "Sorry, what?"

Brenda smiles kindly. "How do you see the next five years going? You don't have to stick to the plan, of course, but if you imagined your life in five years, what would it look like?"

"Take your time," Mr. Grendel says encouragingly. "We understand it's a loaded question."

But it's not a hard question. I made a five-year plan long before Pop got sick, and even earlier this year, when he was starting to return more to his old self, we talked about what I would do in college, the first four years and then after—master's degree versus PhD.

"You could be a doctor," Pop had said with a laugh of *Isn't that fantastic? My son . . . a doctor!*

"I'm not trying to be on *Grey's Anatomy*."

"No, a PhD doctor . . . a doctor in the philosophy of astrophysics . . . I can't think of anything cooler than explaining how a star is born."

"Wouldn't that take forever?"

"You're young; you've got forever."

Pop said I could teach somewhere and do research. *Research is the cool stuff. It's like being paid to play.*

"That's very ambitious," Brenda says when I lay out the plan. "But, then, you're very ambitious. Aren't you second in your class?"

"Yeah," I say.

Mr. Grendel whistles. "Impressive."

"Thanks." I bolster up because I see my way in. "You know what else is impressive?"

Mr. Grendel looks up from his notes "What?"

"Working four years straight, including every Saturday, without taking a break. That's pretty impressive."

Brenda nods politely, but she doesn't seem to follow. "And you know what else is impressive?" I continue.

Silence.

"Cutting off all your hair, wearing pants that fit, in, like, an uncomfortable way, and changing the way you speak because a job—no, an opportunity—means so much to you, especially when you go around telling everyone that this is the opportunity of a lifetime."

Brenda glances at my hair, which is its usual length. She exchanges a confused look with Mr. Grendel. "Did you cut your hair, Marco?"

"Me?" I laugh. "No. I'm also wearing baggy pants with stains around the ankles." I point to the food stains on the cuff. "And I've always talked like this. And I missed two Saturdays last year because I got sick."

"So . . . ?" Mr. Grendel says, an eyebrow inching higher. "Who's this impressive?"

"*Diego.* He's worked here just as long as me, just as hard

as me. He's never missed a day. Why"—I look at Brenda—"didn't you recommend him?"

Her mouth falls open.

I continue. "He's the one who came up with the idea to make those prepackaged recipe kits—you know the ones that go with those recipe cards we have in the meat department. You guys do know that?"

"Is that true?" Mr. Grendel asks Brenda.

"Um." She pauses to think back. "It's been a few years, but wasn't that you, Marco?"

"No. When I told you, I said, 'Here's Diego's idea.'"

"Really?" Brenda says. "I guess I remembered it incorrectly."

"Check it," I say to Mr. Grendel. "Customers would come in and pick up the recipe card, and they'd ask us about where various ingredients were located, and one day Diego said, 'Why don't we put this in, like, a box. Then people won't have to ask us for it.' And I thought that was a good idea, so I told Brenda what Diego had said. I called it, Diego's Great Big Idea."

Brenda's eyes glaze over for a second. When her focus returns, she looks at Mr. Grendel and says, "You know what? I remember that. I do."

"And," I point out, "it was Diego who trained Alex."

Mr. Grendel cocks his head to one side and murmurs, "I like Alex."

"So"—I look at Brenda again—"why did you speak up for me?"

Brenda shakes her head. "I don't know. You're a good employee too."

"Yeah, but I'm not better than Diego. I'm just a little more"—I inserted air quotes—"cleaned up."

"Appearance is important," Mr. Grendel says.

"So is talent. Appearances can be changed," I say, and then I channel a bit of Sookie by adding, "And that's not even addressing the cultural biases that determine what appearances are 'desirable' and what 'cleaned up' means. But no matter that for now. The point is, Diego made himself over to look more like me—way more 'professional' than me, in fact—but you're still not seeing the talent. You guys are kinda obsessed with me."

Mr. Grendel laughs so hard he slaps his hand on his thigh. "You sure you don't want to become a lawyer?"

"I'll be a lawyer for the universe," I say with a smile.

"I daresay you will be, Marco," Mr. Grendel says. "I daresay."

Middle School

30. FRAGMENTED AFTERMATH II

WE WANDERED OUT TO THE PARKING LOT ten minutes after the ambulance left. We found confusion, parents talking in clumps, officers taking statements, and in a corner was Diego with his arms around Jade.

Jade was crying.

And we knew as we walked over that something big had happened, something that would burst our small bubble of happiness, happiness that was already wrapped in the bittersweetness of impending heartbreak.

But still, we pushed forward, picking up the pace with every step that brushed the ground. When Sally broke away to rush toward Jade, I stopped and looked around.

Where was Pop? He wouldn't leave. I knew that. If he said he'd wait for us, he wouldn't leave.

"Marco," Diego called when I was still a few feet away. "Where were you? I've been texting you like mad."

"Have you seen Pop?"

Jade buried her face deeper into Diego's collar, the sobs growing louder. Sally patted her back. A female voice called out, "Diego? Diego?"

"Mom!" Diego shouted, and Mrs. Sanchez pushed her way through the crowd until she pulled him and Jade—still clinging—into a tight embrace. Mrs. Sanchez looked at me. "*Lo siento, Marco. Lo siento.*"

I scanned the crowd, panic rising. Then I pushed forward, trying to reach the cruiser, but the crowd was too thick, and all I could see were bits and pieces—the lights spinning, a man seated in the back seat of the car. I couldn't see who, though. I shoved my way to the right and saw Pop's borrowed car and a man in uniform bent down on his knees to inspect the front bumper.

"Pop?" I shouted out. But there was no answer. "Pop!" I spun around, screaming his name again and again, trying to push through, but I was too small. I couldn't make it.

It was Diego who stopped me. He caught me by the arm and held on to me. "Bro," he said. "I'm sorry. I'm sorry. That ambulance was for your dad."

"Mom?"

"Marco, he's going to be all right. He's in surgery, but the doctors think he'll be okay."

"But, Mom."

"Oh, Marco, I know. I know. It's okay. It's okay. Hush. It's okay. I know."

• • •

Diego said, "Mr. Acosta showed up, and he was like, 'I'll drive Jade home.' But dude was messed up. Eyes half down and wobbly as an octopus. You know how it is. Pops was like, 'I got it. Go home. Sleep it off, man.' And it was back and forth like that for a bit. But then Jade's dad got hyped. All like, 'That's *my* daughter.'

"Man, you couldn't hear that inside?"

"Mom?"

"It's a little worse than the doctors thought, but he'll get better. There'll just need to be some . . . adjustments."

"But we'll be okay?"

"We'll always be okay, Marco. I promise you."

"I think they're going to charge Jade's mom with child endangerment and her dad with child abuse," Sookie said. "Because Jade told them he's been . . . hitting her. Did you know he was hitting her . . . ? My parents are going to try to help, because most of her family is in Antigua. But Mom says maybe we can register to become a foster family. . . . There's a bunch of how-to videos on YouTube about becoming a foster family. I don't think it will be too hard. . . . But did you know, Marco? About the hitting?"

"Marco, try not to think about that now," Sally said.

"No, because . . . it's all I can think about. . . . You were right, and I should have told him . . . but I didn't. . . . And he was stuck out there in that parking lot waiting for *us*. . . ."

"*Marco.*"

"I could've done better."

"*We* could've done better."

"When Mr. Acosta grabbed Jade by the arm, your pops just went off and gave him a shove. And Mr. Acosta sucker punched your dad. One hit. But your pops fell—just bam!—right onto the bumper. Shit. I can't believe it. Just one hit."

"Can we sleep in here?"

"You guys scared?"

"Yeah, and Lito snores."

"And why does he have to sleep in Mamá and Papá's room?"

"He's helping us out. Mom asked him to."

"But why can't he sleep at his own place?"

"Because we have to have a grown-up here at night."

"You're grown up."

"Nope. I'm not."

"But you're big."

"Bigger than you, yeah."

"But when's Papá coming home? I miss him."

"I miss him too."

"Can I sleep in your bed?"

"Me too."

"There's not enough spac—*hey. Hey, now.* Okay, we'll

make space. Domingo, you sleep at the bottom and, Lil' Jay, you sleep at the top with me. We'll fit. Okay? Don't worry. We all fit."

"I don't want to go tomorrow. I don't want to live in North Carolina. I don't want to leave you or here. . . ."

"I don't want you to go either."

"Then I won't go."

"Good. Don't go."

"But even if I do go, you won't forget me?"

"I will never forget you."

There are moments when everything changes. You step over a threshold into a new world. All possibilities that were open before suddenly close. But that's okay when you've chosen correctly, *thoughtfully*.

But if you don't choose thoughtfully, everything can change. You can jump the track into a parallel world, and the one you had before—the one with a pop who helps you dream up a future, tells you to accelerate, gives you hugs that are way too tight—that can disappear.

What I'm trying to say is this: If I could go back in time and give myself one piece of advice, it would be that life is fragile. Choose carefully.

Senior Year

31. SAY ANYTHING

ON FRIDAY MORNING I GET UP EARLY, AND with Pop's old boom box and trench coat, I drive over to Diego's. You might be saying, *Marco, what does your pop know about that trench coat life?*

I'll tell you.

Back in the day, Pop loved grunge, and in that grunge-loving stage, he wore trench coats and combat boots and hair that was long and greasy.

I know. Mom showed me a picture of it this morning.

Inspiration, Diego might have said in better times.

Packrat is what Mom said in current times, when she explained why that boom box and trench coat live in our house.

Anyway, that's how I roll up to Diego's: trench coat on, boom box raised to the sky.

If you don't know where this is going, I'll let our good friend Marta tell you.

Marta: *It's a freaking scene from the eighties classic* Say Anything.

And the definition of a grand gesture, which might prove Diego right about our relationship being bromance goals.

But whatevs.

This wasn't even my idea, to tell you the truth. This time when I woke up an hour early—again—and padded my way into the kitchen to make a pot of coffee—again—Pop was the one who found me. And he did what Mom did—wiped sleep from his eyes and sat down beside me. Then we both watched the sky lighten.

Eventually, when the sky was layered with color, Pop said, "Marco, your mom is saying you might not go . . . to college."

"What?" Black liquid splattered the table. Pop didn't notice. He just added, "But you can't do that."

For the record, I am going to college. Maybe not Wayne. Maybe somewhere here. Maybe I'll work at Grendel's, not as an MIT, but as a dude who stocks shelves on the regular, forty hours a week. I didn't tell him that, though. I just grabbed paper towels to wipe up the coffee.

When I sat back down, I watched him watch the world outside. That first light hitting him bit by bit: the corners of his mouth, the lashes framing his eyes, and finally his whole face.

"Hey, Pop," I said. "What are you thinking about?"

"I don't know," he murmured after a while. "You, your mom, Domingo, Lil' Jay . . . all of it . . . I guess."

"What about all of it?"

He smiled wider. "I'm thinking . . ." And then for a while he didn't say anything. "It's been, you know . . . unexpected . . . but good."

Hopefully this grand gesture would be unexpected but good too. I take one last look at the boom box. I hit play. A song blasts—not Peter Gabriel's "In Your Eyes," if that's what you're thinking. Nineties grunge masters like Pop wouldn't have something that sappy on cassette—or, at least, that's what Mom said when she pulled the boom box from the closet.

See, after the sun rose, my mom came into the kitchen and found Pop and me sitting there, holding hands. Okay, so Pop was holding my hand. He had grabbed it about a minute before Mom stepped into the room. But to be straight with you, I held on too.

"So, two days in a row?" Mom said. "Getting those prom jitters?"

And that's when I told her and Pop—who just nodded—about my hard times with Diego. That's what I called it, "hard times."

"So you fought over Grendel's . . . ?" Mom asked.

I shook my head. "I don't think it was that so much as me just . . . I don't know. It's hard to explain."

"Your not telling him stuff?"

"I guess."

"Because you didn't think he was good enough for the job?"

I look down, ashamed.

"It's okay," Mom said, leaning over to rub my shoulder. "Sometimes we don't see people for who they are now." She chuckled. "Diego was kind of an idiot when you were in middle school, but he's grown into a pretty solid young man."

I nod, because that was part of the big thing I was working out this morning. And the other big thing was coming to understand that maybe I had trouble seeing things as they are in the *now* and not tying it all back to the *before*, not slipping into those wormholes of the past. The past may have made us who we are, but the past was gone.

Mom didn't realize I was having internal epiphanies, so she continued wisely. "And friendship is built on trust. That's a saying for a reason. Come to think of it, everything is built on trust."

Finally, Pop spoke. "You can't break his . . . trust. He's a good . . . friend. He's always there for you . . . for all of us."

"I know, Pop."

"Maybe a grand gesture?" Mom said jokingly.

And that's how I ended up here, a boom box hoisted over my head, the speakers blasting "All Apologies" by Nirvana.

The neighborhood comes to life. Heads creep out of doorways. Old ladies yell to, "Cut it out!" and "*Cállate.*" I'm cursed out in English, Spanish, and Creole before

Diego comes out of his tiny house to stand in his tiny yard. He stares at me while I hoist the boom box up to the sky and, with one agile finger, turn up the volume.

"This isn't even the scene. The scene—probably the most iconic scene of the eighties—is romantic. Romantic!" he shouts. Then he glances at his neighbors filing out of their houses.

I can see him thinking, *This isn't* the *scene, but it is* a *scene.* And Diego hates scenes, especially after the "big scene of July 5, 2015." That's the day the police came for his dad.

So maybe this boom box over my head is a misstep? Maybe I should have given it more thought? At the same time, he's talking to me. Okay, shouting at me. But we're in it. We're communicating.

And wasn't it Diego who said that I needed to earn my PhD in communication?

So, this is me, getting my PhD.

Neighbors start to yell to "Shut the eff up" and that I was a piece of "*come mierda*" and other words that Diego's church-going mom would not like. Diego, though, is ranting about how I've "ruined" *Say Anything* for him. How it's not enough to try to steal Grendel's from him, I have to steal this too. How I even got the song wrong. "Who gets the song wrong?"

"It's a gesture. A grand gesture!" I get out before Diego snags my shirt. I manage to slip away.

"Bro, you're being such a douche bag right now!"

"You're the douche bag!" I shout back. "Accept my apology!"

"*That's* an apology?"

He tackles me to the ground. My bad karma comes at me as stabby twigs and skin-shredding greenery. By the time I hit the grass, I'm bleeding. But in some ways my tumble into the bushes is a blessing because the boom box doesn't crash onto us—it gets tangled in the spindly leaves. Nirvana continues to blare as Diego pins me to the earth.

"It wasn't cool." His arm cuts across my chest; his knee digs into my hip.

I twist and turn, trying to right myself, but Diego is twice as wide and three times as muscular. "I was trying to . . . grand gesture . . ." Somehow I manage to flip him onto his back.

"Tell me something new!" He grunts from beneath me. We glare at each other. The music suddenly stops. Above us is a shadow. The shadow of an older woman, Ms. Debois. Her finger is on the stop button. "You boys are going to wake my Georgie." Georgie is her geriatric partner, known for her bulky hearing aids. A bomb could drop on the neighborhood and Geriatric Georgie would snore right through it.

"We're sorry," we both mutter, because that's how our moms raised us.

After Ms. Debois shuffles off, Diego pushes me away. "If my mom weren't at work, she'd get my dad's belt from the closet and whoop you up and down the street for this nonsense."

I stand, brushing dirt from my pants. I pull the boom box from the bushes and use the sturdy box as a seat. "I'm sorry."

Diego sits on the grass, knees tented, trying to catch his breath. "Not good enough."

"What would be good enough?"

He glances around his yard, the neighbors still crowding the fence. "We're done," he shouts. "We'll quiet down!"

"Little shits," a woman from across the street mutters, clutching her chest as she walks away.

"You should go door to door and tell them you're sorry!" Diego snaps, flopping onto his back. He stares at the sky, one hand protecting his eyes from the sun.

"If that's what it takes."

"If that's what it takes," he parrots.

"Diego, come on. I should have told you the first time Mr. Grendel approached me. Okay? You're right. I should have been honest."

"But you weren't because you don't think I'm good enough for the job."

"You are, though."

"But you didn't think that, right?"

"I thought . . . I thought . . . I saw you, how you . . . the way you were, the way you used to be when we were young. I didn't see how you are now."

"You know what I think?" Diego gives me that hard

stare again. "We both lost our dads that summer, but all you see is what *you* lost. But I had to grow up too and figure out all this manhood shit alone."

"You've done a pretty good job. Way better than I'm doing."

"You know what else I think?" Diego says after a while. "I think you're scared."

"Yeah," I admit. "I'm scared. I'm scared to leave Pop like he is. Scared to leave Mom alone with everything on her. Scared that the boys are gonna end up in juvie. I think those are pretty good reasons to be scared."

"Yeah, okay," Diego says. "But your mom's not alone. Neither is Pop or the boys. They've got Lito, me, Old Mrs. B, Jade, Sookie." He pauses. "No. I think you're scared to leave Seagrove, find out who you are *out there*."

"What?" I chuckle at Diego trying to drop some deep knowledge on me. "That's not it."

Diego stands. "Yeah? *So* . . . who are you if you're not taking care of Pop and your family? Who are you if you're not being all model friend to me and Jade and Sookie? Who are you if you're not mowing Old Mrs. B's lawn or fixing her mailbox? Or being Erika's boyfriend, even if you don't love the girl."

"What's Erika got to do with this? You don't know how I feel."

Diego gives me the side-eye. "Marco, you better be careful, or your whole life could go by without you actually in it. You'll miss a helluva lot if what you care most is not letting people down." He stands, wiping off his jeans. When he speaks again, his voice is low. "You can't fix your pop by being perfect now. No matter what you give up for him, he's always gonna be like he is." He watches my face, and maybe there's something there, because he puts a hand on my shoulder.

I look away, at the street and beyond. Sometimes it's hard to see what's there.

"It wasn't your fault, okay?" he says. And then he says it again. "It wasn't your fault."

It wasn't your fault.

It wasn't your fault.

It wasn't your fault.

Over and over. And he doesn't let me brush that hand away. Won't let me step away. Instead, he holds on tight.

And it feels the way it did when we were three, going down that slide, holding on to each other because we wanted to be brave when, really, we were just afraid.

It's a good while later when he says, "Jade told me tomorrow *has* to work. That we can't be, all, mortal enemies at prom. All right, Lloyd Dobler?"

"So, we're good?" I push out, my voice smaller than I'd like.

"Bro, even when I hate you, we're good." He punches me on the shoulder, sending me back a step. When I look at him, he smiles.

"What's that for then?"

"Them twelve G's." He puts his head between his hands, like he still can't believe it.

"I know," I say. "But I did what I had to do."

"You were almost free, though."

I check him with my shoulder. "I can't be free if they're not free too."

Even later, when I'm lying in bed, staring at that ceiling fan spinning around, I realize this: I didn't lose my pop like Diego said. Pop is different, yeah. He's quieter and slower to speak, but he's still here, on the inside. He hasn't gone away like Diego's dad.

He's *here*.

My pop.

Middle School

32. THE PACT

TWO WEEKS AFTER POP'S INJURY, I LEFT MY mom in some neurologist's office, cupping a mountain of tears as she tried to understand how much damage had been done to Pop's brain by that one hit—not Mr. Acosta's fist against Pop's skull, but the bumper, the sharp edge of metal.

I couldn't take the look on Mom's face, so I wandered the hospital's pastel halls until I found the elevator bank, and I took the car up to the rooftop observatory. There I found my oldest and dearest friends—sky and sun and the faint white moon and the stars, which, on that day, also couldn't be seen quite yet because of the sunlight's glare. But they were present. They *are always* present.

I walked toward the security rail, the blueness of the sky like an ocean above me. Below me everything was made for my brothers' playsets: toy cars, toy ambulances, plastic people. Nothing seemed real, except for me, stretching upward, rising onto the balls of my feet, only my toes connected to the ground.

This was when I made my first attempt to walk the perimeter of the rooftop, telling myself—for whatever superstitious reason—that if I could walk the whole edge on the points of my feet with my eyes closed, Pop would probably be okay. But if I could remember every name of every star that he had ever shown me, then without a doubt, he would surely be okay.

I was grasping at some hope built on superstition. Like I could send a message to the universe that said: *Look, I remember everything he ever taught me, so please help him remember everything that he taught me too. Let him remember me.*

I began by imagining the three points of the Summer Triangle—Altair, Denab, and Vega. Pop had taught me about asterisms like the Summer Triangle when I was very little, but I had a hard time pronouncing the word correctly. I'd call it "asteroids" or "asterisks." By the age of eight, I was able to say the word with confidence, and I knew that an asterism was a series of unique stars that were both a part of one constellation or multiple constellations and pulled together to create something new. The same way Mom and Pop came together from their own constellation families to create me. (That's how Pop explained it back then.)

Tips of toes to the ground: *Denab, from Cygnus, and Vega—*

"Um, Marco?" a voice said from the toy world.

And Vega from Lyra—

"Marco . . . ?"

I opened my eyes, blinked in the daylight. And there was Erika—that other version of her, not the one in the now, the one who's struggling to know me after five years of friendship and six months of dating. No, this was Before Erika—Sookie's nemesis, Sally's track teammate, the girl who once asked me to a middle school dance.

I was my other version too: the still growing me. I had, except for the dance, never seen her outside of school. That was probably because she lived within walking distance of Seagrove Middle, while I took the bus with the tribe. But here we were together, and of all places at the hospital.

I stared at her: messy, light-brown hair wrapped like a knob atop her head, mascara slightly smeared beneath the curve of her eyes. She kept swiping at her eyes, so I asked if she was okay, and she glanced up at the clouds and said softly, "My grandma died."

"Oh." I rose back up, onto my tippy-toes, and tried to push away this new bad thing.

"She's been sick since forever and she was old . . . but *still*."

"Sick forever" would be explained much later. The day that *forever* began would be traced all the way back to the day she spit a loogie at Sookie, but on the day of our strange meeting at the hospital, she didn't say much more, just waited for me to talk all her troubles away. But nothing I said mattered; she cried anyway.

If Mom started crying, Pop would put his arm around her. I hadn't put my arms around my mom, though, when she was cupping her mountain of tears in a neurologist's office, and maybe it was my guilt that had me slipping my arm around Erika's shoulders. But that's what I did, and I said, "I'm sorry about your grandma. I really am." *Pat, pat, pat.*

She buried her face in my chest, and our bodies aligned, fitting in a head-to-toe way that left behind no remainders, no messy trail of fractions or decimals.

After a while she raised her head and studied my face. "You're crying."

I rested my ear against her hair, hoping she would let me be. But she said, "It's okay. You can talk to me."

I didn't know how to say it—*My dad. My dad almost died . . .* because *of me*—

But she pushed, and finally I managed to say something that felt true. "I almost lost a part of my asterism."

She nodded. But if she had asked me to tell her more, I might have confessed my part in it, and maybe if I had that would have freed me. But the next question was, "But *what's* an asterism?"

"It's all the pieces that make you whole," I whispered.

"Like my grandma," she said in a crackly voice.

And then there was this coughing, snot-running bit.

Maybe she cried; maybe I did too. Maybe it went on for a while, and maybe that's why after that day it felt like we had made a pact to be there for each other.

A pact that was never spoken or written in words but still existed.

A pact written in the language of loss, of the dead and dying.

WORMHOLE V

BUT IF I CHOSE TO TRAVEL DOWN THAT wormhole, go back in time and "jump the track," I'd have to accept the casualties.

Lil' Jay and Domingo would never come into the world.

It's possible that Jade, Diego, Sally, and Erika might not exist either. The ripple effect can be unpredictable. But even if they did exist, would we know one another? Is cosmic coincidence so strong that we would find one another in this new world?

Or would all our stories—the ones that we've written alone, the ones that we've written together—disappear?

Because in this new world, the one of self-sacrifice, my current life would be gone.

And maybe I don't want my life to be gone.

Maybe I just want it to be better.

Maybe the goal shouldn't be to fix the past but to accept it, learn from it.

Maybe mistakes make fertile soil.

Because one of life's other paradoxes is this: We want to change the past *because* we survived the aftermath. And in the process, we grew up.

Senior Year

33. PROM

IF MY FRIEND MARTA WERE HERE RIGHT now, she'd probably say, "Marco, you're messing everything up. Like *everything.*" And then she'd tell me a story about that one time she messed everything up, too.

And that story would probably start months before the mess-up occurred, kind of like my own story started a month before prom.

Before Pop got hurt again.

Before I held Sally's hand.

Before those lies of omission.

But maybe at the end of Marta's story, she'd say, "Don't worry, kid. We all make mistakes."

At least that's what I hope she'd say. Right now I'm not sure about anything, except that if Diego is right, if I am living my life trying not to disappoint everyone while, somehow, disappointing everyone . . . Then I must be making mistakes—colossal mistakes.

Typically, I'd bury these sorrows in work. But today is prom, and Mr. Grendel has given me the day off. So I have to be creative about finding work. And that's why Old Mrs. B finds me shoving her mailbox into a fortified hole when she pulls into her driveway that afternoon.

She smiles and waves as she continues on into her garage. A few minutes later she meanders out to the front yard to take in my handiwork. "This is a nice surprise," she says, watching as I fill the hole with dirt, patting the ground with the blade as I go.

"I'll come back next week and drop some cement on top."

"Okay," she says, "but shouldn't you be getting ready?"

"Plenty of time," I say, thinking of Erika, already at some beauty salon. And Jade and Sookie, who started their prom prep last night.

Me? I just have to shower and slip on the suit Mom pressed for me last night.

"Sorry it took so long to find a permanent solution to the mailbox," I tell Old Mrs. B.

"Well," she says gently, "it's not really your job to find permanent solutions to my problems, but I appreciate your help. How's your dad's rehab going?"

I lean against the mailbox (a test of its sturdiness) and say, "Same as last time—slow but, you know, some progress."

"And school?"

"Got to finish a physics project, and then I'm free."

"Tea?"

I follow Mrs. B into the garage, settling the shovel back into its spot beside a rusty backhoe.

As I pass the hood of her Oldsmobile, I rest my palm on the silver metal, still warm to the touch. The garage door slides down, and Old Mrs. B motions for me to follow her into the house. There, a cold gust of air washes over our skin, and for a second I feel soothed.

She turns the corner, heels clicking on the white tile, but I stay in that gust of air, flapping my arms up and down, an attempt to air out my armpits. Then I move on to the kitchen, a small, bright space with white counters and a good deal of light from the window above the kitchen sink.

Outside that window, in a small garden, is a teak bench that sits beneath an oak tree. The tree's arms are raised in a "hallelujah," as if the tree is saying, "Let me just sit here in a state of eternal worship."

Old Mr. B used to like sitting beneath that tree when he was alive, which is why he put that bench there—"a memory bench" is what he called it—for their fortieth anniversary. When Old Mr. B died two years ago, at the start of my tenth-grade year, Old Mrs. B sat on that bench every day for a year. She said that it made her feel closer to him.

Right now Old Mrs. B sets a mason jar in front of me. "What does it mean?" I ask, after my second long swig.

"What?" She tips the pitcher of tea into the jar again,

and the amber liquid rises above the ice cubes once more.

"That saying?" I struggle to remember the exact quote Mr. B had engraved on the wood. If Sally were here, she'd recite that quote word by word—a photographic memory suddenly called to duty. "'Love is a flower and friendship a tree?' Something like that."

"Oh." Old Mrs. B smiles. "That."

"Yeah." I place my wet fingertips to my temples. "That."

"The quote is 'Love is flower-like; friendship is like a sheltering tree.' Well . . ." She grabs a glass from the shelf, fills it to the top, and takes a sip. "I suppose that it could mean a variety of things. You want me to tell you what it means to me?"

I rest my elbows on the countertop and give her a nod. She takes another sip before saying, "Okay, well . . . 'love is flower-like'—that's the first part, right? So I take that to mean that love possesses the qualities of a flower—beautiful, fragrant, intoxicating at full bloom, but not constant."

"A flower that blooms but then wilts?"

"Exactly. That's the natural cycle of a flower's life. If you're patient with the plant . . . if you take care of it even out of bloom . . . you'll see flowers again. But you'll also come to realize that there's an ebb and flow to the plant's beauty. That, in my experience, is a lot how love feels."

"Ebb and flow?" I repeat, trying to visualize this cycle like there's a concrete place where love's ebb and flow lives. A place somewhere that has dirt and the sprouting bud of first love. And we'll say that bud is tender, a fragile little thing that might make it, with protection, with time. When that bud becomes bold, thick, sturdy, it pushes its way into the world, knowing how to lean into the wind's currents, instead of fight them. Knowing how to dance with the rain, instead of drown, to see the sun as a cure for hunger. It seems an impossible feat.

I smile. "It's kind of a miracle, huh? When a plant flowers."

"I'd like to think so."

"I wonder how many almost-flowers there are."

She laughs. "Probably a number near the amount of almost lovers. Things have an amazing ability to not stick."

"Yeah," I say, thinking if Diego were here, he'd snap his fingers together and say, "Bro, mind blown." A pantomime of a bomb blowing up over his brain. But I just grin stupidly.

"So what about the part that has the tree?"

"Oh, that part? 'Friendship is like a sheltering tree.'" Old Mrs. B shakes her head, and little crinkles of amusement wave out from the corners of her eyes. "That's what keeps love together. If your love is protected by a true friendship, then in the worst of times, the times when the wind kicks up, the rain pelts sideways, the flower or the plant that will one day carry the flower, will keep because the tree will shelter it through the storm. The flower can bloom and wilt and bloom again *because* of the tree."

"Because of the tree?" I repeat.

"Yes." She smiles, but her eyes are knowing. "So why the questions?"

"Huh?"

She gives me a searching look. "Why are you so interested in this quote now? It's been there, on that bench, for years."

I shake my head. "I don't know. It caught my eye."

"Today of all days? Prom day?"

"Prom day."

"Still taking Erika?"

"Yep." I cough. "Why?"

"Curious," she says, and sets the tea back in the fridge. "How about Sally?"

"How about her?"

Old Mrs. B shrugs, like this is a question she'll let linger. "It's a good day for a dance," she says, looking at the azure sky outside.

"It is." I down the last of my tea and set the jar in the sink. Then I take a few steps out of the kitchen. Thankfully, there's a buzz in my pocket, an indication that it's finally time to get ready. "I have to go. It's time now, I guess."

I glance back at the tree, stuck again by the miracle of it. So much so that I walk back to Old Mrs. B, wrapping my arm around her waist to pull her gently into a bear hug.

It's really an impulsive moment for me, but it feels right.

She chuckles. "What's that for?"

"I don't know," I say, but then I feel that I do. "Because you're part of the miracle."

She squeezes me tightly, "And so, dear Marco, are you."

"So this is prom," Diego says the minute we step into the hotel's ballroom.

The tribe pauses to look around at the gleaming chandeliers that hang from the high ceilings, twinkling above us like stars in the night.

"It's *all right*," Diego says, and Jade laughs.

"It's more than that," she says. "It's beautiful."

And there is something beautiful about the spaciousness that comes with the room and all that light reflecting off particles of glass and silver, not just on the chandeliers but on the tables, on the necks of the girls, on the reflective material of their dresses. And look at all the dudes, polished up in sharp suits and shiny leather kicks. Erika squeezes my hand, and I squeeze back, caught up, too, in all this magic. Because I've given myself a free pass. A pass that says I don't have to have all the answers. I only need to be here, in this now. And tomorrow I'll start again, look at all the questions that still need answers. But for tonight I'm gonna be a kid. Just for one last night.

"Where'd Sookie go to?" Jade asks, looking back.

"She said she had to meet someone real quick," Erika replies.

"Who?" Diego asks, and does a head count. "We're all here."

"Let's snag a table, and I'll text her," Jade says. "But where?" She scans the tables. All of them are filling up quickly.

"I got this," Diego says, and beelines for a table in the center of everything.

"What?" he says, when we bring up the rear. He nods to Jade and then taps a palm to his chest. "I'm not hiding all this brilliance in a corner."

Jade blushes and wraps her arm around his neck. She plants a kiss on his lips, quick though, because as she said earlier, "I'm still scarred by that damn Care Bear test in middle school."

We sit, filling up only half the table. A few minutes later Sookie shows up with a guy, who smiles broadly. "So, you guys know Ari!" Sookie announces brightly.

Jade leans in to whisper, "She did not mention this to me last night!"

Sookie sighs, reading Jade's mind or her lips. "We just decided to come together last night. I don't have to tell you guys everything."

"Nope, you don't, Sooks!" Diego agrees. "But damn if you always do."

"Hey!" Sookie says, and glances shyly at Ari. "I don't tell them *everything*."

"Sooks, you so chatty, I know if you're backed u—"

"Backed?" Ari says, smiling like he's confused.

"*Diego!*" Sookie hisses.

"Just saying. Prunes. That's all it takes. A handful a day."

Jade busts out laughing, and Erika covers her mouth and lets out one long snort.

Sookie narrows her eyes and turns to Ari. "Want to get a drink?"

"Sure," Ari says, all grins.

"What?" Diego asks when Sookie leaves. "I'm like her big bro. It's my job to embarrass her." He claps his hands together. "But, man, I like that kid Ari. Who says you can't give someone another shot?"

I glance at Erika; her smile has slipped. I remember the last time we talked about Ari and second chances. This time I squeeze her hand, but she doesn't squeeze back.

Diego points to two extra chairs at our table. "Better move 'em or we gonna have some randos tryin' to sit with us, and we'll have to be all, *You can't touch this.*"

Jade laughs. "Hey! Stragglers need friends too."

"Girl. *You. Can't. Touch. This.*" He scans the crowd, looking for a taker. "Lil," he calls out. "Do you need a chair?"

"Yeah, thanks!" she says, and carts it off.

Another kid approaches for the last chair, but Sookie returns with a soda in one hand and Ari's palm in the other, and says, "Sorry, Kendrick. We need that."

"For who?" Erika asks.

"Sally," Sookie says brightly. "I told her she should sit with us."

"She's coming?" Erika glances at me accusingly.

"I thought she wasn't sure?" Jade looks at me. "We hung out with her last night. She wanted to talk about . . . stuff. You know, catch up on all that we missed . . . when she was . . . away."

Erika's lips press flat now. "When she ghosted?"

"You don't know the story," Sookie pushes back.

"But that's it. It *is* a story," Erika retorts, and Sookie narrows her eyes.

"Dude," Diego says to Erika. "Lay off Sooks."

"I'm just saying—"

"Sals is sitting with us," Diego snaps. "Drop it already."

Erika gives me a look like, *Aren't you going to defend me?* When I don't, because I think Sookie is right, she takes out her phone and starts texting.

A few *ping*s later, she announces, "Gabby *and* Manny are on the other side. I'm gonna sit with them for a bit."

"A bit?" I say.

"Yep, a bit." Her voice is cold.

"Just let her go," Diego says, when I make like I'm gonna follow. "That girl is the definition of FOMO-OM."

"FOMO-*OM*?" Jade repeats, the last syllable stressed like a Buddhist chant.

"Yeah, fear of missing out on Marco."

The whole table laughs, Diego the hardest. "And is she still trying to make you jealous with that Manny shiz?"

"D, drop it."

"What? It's true. She's like . . ." He pauses, his mouth falling open.

I twist in my seat to see what he sees: Sally, cutting across the dance floor. No, make that striding. She wears an emerald-green dress that catches every bit of light as she passes beneath the chandeliers. Her hair, back to its original blond, seems to catch the light too.

"Damn," Diego says, and Jade nudges him with her elbow, but then she also adds, "She does look good."

Sookie smiles. "I sent her the link to that dress and helped her dye her hair."

"Well, babe," says Ari, "you've got great taste in dresses."

"Did he just call Sooks 'babe'?" Diego whispers.

Sookie stands, glaring at Diego. "You act like I'm asexual or something."

Diego shrugs. "I don't even know what that is."

And then Sally is upon us. She smiles brightly. "Asexual is when someone lacks sexual desire or attraction. And that"—she looks at Sookie—"would be the opposite of you."

"Look at Sals, coming up here all savage," Diego says admiringly.

"If you're lucky," Sally says brightly, "I might even interpret some dreams for you later."

"*Guess who's back, back again . . .* ," Diego sings.

"You look gorgeous," Sookie says.

"Yeah," Jade agrees.

And it's true. Sally does look beautiful.

Sally, who, for what it's worth, maybe still loves me.

Sally smiles her way around the table. When our eyes

meet, her gaze lingers for a second, and then she sits in the empty chair between Sookie and Jade.

"Did they serve dinner yet?" Sally asks.

"Nope," Sookie says.

"Wait. All this fancy comes with a dinner, too?" Diego asks.

"See?" Jade says. "Every time you wouldn't come to a dance with me, see what you were missing?"

"Girl, all you had to do was tell me about the meal." Diego nods to someone coming up behind me. I turn around to see Erika headed our way. Her eyes are on mine. She's got a fake smile on her lips.

"Hey," she says when she takes the seat beside me. "What I'd miss?"

"Not much."

"Hi," Sally says, and Erika gives her a stiff nod. Diego rolls his eyes.

A second later the waiters appear, setting down muffins and warm bread and pouring water into our glasses. "Warm muffins too! Man, today is like some fairy tale," Diego says. "This and Grendel's."

"Wait!" Sookie claps her hands together. "Did you get the job?"

"Oh, yes, he did!" Jade says. "And they're giving him a scholarship to go to college!"

Sookie looks at me, her eyes wide with concern. "Are you bummed out, Marco? About not getting it?"

Erika's butter knife falls with a *clang* against her plate. "What?"

I glance at her—that familiar disappointment in her eyes. "Mr. Grendel asked me again to interview for it."

"And you did?"

"Yeah, but not because I wanted it. Because it was the only way he'd give me a raise. . . ."

"And," Diego says, "Mr. Grendel also gave Marco a five-thousand-dollar scholarship for cost of living and stuff. He just has to work every summer and long break at the store."

"Oh, that's awesome—" Sookie begins, but Erika cuts her off with, "Every summer and long break?"

"That's really cool, right?" Jade says, trying to silver-line the exchange. "Summer job security?"

"And you said yes?" Erika says. "You didn't even talk to me."

Diego sighs. "Seriously?"

"Diego," Erika snaps. "Can you just not?"

"Can he just not what?" Jade hisses.

Sookie says, "Can we *all* not?"

"It's her," Jade protests. "With the texting and the faces and the drama."

"But why didn't you tell me?" Erika pushes, ignoring everyone but me.

"Maybe," says Sally slowly, "he didn't want to."

Erika freezes. A silence falls across the table. Erika looks at Sally, then me. "Did you tell her?"

"No. I didn't." I take a deep breath and whisper, "Can we just make it through tonight without fighting?" But Erika doesn't answer. She keeps her eyes on her hands, balled up in her lap. I look around the table. "Can we be done with this?"

"Done," Diego says.

Waiters in white suits appear. Diego lifts his fork and knife in anticipation. "Whatever you don't want, I call first dibs."

We all laugh, grateful to move on.

Well, everyone except Erika, who only lifts her eyes. She doesn't speak again until twenty minutes later, when Sookie raises her water glass to toast "endings and beginnings."

"To endings and beginnings," we all say, even Erika, her voice a little sad.

A few hours later, after a series of whispered negotiations and apologies, Erika and I are on the dance floor, swaying our bodies to a slow song. She's got her head on my shoulder when she says, "Do you remember how I asked you to the eighth-grade dance?"

"Yeah?" I take a deep breath, afraid of where this is going.

"Well, you liked Sally back then, remember? Not me." She pauses. "What do you think would have happened if Sally hadn't left? If your dad hadn't gone to the hospital?"

"How can anyone know?" I ask quietly.

"Maybe we wouldn't have happened," Erika says.

I think about back then, how Erika had stopped by my house about a week after we ran into each other at the hospital. She said it was to bring me an extra casserole that had been left over from her grandma's memorial service. She came by several more times after that. Always showing up unannounced, always bringing a little something for the family to eat. Always asking about my dad, picking on my brothers, mostly because she knew that made me laugh. That was the start of our friendship.

And I know that we aren't perfect. But we've been there for each other. Maybe that's why I whisper into her ear, "Erika, no matter what, I'm glad we're here together."

She pulls back to look into my eyes. "No matter what?"

And I realize what I've said. How it sounds. "I just mean, I know that it's been hard lately for us. But you've been important to me. . . ."

"Been important?"

"*Are* important."

"Or maybe it really is *been*?" She swallows hard. "I can't take this. It's like you don't know about us, and your not knowing makes me not know." She looks out to the dance floor, almost like she's talking to herself. "What do you want, Marco?"

I take her by the elbow and lead her to a balcony outside.

It's not too crowded, and I'm able to find a semi-private spot before she starts up again.

"Marco, every decision I've made for my future is wrapped around you, and every decision you're making is wrapped around your family or your friends or . . . Sally."

I look away toward the garden—a couple is walking down there, and I see that it's Jade and Diego. He's got one arm around her shoulders, and the other arm is crossed over his waist so that he can reach for her hand. And that's who they are, always reaching for each other. They don't want to keep their hands or options free. They see thresholds and cross them together. Me? I'm the guy who ran from the Pinterest board.

It's that simple.

"What do you want?" Erika asks again, swiping at her tears, and I know it's time to come clean—to her, to myself.

I take a deep, unsteady breath. "That day you made me grilled cheese. I saw it, your board."

"What board?"

"Your wedding board . . . on Pinterest."

She looks at the garden, her eyes landing on Jade and Diego, and her voice is wobbly when she speaks. "And so what?"

"I ran."

"You did what?" She turns to me, eyes wide.

"I ran."

"Why?"

"Because I don't want that."

"It's just a board, Marco, a future dream. It's not now."

"I know, but I don't want that . . ." I take another unsteady breath, because this next part is hard. "With you. I don't ever want that with you."

Her face falls, and for a second she looks too stunned to speak. But when she does, she asks, "And Sally?"

I gulp. "This isn't about Sally."

"But you want to find out?"

"I don't know."

She nods, her eyes on the floor. "I'm gonna go."

"Where?"

"Does it matter?" she asks, finally meeting my gaze. And I see there, in her eyes, that we're done. I'm surprised by how that feels. The heaviness in my chest that explodes the minute she walks away, leaving me with an ache that spans the last four years—an ache that is partially filled with sadness, partially filled with relief.

And I realize that even when your love for someone isn't enough—even then—the breaking can hurt.

It can hurt like hell.

The week before graduation, I drop by Mrs. A's office to turn in my final project. It's a week late, but that won't affect my grade thanks to an extension Mrs. A gave me after Sookie told her about Pop. I can't say the project is worth the wait, but it's complete, and as Diego keeps telling me, "You make the best choices you can and let the rest flow."

Which means try your hardest.

And I have tried on this project.

And I have tried in this life too.

The rest would have to flow.

I find Mrs. A sorting through papers, separating the sheets into three stacks: wobbly, not so wobbly, and overflowing.

She offers me her own wobbly smile when I walk through the door. "Done?" she asks.

"Done."

"So what did you come up with?" She perches on the edge of her desk.

"A list?"

"Just a list."

"Something to think about?"

The smile grows. "Better," she says. "Better."

I hand her the portfolio: a formal paper on wormholes, a top ten list, and—

"Your notes!" she exclaims. Her eyes grow wide. "I'm honored."

I glance down at the ground, embarrassed. "I . . ."

"I know," she says. "We're human. We're made to share our lives, our worries." She pats me warmly on the shoulder. "Seriously, I'm honored." She peers out of the open door. "Your people?" she says with a smile.

I glance down the hall to Jade, Diego, Sookie, and Sally, waiting near the lockers.

Sally.

Sally, who Diego said I had to make things "100 percent right with."

"Because she's back in with the tribe?" I joked a week after prom. We sat on the stoop of my house, rummaging through a box of Pop's old mixtapes—companions to his boom box.

"Bro, the girls had a sleepover yesterday. So yeah, she's back in. And you know what?" Diego said. "Sals is good people."

Good people.

Later that night, I thought about how Sally's return had sent me down that wormhole into the past.

Before Pop's injury.

Before she disappeared.

Back when the world was still open.

I wanted the world to be open again, and I had Sally to thank for that.

The next day I took Diego's advice and went to her house. I found her sitting in the yard—hair down, feet bare—petting that birthday kitten. She didn't look surprised to see me. It was like she knew I had something to say. Or that the only way for us to move forward was if I got us there. So I took a deep breath and began with, "I thought about what you said. . . ."

She smiled slowly. "I've said a lot."

"Yeah." I chuckled. "You did. And . . . I accept it."

"Okay . . ." Her forehead wrinkled. "What does that mean, accept?"

I had practiced this speech before coming over, but standing in her yard, heart pounding, the words became stuck. All I could do was look around, remembering that day that I found her sitting outside, staring at the For Rent sign. She was so young back then. I was so young. I'd have given anything for her to stay, and now that she was back, I only had to offer up my understanding to have her close again.

I pushed the words out. "I . . . accept . . . that it's possible to do something and not know why. That parts of our lives get hazy. That sometimes survival mode is the only available mode. I get that because . . . because I feel like a part of me's been doing that too, for years, because of Pop. . . . And I didn't always get it right either. I got a lot of it wrong—*a lot.*"

"Me too," she whispered. "But I never meant to hurt you."

"I know that," I said after a pause. "I know that we were both just trying to make it through. I guess I had a lot more help though. . . ."

"It's okay." She smiled tentatively. "I have more help now too."

So, yeah, Sally was back. We all were, that slow

merging of who we used to be with who we've become. And all this on the eve of graduation.

Diego waves his arms wildly, like, *Are you coming already?* Mrs. A laughs, waves back. "Your people," she says again.

"My people," I agree. *"My tribe."*

Senior Year

34. GRADUATION DAY

THE BOTTLE SPINS AROUND AND AROUND, a lazy circle that arcs past Diego, Jade, Sally, and Sookie and lands, crookedly, on me. I sit cross-legged on the itchy grass, the crunchy, hardy kind that Floridians know about—and feel that somewhere beneath my blue-and-gold robe, a fire ant roams. I stand, shake the gown out, and send the ant tumbling back onto the grass. Then I toss my cap to the side, and it lands next to "home base," a lean palm tree where the rest of the tribe's caps lay.

All except for Jade's. "You think I put this much hair spray on to have my look ruined?" She had cried earlier when we'd arrived at the park just after dark, lugging our picnic gear: an assortment of eats from the prepared-foods section of Grendel's; a bottle of Boone's Strawberry Hill Wine, fittingly procured by Sally's brother, Boone; an abused but loved football that belongs to Diego; and a collection of assorted glow sticks.

The glow sticks are Sally's idea—*Remember how obsessed we*

used to be with them?—and right now she is bending them in half so that they crackle and light up like mini–light sabers. She tosses a red one to Jade, a green one to Diego, a blue one to Sookie, and a purple one to me. She crowns herself with the white one and asks, "Are we playing or what?"

I nod, slide the purple glow stick around my neck, and begin to count. I press my face into my hands and lean my weight onto the palm tree. It's a perfectly legit posture, but I hear Jade yell out, "No peeking," and Sally adding, "For real, Marco," and Diego shouting in too, "Remember how he was always cheating and shit when we was little?"

Little.

Much earlier that day, at graduation, Erika had said something to me that was very similar. It was after the ceremony, when all the families were roaming about, and some students were saying good-byes like we'd never see one another again. That's when we found one another. It was somewhere near the fountain at the center of Seagrove Park, a really ornate fountain of a manatee, launching into the air, water shooting out of its mouth. It was a strange fountain, and throughout our nearly four years of friendship, Erika and I had come here to stare at it in wonder, to laugh at it in amusement, and sometimes just to sit with it. I don't know why except to say that we both found something comforting about that damn fountain, especially in the days after Erika's grandmother's death and my father's fall. Maybe because Erika first started coming to the fountain with her grandmother when she was a little girl. And when I was little Pop would bring me there too.

So it made sense that we saw each other there. Maybe I came there to find her. Maybe, she came to find me too.

All I know is that we met at the edge of that fountain and sat on the concrete barrier, staring out at our classmates and their parents taking pictures and laughing.

"It was a nice graduation," Erika said.

"Did you cry?" I asked. Erika had always said she would cry at our graduation.

"Naw," she said, but when I snuck a peek at her, I saw that her mascara was smudged beneath her eyes. I reached out to tap that space—the evidence—with my pinkie, and she flinched, and then I remembered that we couldn't do that anymore. That our bodies didn't really belong to each other like that. And while that felt right, it also hurt a tiny bit.

I guess for Erika that was the case too, because she was silent for a few minutes, and then she said, "Just a little. You?"

I laughed lightly. "Nope, but I felt it." I tapped the center of my chest. "I felt it here." And I was still feeling it—my chest was all tight and my arms all tingly. The graduation and everything that was happening, even standing there with Erika, felt surreal.

She nodded, her eyes watching the crowd. "I'm not going to California. I'm going to FSU. I was able to fix it."

"How?"

She smiled sadly and swung her eyes back toward me. "A miracle."

It was my turn to nod. "You deserve a miracle."

"Don't I?" she said, cocking an eyebrow. "You? You going to Wayne?"

"I am," I said. "But not right away." I decided to defer a year from Wayne. That would be enough time for Pop to finish rehab, for me to work full-time and save money, and to keep cracking the whip over my brothers while handing off the torch to Diego, who promised to fill in the gap once I left. My parents were conflicted about my change of plans, but in the end they understood my decision.

Mom said, "Marco, that was almost everything you had—your college savings. And you gave it to us?" And then she cried for a bit.

Pop said, "I'm . . . I'm glad to have more time . . . but don't tell . . . don't tell Mom . . . I said that."

My brothers said, "Wait! We have to keep sharing a room?"

Old Mrs. B said, "'Do your little bit of good where you are; it's those little bits of good put together that overwhelm the world.' That's what Desmond Tutu would say about this, and who am I to disagree?"

And right there at the fountain, Erika didn't say anything about my staying for that gap year other than this: "Next year will be my first year without you in a long time." She paused and sucked in her breath. "I don't want to stop knowing you. I've known you ever since we were little, and I want to know you even when we're as old as Old Mrs. B."

She was about three feet from me, her pale arms sticking out of her royal-blue gown, her fingers tapping silently on the concrete. I scooted closer, and for the first time in two weeks, I let my hand slip into hers, and she held it there. We didn't look at each other. I think we knew that we couldn't. But I said to her what was true. I said, "I don't want to stop knowing you either."

We were talking about life, that long road ahead—a road on which we were only reaching the end of the beginning. That thought hit me hard in the chest, with that same sentimentality that permeated my father and my father's father before him and so on until time began. But you know what? I didn't mind. Sentimentality makes the world livable. Maybe it's sentimentality that made me decide to stay in Seagrove for one more year, to not go away to college yet, to take some extra time to be with my family and my closest friends. Maybe we're not all meant to leave behind the people we love but to cling to them with both hands. I knew in that moment I couldn't leave Erika behind either. Same as I knew in this moment of pressing my face into my hands at the bark of that tree that I would never leave behind Sookie or Diego or Jade or even Sally.

"Ready or not," I shout, having reached the magical number, thirty. "Here I come." I spin around, scanning the horizon. It's dark now. But the overhead lights that dot the park make it somewhat visible. Still, I don't see any of the tribe—not behind the big tree that we circled endlessly as kids, or on the slide where Jade once snagged her finger so hard it bled for nearly an hour, or over by the swings where me and Diego would pump our legs until we reached the very top, shouting: "Jump! No, *you* jump."

At the edge of the park, I check behind the one-room wooden cabin where Sally and I used to tell each other our deepest secrets and then to the edge of the parking lot, where Sookie learned how to ride a skateboard. There I hear a giggle that is the length of a hiccup—definitely a Jade giggle. I spin around to find her frozen beneath a streetlight. A wicked smile steals across her face, and the giggle expands into laughter. She runs for home base, already so close that she beats me there by several legs.

"Ha!" she shouts, hands on the bark. There is a rustle behind me. I spin around to see Sookie off to my far right, looping her way around the cabin. I decide to wait her out.

"You can't stay at base for longer than thirty seconds," Sookie shouts. "You know the rules."

Rules we developed when we were, like eight, but still I count aloud to thirty, my eyes fixed on Sookie.

"Oh, that's how it's going down?"

"Yeah, Sookie, that's how it's going down."

"Then eat my . . . " She spins her legs like the Road Runner from *Loony Toons*, feet kicking up dust as she dashes off.

It's hard to stop laughing long enough to chase her. Two seconds in, I see Diego to my right, and then Sally somewhere behind him. We run, a nonsensical path past swings and cabin and parking lot and rope tower, and when all is done, I've missed each of them by fractions of a yard.

"That was ridiculous," Sally huffs, one hand on her knee while the other grips the base.

"Bro, that was awesome!" Diego hops in the air and gives Jade a chest bump. She stumbles backward. "Stop, Sookie, or I'm going to pee my pants!" She wipes tears from her eyes. "Where did you learn to do that?"

"What? The Road Runner?" Sookie winks, and finally stops her spinning. "I got jokes . . ."

"You've got insanity," Jade says.

"I've got the spins," Sookie retorts, and grabs for Jade's hand.

"No, seriously, I have a cramp!"

"Don't share 'cause I don't care." Sookie links her hands tightly with Jade's, and this begins the pinwheel: Jade links on to Diego and Diego links on to Sally, who links onto me, until we are all spinning.

And then we are falling—down, down to the ground—a tangled mess of legs and arms and hearts beating wildly against one another's bodies.

And I think that finding *this*—this tribe—is one of the great miracles of my life.

And I think about Sally, about her still, maybe, loving me.

Ten minutes later, we're lying on our backs staring up at the night sky. The giggling has subsided and all seems peaceful—even here, in the center of a city, there is a quiet.

I turn my head so that my ear is pressed flat to the

ground, the grass tickling the side of my face, and I marvel at Sally—stubborn chin, serious eyes, all of her here, *beside me*.

My friend again. My friend Sally.

She catches me staring at her. "What?"

"It was a good night, right?" I ask Sally.

"Yes." She sighs and presses her hands to the center of her chest. "It was good, really good."

"The best . . . ?" I ask.

She smiles and says sleepily, "Yes . . ." And then there is a pause, and she laughs.

"What?"

"The best *yet* . . ."

"Yeah." Jade also sighs on the other side of me. "The best yet."

"The best yet!" Sookie screams, and Diego follows.

And me, I just laugh and hold tight to that promise of *yet*, as if more of this will come. As if more of this can stretch out into forever.

AN ALWAYS SPARK

THE TRUTH IS WE MIGHT NOT HAVE GOTTEN together again, but on the night of Sally's second fall, at approximately midnight, I heard a tap on my window.

She could have texted. I was up. The light was on in my bedroom. And at that point I didn't have a curfew. (We were seven months into our freshman year of college—her at UM and me at Miami Dade College, taking classes that I would later transfer to Wayne.) Finally we were no-questions-asked adults.

I didn't even slip up the blinds. I just slid on my shoes, grabbed my keys, and headed outside. She smiled when she saw me, and I lifted up my finger—made the universal sign for *shh*—and motioned toward my truck.

When we got in the truck, I said, "I thought you were at a meet in Orlando."

She said, "Yeah. We got back today, around ten."

"And now you're here," I said, smiling.

We had grown closer in the past year, nearly as close

as we had been when we were kids. The process had happened slowly—first group hangouts over the summer, but by fall we had begun texting each other directly. Little questions like, "Want to study together tonight?" Always the study sessions were somewhere public—the library, the coffee shop by UM's campus, the picnic tables outside Grendel's on one of my dinner breaks. And then last week a few things happened. It was her birthday, and I bought her a gift—a rose-gold necklace with a little mustang charm to celebrate her return to running.

"Run, Sally, run," she whispered as she dangled it in her hand.

"You remember."

She smiled and looked at me, her serious gray eyes wide.

"I'm nineteen today," she said.

"But you don't look a day over fetus."

"Ah." She laughed, then wrinkled up her nose. "That's disgusting."

"That's biology."

We were parked in her driveway. I had picked her up for her birthday dinner with Sookie, who was back in town for a long weekend, and Diego and Jade, who hosted the party at their new studio apartment—a mostly empty space with nice wood floors and plenty of natural light. "But imagine it, bro," Diego said as we settled down for a candlelit indoor picnic, "with furniture."

Jade laughed. "You mean our blow-up bed doesn't count?"

"Oh, that counts," Diego said, and winked at Jade, who rolled her eyes before smiling.

Then Sookie took a deep breath, asking, "Okay, so are we ever gonna talk about it?"

It was an e-mail Sookie had sent us earlier that semester, describing her new perspective on the word *tribe* or, more specifically, our use of the word to describe our friend group.

At Northwestern, she had enrolled in a course that explored the histories of indigenous peoples, and that had led her to dig deeper into the history of the word—from its Latin root *tribus*, describing the three ancient Roman tribes; to the history of the twelve tribes of Israel, which Sookie was more familiar with; to the devastating effects of European colonialism/imperialism on the indigenous peoples of the Americas, Africa, and beyond, and how their usage of the word downgraded independent nations to "primitive" societies; to the modern marketing of the word as a catchphrase found on T-shirts and coffee mugs across the country; to her uncle, of both Jewish and Native American ancestries, who worked for the Indian Health Services, and used the word solely to discuss issues of vital importance to the country's indigenous peoples.

"The history of the word is pretty complex," Sookie had concluded in her e-mail and again in person, to which Diego replied, "Yeah, Sooks, especially when you bring up the OPs." He paused for one dramatic beat. "Original peoples."

"I can't even with you," Jade said, sighing, and then the conversation went on. And yet for all that followed, our wanting to hold on to the word for what it had come to mean to us—a group who always stood together, who shared a unique way of being, a way of life—we knew that the word was beyond us now.

When the debate was over, Jade said, "How about we just call each other family? I mean, you guys are pretty much that to me."

"Familia," Diego said. "Hmm . . . I'd be down with that." He waved his hand through the air like a showman. "A Tribe Called Family."

Sookie groaned. "Seriously? You just twentieth-century-pop punned me?"

Diego smiled slowly before launching into a rowdy version of "Can I Kick It?" by A Tribe Called Quest, only stopping when Sookie gathered a handful of his ear-length dreads and yanked them.

"Damn, Sooks, careful. I'm growing that out." He touched his hair affectionately.

"But *seriously*, though, I get it. Your uncle is out there fighting the good fight, and you want to show respect to him and the people he's fighting for. I'm down with that." He waited, another one of his dramatic beats. "That's PCC—*people correct choices*."

Sookie laughed and all the tension broke. "So agreed? Family?"

I nodded as Sally leaned in closer. "Yeah," she said, her

pinky tapping across the floor until I found it right next to me.

"Family," I said, because the new word felt right and good, like a reflection of a truth that had already made us whole.

At the end of the night, after I had dropped Sookie off, it was just me and Sally, the motor running in my truck as I watched her unwrap the gift.

There was a card, too, but I told her to open it in her house, afterward.

"Will you put it on me?" she asked, handing me the necklace. She scooted closer, across the bench seat, and pulled her hair up so that the nape of her neck was exposed. I felt my heart shake, but my hands were surprisingly steady when I brought the clasp of the necklace together. "Thanks," she said, and she turned to look at me, our faces only a few inches apart, and then the thing happened—I kissed her.

On the cheek.

It wasn't meant to be on the lips, if you're thinking that I missed. Still, it was a pretty big deal. I had been broken up with Erika for almost a year by then, but I hadn't been out with anybody else. Erika had started dating some dude from track, but I had kept myself solo. I guess I had to fully let go of what *was* before I could see what *might be*.

But that night in my truck, after that cheek-grazing kiss—the one that made Sally laugh this little nervous laugh—I knew for certain that what I wanted was to be with Sally.

She didn't say anything, though, about that kiss. She

just slid out of the car with a wave and an odd smile. I hadn't heard from her since that night. I wasn't surprised. I knew she had a lot coming up—final projects and that last meet of the season. And even though we had started texting each other, we hadn't begun texting each other on the daily. Still, about four days into our radio silence, I cracked and did something else that was unusual: I called.

She didn't answer. I got her voice mail and left a message: "Hey, it's me. Um, calling to wish you luck . . . I mean, it's Marco . . . in case you hadn't got that or . . . anyway . . . okay . . . um, bye ."

I hadn't heard back from her until now. This knock on my window, this girl staring at me with the biggest gray eyes I've ever seen. We're in my truck, a full tank of gas, and all those hours of darkness where nothing can happen because the world is still, but everything can happen because we are not.

"Our park?" I ask, feeling that catch in my heart.

"No," she says, and looks away, almost shyly. "Beach."

We drive north on US 1, the windows rolled down, the wind rushing over our bodies. When we approach the bridge to Key Biscayne, we veer east, stopping only for me to dig enough money out to pay the toll on the Rickenbacker Causeway. And then we are across the bridge, the navy waters of Biscayne Bay to our right and the Atlantic to our left. The roads are empty this time of night, dotted occasionally with streetlights that cast pools of bright white onto the gray concrete.

"There! Go there!" Sally says about ten minutes later. "Right there."

I turn into the beach access and park the truck near the water. Sally hops out before I can even cut the engine. She's left behind her shoes. I slip off my flip-flops and follow. I find her standing at the base of the water, the tide low right now. We draw closer so that the water slips over our feet and then away again.

"I'm not like him," Sally announces.

"Who?" I ask, confused. We hadn't spoken on the drive over, and I didn't know what she meant. I didn't even know why she had come to see me. But I look at her now and see that on her leg is a scrape. "You hurt yourself?"

"I fell," she says.

"Competing?"

"Yep, right there on the track, second time in my life."

"How?" I step toward her, but she steps back. I wait to see what comes next. For a long time she stares at the water, chewing on her lip.

"I couldn't get my head straight for it, for my part of the meet. I was distracted. I was tense. I tried to come in from lane five and I must have—I don't know. Honestly, it's a blur, and I fell. I nearly took out the girl in lane three. It was bad."

"Why couldn't you get your head straight?"

She nods, thoughtful. "My dad came to see me run, in Orlando."

"He came all the way here?"

"It's not that far of a flight from North Carolina, I guess." She shrugs and glances at me with eyes full of hurt. "He brought his new *wife*."

"They got married?"

"Yep. And she thought he should come out and see me run. He follows my career online, knows all about it. He's sorry he put so much pressure on me before. He's glad I'm running again. He's getting help. He's more balanced now."

"He told you that."

"His wife told me that, when he went to the restroom. We went for dinner the first night I was in town."

"Why'd you go to dinner?"

"I was so surprised to see them that when they asked, I said yes. . . ."

"It's okay to love him."

"I know. He's my dad."

"But you're mad?"

"I'm heartbroken, I think, not mad."

"Heartbroken?"

"That she—this new wife—gets the person that I never knew. Like, if they have kids, those kids will get the dad I never knew too."

"You planning on not knowing him anymore?"

She looks at me, surprised. "Why would you ask that?"

"Well, you act like he's gone, but he's not. Maybe you lost time with him, but you've also got more time. You could make new memories. You guys could become something new together." My voice dips. "That happens all the time, you know."

"Like with you and your pop?"

"Yeah. I mean, we had to redefine who we were to each other, and that redefinition didn't happen at once. It happened again as he recovered and then again with this last setback. I think it's something that will happen repeatedly over our lives together. Don't you think?"

"Kind of like us?" she asks.

And this time I don't say anything, but she knows the answer.

"After this fall, I remembered the first time I fell. Do you remember?"

"Yeah, you came to my house."

"At night."

"And we talked at the park."

"About my dad. You were the first person that I ever really told about how hard it was for me. And you made me laugh. You made me feel better."

"I wasn't sure about that at the time."

"You did," she says, sincerely. "You know, I've always secretly been afraid of being like him. Like one day a switch will come on, and I'll be unpredictable and moody and unkind. That was part of it, that year that I went inside myself. But you know what I realized? I realized that if I keep people away to protect them from me, I *will* be like him. And I don't want to be like him. I want to let people in. I *can* let people. . . ." She pauses, chews on her lips, looking at me with woeful eyes. "I can let people in. I can . . ."

"You came back here to let us in," I point out.

"Yeah," she says. "I did, but there's still so much more to say that I haven't."

I step forward, the wet sand grainy between my toes. I touch her shoulder, and she turns her gaze to my hand. "You okay?" I ask, because she's shaking.

"No. I'm petrified, but it's, like, a good thing because I'm trying to get the courage to say something."

"Okay," I say, my body tense. Because I could tell her, too, that I've been trying to get my courage up for weeks, maybe even months. And right now, on this beach with her—her hair tossed up into a sloppy ponytail, the wind whipping strands of curls around her beautiful face—it's hard not to blurt out everything I know to be true about us.

That I think about her more than I should.

That when funny things happen to me during my day, I want to tell her.

That I have conversations with her when she's not even around.

That I've been doing that since the time I was, I don't know . . . forever. That I never stopped doing that even when she was gone.

That when she's like this—open and vulnerable and afraid—some part of me wants nothing more than to take care of her, even though I know she can take care of herself.

That when she does something as simple as hold my stare, it's hard not to blurt out—

"I love you still," she says. "Even more than that day at the park, last year."

She lays her hand atop of mine, the both of us cupping her shoulder. She steps forward so we're toe to toe and a couple inches shy of being eye to eye. She says, "I seem to love you always, Marco Suarez."

When she steps back, I gape at her, my hand falling to my side. Maybe I say nothing for too long because she adds, "You don't have to say it back right now . . . Or you could say it whenever you feel comfortable . . . I can wait . . . or . . ." Her hand moves to the charm on her necklace, the rose-gold mustang. "Or . . ."

"Or . . ." I step forward until my mouth is pressed against her ear. "I could tell you that I love you, too, Sally Blake." I wrap her in my arms and hold her to me. She holds me back.

"Always?" she says.

"Always."

An hour later we're standing at the edge of the ocean, barely talking. My arm is around her waist, and she's holding that same hand. With her free hand she takes my free hand so that we're squeezed together like a pretzel. She says, "When we were little, Sookie was convinced that the ocean was God. Did you know that?"

"What?" I laugh, sneaking a sidelong glance at her. Her

lips have caught that smile again. That same goofy smile she got when I said that I loved her too. I loved her always.

"I don't know. Why not? We're filled with water and so is the world. It's the one thing that separates life from death. There's a nice symmetry there. And there's parts of it that we'll never fully explore. No water, no life."

"You mean, not like we know it," I clarify.

"I guess, but I like the idea that instead of looking up for God, we could find him—"

"Or her."

"Or neither a him or a her," she says with a smile, "right here." It's Sally's turn to give the me that sidelong stare. "How do you feel when you stand here, in front of the ocean? Tell me you don't feel something inexplicable. . . ." She turns to me, runs her hand over my cheek. Goose bumps spread across my flesh. "Really look," she says, and I do.

I stare at the ocean, the dark, endless water, relatively motionless at night but beneath, another world of color and sound and life. A complete mystery to me, but whenever I'm close to it, I still feel . . . "Whole."

She nods. "Me too. Like there's this stillness inside me . . . and that stillness makes me feel . . ."

"Like anything is possible . . ."

"Yeah," she says, and then there's that goofy smile again.

"What?"

She looks at the ocean, then me. "It's how I feel when I'm with you."

"Me too." I bring her hand to my lips and give it a gentle kiss. Then I trace the lines of her palm, diverting from the path to follow a pale-blue vein that runs the length of her forearm—up, up, up—past her shoulder and across her neck until the path ends at her lips.

Her lips. Pink and scooting closer. The promise of softness.

And then we're kissing, her hands in my hair, her hips pressed to my hips. We sink lower and lower into the mystery until we're wrapped around each other and all I can taste is the salt of the ocean and Sally.

EPILOGUE

WHEN GRENDEL'S OPENED THEIR COFFEE bar several years later, I was offered the cushy job of co-managing the kiosk every summer with none other than Alex, who had finally gotten decent at twentieth-century pop song. Unlike the larger store, the bakery-adjacent café has limited hours throughout the week—seven a.m. to seven p.m. So I can take on three twelve-hours shifts and one short Sunday shift each week and still have three days off, the days I primarily spend with Sally.

Then, when we have a lull here, which we do nearly every afternoon between eleven and two, I'm free to do research at one of the bistro tables. I'm taking such a break this very Sunday when I see Marta—yes, Marta of all those long, circuitous stories. Marta, who has kind of been the coauthor of my circuitous autobiography. She is coming down aisle nine, chatting away into a Bluetooth hooked over her ear. Her mouth opens wide, and she bursts out laughing—one hand pushing the cart, the other holding on to a cereal box.

I lean forward to read the brand name, because really, what kind of cereal does a chatterbox like Marta eat?

Cheerios. Just good old-fashioned Cheerios.

And you know what? It's good old-fashioned Marta too. Her hair still zigzags all the way down her body until it settles somewhere at the curve of her back, and her fingernails are still long and painted a neon yellow that can be seen all the way over here. Maybe she's an inch taller and ten pounds lighter; with the baby fat missing from her face, she looks more womanly with her curves. But even so, it's still good old-fashioned Marta.

"Marta?" I call out in a loud whisper.

She glances around but doesn't recognize me sitting at the bistro table about ten feet to her left, so her eyes roam past me. I stand and say again, "Hey, Marta." This time when our eyes meet, I imagine what she sees—not the scrawny preteen she once knew or the taller, more muscular teen she never knew. But me, this adult version of me, with a full-out beard (unnecessary in south Florida, but hey, I can finally grow one!), a tiny bit of a love belly, and that ten inches of height I had gained since the last time I saw her. I am twenty-one now, soon to be a graduate of Wayne University, and if all goes as planned, I'll join Sally at the University of Miami this fall. She'll get her master's in library science, and I'll work my way toward a PhD, studying what I've always loved, the cosmos.

Marta steps closer, her cart pushing against the courtesy rope that separates the café from the rest of Grendel's. "Do I know you?"

"Well, do you? I don't know. I guess to get to the answer, let me take you back about to that time when I was seven and first saw a blowfish on a trip to the Miami Seaquarium and this little curly haired girl wouldn't stop telling me about the first time she saw a blowfish. . . ."

And then she smiles—ear to ear, forehead to chin.

"Marco?! Wow!" She laughs. *"Mami!"* Her gaze dips to the right as she speaks into her phone. "You'll never believe who I just ran into! No, no, it's Marco. Marco Suarez! From Seagrove Elementary! Yeah, *yeah*. Okay, I'll call you back." Her Bluetooth dims, and she flicks her wrist, sending her Cheerios sailing into her cart. Then she barrels over to me, wrapping me in the biggest bear hug I'd experienced since . . . well, since the last time I saw her, at the end of sixth grade, before she moved a little north to Broward County and I stayed exactly where I've always stayed until I finally went off to Wayne. This time when we hug, though, I don't leave the ground; she does. I make sure of that.

"I can't believe it's you," she says.

"I can't believe it's you either. You look exactly the same."

"And you look completely different. You're . . ."

"Grown?"

"Tall."

"Distinguished?"

"Hairy."

"Intelligent around the eyes?"

"Okay, *that* I'll give you. . . ." She laughs again. "But, man, you look like your dad, now that I think about it." She sighs, and it's like it always is when I see someone for the first time after my dad got hurt. There are the questions, which I'm okay with now. The thing with my dad is like my mom always says, *It is what it is.*

"I heard about him," Marta continues. "About what happened with Jade's dad and . . . I know that was a while back, but how is he? How is everyone—your whole family?"

"Pop's better. It's been a while, you know? Time and therapy have really helped. Now that old dude is auditing college classes at Miami Dade, like some young buck. Can you believe it? And he's doing some writing in a journal, which he won't let us read—a very productive retirement since he doesn't work anymore. Twins are about to graduate, which is a miracle, and Mom's still sewing, but she does it from home now, branched out on her own a few years ago, if you've got some sewing jobs that need done."

I never miss a chance to promote Mom's business. Her being able to work from home was the best thing that ever happened to us, and believe it or not, it was Diego's idea. "Bro, we got like one hundred and twenty-five employees in this store, and they got families, and their families got families. We spread the word that your moms has the best hands this side of Bird Avenue and you'll see what's what!"

Diego even set my mom up with a social media presence and her own Etsy store, where she sells her original creations. Turns out Diego has a head for business and Mr. Grendel made the right choice sending him to business school. Since Diego took over as assistant manager of the entire store last year, sales and customer satisfaction ratings are up. And this café, the café that only breaks even in sales but brings in more shoppers, was also his idea.

"Of course," Marta says. "I have, like, ten little cousins about to have their *quinceañeras*. But what about you? I thought . . . Boy . . ." She laughs, the edge of her voice spinning upward. "I thought you'd be out of here."

"Well, I am, sorta. I go to school in California." And because I know Marta loves a good story, I say, "Actually, I was supposed to go with Erika Richards? She was my girl for a while."

"Erika?" Marta pauses for a few seconds. "Hmm . . . Ran track, right?" Her eyes pop wide. "*Oh*, she's the one who spit in Sookie's hair. Remember that?"

Shows you how long it had been since I had seen Marta and also how good of a memory she has.

"Ha! I remember that. Pretty sure Sookie does too."

"Where is she now?"

"Who? Erika?"

"Erika, Sookie. What about Jade?"

"Well, Erika's at school at FSU, not spitting on anyone—at least, not the last time I talked to her. And she did apologize to Sookie," I add as a parenthetical aside.

"But she's good. She's studying sports management, been dating some track star for a while now. Sookie graduated from Northwestern, accelerated, and is heading to law school to become a lawyer—either civil rights or constitutional law. Jade is married to Diego—"

Marta stops me by clapping her hands. "I can't believe that," she says, the glee spreading across her face. "She finally snagged him, huh?"

"Believe," I say, "but Jade would kill me if I didn't tell you she's still getting her school on. She's studying to be a child psychologist. And me, I'm here every summer."

"So tell me about you, about this." Her hand sweep includes Grendel's and the books by our feet.

"Well, that's a long story." And then I get to say the words that I've always wanted to say to Marta. "You got time for a long story?"

Marta rolls her eyes, and I swear that arc is so wide, she must have seen every corner of the ceiling. "*Please*, I got all the time in the world."

Instinctively, I glance at her cart, no perishables.

"Okay." I walk back to my table. Sitting, I offer her the seat opposite mine. I clear away textbooks and notebooks, setting them at my feet. Then I lean forward and begin. "Well, for starters, I have a new love. And you're going to like this. . . . It's Sally Blake."

"Sally Blake! *Ooh*." She leans forward too, cozying up so that her elbows rest on the table and her chin on the bridge she forms with her hands.

"Okay, well—" Her Bluetooth lights up, vibrates urgently against her ear. But she never breaks eye contact; she tugs it swiftly from her lobe and sends it sailing toward her cart. I watch it land somewhere between the Cheerios and a loaf of Cuban bread. "Go on." She snaps her fingers so that our eyes connect again. "It's fine. Don't stop."

"Well, in order to understand that story, you'll have to understand that it began with a kiss . . . a first kiss . . . very long, long ago."

"Yes," Marta says. "I like this story! Continue!"

"It wasn't just a kiss. It was a spark really," I say, and I know she's hooked. I can see it in her eyes. I glance away and see that Alex, who has arrived to take over the café for the day, stops his work behind the counter and also leans over, listening. It's a slow afternoon at Grendel's, so why shouldn't he listen? And well, once in a while you have to tell a story, a really long story. A story about love, about family—the ones you're born into and the ones you make along the way. You have to tell these stories to stay connected to those you love and those who love you. And this is a story I know so well. I've told it so many times in my head. So I clear my throat and in my best storytelling voice, I say, "The first time I kissed Sally Blake was on a hot summer day . . . *in early August. . . .*"

And, well, you know the rest of the story. After all, you were there.

There are only two ways to see your life:
One is as though nothing is a miracle.
The other is as though everything is a miracle.
—Albert Einstein

The Universal Laws of Marco

1. Keep moving forward because *life is now.* —Pop

2. People like that, they look for reasons to be angry. But you hear me, Marco: There are as many reasons to not choose your anger. You remember that. —Mom

3. We've got to fight to make things right, to make them better. —Sookie

4. Marco, physics *is* wisdom. —Mrs. A

5. We imagine that we can wait on things, but that's you believing that those things will wait for you too. But some of that could disappear while you're waiting to be ready. Sometimes we have to do things when we're not ready. —Sally

6. Strategy is everything. Strategy is how you win the long game. —Jade

7. Remember, it's never too late to start again. Sometimes a stop can also be seen as an extended pause. You just have to hit the unpause button. —Principal Johnson

8. It's more grown-up to walk toward the things that scare us than to run away from them. —Mrs. B

9. When it's do-or-die, you grab on to your future and hold on tight. —Diego

10. A man can protect and be brave, but a man can also be sad. For what is any of this for if you can't feel it? —Lito

All of life is a practice. You don't have to get anything right the first or second or third time. You just try to get better every day. You do that and you'll be fine.

—Mrs. A's grandmother

Acknowledgments

Special thanks to former editors Jennifer Klonsky and Michael Strother. Jen for believing in this project early on, and Michael for picking up where Jen left off, helping to develop the project into a manuscript that had heart.

A debt of gratitude to my current editor, Jennifer Ung, for loving Marco as much as I do. I could not have completed this novel without your patience, guidance, and support—a million thank-yous!

Tremendous thanks also to publisher Mara Anastas, deputy publisher Chriscynethia Floyd, and editorial director Liesa Abrams, plus the rest of the Simon Pulse team: Jessica Handelman, Nicole Russo, Caitlin Sweeny, Lauren Hoffman, Alissa Nigro, Christian Vega, Elizabeth Mims, Penina Lopez, Christina Pecorale, Emily Hutton, Michelle Leo, Anthony Parisi, Anna Jarzab, and Danielle Finnegan.

To my agent Steven Chudney for sending my work into the world and bearing with me through this long revision process.

To early readers Meagan Simmons, Jenny Prendergast, Joyce Masongsong-Ray, and Nathan Johnson for providing feedback and encouragement to move forward. To Dr. Richard Tran for help with medical terminology. To Brett Poche for patiently walking me through the science. To Sam Brewster for insight into the complex history and meaning of an important word and the discussion of the power of words in general. To Kate Rogers for help with branding. To my aunties, Iris Diaz, Carmen Iglesisas, and Marta Rivera, for help with my Spanish.

To Amy Risher for listening to daily rewrites, talking through revisions, and reminding me to have fun on occasion. Much love to you.

To Alison Harney for writing retreats, weekly chats, manuscript read throughs, pep talks, and mutual love of all things related to the spirit and universe. Thank you, thank you, thank you.

To my family for their continued support and love. To my brother, Walter, for buying multiple copies of my novels and handing them out to coworkers. To my sister Aria, for asking librarians to stock my books. Special thanks to my "twin" sister, Suzi, and my mom, Zulma, for reading the book again and again and offering the right cocktail of compassionate/tough love. You two know me so well! Thank you for believing in Marco and me.

Finally, to anyone I have forgotten unintentionally, thank you and forgive me.

About the Author

Carmen Rodrigues lives and plays in the great urban wilds of Northern Virginia, where she is a writer by day and an educator by night. She earned her MFA from the University of North Carolina Wilmington. *The Universal Laws of Marco* is her third young adult novel. Visit her at carmenrodrigues.com.